Two Wars

and a

Wedding

ALSO BY LAUREN WILLIG

Band of Sisters

The Summer Country

The English Wife

The Other Daughter

That Summer

The Ashford Affair

The Pink Carnation Series

Two Wars
and a
Wedding

❧

A NOVEL

Lauren Willig

wm

WILLIAM MORROW

An Imprint of HarperCollins*Publishers*

HarperCollins books may be purchased for educational, business, or sales promotional use. For information, please email the Special Markets Department at SPsales@harpercollins.com.

FIRST EDITION

Designed by Nancy Singer
Map by Jeffrey L. Ward

Library of Congress Cataloging-in-Publication Data

Names: Willig, Lauren, author.
Title: Two wars and a wedding: a novel / Lauren Willig.
Description: First Edition. | New York: William Morrow, [2023]
Identifiers: LCCN 2022016132 | ISBN 9780062986184
   (hardcover) | ISBN 9780062986207 (ebook)
Subjects: LCGFT: Novels.
Classification: LCC PS3623.I575 T96
   2023 | DDC 813/.6—dc23
LC record available at https://lccn.loc.gov/2022016132

ISBN 978-0-06-298618-4

23 24 25 26 27 LBC 5 4 3 2 1

To all the librarians,
past, present, and yet to be.

But most especially
to my Angel of the Bibliography,
Vicki Parsons,
without whom this book would not be here.

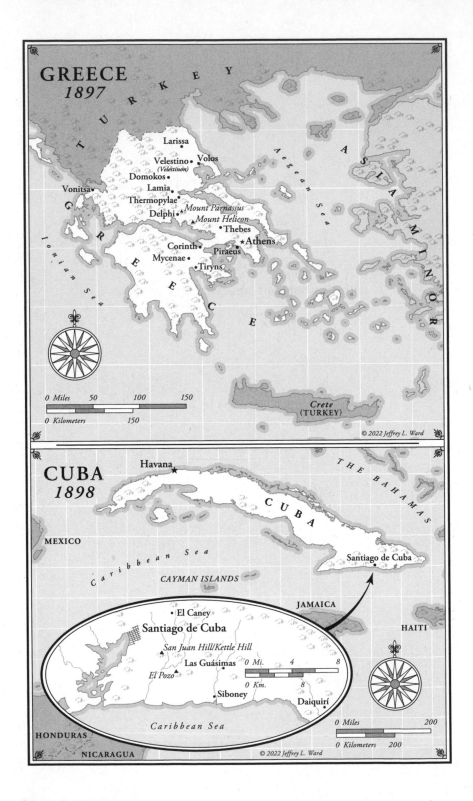

GREECE
1897

TURKEY

ASIA MINOR

GREECE

Larissa
Velestino
(Velestinon)
Volos
Domokos
Vonitsa
Lamia
Thermopylae
Delphi
Mount Parnassus
Mount Helicon
Thebes
★Athens
Corinth
Piraeus
Mycenae
Tiryns

Aegean Sea

Ionian Sea

0 Miles 50 100 150
0 Kilometers 150

Crete
(TURKEY)

© 2022 Jeffrey L. Ward

CUBA
1898

Havana★

CUBA

THE BAHAMAS

MEXICO

Caribbean Sea

CAYMAN ISLANDS

Santiago de Cuba

JAMAICA

HAITI

El Caney
Santiago de Cuba
San Juan Hill/Kettle Hill
Las Guásimas
El Pozo
Siboney
Daiquirí

0 Mi. 4 8
0 Km. 8

HONDURAS

Caribbean Sea

0 Miles 200
0 Kilometers 200

NICARAGUA

© 2022 Jeffrey L. Ward

Two Wars

and a

Wedding

CHAPTER ONE

Betsy,

I had thought it best you hear from me before you read it in the Smith College Monthly. *Now that our country has officially declared war on Spain (yes, I know you never read the papers: we're at war with Spain, in case you haven't noticed, which you probably haven't), the New York Red Cross has put out a call for volunteer nurses.*

I have volunteered. We are to undertake a training course at the Red Cross Hospital in New York and all those who pass the course will then take ship for Florida, and from there to Cuba to serve in the coming conflict.

I will be trained—properly trained—and we are to be paid for our services.

I'm not saying what you said in Athens is right. But there might have been something in it.

Now you won't be able to tell me I didn't try.

> *Yours,*
> *Ava*

—From Miss Ava Saltonstall, Smith College '96, to Miss Betsy Hayes '96

Tampa, Florida
June 2, 1898

BETSY HAYES ARRIVED IN FLORIDA with a single carpetbag and sick on her skirt.

The sick wasn't hers. It was courtesy of a three-year-old who'd been in her compartment since Savannah. The one benefit to her noxious state, as far as she could see, was that the other passengers tended to give her a wide berth. Betsy's dress felt stiff with sick and her legs felt stiff with sitting and her brain felt stiff with trying to make sense of a situation that didn't make sense at all.

Betsy wasn't supposed to be in Florida, barreling toward a war she knew nothing about. She was supposed to be in Greece, digging up antiquities and showing the Harvard boys how it should be done. One minute, there she had been, a newly minted graduate of Smith College, one of only two women at the American School of Classical Studies at Athens, all prepared to batter down the prejudices of the male establishment—but then it had all gone so very wrong and now here she was, on a train in the middle of nowhere, covered with someone else's vomit, trying to stop her best friend from making the same mistakes she had made.

She had to find Ava and stop her from sailing to Cuba.

We're at war with Spain, in case you haven't noticed, which you probably haven't, Ava had written, and, of course, Ava was right, as Ava so often was. From the chatter on the train from New York to Florida, Betsy gathered the war was something to do with the Spanish oppressing the Cubans. Or possibly something to do with the Spanish blowing up an American ship and then lying about it. Betsy didn't like to ask and she didn't much care. She'd learned in Greece that it wasn't the cause that mattered; even the best of intentions wouldn't stop wounds from festering and disease from spreading.

Two miles to Tampa, the conductor had said. But that had been an hour ago, before the train had stopped with an abrupt jolt, and here they were still. Not moving. Stuck in the middle of nowhere in an endless night made hideous with the belch of coal smoke and enough shouting and clattering and clanking to keep even the most exhausted awake.

"Hey diddle diddle, the *train* and the fiddle," sang the loathsome tot who had been ill on Betsy's skirt, singing the wrong words and then hooting as though he'd done something clever.

The child's mother was heavily pregnant and feeling it. As Betsy watched, the little boy bumped up against his mother's arm and, green-faced, weary, the mother lifted her arm so he could snuggle against her, bump in the belly and all.

Betsy's eyes stung. With the smoke, the blasted smoke. Good heavens, did no one know how to open a window around here?

Rising abruptly, Betsy grabbed her carpetbag off the rack overhead. She didn't care if it was two miles to Tampa. What was two miles? She'd walk if she had to. If she didn't get out of this compartment soon, they would clap her straight into one of those depressing places where they prescribed cold baths and electrical shocks and called it healing.

The pregnant woman lifted her head from her son's. Betsy could see the fine lines the boy's hair had made on her cheek, imprinted on her. "Where are you going?"

"I'm finding out what's going on out there," Betsy lied.

The woman blinked at her. "With your case?"

Betsy pretended not to hear. She swung herself out of the compartment and onto the ground. She had failed to take into account that there wasn't a platform there, so it was a longer way down than she'd expected. She landed hard on her left foot and staggered before righting herself. The ground on the side of the track was dirt and scrub, studded with chunks of coal that bit through the thin soles of her boots.

She wasn't the only one taking a break from the train. Half the US Army appeared to have had the same idea. She could see them as dark shadows, as the red circles of cigar butts glowing in the darkness. But even if she hadn't been able to see them, the smell of an army on the move was unmistakable: unwashed bodies and tinned beef; black powder and oiled leather.

Despite the heat, Betsy was suddenly cold through, shivering in her sick-stained, sweat-soaked dress. Her hands felt numb and bloodless; she rubbed them together, dragging in tortured breaths of thick, smoke-clogged air. Florida. She was in Florida. Not Greece. Two miles from Tampa. Just two miles. Two miles to go.

She drew herself up. She'd been traveling for days, from train to ship to train. Enough to make anyone dizzy. She was fine. Fit as a fiddle. She'd walk to Tampa if need be.

Betsy flexed her hands, grabbed her carpetbag, and squinted down the track. By the light of the train lamps, she could vaguely make out semitropical trees and dense scrub, crowding close to the tracks. And ahead, as far as the eye could see, train after train after train, backed up all the way to Tampa.

Well, that was it, then. All she had to do was follow the tracks.

She'd scarcely gone more than a yard before one of the dark shapes peeled away from the shadows, blocking her path. "Ma'am. May I help you back into your compartment? This is no place for a lady."

Ha. She hadn't been a lady in years. Possibly ever, if her brother was to be believed.

Betsy straightened, trying to ignore the way her hair straggled down the back of her neck, half out of its pins. "It's very kind of you, but . . . no. Good night."

Those particular cut-off consonants had always had great success in squashing the pretensions of university men who believed her to be a sweet little thing. Little, yes. Sweet, no. Unfortunately, this man seemed to be made of tougher stuff.

"Let me help you back in," he said, and made the mistake of reaching for her elbow. Betsy jerked her arm out of the way. The man stepped back, saying carefully, as to someone delicate and nervous, "Is your chaperone in the compartment?"

Betsy had given up chaperones years ago, along with her illusions. "If you *must* make yourself useful, I need a cart or wheeled conveyance. It doesn't need to be anything fancy. Just something sufficient to take me the two miles to Tampa."

The man looked at her as if trying to figure out if she was joking. "Ma'am, everyone is trying to get to Tampa."

"Yes, but there are a great number of you, and just one of me," said Betsy, quite reasonably, she thought.

Another man ambled up out of the darkness. "Holt, what are you—" He stopped abruptly, leaning practically double to squint at Betsy. "Betsy? Betsy Hayes?"

Betsy's stomach dropped. She'd know that loping walk anywhere. "Paul? What on earth are you doing here?"

"What do you think I'm doing here? Fighting the Spaniards," Paul said happily, the same way he might have said, "trouncing Harvard," as if this were the Yale-Harvard game and not a war, not a hideous excuse for men to exterminate their fellow man and leave them bleeding. "I'm with the First United States Volunteer Cavalry."

He was bouncing on the balls of his feet with excitement. Betsy would have taken him by the shoulders and shaken him if they'd been alone. And if she could reach.

"What made you do an idiot thing like that?"

"Betsy! We're going to free Cuba!" Paul laughed. He actually laughed, as though it were all a joke, as though they were in the dining room of Delmonico's and not on a humid train siding somewhere in Florida. "What are you doing down here? Not that I'm not happy to see you, of course, just, it's not the place for a lady."

Betsy rubbed a hand inelegantly across her nose. "So I've been told."

"Oh, I forgot to introduce you!" Paul clapped the other man on the back in an excess of hail-fellow-well-met. "Miss Hayes, may I present to you my comrade in arms Private Holt, also of the First United States Volunteer Cavalry. Holt, this is Miss Elizabeth Hayes of Smith College, who once did me the honor of being my guest for Yale prom."

The other man was slighter than Paul, but what he lacked in bulk, he made up for in sheer disapproval. "You're a long way from New Haven, Miss Hayes."

"Really? I'd hardly noticed."

Paul gave a happy chuckle. "We've so many Yale men about you'd think you were at Mory's. There's Thede Miller—did you ever meet Thede? He was a year behind me. And Teddy Burke and David Goodrich. . . . We've more than our fair share of Harvard men here too, but we've decided to count them friends under the circumstances."

"Given that the same people will be shooting at both of you." Betsy's mouth felt very dry. All the chivalry of Yale and Harvard, to be turned to food for buzzards. Did men learn nothing through the generations? They'd died to a man at Thermopylae and called it honor.

Paul ignored her, too buoyed up by his own excitement. "And then we've the real cowboys, like Holt here, men who've studied at the University of Experience."

"A degree in cattle rustling, I take it?"

"Don't be a snob, Bets. You must have heard of Private Holt. Hold 'Em Holt? The man who single-handedly hunted down the Jakes Brothers?"

"It wasn't single-handed," interjected the object of Paul's adoration.

"As good as!" In the light of the train lamps, Paul's eyes shone with hero worship. Paul's enthusiasms, when they lasted, tended to be all-consuming. In her case, it had involved whole hothouses full of flowers and reams of letters speckled with detailed accounts of his sporting activities, which he had assumed, for some incomprehensible reason, must be of interest to her.

It had suited them both, at the time. Paul had wanted a woman on his arm; Betsy had wanted an invitation to Yale prom, largely to annoy Ava. It had been such fun annoying Ava, and so ridiculously easy. Besides, Ava had enjoyed it too. Nothing made her happier than getting to be all purse-lipped and disapproving. It was how their friendship worked. Betsy did something appalling and Ava clucked at her and they both felt entirely themselves.

Then. Back before it all went wrong. So very, very wrong.

I'm not saying what you said in Athens is right. Betsy had Ava's letter in her pocket, folded into eighths, read and reread until the scrap of paper had all but disintegrated. *We are to undertake a training course . . . take ship for Florida . . .*

"Brilliant." Betsy cut Paul off mid-encomium, something about hornswoggling or hog-tying, goodness only knew. "I'm sure Annie Oakley will be terribly impressed. Do you have Buffalo Bill here too?"

"Did someone forget to feed you? Miss Hayes gets cranky when she's hungry," said Paul to his friend, which was all the more annoying because it tended to be true, she did get cranky when she was hungry, although she hadn't felt properly hungry, not for months and months.

Hunger felt like a betrayal, an obscene indulgence. There were times when she hated her legs for moving, her skin for being warm, herself for being here when others were not.

"I'm fine," she said.

Private Holt gave her a long look. "You're on a train siding in the middle of the night."

Paul blinked. "That's a good point. You never said why you're here. Why are you here?"

Betsy felt a rush of exasperated affection. The emotion felt rusty, but it was there, and she wasn't sure if she liked it.

"I'm with the Red Cross," she said. It wasn't entirely a lie. She'd worked with the Red Cross, the Greek branch. Now she just had to hope the American branch would take her. A Betsy for an Ava. The American branch was run by Miss Clara Barton, the famous Civil War angel of the battlefield. Betsy had never met her, but she'd seen her picture in the papers, which almost amounted to the same thing. "I need to report to Red Cross headquarters. So, you see, I really *must* get to Tampa."

"Ma'am." It was that annoying man again. Holt. What kind of name was Holt? "If you want to get to Tampa, you need to get on the train. It will get there when it gets there."

"When's that? Sometime after the Last Trump?"

"Better than not getting there at all."

"It's a straight walk down the train tracks. I've walked farther than that—" Hiking up the hills in Mycenae, drinking in the thin air like wine, laughing down at the stragglers below. Betsy lifted her head, swiping irritably at a plume of coal smoke. "I've walked farther than that in worse circumstances."

"In the dark?" The man sounded like he didn't believe her. "There are alligators."

He was making the mistake of assuming she cared about her own safety. "And bears too, I have no doubt? Perhaps an enraged mongoose? A griffin or a basilisk?"

"Only the odd hydra. Ma'am." He held out his arm to her, and before she knew it, Betsy was back up in that compartment, carpetbag and all.

She could have screamed with frustration. But that would have given the man far too much satisfaction.

On an impulse, she leaned out the door. "Paul—"

The words she wanted to say to him burned on her tongue: *Go home. Get out. Run for the hills. Run away from the hills.*

But she couldn't say any of them. Lamely, she raised a hand. "I'll see you in Tampa?"

Paul beamed at her, assuming her worry was on her own part, not his. Or just not hearing it at all. Men were very good at not hearing what they didn't want to hear. "It will be like old times."

Only with more senseless death. "Quite."

Inside the compartment, the child had finally spent his energy, falling asleep curled up against his mother. He fit neatly into the space beneath her arm, his head on her swelling stomach. His mother had wrapped herself around him in sleep, sheltering him with her body.

Betsy's chest hurt. The smoke rasped at the back of her throat. Dragging a shawl from her carpetbag, she flung it over her head, the way she used to pull her covers up over her face as a child, as if the cloth could keep the ghosts at bay.

Curling into a corner of the seat, she fell asleep to the sound of goods being moved, soldiers snoring, engineers shouting, and a little boy sighing in his sleep.

Port Tampa, Florida
June 3, 1898

"WE DON'T TAKE VOLUNTEERS." THE nursing sister in charge, Sister Bettina, backed away from Betsy and the strange smells emanating from her garments.

Betsy couldn't blame her. It had taken Betsy hours to track down the Red Cross headquarters, which had turned out to be not in Tampa at all but on a ship. A ship confusingly called the *State of Texas*. It wasn't in Texas. It wasn't even near Texas. It was anchored in Port Tampa, which was all of eight miles from Tampa but might as well have been the moon as far as Betsy was concerned, with all the roads clogged with soldiers. Betsy had floundered around in the June heat, still lugging that dratted carpetbag, still with sick on her skirt, until she finally found a carriage willing to accept an exorbitant amount of money to take her.

Betsy thrust a crumpled wad of paper at Sister Bettina. "Here—read this. You'll see I have considerable experience."

"Have you?" Sister Bettina might have tried to sound happier about it.

She had a hint of a foreign accent, something European. She was, Betsy realized, not much older than Betsy, and not much taller, but the uniform, the accent, and her uncompromising tidiness made Betsy feel like a schoolgirl brought before the headmistress.

Betsy could see Sister Bettina taking in the Paris traveling suit, which had been beautifully fitted two years ago, when Betsy had stopped to shop in Paris on her way to Greece and academic glory. It hung from Betsy's reduced frame.

"You're not sickly, are you?"

Betsy put her shoulders back and bared her teeth. "Strong as a horse. Although I be small, yet I be fierce."

"Hmm," said the nursing sister. She shuffled through the papers in front of her, pausing at one. "You come very highly recommended—by Queen Olga of Greece?"

Betsy gave a modest wave of her hand. "I did some work with the Red Cross there."

Sister Bettina's eyes narrowed. "Bandage-rolling parties are all very well, but our work here requires skill and dedication. We face hardship and spartan conditions in a climate that can only be termed *inhospitable*."

Betsy cut the nursing sister off before she could say more. "It was hot in Greece too." Did the woman want hardship and spartan conditions? She could tell her about all of it. About the smell of putrefying flesh, the sound the flies made as they buzzed closer, drawn by blood. "It doesn't matter if they're speaking Greek or English. I've seen men die before."

Sister Bettina was not impressed. "Our goal, Miss Hayes, isn't to watch them die but to keep them alive."

Sometimes there wasn't much choice. Sometimes they died anyway.

But she couldn't say that. Not when she needed Sister Bettina to take her on. "I'll do my best." When the sister looked unconvinced, Betsy added, "I spent three months patching up wounded men in the midst of a war zone. I have some experience with field dressings."

She didn't mind mangled limbs. There was something strangely satisfying about sewing together torn flesh and watching it knit. It was the fever that terrified her, that invisible foe, leaving men sweating and gasping, convulsing as the enemy attacked from within. A familiar face made strange with pain, eyes glassy and unseeing.

Sister Bettina sighed. "We're not so well-staffed we can turn down a trained nurse."

"You're taking me on?" Betsy didn't know whether to be delighted or run away screaming.

"Final approval will rest with Miss Barton, but . . . yes. Collect a uniform and we'll find you a berth."

"A berth?" Betsy was still making sense of the ship as a temporary hospital; she certainly hadn't expected to live there. "But—I've booked a room at the Tampa Bay Hotel."

"You'll just have to cancel it, then. We all live and work here on the ship," Sister Bettina explained. "Our work calls us at all hours and we must be here for it."

"But the war hasn't started yet." This was not good. How was she meant to grab Ava, talk some sense into her, and shove her onto the nearest train for Boston if they were stuck on a ship?

Sister Bettina regarded her with something very like impatience. "Men don't wait for the bugles to blow to fall ill. There are refugees and prisoners of war in dire straits. They won't wait for us to come from the Tampa Bay Hotel."

She made Betsy feel about six inches tall. In another life, Betsy might have agreed with her. She'd felt that way once. Full of zeal for the cause and scorn for those who shirked their duty. Had that only been a year ago? It took Betsy a moment to remember that she was twenty-four. She felt as ancient as a sibyl.

Betsy put back her shoulders and tried to look like the old Betsy, the one who was ready for anything. "Right. Never an idle moment."

Sister Bettina took a deep breath and looked as though she wished she hadn't. "You'd best stay the night at the hotel and join us in the morning." Sister Bettina waved over another woman garbed in the traditional white pinny with the Red Cross insignia on a tight band on her left arm. "Miss Carson. You'll find a uniform for Miss Hayes."

"Yes, Sister Bettina." Miss Carson turned a friendly face to Betsy.

She had curly brown hair stuffed beneath her white cap, and a pleasant, crooked smile. "Hallo there. Let's get you kitted up."

"Miss? Not sister."

The other woman grinned, revealing a deep dent in one tanned cheek that was almost a dimple. "I'm here under false pretenses." She stuck out her hand. "Kit Carson of the *St. Louis Star Ledger*. I'm here to report on the war."

Betsy looked at the other woman's uniform, then back at Sister Bettina. "But then why . . ."

"Because I couldn't get over any other way." Kit caught Betsy's look over her shoulder. "Oh, Sister Bettina knows. Miss Barton said she'd take me along as a nurse, provided I write up the Red Cross. And do my share of bandage rolling. Sister Bettina gave me an abbreviated version of the usual course. But I gather you're the real thing."

"I've rolled my share of bandages." So much for skill and dedication. Apparently those counted for less than a few inches of newsprint. Betsy followed along after the other woman to a room filled with sundry supplies, all neatly labeled. "Since you've been here—have you met a nurse named Ava? Ava Saltonstall?"

"No Avas or Saltonstalls. I'd remember a name like that." Kit Carson was shaking out aprons, trying to find the smallest of the bunch. "Here's one that won't swamp you. Why do you want to know?"

"We were at Smith College together." Betsy stuffed the apron into her carpetbag, on top of two much-abused dresses and a set of combinations. "She told me she'd be here."

"College women." Kit gave a whistle of admiration. "She might be in the next batch. There's a whole detachment of nurses being sent by the New York Red Cross—or that's what Sister Bettina says."

"That's the one. Do you know when they'll get here?"

"No one knows anything about anything right now," Kit said

cheerfully. "Not even the generals on the porch of the Tampa Bay Hotel."

"The Tampa Bay Hotel? That's where I'm going. Where I was meant to go." Betsy's head itched with dried sweat and what she suspected might be something else entirely. She needed a bath. And someplace to think. "Sister Bettina says I can stay the night there before coming back to the ship. Do you know how to get there? I just got in this morning and I have no idea where anything is."

Kit stretched, her hands on the small of her back. "Honey, you can't miss it. It's the monstrosity that looks like a cross between the Brighton Pavilion and a Turkish harem."

Betsy vaguely remembered seeing something like that. "It's not in Port Tampa, is it? It's in the other Tampa."

"Right at the end of the train line. You probably saw it when you came in." At Betsy's look of bewilderment, Kit took pity and slid her arm through Betsy's. "I'll take you. Come along with me."

Blinking, Betsy followed Kit up onto the deck into the bright sunlight. For a moment, the intensity of the light reminded her of Greece, in happier times. If she closed her eyes, she might be there again, twenty-two and fearless, ready to take on the world. . . .

How on earth had it come to this?

CHAPTER TWO

Darling Ava,

I've already made the local papers! The headline read, "Miss Hayes, one of the most famous bicyclists in Europe, is staying at the Grande Bretagne." All this because I decided to ride my wheel from the Hotel Grande Bretagne to the American School. Before you ask, no, I wasn't wearing my bloomers. I was very respectably attired in all that was modest and inconvenient.

But it is glorious here, Ava. You couldn't imagine anything farther from Northampton. We have an olive grove behind the school—and a herd of goats to go with it! The goats are meant to produce milk but largely produce chaos instead. I hear they've been known to eat papers, particularly when said papers are overdue.

Dr. Richardson is a bit of an old stick—doesn't think women's temperaments are suited to the work. Ha! A month at Smith would set him right. But what can one expect of a Dartmouth man?

With love,
Betsy

—From Miss Betsy Hayes '96 to Ava Saltonstall '96

Athens, Greece
September 1896

BETSY REALLY DIDN'T SEE HOW it had come to this.

She stood in the office of the director of the American School of Classical Studies at Athens, trying to put in clear, simple terms that even a man could understand just why she should be allowed to excavate like any other member of the American School.

"I don't see why I can't go along. Corinth is to be excavated by the American School. I am a member of the American School. It's really quite simple."

"Miss Hayes." Dr. Richardson looked deeply pained. "Women do not dig."

He had no idea what she could do with a shovel. But, then, the poor man taught at Dartmouth. He hadn't had the benefit of female students before. "I assure you, we don't faint at the sight of a bit of dirt."

"Your constitution . . . your clothing . . ." Dr. Richardson appeared to be having trouble mustering words, which Betsy thought was a distinct disadvantage in someone meant to be heading an intellectual institution. "Have you ever considered a career as a librarian?"

Betsy stared at him. "A librarian?"

Dr. Richardson visibly relaxed. "Yes, a librarian. You have some facility with Greek, I understand."

Some facility? She'd been reading Herodotus in the original before she was in long skirts.

Dr. Richardson warmed to his theme. "Think of the role you could play in cataloguing the vast store of knowledge for future generations."

Future generations were all very well, but it was the past that interested Betsy. "I came here to excavate. If I wanted to work with books, I could have stayed in Northampton."

Where she was surrounded by people of sense. Otherwise known as women.

"A translator, then," said Dr. Richardson hopefully. "A trained classicist, familiar with the language, can be a great aid to the men in the field."

There was no point in being subtle. "I don't want to transcribe other people's finds. I want to find them myself."

Dr. Richardson chuckled benignly. "My dear, the rigors of the field . . . the strenuousness of the endeavor . . . None of these are the least suited to the gentler sex. What was that, Miss Hayes?"

"Nothing." Betsy bit back a sharp retort. She needed Dr. Richardson's goodwill. As the director of the American School, he had the final say. And she refused, absolutely refused, to have come all this way to do nothing more than read the same texts she could have read back in Massachusetts. What was the point of being in Greece if one couldn't dig?

She could hear Ava's voice in her head, saying that the point was climbing the Acropolis, walking where Plato and St. Paul had walked (not at the same time, of course; that would have been ridiculous, and quite possibly acrimonious; she really didn't think they would have got along), attending the lectures given by the professors of the various schools, enjoying the company of other scholars.

Yes, the American School had a brand-new dig site in Corinth that was just begging for a talented excavator to come along and explore its mysteries. But it was only one facet of the school's offerings. And she was in Greece! The land of Homer. The land of so much still undiscovered.

Betsy meant to uncover it.

She had been eight when her father had first given her Schliemann's report of his excavation at Mycenae. She could remember the weight of the volume in her hands, the maroon cover embossed in silver and gilt, that precise moment when it dawned on her that the ancient world wasn't merely a charming tale to be told at bedtime. It was still there, under the soil, waiting to be discovered. It had felt like reaching out to a mirror to find the figure in the mirror reaching back to you, something static and flat suddenly coming alive.

Betsy had known then and there that this was what she was meant to do, and she wasn't going to allow anyone to stop her.

Cunningly, Betsy said, "I hear Dr. Sterrett is leading a trek in the Peloponnese."

Dr. Richardson eyed her warily. "Yes. He means to take a party to Tiryns and Mycenae. The excavations there . . ."

"Yes, I read Herr Schliemann's reports." Drat, that had been too curt. Betsy tried again. "I'd like to go with them."

"My dear, this is not the sort of travel to which you are accustomed." He looked at her shirtwaist with its puffed sleeves, the elaborate braiding on her skirt. "The inns are little more than stables; the terrain is ruthless. These are treks, not pleasure jaunts. Ah, I'll never forget tramping from Phocis to Thermopylae and then back round through Boeotia a few seasons past. Two hundred and fifty miles in ten days, pouring rain all the way. And the places we slept! We had so many bedbugs, we named them the Persians."

"It sounds delightful," said Betsy. It sounded awful.

"It was, it was. Tramping in the rain, singing our way through the Carmina Collegensia." Richardson burst unexpectedly into a rumbling baritone: "*We will give three cheers for old Dartmouth, old Dartmouth, a tiger and three times threewith!* There was Brownson bellowing out his Yale glees and Gilbert, not to be outdone, with his *I wish I was in Boston city, where the girls they are so—*ahem."

Richardson recalled himself to his present company with a violent fit of coughing.

"Smith has songs too," Betsy pointed out. "And I am perfectly capable of singing them in all conditions and all altitudes."

Looking thoroughly discomfited, Professor Richardson took refuge in delay. "You'll have to speak to Professor Sterrett."

Betsy beamed at him. "Oh, I shall. Thank you, Dr. Richardson! I'll be sure to tell him you sent me."

"But—I didn't—"

"I won't keep you a moment longer. I know you have important . . . papers to attend to." She turned on her heel before he could recover himself. After all, he had told her to speak to Dr. Sterrett. So he had, in fact, sent her to Dr. Sterrett. Which was nearly the same thing as suggesting she accompany the expedition. Betsy was sure Dr. Sterrett would see the sense of it.

She whisked out the door, turning only to twiddle her fingers in farewell, which was why she didn't at all see the man coming from the other direction until she had launched herself straight at him, landing in a flurry of papers and a tangle of limbs (his) and petticoats (hers) on the hard floor of the corridor.

"Ooof," said Betsy eloquently.

She shoved herself up on her elbows, and then to her knees, and found herself facing a man similarly situated. There was no mistaking the man for anything but an archaeologist. His hair, naturally a rich chestnut, had been faded to tow in places, and his eyes bore the unmistakable white lines of a man who spent a great deal of time squinting into the sun.

"A million pardons, mademoiselle." He spoke English with a light French accent and a very heavy British one.

"One would have sufficed." Since she was on her knees already, Betsy decided she might as well gather the fallen papers, so she did, practically bumping heads with the Frenchman, who seemed to have had the same idea. Nose to nose, his eyes were a very pleasant shade of brown, like her father's whiskey, and just as full of forbidden promise. "And it was my fault, not yours."

He rose, holding out a hand to her. "I've seldom been felled by so charming an obstacle."

Betsy grinned up at the Frenchman, feeling all the more charming for being called so. "Tell that to the next tree stump you trip over. Au revoir, monsieur."

Betsy couldn't resist looking after him as he let himself into Professor Richardson's office. The man had to be a fellow of the French School, of course. They were here too. The national schools did a good line in mutual aid, scholarly ribbing, and cutting one another out for dig sites. It was all in good fun, except when the French School shamelessly stole the permit for excavating Delphi out from under them.

It gave Betsy a thrill to think she was about to be one of them, this elect group of explorers who coaxed the secrets of the past from the soil, turning myth flesh with their finds. That someday not too distant, she might be striding through the American School and some new girl, fresh from Vassar or Wellesley, might bump into her and look at her sunburnt skin and know her for an archaeologist.

"Betsy?"

Betsy came down with a thump to solid ground. Ethel, the only other female student at the American School, hailed Betsy from the end of the corridor. "Have you seen Jane? I left her on a table in the library and now I can't find her anywhere."

Jane wasn't a person but a book—Jane Harrison and Margaret Verrall's *Mythology and Monuments of Ancient Athens*—which was required reading for all members of the American School. Jane was constantly being taken for walks or going missing and turning up in odd places.

"Wingate must have filched her when you weren't looking." Betsy had bought her own copy of Jane, now heavily underlined. She wasn't risking it to the uncouth hands of any of the Harvard men, who made up nearly half their cohort of nine students and took up more than their fair share of space and library materials. "Last I saw, he had her in the olive grove."

"Bother." Ethel shoved her spectacles up her nose, looking decidedly put out. "The goats have probably eaten it by now."

"They'll have got more out of it than the boys will," said Betsy. "I got into such an argument with Wingate over her interpretation of the Aiora festival. He claims that vase was a depiction of a Dionysian bacchanal and nothing to do with Erigone."

"We don't really know one way or the other," said Ethel, coming to Wingate's defense. Betsy blamed coeducation. Ethel had spent her undergraduate years at Cornell. Betsy couldn't fault Ethel's scholarship but felt that her spirit had been irreparably dampened by the disadvantages of having her formative academic years spoiled by men in the classroom.

"It's bunk," said Betsy bluntly. "Why *are* men so fascinated by bacchanals, when they'd never participate in one themselves?"

"Most likely because they'd never participate in one," said Ethel sensibly. "The ones who participate aren't reading about them."

"And the ones reading aren't participating?" Betsy decided she didn't need to picture that. "Speaking of nonsense . . . our esteemed director informed me that women aren't welcome at the excavation in Corinth."

"Did you think we would be?"

Betsy frowned at her colleague. "It's the school's excavation. We're members of the school. We earned our entrance fair and square, just like the rest of them." More than some of the rest of them. She and Ethel had to prove themselves and prove themselves and prove themselves again. "Can you believe Dr. Richardson asked me if I wanted to be a librarian?"

Ethel looked at her steadily. "I do want to be a librarian."

Betsy felt the tips of her ears go pink. "Well . . . yes, if that's what you want. But if you wanted to excavate, wouldn't it madden you to be told you couldn't?"

"But I don't want to excavate," said Ethel matter-of-factly. "I couldn't think of anything I'd like less."

Betsy could think of many things she would like less. Long donkey rides. Naming her bedbugs after Persians. That peculiar sandwich filling beloved of the men of the British school that tasted rather of old socks.

There was no accounting for taste. "So I suppose that means you don't want to come on the trek to the Peloponnese with me?"

It would have been much easier to convince Sterrett to take both of them. Men had this strange idea that women needed to travel everywhere in pairs, for the sake of their virtue, as though two could get in less trouble than one.

"Of course I'll come," said Ethel calmly.

Betsy stared at her. "But you said you don't want to excavate."

"Just because I don't want to dig it up doesn't mean I don't want to see it once somebody else has." Ethel changed the subject. "Have you found new lodgings yet?"

"No, not yet." Betsy thought it thoroughly unfair that the male students got to lodge in the school while the women were left to shift for themselves as they would. She had been living at the Hotel Grande Bretagne and would have been happy to stay there indefinitely, but she had noticed the way it raised brows among her fellow students. The last thing she wanted was to be thought a wealthy hobbyist. Wealthy, yes. She never pretended otherwise. But a hobbyist? No.

"There's room with Reverend Kalopothakes," offered Ethel.

"I'll bear that in mind." It might make it easier to befriend Ethel if she were rooming with her, but "boarding with a Presbyterian minister" was high on Betsy's list of things she'd rather avoid. "Would you like me to come help you find Jane? I think the boys have been hiding her deliberately."

"They wouldn't do that," said Ethel, even though Betsy was quite sure they not only would but had. "It's all right. I probably left it in the olive grove myself and forgot."

"I should probably go anyway." Betsy tried to pretend she didn't feel snubbed. "I'm engaged to pay my respects to an acquaintance of my father's. A Mrs. MacHugh. She's invited me to tea."

The woman had left a card for her at the Grande Bretagne. Betsy hadn't the slightest idea who she was. Her father had had a large and varied acquaintance, most of it conducted from his writing desk in Boston. Betsy could imagine this Mrs. MacHugh, undoubtedly the widow of an importer like her father, seventy if she was a day, all that was proper, bringing a bit of Boston to the heart of Athens.

"At least you might get a decent meal out of it," said Ethel. "Something not drowned in olive oil."

Betsy rather liked olive oil. "If there are little sandwiches, I'll drop some in my pocket for you."

"You wouldn't—would you?"

Betsy left Ethel looking equal parts horrified and skeptical. Ava would have known she was joking. Ava would have told her what she thought of such frivolousness in no uncertain terms.

Goodness, she missed Ava. After four years together, being apart was like being without a piece of herself.

Betsy felt a surge of longing for Northampton and the glorious fellowship of women. Of course, she'd known the American School wouldn't be like Smith—but she had rather thought the men would be more like her Yale prom date, Paul, ready to be teased and charmed, quick to bow to her superior wit, not convinced of their own.

Well, she would just have to win them over, Betsy told herself. There was no point in repining. She was in Greece! Just where she'd always meant to be. And she was late for tea.

Betsy quickened her step, stopping at the hotel just long enough to change her sensible shirtwaist—it was sensible, whatever Dr. Richardson might think—for one of her new Paris suits, a bright, defiant purple elaborately banded with scrolls of black braid. It was cut to perfection, giving her figure an illusion of the hourglass silhouette that nature had declined to bestow.

She pinned on the matching hat and retrieved her faithful bicycle from the hotel staff, swooping happily past carriages and carts, horses and donkeys.

It was a very short ride to Academy Street, to a house that—well, it wasn't a house, really, was it? Not in the way Betsy understood houses, the narrow brownstones of her youth, with their three floors up and the area beneath the stairs where the cook would pop out above the railings when the butcher's boy came calling. This was a mansion, of white marble, comparatively restrained in its facade, but a mansion nonetheless.

A maid took Betsy's bicycle. Another maid led her across a mosaic so fine that she wanted to stare at it rather than step on it. An arched door opened into a thoroughly European drawing room replete with red velvet furniture and insistent aspidistras.

A woman reclined on a chaise longue in a gown that Betsy knew wouldn't suit her in the slightest, but coveted all the same: a tea gown in the aesthetic style, with a red silk overdress embroidered in gold thread hanging open over a high-necked gown of cream-colored voile.

Betsy ventured into the room, completely flummoxed by the difference between the woman in her head and the one sitting before her.

"Mrs. MacHugh?"

This woman couldn't be more than a decade older than Betsy, thirty or so to Betsy's twenty-two. Her rich black hair was piled on top of her head in loops and coils and she rose with a sinuous ease—aided, no doubt, thought Betsy enviously, by the lack of corset. It made her Paris suit feel uncomfortably tight and fussy.

But for all that, there was something very big sisterly about the woman advancing toward her, who regarded her with frank interest.

"You must be our famous bicyclist—Elizabeth Hayes." She pronounced it in the Greek way, with a hard *t*.

No one called her Elizabeth. It had been her mother's name. Her brother had always made clear to her he felt she had no right to it; that having taken their mother's life, she shouldn't also have her name.

"Call me Betsy," Betsy said quickly.

"Betsy," her hostess repeated. "And I am Aikaterini."

"Aikaterini MacHugh?" Betsy blurted out, before she had the sense to stop herself.

The amusement in her hostess's eyes turned into a full-blown smile. "My husband is the Scotsman. As for me . . . my mother was maid of honor to Queen Amalia."

Betsy didn't know the slightest thing about any Greek monarchs more recent than Agamemnon. She had a vague idea that the current royal house was roughly as Greek as she was—German? Belgian? Danish?—but that was about the extent of it.

"Goodness," she said, for lack of anything better. She sank into the seat her hostess indicated, feeling very American.

"You would like tea, I imagine? It is a dusty ride in the heat of the day. On your famous bicycle." Her hostess rang a bell and a maid appeared almost on the instant, rolling a trolley piled high with sweetmeats of various kinds.

Betsy stripped off her gloves. "It's really just a bicycle. I'm not famous."

"You are to me," said Mrs. MacHugh, calmly pouring tea. "When I saw your name, I knew you at once, and was delighted. Your father did me a great kindness."

Her father had lived in Athens only in his dreams. Betsy accepted the cup her hostess handed her. "How did you know my father?"

Mrs. MacHugh settled comfortably back on her sofa with her own cup of tea. The soft folds of her dress moved with her. "He and my father were business partners—oh, a very long time ago! But the partnership was only prelude to a friendship that was valued, I think, far more than their profits."

Yes, that had been her father. He had come to business reluctantly, bound to it by birth and driven onward by obligation, but he had reserved his energies for his studies, his circle of correspondents— and his daughter. Well, there had also been her brother, Alex. But Alex's temperament and her father's had never aligned. He'd resented their father's passion for the antique past, and the time it took from his work and his children. Betsy had understood, as Alex hadn't, that their father expressed his affection with articles and epigraphs. One of her earliest memories was sitting curled up in her father's lap in his favorite chair as he read aloud to her in ancient Greek, his finger following under the letters, so that she had read Greek before she had read English.

Heathen, the maids called it.

Inappropriate, Alex called it.

But her father had never once suggested that Betsy was any less capable of learning than a man. He had been so terribly proud when Betsy had passed her entrance exams for Smith.

"Perhaps," said Mrs. MacHugh, "you heard him mention my father. Georgios Damala."

"But of course!" Betsy sat up straighter in her chair, nearly upsetting her teacup. "I never saw him so animated as when your father's letters arrived."

"They were as like as two drops of water. They had some lively discussions, did they not?"

"They fell out over Odysseus," Betsy said reminiscently.

"And fell back in again." Mrs. MacHugh's eyes met Betsy's in a moment of perfect mutual comprehension. "Your father sent me a very kind note upon my father's death. I keep it with me still. I had hoped to thank him if ever he came to Athens."

Betsy's throat felt scratchy. "He passed away a year ago."

"I'm so sorry."

"I am too." If her father hadn't been obligated to chase after her to Northampton in the middle of a frigid February . . . Betsy cleared her throat. "I know he would be glad I'm here. It was always his wish to take part in an excavation."

"Why did he never do so himself?"

They had planned to sail to Greece together, once Betsy graduated.

Betsy shrugged. "There was just never time, I suppose."

"And you? You are fulfilling your father's wishes." It wasn't a question.

"And my own," said Betsy defensively. "If they'll let me."

"They?"

Betsy grimaced. "The esteemed director of the American School."

Mrs. MacHugh looked so sympathetic that Betsy would undoubtedly have said more—much more—but the same servant who had brought her in was hovering at the door, followed closely by a man Betsy had last seen from a rather more prone position.

"Monsieur de Robecourt," announced the maid, and effaced herself again.

The Frenchman regarded Betsy with mingled surprise and delight.

"Mademoiselle de la Souche." Betsy didn't need any translation. Miss Tree Stump, he had called her. "I trip over you again."

"You didn't trip over me. I bumped into you."

Mrs. MacHugh looked from one to the other, intrigued. "I take it you have met?"

"Somewhat forcibly," said the Frenchman, and Betsy could see the laughter in his eyes despite his grave tone. "But we have not, I think, been properly introduced."

"An omission which should be remedied." Mrs. MacHugh rose gracefully from her seat, the silk of her tea gown whispering against the Turkish carpet. "Miss Hayes, may I present to you Monsieur de Robecourt. Monsieur de Robecourt, Miss Hayes."

Monsieur de Robecourt bent over Betsy's hand, brushing a kiss across the back. The shocking intimacy of his lips against her bare skin sent a tingle straight up her arm.

Still holding her hand, Monsieur de Robecourt smiled into her eyes, as though they had a shared secret. "Shall we start again, Miss Hayes?"

Something about his voice made it sound like an invitation to forbidden pleasures. Betsy could feel her cheeks go faintly pink. "I will if you will. I promise not to bowl you over this time."

"I shouldn't be so sure of that." With a bow, Monsieur de Robecourt relinquished her hand, and took the seat his hostess indicated. "What was it that you said to poor Rufus to make him look so fatigued?"

Striving to regain her composure, Betsy smoothed her skirt down over her legs. "Nothing the least bit outrageous. I simply asked to be allowed to participate in the excavations in Corinth. You would think I had suggested performing a cancan outside the palace!"

Monsieur de Robecourt raised a brow. "An intriguing prospect. Might anyone attend?"

"Their majesties might have something to say about that," countered Mrs. MacHugh, struggling to hide her smile.

"*C'est bien vrai.*" Monsieur de Robecourt's eyes slanted sideways to Betsy. "One would not want to cause a riot outside the palace."

"I would hardly do that," protested Betsy. Just the prospect of it made her feel terribly worldly and daring. It was heady stuff. "I only meant that I don't see why my wearing a skirt should impact my ability to perform a task. The Romans wore togas. The Scots wear kilts."

"Not all the time," interjected Mrs. MacHugh, her eyes dancing with amusement. "I can assure you on good authority. They've been subjected to trousers."

"Even so. Men's clothes can be just as confining as women's. Look at those ridiculous cravats you wear and those stiff collars." Betsy turned to Monsieur de Robecourt, waving her teacup in the direction of his throat.

Monsieur de Robecourt fingered the silk of his cravat. "Like the plumage of a bird—designed to attract the attention of the fairer sex." His eyes followed the curves exaggerated by Betsy's Paris suit with frank appreciation. "We have fewer natural advantages."

"That's beside the point." What was the point? Betsy tried to remember what she had been talking about. She was suddenly very aware of the way her breasts pressed against the fabric of her chemise. "The point is that there is absolutely nothing that makes women constitutionally incapable of the art of excavation and I mean to prove it."

Monsieur de Robecourt leaned back in his chair. "And how do you intend to go about that?"

"Strategically." Belatedly, Betsy remembered that her new companion was on first-name terms with the director of the American School. Just because she had bowled him over, quite literally, didn't make him an ally. "You aren't going to tell Dr. Richardson, are you?"

"I shouldn't dream of it."

"Monsieur de Robecourt is quite trustworthy," Mrs. MacHugh assured her. "For a Frenchman."

"This from Greeks bearing *gâteaux*? Ah, thank you." Monsieur de Robecourt accepted the tea cake his hostess offered him. "May I aid in your grand strategy?"

Betsy swallowed a mouthful of scone. Ethel would be terribly jealous; it really was very good. "Why should you do that?"

"To discommode Rufus, of course. And to oblige a lady."

There was a crumb on her lip; Betsy licked it off. "Dr. Richardson would say that to wish to participate fully in the work of the school makes me nothing of the sort."

Monsieur de Robecourt set his cake plate down on one knee, all mockery gone. "Then he and I have a very different definition of what it means to be a lady. One of my ancestresses went on Crusade with Queen Eleanor. She rode bare-breasted to Jerusalem. We have, I believe, a different idea of what it is to be a lady."

Betsy could feel little pinpricks all over, as though she'd been asleep and was only just waking up. She'd been told what ladies did and didn't do, but no one, not even her father, who believed she could do anything at all—as long as it had to do with classical studies—had suggested to her that perhaps a lady might be something different from the petted creature on a pedestal she had scorned to become. That a lady might do instead of just be.

"I'd never thought of that," said Betsy wonderingly. "It's rather like the classical concept of *virtu* as opposed to the modern idea of virtue. We praise people for what they refrain from doing rather than rewarding them for what they dare."

"What would you dare, Miss Hayes?"

"Well, I don't intend to excavate bare-breasted, that's for certain," said Betsy, without thinking.

"*Dommage*," murmured Monsieur de Robecourt. Betsy's cheeks flared. "You could set a fashion."

"I'm not that fashionable," said Betsy hastily. She had a mad, fleeting image of riding bare-breasted in the Greek sunshine, or lounging like Mrs. MacHugh, uncorseted, in soft silks. "Professor Sterrett is leading a party through the Peloponnese to Tiryns and Mycenae. I have been informed that this is a grueling expedition requiring a great deal of mud and the loud singing of college songs."

Mrs. MacHugh clapped her hands together. "And you mean to go along?"

"I can sing as loudly as anyone."

"I imagine you can." Something about the way Monsieur de Robecourt said it made it sound like a compliment. "What about the mud?"

"I don't adore it, but I don't mind it."

"I feel that way about a number of people," murmured Mrs. Mac-Hugh.

Monsieur de Robecourt sent her a look of mock distress. "Is that my cue to depart?"

"Not you, Charles—nor you, Miss Hayes. I haven't been so entertained in a fortnight." Betsy doubted that. Mrs. MacHugh seemed like the sort of woman who never failed to milk enjoyment from any circumstance. After the anxious atmosphere of the American School, Betsy found her immensely refreshing. This was a world of which Betsy knew nothing, of sophisticated banter, of royal courts, of casual erudition.

Of ladies who rode bare-breasted on Crusade. Or had. Several centuries ago.

Reluctantly, Betsy set her teacup down. She had stayed far longer than the half hour acceptable for a first call. "I should be getting back."

Mrs. MacHugh rose with her. "Do you still lodge at the Grande Bretagne?"

"For the moment." It was rather a sore point. "I shall have to find some more permanent accommodation, but the options are limited. The American School doesn't see fit to house its female students."

"Where shall you go?" asked Mrs. MacHugh.

Betsy made a face. "There's a Presbyterian minister with a room, I gather."

"I doubt he'd approve of the cancan," said Monsieur de Robecourt blandly.

"Hush, Charles." Mrs. MacHugh thought for a moment and then said decidedly, "It's very simple. I can't imagine why I didn't think of it before. You must stay with me."

Betsy stared at her, at the ormolu ornaments and the classical statuary and the peacock feathers in vases. "Here?"

"But why not?" Having had the idea, Mrs. MacHugh seemed quite enchanted by it. "There are rooms enough and not nearly enough people to fill them. It will be just the thing—for both of us. I have four sisters, all gone off in the world, and I miss them terribly. You can entertain me with your strategies."

"But what of Miss Hayes?" interjected Monsieur de Robecourt. "She is here to engage in serious study. What must she think of your menagerie?"

"Menagerie?" asked Betsy, glancing around as if expecting a tiger to appear at any moment. It wouldn't have surprised her.

"Artists and authors and cabinet ministers . . ." Monsieur de Robecourt shook his head sadly. "I don't believe there's a poet, politician, or courtier who hasn't made his way through Madame Mac-Hugh's salon."

"Including French classicists?" Betsy entered the fray on her new friend's behalf.

Monsieur de Robecourt bowed. "A veritable hit."

"Very well done!" said Mrs. MacHugh approvingly. "You'll do splendidly. Do stay."

Betsy did rather think it would do splendidly. It was certainly better than boarding with the Reverend Kalopothakes. Why should she question good fortune when it came calling? she thought giddily.

This, at last, was life. This was the world in all its glory and it was welcoming her in.

"You'll have to let me pay for my board," Betsy said firmly. Foreigners—aristocratic foreigners—might go living in one another's houses, but she was a Yankee and independent, and it was best her hostess knew that from the outset.

"Certainly," said Mrs. MacHugh gravely. "One peppercorn the quarter."

"Fifty drachma and no less."

"Fifty drachma and you let me introduce you to my dressmaker."

"Done," said Betsy, and held out a hand to seal the bargain.

She had a feeling this was the start of wonderful things.

Chapter Three

The world has congregated on the verandah of the Tampa Bay Hotel, with everyone from foreign diplomats to your own humble correspondent, as we all wait, in the Florida heat, for the answer to that great question: When will our brave boys set off to liberate Cuba?

One thing I can tell you: the waiting period has been considerably enlivened by the recent arrival on the scene of those riotous roisterers, Roosevelt's Rough Riders, who chugged into town this week with a lion cub, a dog named Cuba, and those relentless high spirits for which they are famed.

It's not surprising their mascot is a lion: this ragtag band of cowboys, Fifth Avenue dandies, and Harvard men are the lions of the camp. Everyone is angling for a glimpse of them and their charismatic commander. . . .

—*Miss Katherine Carson for the* St. Louis Star Ledger, *June 3, 1898*

Tampa, Florida
June 3, 1898

BETSY HAD A FEELING THIS was the start of terrible things.

She felt as wobbly as if she were still on the water as she followed Kit Carson down the makeshift pier. The tropical sun shone through the dust, giving everything a curious haze, as though she were fighting her way through glazed glass.

"You all right?" Kit put a hand on Betsy's elbow. "You look like you're about to keel over."

Betsy forced a smile. "I forgot to eat breakfast. Or lunch."

She wasn't sure when she'd last eaten anything at all. Some bread and cheese on the train. Horrible train coffee, tasting of chicory and served with milk that clumped. She'd held it for the warmth and dumped it out the window when it had gone cold.

"Here." Kit dug in her pocket. "I always keep something handy. . . ."

"No, really. There's no need—" The thought of chewing, of swallowing, was overwhelming. Betsy had geared up all her energy, all her courage, for this one grand sacrifice: offering herself up in place of Ava. But one couldn't offer oneself up in place of someone who wasn't there.

What was she meant to do now?

Kit stuck something into Betsy's hand. "Here. Reed's rolls. Butterscotch. It'll rot my teeth out someday, but it's worth it."

Fumbling with the paper, Betsy unwrapped it and put it in her mouth, feeling the sugar dissolving on her tongue, sending a rush of warmth through her. The butterscotch tasted of fall evenings on campus, of hot buttered cider and bread toasted on the fender and dried leaves crunching underfoot.

"Thank you," she said. The words felt rusty, and not just because she was talking around a large block of butterscotch.

"Think nothing of it. You gave me an excuse to escape the abattoir." Something in Betsy's face made Kit say quickly, "Just joking. It hasn't been as bad as all that. We get a lot of scalds and burns—boys who've never cooked around a campfire before. We've had synovitis of the knee, necrosis of the bones of the leg, sixteen ear infections, and a partridge in a pear tree. But you must have seen all this before."

"Not so many partridges in Greece. And I'm not even sure what synovitis is."

"Neither am I," said Kit cheerfully. "I'm just repeating what I heard Sister Bettina writing in her report. I'd thought necrosis sounded pretty dire, but it's just something to do with the joints. It'll impress the readers, though. Look, there's the train."

"The train?" In her addled brain, Betsy wondered for a moment if Kit had been given orders to pack her off to Boston. "I thought— weren't you showing me the way to the hotel?"

"This *is* the way to the hotel," Kit said, picking up speed, her eyes on the train belching black smoke at the station. "Good, you've got some pink back in your cheeks. The easiest way from Port Tampa to Tampa is by train. The roads are clogged with military. The trains are clogged too, but they're still better than the roads."

Betsy stumbled along in a clumsy half jog, her carpetbag bumping against her leg. "I didn't mean to take you so far out of your way."

Kit stopped on the platform with a sigh of satisfaction. "Phew, we haven't missed it. They're still unloading. And it's no bother. I was looking for an excuse to go that way anyway. It's where the news is. Such news as there is."

"Such news as there is?" Betsy echoed. Her corset was soaked through; her carpetbag, with the additional burden of her new uniform, weighed approximately ten tons. She felt a million years old, all the energy that had buoyed her on the long journey gone.

"I've seen children's parties organized more effectively than this war. No one knows whether they're coming or going. You should have seen the number of orders sent and canceled just since I've been here! Although the men do drill nicely." Kit waved a hand in the direction of a group of soldiers standing nearby. "Hiya, boys!"

Several of the men grinned and lifted their hats in reply. "Miss Carson!"

"It's missus, really," Kit confided to Betsy, waving to friends along the way as she took Betsy's arm and hurried her along the platform toward her preferred train car. "But you know how men are. Mention you're a mother and suddenly it's all 'ma'am' and foot shuffling and they won't tell you a thing. This way I'm like their kid sister and they blab their little hearts out."

"You're married?" Betsy was still trying to get her breath back.

Kit swung herself up easily into the train. "And two kids. Boy and a girl. I'd show you their pictures, but that would ruin my image."

"How old are they?" It was the sort of thing one asked.

"Six and four. Limbs of mischief, both of them." Kit looked at her sideways as they jostled their way to their seats. "Are you going to tell me I should be home with them?"

"Why should I?"

Kit gave her a look of surprise. "Most people do. But I was a reporter before I was a mother, and I'll be hanged if I'm going to give it up." Kit plopped down in the seat next to Betsy. "What about you? Husband? Kids?"

"None that I acknowledge."

Kit hooted. "Funny."

Betsy hunched over her carpetbag, cradled in her lap like a baby. "My brother wouldn't think so. He had his sense of humor surgically removed when he started at the Harvard Law School."

"He knows you're here?"

"He will when he gets the bills." At Kit's look, she added defensively, "It's my money. He can't touch it. But he's trustee."

"All the responsibility, none of the authority? He must love that."

"He's just waiting for me to overspend my income so he can refuse to disburse the principal."

"Is that what you're here for? To annoy your brother?"

Betsy glanced out the window, at the smoke-smudged landscape, trying to think of a convincing reason that sounded less crazy than the truth. *I'm here because I dared my best friend to take some risks for once in her life but I didn't mean this, not this, never this, and now I'm afraid she's going to die and it will be all my fault and she'll haunt me forever.*

Kit laughed. "Honey, you look just like my six-year-old when I catch her with her brother howling, swearing right and left she never took his toy, when it's right there behind her back."

"Maybe I just want to nurse the sick."

"And maybe the moon is made of green cheese. You've met the sisters. There's a certain air of zealotry about them. You, not so much. I know why I'm here; I know why they're here. Why are you here? And what does this Miss Saltonstall have to do with it?"

Betsy forced a smile. "I'm not a war story."

"Anything can be a war story." At the look of alarm on Betsy's face, Kit backed up. "Don't look like that! I'm not going to make you a women's page feature. Unless you give me good reason."

She was joking. Sort of. Betsy suspected that if it suited her, if it got her a larger headline, Kit Carson would have no compunction about making her a women's page feature—and no shame about it either.

A woman had to do what a woman had to do to survive in a man's world.

She respected that—but that didn't mean she wanted her private torments pasted over the yellow press. There was too much in her past that didn't bear inspection. Greece. Turkey. Switzerland.

Betsy narrowed her eyes at Kit. "How are you keeping up with the work? If you're not really a nurse."

"Any mother picks up a certain amount of practical nursing." Kit grinned, and Betsy found herself fighting liking her. Two years ago, she wouldn't have thought twice; she would have taken to Kit immediately, just as she'd taken to Aikaterini. Back before. "Don't worry. I'm not going to bore you talking about my babies. Or maybe just a little. I have to talk about them sometimes, get it out of my system."

The coal smoke made Betsy's throat feel scratchy. "Do you ever worry you might not make it back?"

Kit shrugged, looking away. "I worry I might not make it over there. Do you know that they won't let any women reporters near the encampments? Not even here in Tampa. What do they think? We'll swoon?"

"There are more women reporters here?" Betsy asked, grabbing at the back of the seat in front of her as the train rocked forward.

"At least four of us I know of. All trying to get the story of the century. If one of those bloated buffoons bunking with the boys doesn't scoop us first." Kit's foot tapped impatiently against the sticky floor of the train. "They've got William Randolph Hearst and Stephen Crane up there on the verandah of the Tampa Bay Hotel, cozying up with the brass, and every bit reporter you can think of sharing tobacco chews with the troops. They've even let in a cameraman from the Edison Kinetoscope Company! But no women. Not one."

"Maybe they think our constitutions are unsuited to the rigor of warfare."

Kit gave her a surprised look. "Don't you know it! You sound like you've heard it before."

"I used to be an archaeologist." No, that wasn't entirely true. Betsy licked her dry lips. "I *wanted* to be an archaeologist. They told me women don't dig. They told me to try training as a librarian."

"They told me I could write for the women's pages. This month's hats and next month's shoes."

"What did you do?"

"I wrote it." At Betsy's expression, Kit gave a quick, sharp laugh. "Honey, I can write about hat trim in my sleep."

"Why?"

"Because they wouldn't let me on the paper any other way. I'd have written about the life cycle of the ladybug if that was what it took. What matters is getting your foot in the door."

"But what if they won't let you stick the rest of you in and you're just stuck with your foot clamped in a door?"

Some of the determined girlishness drained from Kit's face, leaving her looking much older. Older and grim. "Then you just find your own door. Like volunteering with the Red Cross and hoping for a scoop." Pulling herself together, she said brightly, "Did you know the famous Rough Riders arrived last night?"

"The who?"

"Teddy's Terrors. Roosey's Red Hot Roarers. Roosevelt's Rough Riders." The train juddered to a halt. Kit pulled herself up by the back of the seat in front of them. "You know, Teddy Roosevelt's volunteer cavalry troop. The boys in the blue bandanas. You must have heard of them. Everyone's mad for them. I'd give my little finger for an interview with one of them."

"What's so special?" Betsy picked her way carefully down off the train. The butterscotch had helped. And maybe, just a little, the conversation with Kit. She no longer felt light-headed, just very, very tired. "They're all marching off to the same place."

"Oh, come on. If anything makes good copy, if there's anything every boy and girl in America wants to read about, it's Roosevelt and his Rough Riders. You must see the magic of it. The whole panorama of American manhood coming together in a common cause, sitting at the same mess. Senators' sons, cowboys, Yale men, desperadoes . . ."

Betsy got a better grip on her carpetbag. "What makes you think those categories aren't all one and the same?"

Kit's dimple appeared in her cheek. "A senator's son–cowboy– Yale man–desperado? Now that I'd like to see. You find me one of those, I owe you the finest dinner in town. Here's your hotel."

The hotel was, as Kit had said, unmistakable. Although it didn't look anything like any Turkish harem Betsy had seen. This was a Western fantasy of the exotic, coupled with the homey comfort of a wraparound porch.

Kit gestured grandly at the verandah. "This is where they all are: the generals, the foreign envoys, the wealthy curiosity seekers. I'm off to try to scrounge up some interviews. You'll be okay from here?"

A shadow fell over Betsy, a man-shaped shadow in a broad hat. "Miss Hayes?"

Betsy turned and found herself facing a brown canvas-covered chest. She looked up from a blue silk bandana to a face shadowed by a wide slouch hat bearing the insignia of some regiment or other. She could just make out a thin face, a thin nose, a thin cavalryman's mustache, a thin scar on one cheek.

This was all she needed. Paul's self-righteous cowboy friend.

Tampa, Florida
June 3, 1898

"IT IS MISS HAYES, ISN'T it?" Holt repeated, wondering if he'd accidentally accosted the wrong woman.

"No, it's an Eskimo," the woman said, and Holt knew, without a doubt, that this was the woman he'd met outside the train last night.

He'd seen her standing there, small and indomitable—it was the stance he'd recognized, more than anything else—and thought he ought to say hello, see how she'd fared, but when she just stared at him, he began to wonder if he'd made a mistake.

He'd definitely made a mistake. He should have just pretended not to recognize her and kept on walking.

"I'm glad to see you made it here safely."

It was a bit of a stretch. Miss Hayes looked like she'd been put through a wringer and come out the worse for it. Her purple hat listed to one side, revealing an equally lopsided chignon beneath. The blond hair looked dry and brittle, like a bird's nest.

Once, as a child, Holt had rescued a bird's nest. It turned out it didn't need rescuing at all, and the mama bird had swooped at him with all her feathers bristling and a look of mingled fear and fury that reminded him strangely of Miss Hayes. Fragile but fierce. Ready to peck.

He ought to stop trying to rescue things, Holt thought wryly. It never did end well.

The nurse standing beside Miss Hayes poked Miss Hayes in the ribs. "You didn't tell me you knew one of Teddy's Terrors."

Holt winced. He hated that name. He hated the crowds lining the train tracks shouting their names, the articles in the papers extolling them for exploits they hadn't committed, vilifying, deifying, making up stories when there weren't any to be had, turning them from ordinary men into pocket heroes, modern-day Robin Hoods, part bandit, part saint.

"I don't," said Miss Hayes flatly. "I didn't even know they were— whatever you called them. I only met Private Holt because he wouldn't let me get off the train last night."

"Wait. Did you say Holt? Not Hold 'Em Holt?" Miss Hayes's friend grabbed his arm. "Kit Carson, *St. Louis Star Ledger.*"

"Ma'am." Talking to reporters was always a mistake. Even ones dressed up as nurses. Disengaging his arm, Holt turned back to Miss Hayes. "Well, if you're all right . . ."

"Other than near asphyxiation from the close atmosphere of the train compartment, I'm perfectly all right, thank you."

Holt didn't quite understand how she managed to make him feel as though he were in the wrong. "It wouldn't have been safe to walk that way in the dark."

"I got back on the train, didn't I?" Miss Hayes folded her arms across her chest, emphasizing how loosely her jacket hung on her thin frame. "You didn't follow me here, did you? There's no need for more knight errantry."

"It wasn't knight errantry. It was just common sense." He was definitely going to stop rescuing people. Next time he met a woman on the train tracks, she could waltz off into the wilderness. "And I wasn't following you. I'm taking a message to Lieutenant Colonel Roosevelt."

"To Colonel Roosevelt?" Miss Carson elbowed past her companion to get to Holt. "What is it?"

"That, Miss Carson, is for Lieutenant Colonel Roosevelt's ears." Holt's head was beginning to ache, and not just from the sun. He really hoped it wasn't a migraine. He turned back to Miss Hayes. "In that case, I'll bid you—"

Miss Carson jumped in before he could complete his farewells. "You wouldn't care to give me an exclusive interview, would you? As one of the most notorious of Roosey's Red Hot Roarers?"

Holt couldn't help himself. *"Notorious?"*

"Celebrated, then. The man who stopped the Jakes Brothers from terrorizing the New Mexico territory now turns his talents to de-

fending the innocents of Cuba from the heavy fist of Spain." Holt
wasn't sure which was worse, her prose or the pain in his left temple,
which was growing more acute by the moment. Miss Carson leaned
forward, intent. "What do you think of the Fifth Avenue Boys? Are
they up to the job or are they too soft in the hoof?"

"I think we're all here with the same goal and we're all going to
work as hard as we can," said Holt, trying to keep his voice pleasant
with the blood pounding in his temple, sending red-hot pokers of pain
through his scalp. "And I don't mean for you to quote me on that."

"If I'm not going to quote you, could I at least say something about
seeing you?" said Miss Carson hopefully. "The celebrated lawman
Hold 'Em Holt delivering messages for his commander, wearing the
signature blue bandana of this dashing troop of daring deliverers?"

"I'm not a lawman." No, he'd seen to that, hadn't he? He and
the law had no more than a passing acquaintance these days. "Don't
write about me. Write about the men who died on the *Maine*. Write
about the Cuban women and children starving in Spanish reconcentration camps. That's why we're here. That's what we should be reading about."

Miss Carson batted her eyelashes at him, all girlish innocence.
"But the fact that you're all here to avenge them—that's a story too.
Don't you agree?"

"I'm not interested in stories. These aren't stories—these are
people's lives at stake."

"Your life too." Miss Hayes's voice rang out rough and raw, like
something scraped off the bottom of a shoe. "It's your life and the life
of every man here."

Holt looked at her sharply. "It's what we signed up to do. For the
women and children of Cuba." He'd seen the images of Cuban children more skeleton than flesh, grieving mothers clutching their starving babies. In an effort to curb rebellion, the Spanish authorities in

Cuba had torn hundreds of thousands of civilians from their homes, herding them into barbed-wire reconcentration camps, where those who didn't die of starvation were ravaged by disease. No one should have to live in that sort of want and fear. "Now, if you'll—"

The bones of Miss Hayes's face stood out too clearly in the sunlight, like a skull. "That's all very well, but what about the women at home? What about the children who'll never see their fathers again? You go waltzing off, playing at soldiers . . ."

Holt fought down his irritation. "We're not *playing soldiers*. We're the US Army." Admittedly, a rather irregular branch of it. But that was the American spirit for you. "What do you think we should do? Ask Spain nicely to treat the reconcentrados better? We tried that. It didn't work."

"So you're going to go in with guns blazing. They have guns too. And they probably know how to use them a good deal better."

Holt frowned at her, not quite sure he was hearing what he was hearing. "Are you saying we're going to lose?"

"There's no winning, don't you understand? Even if you win you lose." Miss Hayes looked straight at him, speaking with the detached authority of an ancient oracle. Her eyes weren't the blue one would expect with that hair but a deep gray, almost black. "The man next to you might be the one to fall. Or it might be you. Gone. Like that. And for what?"

"Maybe some things are worth dying for."

Miss Hayes shook her head, her hat wobbling. Holt had never seen anything so bleak as those eyes. "Like the Charge of the Light Brigade. They can write a lovely poem about you when you're all rotting beneath the palm trees."

With that, she turned and marched up the steps to the hotel, leaving her words to settle around Holt like a chill in the heat of the day.

Chapter Four

Darling Ava,

Look on ye mighties and despair! I've been walking in the steps of the Titans this week—gods and heroes and Cyclops.

Don't mind me. I'm antiquities drunk. It's intoxicating, seeing all of this in situ and not just in fuzzy photographs and artists' illustrations. It feels quite different when you're standing in the midst of it. That's when the true wonder of it all hits you. These were people, Ava. Actual people, not just creators of vases and myths left for future generations to puzzle over. They lived and ate—and bathed! Oh, the baths I've seen. I'm giddy with it.

We saw Tiryns today and we're bound for Mycenae tomorrow, Professor Sterrett, the Harvard boys, Ethel, and me. There is also a scholar from the French School who has happened to join us. The boys call Ethel the Coffee Angel. She managed to coax the beverage into being over a spirit lamp and served it in a Minoan jar (all right, it wasn't actually a Minoan jar, but it was its near descendant) and they're now her devoted slaves and carry her pack for her in the hopes of future favor.

More anon. Don't you wish you were here? You could be here; I'd arrange it all.

All my love,

Betsy

—Miss Betsy Hayes '96 to Ava Saltonstall '96

Athens, Greece
October 1896

THE MORNING CHILL FELT LIKE heaven on Betsy's flushed cheeks.

She'd been late, of course. She'd had to run like anything for the steamer, but she was here now, and had been clouted amiably on the shoulder by one of the Harvard boys, frowned at by Ethel, and harrumphed at by Professor Sterrett, although she thought she'd gotten the better of that one when she'd pointed out that she was proving her stamina for the rigors ahead by showing how she could run. He'd been bemused rather than cross, which Betsy thought boded well for their future association.

"Pardon me—excuse me—" Betsy wove her way past an entire herd of goats, holding her bag high above her head so they wouldn't scent the treats Aikaterini's cook had pressed on her.

She did love living with Aikaterini, and not just because of the cakes.

"You don't have to apologize to the goats," Ethel pointed out, as Betsy joined her at the rail.

"It's really more their boat than ours." Not just the goats, but at least one bewildered cow, several chickens, and an entire regiment of soldiers. There were old ladies in rusty black with their heads veiled carrying straw baskets, and irritated donkeys laden with pallets, and the clothes, oh, the clothes! The men sported wide red sashes and baggy trousers and sometimes a sort of skirted garment. Athens was marvelous, with its antiquities jostling against the grand, modern marble mansions that had been erected in the past few decades, but this—this felt like Greece as she had imagined it.

Betsy elbowed Ethel, too excited to pretend to be blasé. "Look at that man over there, the one in the beard. Doesn't he look straight off an Attic vase?"

"That one's more a marble head," said Ethel. "He looks like a bust I saw once in the Metropolitan Museum."

Betsy tried to look everywhere at once, drinking it all in. "I wonder what all those soldiers are doing here. Ought we expect pirates?"

"Not pirates," said a voice behind them. "But possibly Turks."

Betsy turned too fast and tripped over her own skirts. Monsieur de Robecourt caught her before she could fall, his hands warm on her upper arms.

"We seem destined to collide," he said, smiling at her from beneath the brim of his hat.

Betsy tilted her head up at him. "Only because you keep sneaking up behind me."

"Shall I depart?" he offered, his hands sliding down her arms to her elbows.

"Certainly not." Betsy suppressed an absolutely ridiculous impulse to rise up on her tiptoes and wrap her arms around his neck. "It's safer to keep you where I can see you."

Monsieur de Robecourt looked deeply into her eyes. "But am I safe from you?"

"You can always call the soldiers," Betsy suggested breathlessly.

He held her out at arm's length, examining her with mock seriousness. "You make a very unconvincing Turk."

"It's never been one of my aspirations," said Betsy, basking in the admiration in his eyes. "Is that what they're here for, these soldiers? To fight the Turks?"

Monsieur de Robecourt looked at her in surprise. Even worse, he let his hands drop. "But who else? The revolution wasn't so very long ago."

Betsy was vaguely aware that at some point the Ottoman Empire had occupied Greece and gone on occupying it until Lord Byron had made them stop. Or something of that sort. Betsy didn't much care. She wished they could go back to the bit where he was holding on to her arms and teasing her.

"It's rather like Leonidas and Themistocles, casting Xerxes back into Persia," said Betsy, trying to twist the conversation back onto familiar ground. "Two thousand years on and the heart of democracy still stands stalwart against the tyrant."

"Greece is a monarchy now," said someone to Betsy's left.

Ethel. Betsy blinked. She had forgotten all about Ethel. Ethel was standing there with her arms folded across her chest looking distinctly put out.

"Only a very mild sort of monarchy," Betsy said hastily. "Oh, goodness, where are my manners? Miss Ethel Lewis, Monsieur de Robecourt. He's one of those vandals from the French School that stole Delphi from us."

Ethel gave her a long, measuring look before holding out her hand to Monsieur de Robecourt. "Monsieur."

Monsieur de Robecourt bowed over her hand, but he glanced at Betsy as he spoke. "Are you, too, determined to prove that skirts don't prevent one from pursuing archaeology?"

"No," said Ethel crisply. "I have no interest in digging up the dead—only their words."

"A sanitary and sane pursuit." Something about the way he said it, however gravely, made Betsy feel like they were in a conspiracy together, the ones who didn't bow to the sanitary and the sane.

"Have you dug?" Betsy demanded.

"What she means," said Ethel, giving Betsy a look, "is have you participated in excavations."

"From here to the Valley of the Kings. I dabbled in Egyptology before following my heart to Greece."

Betsy burned to know just whose heart it was he had followed, but she couldn't ask, so she demanded instead, "You never did say what you're doing here. On this boat, I mean."

"Going on a trek to the Peloponnese, of course," Monsieur de Robecourt said lightly.

"With us?" That had sounded a little too eager. Betsy made an attempt at sangfroid. "Isn't this old hat for you?"

"Greece?" He held her gaze just a moment too long. "Greece never grows old. He who is bored with Greece is bored with life."

"You stole that from Dr. Johnson," said Betsy severely. She had to work very hard at being severe. His presence gave the cool morning air a fizz like champagne. Betsy could feel it going straight to her head.

"Did I?" He moved closer to avoid a pack of goats on the move. Betsy could smell his cologne and feel the warmth of his skin through the fine wool of his sleeve as his arm brushed against hers.

"Pure thievery."

Monsieur de Robecourt bent his dark head to speak to her above the din. "But he's dead; he'll never notice the loss of it. Besides, isn't that what archaeologists do? We rob the dead to delight the living."

Betsy thrilled to that *we*. "I think of it more as safeguarding their remains for them, making sure they're studied properly. It's for their own good, really."

Monsieur de Robecourt raised a brow. "Theirs? Or yours?"

"Does it matter?" asked Ethel, sounding rather exasperated about being left out again. "They aren't here to complain."

"An intriguing point." Something Betsy couldn't read passed across Monsieur de Robecourt's face. He took a step back, nodding to Betsy and Ethel. "I should pay my respects to my host before he thinks me impossibly rude."

And with a tilt of his hat, he was off to Professor Sterrett, leaving Betsy with Ethel, feeling bemused and slightly giddy.

"He does flirt," said Ethel calmly, and Betsy came back down to earth with a thump.

"Well . . . the French," said Betsy, as though she'd never thought anything of it, and went off with Ethel to join the Harvard men, although their company felt distinctly flat after the intoxicating worldliness of Monsieur de Robecourt.

THEY DOCKED THAT NIGHT OFF Nauplion, and went the next morning to Tiryns, trekking up to the ancient city in the clear, pure light of dawn.

"Famed for its walls," murmured Betsy, staring up at the massive fortifications, kissed with the light of the rising sun. Every now and then, Homer did get something right.

"It doesn't actually say *famed*," pointed out Ethel. "A more accurate translation would be well-walled."

There went romance. Betsy frowned at Ethel. "That's like saying Versailles was well-gilded. It doesn't convey the awe of it at all."

There were only the bare remnants of rooms remaining, the outlines of walls and scraps of frescoes, but Betsy could see them growing, becoming whole again. They ran around like schoolchildren, shouting and pointing, speculating and guessing. There, that had been the circular hearth in the *megaron*, or great hall. There, those were the remains of the temple of Hera, built onto the *megaron*—but later, so therefore less interesting. And there, that was what Professor Dörpfeld, who had excavated after Herr Schliemann (and was very careful not to be critical, although one could tell he wanted to), said was a bathing chamber. And, goodness, was that a sort of public latrine over there?

"Look," said one of the Harvard boys, forgetting to be superior in his excitement. "This is what old Dörpfeld was talking about. See that stone slab? They tilted it like that so the water from the bath would drain down there."

Ethel had her copy of *A Dictionary of Greek and Roman Antiquities* open to the section on Tiryns. "This says the bath itself would have been made of red clay decorated in a spiral pattern."

They wandered off together toward the women's quarters, bickering over Ethel's guidebook and fighting over how many pillars would have held up the main room. But Betsy lagged behind, looking at that perfectly tilted, smooth sanded stone floor, marveling at the wonder of prehistoric engineering that had been expended, not on the defenses of the fortress, not on stone carvings for the glorification of the ruler, but so that they could have a nice bath, with scented oils in stone jars, and not worry about the floor being all sloppy afterward.

Someone, three thousand years ago, had soaked here in a red clay bathtub, toes sticking up out of the tub, scrubbing off the sweat of a summer day.

Someone touched her shoulder.

"What?" Betsy turned, looking for Ethel and the boys, but found Monsieur de Robecourt instead. Flustered, Betsy scrabbled for her self-possession. "Did you say something?"

"Nothing of importance. You were away in the moon."

Betsy looked at the stone slab. It was just a stone slab again now. "Not the moon. Just three thousand years ago."

"Where's your hat?" Betsy felt her head. She didn't remember losing it. Monsieur de Robecourt set his own panama hat upon her head. "Here. And drink this. You look sun-dazed."

"Not sun-dazed. Antiquity dazed." Betsy drank the water without tasting it, staring out at the countryside falling away around them. The palace was at the very top of the citadel. In the fields below, a man was pushing a plow that might have been used in Homer's day. Past and present wove around each other, the boundaries uncertain. "Does one become acclimated through long acquaintance?"

Monsieur de Robecourt stood beside her, looking with her over the fallen walls of the once-great citadel. "A bit. But, no—not truly. It still awes me. This was old when Charlemagne was young."

"And Boston not even thought of yet. We're just specks in time. But this—it makes everything we've built feel so flimsy, so fleeting." Betsy thought about the ancient craftsmen who had built these walls, men toiling to get these stones into place, cursing as they jostled them, breaking off for a skin of wine, only to be yelled at by the foreman. "They lived on a different scale than we do."

"In the days of heroes—and goddesses."

Betsy could almost see the armies gathered below; the gods in state on Mount Olympus. She didn't realize she had swayed on her feet until Monsieur de Robecourt put a hand to her back to steady her.

He looked sideways at her. "It is dizzying, is it not? It's said that the Cyclops built these walls. No mortal man could have moved them."

"But someone did." It was hard to think sensibly when she was so very aware of Monsieur de Robecourt's fingers fanned out across the small of her back. "I'm more likely to believe in a pulley and tackle than a Cyclops."

"There speaks the cold pragmatist, plucking the heart out of old mysteries."

Betsy didn't like being called cold. She put her hand impulsively on his arm. "I didn't say I don't like the old myths! They're fascinating. But that doesn't mean I need to believe in them. I just need to believe that the Ancient Greeks believed."

"But you, mademoiselle, are above such base superstitions?"

"I wouldn't say that. I'm sure I'm crammed full of what people two thousand years from now would consider base superstition. But they're my superstitions and not anyone else's."

Monsieur de Robecourt's lips twisted in a wry smile. "You don't bow at the altar of Zeus, then?"

Betsy crinkled her nose at him. "He wasn't terribly reliable, was he? I don't want to be turned into a swan or visited with a shower of gold."

"The gods aren't kind to those they love," murmured Monsieur de Robecourt.

"I don't think you can call it love," said Betsy. "Not Zeus and his women. He only wanted them until he had them. That wasn't love; that was just desire."

Monsieur de Robecourt looked at her intently. "Just desire?"

Betsy was suddenly very aware of her hand on his sleeve, his on the small of her back. As if they were about to waltz. Or embrace. If either of them were to lean the tiniest bit forward . . .

"It doesn't do to underestimate desire." Monsieur de Robecourt's hand fell from her back. "One might as well say these are just walls."

He began walking and so Betsy did too, picking her way carefully around the fallen masonry. She felt dizzy, and not just with antiquities. Flirting, Ethel had called it. Betsy had done more than her share of flirting in the past, but she'd never felt anything like this, this elemental urge, this . . . desire.

Betsy cleared her throat. "Did you see the bath?"

"The bath?"

"Yes, that big stone slab I was looking at when you found me." Before she had gone mildly mad. "It's really rather marvelous, isn't it? Someone, three thousand years ago, soaked in that bath and rubbed oils from those jars on her skin. . . ."

"I saw the stone," said Monsieur de Robecourt slowly. "I knew that it was meant to have been a bath. But I did not see it. Not until you showed me. And now I can see it as if it were here before me, every drop of water, every trace of oil."

Betsy felt as though she were in that bath, her limbs soft with scented oil, the steam rising around them.

"There you have it. That's what archaeology is meant to do," said

Betsy briskly. "We make people see the past. People slept and washed and ate here. If we looked, I'm sure we could find bits of the jars they stored their oil in, the plates off of which they ate their meals. . . . Maybe even combs and bits of buckles from their clothes. All the bits and pieces we throw out and don't even think about after."

"Wouldn't you rather find royal regalia and treasures of state?" They'd come out of the palace complex now, onto a projecting bastion with a marvelous view of the countryside below. Betsy felt as though she were floating on the top of the world. "Think of the shaft graves Herr Schliemann found at Mycenae. Wouldn't you rather a golden mask than potsherds?"

Betsy stopped, leaning against the old bastion. "Those were stunning finds, and they look very well in a glass case. But don't you see? The treasures are the exceptions, the rarities. That makes them less valuable—from the point of view of figuring out how people lived, I mean," Betsy said hastily.

"So you shall search for . . . kitchen things?"

She'd never really thought of it quite like that before, but now that he'd said it, Betsy felt a wonderful sense of rightness, like stepping into the proper pair of shoes after trying on ones that pinched. She could pioneer a new sort of archaeology, not jostling for showy finds but painstakingly putting back together the lives of ordinary people, people like her.

Betsy glowed up at him, alight with her new inspiration. "Didn't your own Napoleon say an army marched on its stomach? An army marches on its stomach and everyone needs kitchen things."

Monsieur de Robecourt looked at her wonderingly. "Napoleon never said *that*."

"No, I did." Betsy beamed at him, dazzled by her beautiful new idea: the history of ancient Greece, told not through epics, but through the little daily things.

Monsieur de Robecourt lifted her hand, as if it were something infinitely rare and precious. Betsy thought he meant to kiss it, as he had before, in Aikaterini's drawing room. But he didn't.

Holding her hand in his, he said softly, "Wait until you see Mycenae tomorrow before you swear off royal regalia. Or better yet . . . come to Delphi with me next month. We'll see if one of the most sacred places in Greece can make you change your mind about kitchen things."

Betsy tilted her head back, looking Monsieur de Robecourt in the eye. "I don't change my mind easily. But you're welcome to try."

His fingers twined with hers. Betsy closed her eyes against the glare of the sun, letting herself sway forward.

There was a pointed cough behind them. Ethel tapped Betsy sharply on the shoulder. "Betsy. *Betsy.* You dropped your hat."

"Bless you," said Betsy, feeling thoroughly bemused. "Now Monsieur de Robecourt can stop courting sunstroke."

"Are you sure sunstroke is all he's courting?" asked Ethel.

CHAPTER FIVE

The Red Cross ship the *State of Texas*, filled with food and clothing for the suffering Cubans, daily awaits the order to sail—as do our troops.

The *State of Texas* is not, as people suppose, a hospital ship, but was chartered solely to carry medicines, clothing, and food to the reconcentrados, about whose plight you can read in last week's edition. However, the troops were so convinced that any ship bearing the insignia of the Red Cross must be intended for the treating of their ills that the doctors and nurses on board bowed to the inevitable and converted the smoking room into an operating room, the purser's room into a dispensary, and state rooms into wards where our patients might receive rest, quiet, and watchful care under the expert eye of the nursing sisters.

Nonetheless, none of us has forgotten our true mission, or that of our brave boys in uniform: to free the people of Cuba.

Due to a lack of transports, not all of our boys will make it over, and it would do your heart proud to see them fight over who should have the honor of liberating the reconcentrados from the suffocating yoke of Spain. . . . Millionaires' sons and cowboys alike beg for the privilege of firing a shot for freedom.

The word about who will go and who won't changes daily, but this reporter has heard that among the chosen are William Tiffany of the New York Tiffanys, Oklahoma broncobuster Bill McGinty, Harvard football player and famed yachtsman Woodbury Kane, and the fearless bounty hunter Hold 'Em Holt, who brought the Jakes Brothers to justice.

Let's hope he can do the same for the reign of Spain. . . .

—*Miss Katherine Carson for the* St. Louis Star Ledger, *June 7, 1898*

❧

Tampa, Florida
June 8, 1898

"BETTER PUT ON YOUR HAT before you get sunstroke," said Holt.

Paul obediently crammed his hat down on his head, squinting along the tracks. "I'm sure the train will be here any time now."

"Uh-huh," said Holt. There was dust in his eyes, dust in his nose, dust in places he didn't want to think about there being dust. They'd been standing on this train siding since midnight the night before, waiting for a train they'd been told was coming to take them the nine miles to Port Tampa for immediate departure for Cuba.

"You don't happen to have a cracker on you?" asked Paul hopefully.

"Not a crumb." They'd left in such haste, so sure they'd be on shipboard by dawn, that no one had bothered to pack any provisions. It was the coffee Holt missed; it helped keep the headaches at bay.

Paul shrugged that aside, undaunted. "It could be worse. At least we get to go. Think of those poor mugs back in camp missing all the fun."

"You call this fun?" But Holt knew what he meant. Back at the camp were men who'd rushed from all over the country to join up, and, after all that, they wouldn't even get to be part of the big moment. There'd been a problem with the boats, the problem being that there weren't enough of them. There were rumors that Colonel Wood and Lieutenant Colonel Roosevelt had tossed a coin to see which troops would go.

But Troop L was safe. Troop L was without their horses—there was no room for horses—clumsily hauling unaccustomed packs, staggering bandy-legged on boots that felt odd without their spurs, but they were on the move.

Paul raised his voice to be heard over the rattle of a series of coal cars chugging up the line from Port Tampa. "You'll see; Lieutenant Colonel Roosevelt will get us over there."

The coal cars clanked to a stop. And then came the distinctive voice of their lieutenant colonel, who was waving his hat and shouting, "All aboard! Our chariot awaits!"

There was a mad scramble for the coal cars, men hoisting themselves up over the sides, grappling and slipping, plunking themselves grimy but triumphant on top of the mountains of coal. A cheer went up from the men as the train began chugging backward toward Port Tampa, laden with coal and volunteer cavalry.

"Told you he'd do it!" Paul bounced on his throne of coal, waving his hat and cheering himself hoarse. "Told you our Teddy would find a way!"

"Bass-ackwards," said Holt drily. Lieutenant Colonel Roosevelt and Colonel Wood were leading their regiment from the caboose, to the great hilarity of all.

"Yes, but it's getting us there, isn't it?" said Paul blithely. "And that's all that matters."

"Right," said Holt, and tried to mean it. Ends and means and all that. It wasn't the manner of their going that mattered. It was that they got there.

They'd be all right once they got to Cuba. Once they were there, on the ground, doing what they were trained to do.

Without their horses. Without most of their gear.

Facing Spaniards far more experienced and far better trained than they.

Just like the Charge of the Light Brigade. They can write a lovely poem about you when you're all rotting beneath the palm trees.

"That friend of yours," Holt said abruptly. "The girl."

"Girl?" Paul was extracting a large piece of coal from a sensitive part of his posterior. "Ouch! You mean the one from Ybor City who—"

"No. The one we met at the train the night we came to Tampa." Those big, hollow eyes. Holt saw them in his nightmares. He'd roll over on his bedroll in the tent he shared with Paul and there she'd be, like a drowned woman, floating just beneath the water. "The one you took to the Yale prom."

"What, Betsy?"

"Yes. That's the one. Is she all right?"

"Why wouldn't she be? Betsy is . . . well, she's Betsy." Seeing that wasn't going to do, Paul added heartily, "She's bully, just bully."

Paul had adopted a tiresome habit of imitating their assistant commander in all his more obvious eccentricities. Holt was only surprised Paul hadn't started sewing fifteen pairs of eyeglasses into his hat and the lining of his clothing in emulation of the famously near-sighted Roosevelt.

Holt refrained from comment. "She didn't seem that bully to me."

"Well, she'd just got off a train. Betsy's a great girl. Almost not like a girl at all." Paul grinned, his teeth very white in his coal-grimed face. "It's hard to imagine her nursing, though. Can't think why she took it up. She's not exactly the sort to mop the old fevered brow. She's more likely to order you to get well and then scold you if you don't."

The haunted woman he had met outside the Tampa Bay Hotel had nothing at all in common with Paul's great girl. Except possibly the scolding. "She didn't seem well."

"Don't let her lack of inches and that milk-and-water complexion deceive you," said Paul wisely. "She's strong as a mule and just as stubborn. Hoy! Why are they pulling us over?"

Their dusty cavalcade was shunted to a siding as a passenger train barreled past, bearing the 71st New York Volunteers. The men leaned out the windows, waving madly and shouting, "It's the Rough Riders! Hallo, Teddy! Speech! Speech! Show us your teeth, Teddy!"

Laughing, they left the Rough Riders behind in a cloud of dust.

Paul scrambled up to his feet on the pile of coal, cupping his hands around his mouth to shout, "We'll see you in Cuba!" and then overbalanced as the train started up again, sliding madly toward the ground.

Holt grabbed him by the collar before he could tumble over the side. "Fine lot of good you'll do us in Cuba with a broken leg."

Paul plunked back down on his bottom, bright-eyed and energized. "Right you are. Don't want Betsy to bandage me up. She'd probably break the other one as a lesson to me for being so stupid."

Was he going mad? Maybe Holt was the one suffering from heat exhaustion. He'd experienced that his first month in the New Mexico territory, when he was too stupid to know to get out of the sun.

Paul was right; the woman had just come off a sleepless night on a train, followed by a strange city and oppressive heat. She was tired, she was cross; it was Holt's own demons that made him see a damsel in distress where there was none.

Guilt stabbed him in the gut, still sharp after all this time. Over the past three years, he'd tried to drink himself numb; he'd tried to fight himself clean; he'd tried to escape by putting miles in between. But if he'd learned anything, it was that there was no wilderness far enough, no oblivion deep enough; he took his sins with him, like the pack on his back, welded there for eternity.

The coal cars shuddered toward the end of the line. Holt could see the gleam of water, the harbor thick with ships, waiting to carry them across to Cuba. To free starving women and children from the yoke of Spanish tyranny.

If he could strike a blow for them, if he could relieve one woman of her suffering, he would have, not atoned—there was no atoning— but he would have done something. He might be able to look himself in the mirror again.

And as for Miss Betsy Hayes, she could just take her pronouncements of gloom and doom and stick to splinting legs.

In a spirit of exaltation, Holt swung himself off the coal car— and sank ankle deep into the sand. He had to do a fancy quickstep to keep his pack from bowling him over backward, flailing in the sand like a bug on his back.

Around him, the rest of the troop was floundering, trying to get their footing. One man fell flat on his face and was hauled up, spitting out mouthfuls of sand.

"I knew I should have brought my bathing costume," gasped Paul. "Which one of these transports do you think is ours?"

"I don't know." Holt looked around for someone else who might.

It was hard to miss General Shafter. He had settled his bulk on a makeshift chair composed of two cracker boxes, overseeing the operation from a packing crate. He was surrounded by indignant, redfaced officers all demanding to know what to do with their troops. As for the twenty-odd thousand troops of Shafter's army, ranks had long since broken. Some men made a beeline for the water, wading fully clothed into the surf in a desperate attempt to cool off; others had wandered off to a row of shanties that seemed to have sprouted from the sand overnight.

One of the other members of the troop came slinking over. Bill called himself a cowboy, but he was, as far as Holt could tell, more of a two-bit card shark, long on stories, short on action. He'd been running a good trade in bilking the credulous Ivy Leaguers, dazzled by their brush with the real Wild West.

Ignoring Holt, Bill sidled straight up to Paul. "This looks like it's gonna take a while. You wanna come get some General Miles grape juice?"

The residents of Tampa, unnerved at the reputation of Roosevelt's men for rough drinking as well as rough riding, had begged that spiritous liquors not be served. So the good bartenders of Tampa had gotten around it by creating innocent-sounding libations with a kick like a mule.

Paul's flushed face lit up. "First round's on me. General Robert E. Lee milkshakes all around!"

"Whoa." Holt grabbed his bunkmate by the sleeve. Sweat dripped down his forehead, stinging his eyes and blurring his vision. "You want to miss the call to board?"

"Doesn't look like we're going anywhere fast," said Bill, defending his right to Paul's company, or, more accurately, Paul's wallet.

Holt felt like a very unlikely nursemaid. But Paul was one of life's innocents. It would be plain wrong to let him be fleeced by Bill. Besides, if Paul didn't make it over, he might have to share his tent with someone else. "You never know. You want to tell your kids you didn't make it to Cuba because you were caught with your pants down in a one-room whorehouse?"

Paul scratched his chin. "You put it that way . . ."

"We've come this far." To rot beneath the palm trees. Holt pushed Miss Hayes's voice out of his head. "Think of the boys back in camp cursing because they didn't get to join us."

"Well, if *Holt* says you can't come out and play . . ." Bill shrugged, looking around for another Easterner to pay his bar bill. "Your loss."

Paul looked longingly at a shack selling General Miles grape juice. "Maybe just a small one?"

"You drink liquor in heat like this, you're going to feel a thousand times worse," Holt said tersely. "What you want is water and lots of it. Coconut milk's fine as long as no one's put rum in it. Or juice. Actual juice."

Paul looked at him as though he were an early saint dispensing the gospel. "Good thing I've got you to show me the ropes."

"It's just common sense." He had never asked to be held up as an icon of the Wild West. He was about as much of a real cowboy as Paul. "Doesn't take a genius to tell you that dehydration isn't your friend."

"My old nanny used to say there's nothing common about common sense," said Paul blithely. "Oh, look! What's that?"

That was Lieutenant Colonel Roosevelt, sprinting for all he was worth, shouting, "The *Yucatan*! The *Yucatan*! You! You there! Take a group of men and guard the train with our supplies! You! Round the boys up and get 'em on board! Double-quick! Step lively, men! Time and tide wait for no man!"

With a whoop, the Rough Riders charged toward the ship, fatigue forgotten, heat forgotten, their thick coating of coal forgotten, hats waving, voices hoarse with cheering as they picked up the cry, "The *Yucatan*!" They thronged the gangway as the ship moved with painful slowness to the dock, and two other groups of soldiers advanced.

"Guard the gangway, boys," muttered Lieutenant Colonel Roosevelt, striding to the front, as the men clustered around the gangway in the unforgiving sun.

"Tell your men to move aside," barked the colonel in charge of the 71st New York. Holt recognized some of the men who had been shouting for Teddy that morning as they chugged past the Rough Riders on their comical coal cars. "We've been assigned this ship."

"So were we," said Roosevelt serenely. The gangplank was being laboriously attached to the ship. Roosevelt made shooing motions behind his back, urging the men to board. "You may have been assigned it, but we seem to have it."

"Wait!" It was the commanding officer of the 2nd US Infantry. "Just a minute! That's our transport! As your ranking officer . . ."

"I'm sure we can fit some of your boys aboard," said Roosevelt calmly. "After we get settled. You over there! What are you young men up to?"

Two men were in the process of setting a hand-cranked camera on a tripod by the side of the gangplank. One looked up from his work. "We're from the Vitagraph Company, Colonel Roosevelt," he said tentatively, as if waiting for Roosevelt to bite. "We're going to Cuba to take moving pictures."

The lieutenant colonel stepped aside, motioning them to proceed up the gangplank. "I can't manage a regiment, but I'm sure I can squeeze in two more," he said genially.

"This is absurd," blustered the commanding officer of the 71st New York. "It's nothing short of highway robbery!"

"My apologies," said Roosevelt, showing all his teeth, just as the men of the 71st had demanded that morning. Holt doubted they liked it so much now, standing there in the sun, balked of their boat. "I'm under orders from my commanding officer to hold the gangplank. My hands are tied."

He spread his hands, which were very clearly not tied. Colonel Wood might technically be commanding officer, but there was very little doubt who really ran the regiment.

The commanding officers of the 71st and the 2nd US Infantry stomped off to complain to General Shafter as the Vitagraph men cranked their camera and Roosevelt turned his wide grin to his men.

"Individual initiative, boys. That's what it's about. Now let's get our gear on board before someone else tries to steal our ship!"

A great cheer shook the ship. Men were hanging from the sides, hollering their approval, as the weary 71st tramped away in search of another transport.

From the ship, the dock looked even more chaotic than before, companies broken up between ships, men staggering out from the makeshift bars trying to find their regiments. Holt found himself wondering whether individual initiative was really the best way to organize an invasion and hoping that wouldn't be the order of the day when it came to battle.

Paul slung an arm around Holt, yanking him into an exuberant hug. "You're my lucky charm, Holt. Just think if I'd had my pants down and missed this! Huzzah for Colonel Roosevelt! Huzzah for the Rough Riders!"

As the *Yucatan* began to back slowly away from the pier, toward Cuba and glory, the 2nd Infantry's band struck up the opening strains of "A Hot Time in the Old Town." It did seem a bit skewed to Holt that there hadn't been room for the 71st on the ship, but they'd managed to fit in the Vitagraph men and the 2nd Infantry band.

"You're singing it wrong!" shouted Paul with glee. "There'll be a hot time in Cuba next week!"

And the whole company took up the refrain, "A hot time in Cuba next week!"

Port Tampa, Florida
June 16, 1898

"CUBA? NOW?"

"What else could it be?" Kit shoved an armload of bandages into the cupboard and slammed the door with a triumphal bang. "Miss Barton is finally back and the stevedores have been loading like nobody's business."

Betsy stared dumbly at Kit, her own burden of blankets all but forgotten. They'd been on the *State of Texas* for two weeks now, long enough for their life on the ship to settle into a routine. "But—we can't leave. We haven't got orders. And what about the other nurses? The New York contingent?"

"You mean your friend?" Kit asked shrewdly. "I guess they'll join us when they join us. You really think Clara Barton is going to wait around for a group of auxiliary nurses when the army is on the move?"

"But are they? Really?" The army had boarded over a week ago and been sitting there, sweating on their ships, ever since. There'd been news of a Spanish warship sighted. Betsy knew it was unpatriotic but she was grateful for that Spanish warship if it kept the fleet from doing whatever it was fleets were meant to do. "They've said they're going before and haven't."

"This time it's for real." Under her tidy cap, Kit was fizzing with excitement. "They've sailed already. No one knows where they've gone. Goodness only knows if they know where they're going! But wherever it is, we'll be there too."

"I thought the secretary of the navy hadn't answered any of Miss Barton's letters." The scuttlebutt among the nurses was that their services had been tendered to the army—and ignored.

Kit grimaced. "He still hasn't. Just like a man. But Miss Barton is made of sterner stuff. When he changes his mind, we'll be there."

"But . . ." Betsy looked down and realized she'd unraveled a whole corner of the blanket. They couldn't be sailing. Not yet. Ava wasn't here.

She should be glad of that. Ava wasn't here. That was the whole point, wasn't it? To stop Ava coming to Cuba.

Only, Betsy realized, with a sickening lurch of her stomach that had nothing to do with the movement of the ship, it wasn't. Not really.

She hadn't come to save Ava. She'd come because, as much as she'd hurt Ava, as much as she'd pushed Ava away, she'd hoped, deep down, that Ava would say, "Oh, Betsy," in that exasperated way of hers, and then hold out her arms and let her rest. She'd come because she'd trusted that Ava would forgive her, as she'd always forgiven her before. Even if the offenses this time had been so much worse.

If she didn't have Ava, she didn't have anyone.

"Are you all right? You're looking green about the gills."

Betsy made an effort to pull herself together. "Is that your official assessment as a trained nurse?"

"That's my assessment as someone who's held more heads over buckets than you've had hot dinners," said Kit, unimpressed. "My oldest gets sick the second she gets in a carriage. She goes about the same color you are now."

She'd told herself she didn't need anyone. She'd told herself this was all a noble act of self-sacrifice. But it wasn't. Betsy could feel the despair pulling her under. She couldn't even do noble sacrifice right.

You've been given everything, Ava had said furiously. *You've been given everything and you're throwing it away.*

"Look," said Kit, putting a hand on Betsy's arm. Her fingers were stained with ink from the dispatches she'd been writing up in between her nursing shifts. "There's no guarantee we'll be in on any fighting. We're a relief force. There's always a chance it will be all over by the time we get there and we'll go in with our medical supplies and our barrels of jerked beef and tour orphanages and feed hungry children like Miss Barton meant to do in the first place."

Betsy made a choking sound she hoped would pass for a laugh. "If there's no war, then what will you write about?"

"Angels of mercy saving starving children," said Kit calmly, but Betsy could tell she was watching her. "Readers love that sort of thing. Come on, let's go hear what Miss Barton has to say. The word is that she's going to make some sort of formal address now she's back."

Betsy held up her pile of blankets. "You go ahead. I need to get these stowed."

What she really needed was to curl up in a ball, her arms over her head like a little girl hiding from the monsters under the bed.

"You're sure?" Kit's notebook was already in her hand. Betsy could see her shifting from foot to foot, torn between staying with Betsy and not missing the latest scoop.

"You go on." Betsy did her best to look calm and competent and not the least bit green. Cuba. She'd never bothered to think what would happen if they went. All her imaginings had ended with Ava. "I'll be there in a few minutes."

"All right," said Kit, but she didn't sound convinced. "I'll see you up there. Don't do anything stupid."

She left before Betsy could tell her she already had.

Chapter Six

Darling Ava,

My modern Greek proceeds apace—a very slow pace, but any pace is still a pace. The servants seem to understand me, at any rate, and that's the most important part of the exercise. If I'm ever to have part in a dig, I must be able to speak to the workmen in their own language and remember to keep my g's a sort of y sound instead of the hard g of antiquity. Aikaterini tells me it's harder for classicists to learn modern Greek than the average layman. She also tells me my dress sense is terrible and I was not made for excessive trim. Yes, I know you've been telling me that for years, so don't gloat.

Despite our triumphant trek to Mycenae, Professor Richardson is still unconvinced as to the fitness of the female sex to endure the rigors of classical studies. Mercifully, the gentlemen of the other schools are more broadminded. I am to be given a tour of Delphi by an archaeologist of the French School.

Do you think the oracle will speak to me if I ask it nicely in my very best classical Greek?

> *All my love,*
> *Betsy*

—Miss Betsy Hayes '96 to Ava Saltonstall '96

Athens, Greece
November 1896

"DOES MONSIEUR DE ROBECOURT OFTEN arrange excursions for students of the American School?"

"Charles?" Aikaterini half turned on the pedestal on which she was standing, eliciting an agitated clucking from the woman crouching at her feet. "Yes, yes, I'll stand still."

It had become part of the routine of the house, Betsy joining Aikaterini in her boudoir for her morning dress fittings, happily breathing in the scents of rich fabrics and even richer perfumes. Betsy had grown up in a house of men. There had been only her father and Alex—and the less said of her brother, the better. But with Aikaterini, she felt what it might have been like to have a high-spirited sister to turn to. Someone who would listen and understand, not just about Herodotus, but about everything from the arrangement of hair to affairs of the heart.

Even so, it had taken her weeks to get up the nerve to ask Aikaterini about Monsieur de Robecourt.

Betsy ducked her head over a bowl of sweetmeats, saying casually, "I only ask because he's got up an expedition to Delphi for the lot of us. I wasn't sure if he made a habit of it."

Or if he had only done it for her. Which was a foolish notion to contemplate. But Betsy couldn't help contemplating it, any more than she could help the thrill she felt every time she came down to Aikaterini's drawing room or entered a lecture hall and found Monsieur de Robecourt there, smiling at her, making the room glow as though all the gas jets had been turned up at once. Nice condescension from an experienced archaeologist to a would-be one, Betsy told herself, but there was a frisson she certainly didn't feel with darling old Dr. Dörpfeld of the German School.

Betsy could just see their pictures in the paper in the fashion of that other notorious archaeological couple, Mr. and Mrs. Radcliffe Emerson, both covered in dirt and dust, posing next to a half-excavated column. "Monsieur and Madame de Robecourt at the site of their latest excavation. . . ."

Yes, Monsieur de Robecourt was a good bit older than she was, at least forty to her twenty-two, but what did that matter? Her father had been nearly fifty when he'd married her mother.

"That is . . . surprising." In response to an annoyed exclamation in Greek from her dressmaker, Aikaterini obediently turned so her back was to Betsy before adding, "I've never known Charles to take an interest in nursery parties."

"We're all of us adults," said Betsy indignantly. "He came with us to Tiryns too, and Mycenae."

Aikaterini looked sharply back over her shoulder. "He didn't mention that."

Betsy could feel herself flushing slightly. "Well, you know, the scholars of the different schools do tend to go about together. . . . But I was a bit surprised he should want to come with us. He must have seen Mycenae a dozen times."

"More than that." Cognizant of the pointed tugs on her hem, Aikaterini turned back around, standing very still. To the wall at the back of the room, she said, "He's married, you know."

"He's . . . what?" Betsy gaped at Aikaterini's back.

"Married," repeated Aikaterini. "And has been for some time."

There had to be some mistake. The way he looked at her. The way he spoke to her. She'd thought he was about to kiss her at Tiryns. Even Ethel had noticed.

"He never mentioned a wife."

"I don't imagine he did," said Aikaterini drily. "But he has one all the same."

Betsy drew her knees up to her chest, feeling like an idiot. No wonder Aikaterini had called them a nursery party. He'd been being urbane and she—she'd been fancying herself in love. Had she been very obvious about it? Betsy desperately hoped not.

"I ought to have realized he was married." Betsy pressed her forehead against her knees. "I should have known a man of his age . . . It would be strange if he weren't."

"Strange but not impossible."

Betsy wished Aikaterini would stop being so nice about it. It made it worse. It would be easier if Aikaterini would just mock her as she deserved for thinking a man like Monsieur de Robecourt would pay court to a scrappy thing like her. Alex's wife, Lavinia, was adamant that no man ever would. Too educated, too opinionated.

"It never occurred to me. . . . My father didn't marry until late. But that's different. He was so unworldly everyone wondered he managed to marry at all. But Monsieur de Robecourt—he doesn't seem like that."

"No," said Aikaterini, "he's not. Charles can be . . . very compelling."

There was something in her voice that made Betsy lift her head from her knees and squint up at her, but Aikaterini still had her back turned to Betsy. Aikaterini switched to Greek and said something to the seamstress, who sat back on her heels to listen and then started doing something with the fabric just above Aikaterini's left hip.

Betsy had wondered, sometimes, if there might be something between Monsieur de Robecourt and Aikaterini, if Aikaterini's was the heart he'd followed to Greece.

But Aikaterini, for all her laughing sophistication, seemed genuinely devoted to her dour Scottish husband. Betsy didn't understand Aikaterini's marriage at all. They were such very different people and, from what she could see, led entirely separate lives. John MacHugh was taciturn to the point of grim, a former doctor who now confined his doctoring to the servants and spent most of his time running Aikaterini's family's shipping business. He appeared periodically at supper, but almost never for the fashionable teas, salons, and balls to which Aikaterini was escorted by a never-ending crowd of admirers. Betsy had seldom seen them exchange more than a few words. But perhaps it was different when they were together, on their own.

What did she know, anyway? She didn't have much of a model for marriage. Her mother had died when she was two, and her father had shown no inclination toward remarriage. As for her brother, Alex, and his wife, Lavinia, they were hardly an advertisement for modern matrimony. Betsy had no doubt they were well-pleased with their situation and with each other, but she had no desire to sit on charitable committees while her husband puffed out his chest and basked in his own importance.

And then there was Monsieur de Robecourt. What was his marriage like that he left his bride in Paris while he spent the year in Athens? Did they exchange long letters across the divide? Sonnets and words of love? Long musings on the intricacies of classical civilization?

"Have you met her?" It was like poking at a sore tooth. Betsy knew she shouldn't, but she couldn't quite seem to help herself. "Madame de Robecourt?"

Aikaterini glanced back over her shoulder. "I've met the baroness."

"What is she like?"

"Very *comme il faut.*" As her dressmaker made swishing motions, indicating she could turn back toward Betsy, Aikaterini abandoned her attempt to be diplomatic. "She's a frightful snob. She knows all the orders of precedence and will freeze you with offended dignity should you accidentally offer a deeper seat to someone of inferior rank."

"A deeper seat?"

"Oh, there are rules, you know, about who gets which sort of chair based on the purity of the blood." Aikaterini looked back over her shoulder at Betsy, her dark eyes dancing with amusement. "One wouldn't want to offer an armchair to anyone but a prince of the blood. A stool will do for the minor gentry. As for the merchant class, one might as well let them stand if one has to let them in at all."

Betsy's grandfather had made his fortune by importing expensive carpets and manufacturing cheap ones. She could still remember the mills in Yonkers, the bustle and smell of them, before her grandfather's death had freed her father to sell the lot, keeping only the import end of the business, and move to Boston.

But they had never belonged to old Boston, any more than she belonged to old Europe. She was, when it came down to it, an upstart carpet heiress from Yonkers. She had industry seeping through the pores of her skin. The baroness would probably wrinkle her nose at the stench of it.

"And the baroness?" Betsy demanded. "Is she an armchair or a footstool?"

"Oh, an armchair, of course. Her mother is descended from not one but two of Louis XIV's by-blows and she won't let anyone forget it for a moment. *Plus royaliste que le roi.* And that, my dear, is why Madame la Baronne lives in state in the Faubourg Saint-Germain and Charles comes here and grubs in the mud."

Betsy thought of Monsieur de Robecourt, sun-browned and rumpled, laugh lines around his eyes. She hadn't thought he would mock her for stinking of the carpet mill. "How on earth did they come to marry?"

"It was a family arrangement." At the look on Betsy's face, Aikaterini burst into laughter. "My dear. It's only in the new world that people marry for love."

"But you—"

"Oh, I'm the exception that proves the rule," said Aikaterini airily. A little too airily. Every now and then, Betsy was reminded how little she truly knew of Aikaterini, for all that she felt like family. "And John allowed himself to be adopted into the family. It would have been quite another matter if he had insisted on following his profession. Such are the sacrifices we make for love."

Betsy had fancied Monsieur de Robecourt in love with her, gradually building to a grand declaration. Betsy groaned and buried her face in her hands. "He must think I'm an idiot."

"Charles? If it will make you feel any less a fool," said Aikaterini gently, "he told me he thinks you have a—how did he put it?—a unique and refreshing turn of thought. He says you sweep away his cobwebs and make him see things fresh."

Brilliant. She was something on the order of a patent carpet sweeper, removing dust.

Betsy worried at a cuticle. "Should I not go to Delphi? There's a whole excursion planned, Delphi and Mount Helicon and Thebes. I'd already said yes—and the others too. But if you think—"

"It isn't really the season for it," said Aikaterini slowly. "It gets quite cold on Mount Parnassus in this season. But if it has already been arranged . . . I don't see the harm in it. As long as you go prepared."

"I'll bring my most unflattering woolens," said Betsy glumly.

BETSY DIDN'T EVEN NEED THE woolens to make her unglamorous. Their small party traveled by donkey. Betsy defied anyone to look dashing on a donkey.

Not that she should want to look dashing. After many agonized midnight reflections, Betsy had come to the conclusion that she should be grateful that an experienced archaeologist appreciated her mind—and thought her sophisticated enough to flirt. There was no reason that she couldn't be friends with Monsieur de Robecourt. She had few enough friends in Greece. And no one but Aikaterini ever needed to know what a cake she had made of herself.

Even so, Betsy couldn't help but look with chagrin at her legs in their unflatteringly thick stockings as her donkey jolted down the path, following a convoy of locals leading heavily laden camels.

"It could be worse," she muttered to herself. "It could be a camel."

"Ah, you saw the camels." Monsieur de Robecourt ambled his donkey up to hers. He rode with a supreme indifference to the silliness of his position. "Odd creatures, aren't they?"

Betsy glanced over her shoulder. Jenks and Wingate were riding with Ethel, a little ways behind. Betsy wondered vaguely if they ought to wait for them; now that she knew Monsieur de Robecourt was married, riding together like this didn't feel appropriate.

There she was, being American again. Betsy disliked herself thoroughly. "I hadn't realized there were camels in Greece."

"Didn't you?" It was hard to be stiff when Monsieur de Robecourt was smiling at her like that. "According to Herodotus, Xerxes introduced the camel to Greece."

"Yes, but you can't believe everything you read in Herodotus," protested Betsy. "The man thought India was filled with giant ants digging up gold dust."

He raised his brows at her. "Don't forget the people of Libya who squeak like bats, dine on snakes, and pass their time hunting strange troll-like creatures from four-horse chariots."

Betsy couldn't help laughing. "And yet we call Herodotus the Father of History. He was really just a big old gossip."

"Isn't that what history is? Gossip hallowed by time?"

It was entirely unfair for Monsieur de Robecourt to look quite that debonair with his feet sticking out at an odd angle. "History is about discovering the truth of what happened—of how people lived."

"But what is truth?" Monsieur de Robecourt glanced sideways

at Betsy. "My truth may be different from your truth. Truth lies in recollection and recollection lies."

"Then it isn't truth at all."

"That depends on how one defines *truth*."

"Truth is truth," said Betsy firmly.

"Except when it isn't," countered Monsieur de Robecourt, looking ahead to the heights of Mount Parnassus as their donkeys picked their way up the pass. "The Greeks called it *aletheia*, the art of revealing the concealed. To the Romans, truth was the goddess Veritas, the daughter of Time and the mother of Virtue. And yet, what is it really? What do we mean when we talk about *verité*? About your English *truth*? Are they the same? Or something different entirely?"

It gave Betsy a rather squirmy feeling, as though the ground which she had thought solid was suddenly moving beneath her. "Next you're going to say 'What is the good, Alcibiades?' and I am going to be strongly moved to push you off your donkey."

Monsieur de Robecourt grinned at her from beneath his hat. "*Soit*. I shall cease playing Socrates. I have never liked the taste of hemlock."

"I should hope you've never tasted the taste of hemlock," retorted Betsy.

A wry look crossed his face. "I should think absinthe is a close cousin. I drank enough of that for a time, seeking oblivion where I could find it. But enough. Do you see? The Sacred Way. We'll see if we can convince you to value wonders over potsherds."

The way he looked at her made her feel like a wonder. Her mind, Betsy reminded herself. He admired her mind. "Do you know, I owe you a debt."

"For Delphi?" he asked.

"No. Our discussion at Tiryns—it made me realize what I'm meant to do." It was hard to be frank. It was so much easier to banter and exchange witticisms. "I'd always thought— It was always just assumed that I would go out and do what my father would have done, if he could—that the whole point was to try to find the pieces that would prove the truth of the Homeric legends. Like Herr Schliemann at Troy. My father longed to find Achilles's shield or the pieces of Penelope's loom. But why should the loom have to be Penelope's? Isn't it just as important to find a loom that's just a loom?"

"Or some kitchen things?" Monsieur de Robecourt offered quietly.

"Yes. That's it exactly." Betsy let out her breath in a big rush. "It sounds silly, but I feel like I've been traveling a very narrow path and now I see a whole vista before me."

They had reached the base of the Sacred Way while the others still dawdled behind. Monsieur de Robecourt reined in his donkey. "Why should that sound silly? Most people blindly follow. It's no easy thing to eschew the expectations of others and find one's own way."

Betsy drew up alongside him. "As you did?"

His lips twisted. "I didn't so much find my way as stumble into it." Dismounting, he turned it into a pretty compliment. "I haven't your vision."

He offered her his hand. Betsy hesitated for a moment and then told herself not to be a fool; helping her down from her donkey was what anyone would do, even Wingate.

But he wasn't Wingate. The second their fingers touched, she was shamefully aware of the press of his fingers beneath his gloves, the muscles of his arm beneath his sleeve, the vibration of his throat beneath his collar.

Betsy swallowed hard. "Does your . . ." She'd meant to say "wife" but the word was a stone on her tongue. "Does your family also have an interest in archaeology?"

"No." He released her hand. "To them, I am an oddity."

"We're oddities together, then. My brother always thought my father was selfish for educating me. He and his wife say it unfit me for womanhood." Betsy tried to make a joke out of it, but it didn't come out quite as she'd intended. As much as she despised Lavinia's opinions, there was still a sting in it. "She thinks if I'd spent less time studying Greek, I'd be married by now."

"Do you regret it?"

The direct question took her by surprise. "No. I shouldn't want to marry anyone who didn't want me for anything but what I am."

Monsieur de Robecourt's smile was like European chocolate, bitter and sweet at the same time. "I am glad you are nothing but what you are." He gently touched her cheek. "The world has many Helens, but very few Circes."

As Betsy stood there in complete confusion, he raised his voice, saying to someone behind Betsy, "Ah, there you are. We dismount here."

As Monsieur de Robecourt went to give instructions to the rest of their party, Betsy stood where she was, her back to the others, hoping they would think she was in rapt contemplation of Mount Parnassus and not waiting for her flaming cheeks to return to a socially acceptable shade.

Had Monsieur de Robecourt just called her an enchantress?

Odysseus had left Circe and gone back to his wife, Betsy reminded herself. So much for enchantresses.

Monsieur de Robecourt fell tactfully back, letting the Americans marvel at the sheer scope of the excavations stretching up above them, from the remains of the Temple of Athena Pronaia through the zigzagging path up to the Sanctuary of Apollo. They tripped and scrambled their way up the Sacred Way, between the remains of the treasure houses where the great city-states of Greece had once piled their offerings to Apollo. Wingate had his battered copy of Pausanias out and read aloud from it as they walked, falling headlong over a pile of rubble in his abstraction and having to be hauled up again by Jenks.

It was, Betsy had to agree, majestic. It was incredible to think of all the triumphs commemorated here, all the city-states paying tribute here, all the prophecies uttered here—but she preferred Tiryns, with its homely baths and guardrooms, where people had lived and not just worshipped.

She looked around to tell Monsieur de Robecourt, but he had slipped away somewhere. Well, she couldn't blame him, could she? If this were her site, she wouldn't want to watch the nursery party blundering around and slaughtering passages of Pausanias he undoubtedly knew by heart already.

"Do you have your coffeepot on you?" asked Wingate hopefully, peering at Ethel's pack.

Betsy was suddenly in a terrible mood. "You don't think it's a crime against Apollo to make coffee in his sanctuary?"

"Not if we do it just outside his sanctuary," said Wingate. "Up there, way at the top, in the stadium. There's bound to be a jolly view."

"Fine." Ethel turned to Betsy, resigned to reprising her role as the Coffee Angel. "Would you like coffee too?"

Betsy couldn't bear the thought of sitting there while Ethel plied the Harvard boys with coffee. They were all so loud and brash and American, everything she hated herself for being. She wished she were French and sophisticated. "I want to take another look at the Stoa of the Athenians. I missed it on our way up."

What she really wanted was to be alone. It felt a bit like the time, as a child, she'd put on her father's spectacles and seen the world distorted. That was how she felt with Monsieur de Robecourt ever since Aikaterini had told her about his wife. When she was with him, talking with him, laughing with him, it felt utterly right until she remembered. And then everything went out of focus again.

Maybe, thought Betsy, wandering back down the slope, if she were European, she wouldn't feel that way. Maybe it was just her American way of trying to put everything into simple categories. She kicked at a stone that might once have been kicked by the ancients. Somehow, the thought didn't quite thrill her as it should.

Betsy tried to conjure Ava. Ava would remind her that it was about the archaeology, not the man, and she was just lucky to be here.

She might even have convinced herself of it if she hadn't rounded the corner and seen the man himself, bending over a pile of rock in the shadow of the Stoa of the Athenians. Grubbing in the mud, Aikaterini had called it, but there was nothing grubby about it.

Monsieur de Robecourt looked up. His expression changed at the sight of her, lighting with delight—and Betsy knew, deep down in the pit of her stomach, that she'd been wrong about being wrong. Whatever it was, whatever she'd felt—it was real. It was here between them.

She should turn and walk away. She should make some excuse and go and find the others. But she didn't.

"Hullo," Betsy said in a voice that didn't sound like her own. "Digging out of school?"

Monsieur de Robecourt brushed his hands off against his knees as he rose, his face a picture of amused contrition. "I know. But who can resist the lure of the treasures that still lie undiscovered? It would take more willpower than I possess to keep from searching—even out of season."

Betsy lingered at the edge of the stoa. "After a point, that's not archaeology. That's treasure hunting."

"Only," said Monsieur de Robecourt with mock gravity, "if I fail to note it properly in my records. Properly catalogued, treasure hunting becomes scholarship."

Betsy tried to focus on his words, but it was hard to concentrate when she was painfully aware of every whisper of the fabric of his trousers as he came to stand beside her. They were alone as they had never been before; Jenks and Wingate and Ethel were well away up the slope, far out of sight, out of hearing, out of everything.

"Are you sure there are more mysteries to be found?" Betsy asked, trying to sound normal and failing miserably. "Didn't you have a bad season last year?"

"Winds and rain and mud. Yes. But we found a charioteer made of bronze, of a beauty to make you weep. He had been cast in segments and the segments had come apart, but each was whole and perfect there in the earth, waiting only to be put together again. We are still missing an arm, but that only makes him like any other veteran, battle-scarred."

"You make him sound . . . real."

"Legend has it that Zeuxis painted a bunch of grapes that looked so lifelike that birds blunted their beaks fighting to eat them. If you saw our charioteer . . ." Monsieur de Robecourt spread his hands in wordless illustration. "I wasn't here when Homolle found the statue of Antinoüs. But they tell me he was standing on his plinth, waiting beneath the weight of dirt for someone to find him and dig him out."

Despite her layers of wool, Betsy felt a chill along her spine. She had to resist the urge to look over her shoulder, to see if a classical statue was rising from the dirt behind her. "You speak as though the statues have spirits of their own."

Monsieur de Robecourt's eyes were amber, the sort of amber that held history embedded in it. "Don't they? Here in Delphi, where the oracle speaks?"

She'd told herself she was a practical person, with practical interests. But something in his words struck a chord in her. Standing there, by the ruined ambitions of the Athenians, in the shadow of Apollo's abandoned sanctuary, Betsy took a deep breath and recited from memory, *"Tell the king that the flute has fallen to the ground. Phoebus does not have a home any more, neither an oracular laurel, nor a speaking fountain, because the talking water has dried out."*

Monsieur de Robecourt's eyes were intent on hers. "So you do feel it. The magic."

"Or the loss of it," Betsy said unevenly.

Her skirt brushed against his trousers. She wasn't sure if he had moved or she had. "To lose something, it must once have been."

"Or have been imagined." She should step back. Step away, pretend they were talking about Apollo.

Betsy rested her palms against his chest, feeling his heart beating beneath the layers of linen and wool.

"If one believes in something thoroughly, with all one's heart," said Monsieur de Robecourt quietly, "isn't that enough to make it so?"

Betsy was quite sure it wasn't.

She was also quite sure she didn't have the words to deny it. Magic, he'd called it, and perhaps it was, because instead of using her hands to push Monsieur de Robecourt away, Betsy found her arms sliding up his chest and around his neck, her eyes closing as his lips moved to cover hers, while the ruins stood silent sentinel around them.

CHAPTER SEVEN

This morning, by special invitation from Commander Dunlap, Miss Clara Barton and the staff of the Red Cross were given a tour of the United States naval hospital ship the *Solace*. Miss Barton was kind enough to share her recollections of nursing during the Civil War with the doctors on the *Solace*, with whom she discussed methods of treating wounds, particularly her abhorrence of the practice of amputation, which the doctor assured her is no longer practiced so wantonly as it was in the past. Miss Barton was deeply gratified to hear it.

No sooner had we returned to the *State of Texas* than word was brought to us of a terrible battle fought on the road to Santiago. . . .

—*Miss Katherine Carson for the* St. Louis Star Ledger, *June 25, 1898*

Siboney, Cuba
June 24, 1898

"HAVE YOU EVER SEEN A less inspiring sight than those sentinels?" Paul yawned broadly, cracking his knuckles over his head as he stretched. Reveille had sounded at half past three in the morning and as the sky began to lighten over the fishing village of Siboney, the Rough Riders were still bleary-eyed over their campfires. "I've seen scarecrows better dressed."

Holt glanced over to the guerillos who had been loaned to their regiment by the local Cuban commander. The light of the campfires gave them the chiaroscuro look of Caravaggio saints, all sharp lines and hollows. Neither had a shirt. Their trousers hung off them in peeling patches of fabric.

He took a gulp of what passed for coffee. "Given that they've kept hundreds of thousands of professional soldiers on the run for the past three years with minimal support, I'd say their attire is hardly of primary importance."

"Tatterdemalions," said Paul, oblivious to Holt's tone. "That's what Lieutenant Roosevelt calls 'em. Look at that rifle that man's holding—that has to be, what? Thirty years old, at least. And the other one—he's just got one of those knife thingies."

"A machete," bit off Holt. "It's called a machete. I should think that would make it even more impressive. Give them their due. Neither of us could do what they've done."

Holt should know. He'd spent his childhood in a form of guerilla warfare. It wore on you, being constantly on alert, always knowing that the other side had the advantage. The only thing to do was survive. Survive long enough that hopefully the tables would be turned.

But Paul wouldn't understand that.

Holt shrugged, leaning over to roll up his bedroll, still sodden from last night's heavy rains. "Give us a few months in these jungles and we won't look much better."

They didn't look so great now. Even Paul's face had hollowed out. Weeks crammed into fetid transports with inadequate rations had left them wobbly. It had been six days before they'd finally sailed from Port Tampa, and then another week before they'd made land at Daiquirí, on a ship designed to hold half the number of men, provisioned for a single day's sail. The men who'd had the sense to buy extra rations before leaving had become very popular—and very wealthy. For the others, there was bully beef, in tins that exploded when they were opened, revealing slimy, odorous contents that some swore they'd starve rather than eat.

The forced march from Daiquirí to the village of Siboney hadn't helped either. They'd scarcely had time to get their land legs before General Wheeler had them on the move, a group of cavalry without horses, staggering with their packs in the tropical heat on legs more used to riding than walking. The trail behind them was littered with bedding, books, clothes, and cookpots jettisoned on the road. Technically, General Shafter held command. But with Shafter, uncomfortable in the tropical heat, still on board the ship *Seguranca*, it was General Wheeler who was the senior officer.

There were times when Holt wasn't entirely sure that General Wheeler remembered they were meant to be fighting the Spanish. A Confederate veteran, Wheeler had a disconcerting habit of forgetting his enemy wasn't the Yankees. Or his fellow commanders.

The objective, as Holt understood it, was to take the city of Santiago, and Wheeler was determined that his men would get there first, whatever the cost. Men were already dropping: from heat, from food poisoning, and from fever. But they'd done what General Wheeler wanted; they'd made it to Siboney before General Lawton's infantry and parked their camp that little bit closer to the enemy, closer to glory.

"Join me for breakfast?" Ham Fish hailed them from a neighboring campfire, where smells of food that actually smelled like food were emerging from a tin cooking pot. "I salvaged some cans of tomatoes. We're liable to all be killed today, so we may as well have enough to eat."

"Thanks," said Holt drily.

"Wait, what?" said Paul, who wasn't the swiftest in the morning. "What's that about being killed?"

Fish tapped the side of his nose. "Secret orders. There was a pow-wow last night. Overheard it. That's how I know." Fish still smelled strongly of the sweet Spanish wine he'd been knocking back the night before. The scion of an old New York family, Fish was an amiable alcoholic. "The Cubans skirmished with the Spanish yesterday at some crossroads or other. There's about fifteen hundred of them, they say. We're to hit 'em from one side, and Young's men'll hit 'em from the other."

"Are we supposed to know this?" asked Holt.

"No," said Fish. "But we're due to find out eventually, aren't we?"

There was no refuting that logic.

"Are those tomatoes?" Thede Miller, one of Paul's many Yale classmates, plunked himself down next to Holt. He looked sideways at Holt, squinting at him in the half-light. "I keep thinking we've met before."

They had.

"You've probably seen his picture in the papers," said Paul, who seemed to have appointed himself Holt's press agent. "How's Teddy?"

Their fellow Yalie, Teddy Burke, had stumbled in after dark, delirious with fever, mumbling about a polo match. Thede had made the rounds of the campfires, looking for wine to doctor him, not realizing most available potables were already inside Ham Fish. Holt was shamefully relieved by the change of subject.

Thede grimaced. "Still convinced he fell off his polo pony. I covered him up with a rubber sheet last night, but it didn't do much to keep the rain off. Anyone want to help me move him into one of the huts? I know we're not supposed to but he's in no shape to come along with us, and I don't want to just leave him out in the open."

"You don't want to risk the land crabs." Holt's voice came out even more gruff than usual. That was the effect of sleeping in the rough. Or trying to be the person that Paul thought he was.

That he was, Holt reminded himself. He'd been that person for four years. It wasn't a lie. It just wasn't the whole story.

"I hear they'll eat a man's face off," said Ham, cheerfully eating stewed tomatoes.

"One of those crawled over me last night. Scared the living daylights out of me." Paul shuddered. "Maybe ask Dr. Stringfellow to look at Teddy, Thede. I know the doc's a Princeton man, but . . ."

"Needs must. Hey, Doc!"

With the exaggerated patience that came of being the Rough Riders' junior surgeon, Dr. Stringfellow said, "Yes?"

Dr. Stringfellow wasn't much older than the men he was doctoring, but his prematurely thinning hair and general air of faint irritation made him seem a generation removed. There'd been a certain amount of ribbing early on, but the Rough Riders had come to the conclusion that the doctor wasn't a man to be crossed. When Colonel Wood had told him he had no mules to spare to carry medical supplies, Dr. Stringfellow had quietly found the mule holding Wood's and Roosevelt's bedding, dumped it, and appropriated the animal for the medical department.

Stringfellow was doggedly strapping bundles to the mule in question, and showed no inclination to interrupt his activities. "How may I help you gentlemen?"

"We've got a man down. Fever."

Stringfellow looked at him sharply, his attention caught. "Black vomit?" That was the fear that stalked the army. Yellow fever.

"No," said Thede quickly. "Nothing like that. Just a fever. He thinks he's in a polo match."

"Tell him to keep an easy pace and not to flatten his mallet." The doctor held up his hands to silence their protests. "There's not much that can be done for him right now. He's better off staying where he is, in what shade you can find for him, than attempting the march back to Daiquirí to a hospital ship—if someone could be found to take him."

"There's no one to be spared." Their commanding officer Colonel Wood stalked past, snapping his pocket watch closed. "We leave in five minutes. Anyone who isn't ready will be left behind."

"That's what you get for taking his mule," said Fish.

Stringfellow sighed. "I'll take a look at your friend. Show me where he is?" He gave the men around the campfire a hard look. "Nobody touch my mule."

THEY SET OFF UP A path so steep that some of the men were reduced to grabbing bits of rock or foliage to try to heave themselves along. Guacimos and banyans thick with vines pressed close on either side, the path so narrow they could go only single file as the rising heat turned the damp of last night's storm to steam. Holt's face was slick with sweat, his mustache drooping as though he'd jumped in a pool. The spiky leaves of Spanish bayonet sliced at their legs, leading to indignant yelps of pain as the stiff foliage pierced fabric and skin.

"I guess I know why our guides have no clothes," panted Paul, struggling up the path just behind Holt. He slapped at his neck as a mosquito bit him just above his bandana. "Brooks Brothers won't recognize my kit by the time we're done."

"Stay to the center of the path," advised Holt. "And don't scratch that. It'll only make it itch more."

Alongside the path, an abandoned plantation lay overgrown and silent, the fields clogged with shrubs, dwellings covered with vines. It looked like a picturesque ruin out of an artist's etching. It was hard to believe that a mere two or three years ago, this had been someone's home, someone's livelihood.

All gone. Overtaken by the hungry jungle, civilization crushed and rotting beneath the weight of nature.

There had been a time when Holt would have been all in favor of that. Leave behind the ugly veneer of civilization, the polite lies of society, and live in nature. But he'd discovered that it didn't matter whether a man slept on carved mahogany or on hay; back East or out West people were still people, and there were as many lies and crooked dealings on the range as there had ever been in his father's opulent, oak-paneled office in their Springfield mansion.

Holt wasn't sure what he'd have done with himself if Roosevelt hadn't put out a call to arms. Joined an expedition to the Yukon, perhaps.

The Yukon was sounding pretty attractive just about now. It was barely seven in the morning, but the heat was brutal. Men were straggling behind, falling out of the column, just taking a moment to rest, or so dizzy with heat they scarcely knew what they were doing. Holt had spent a year in the Arizona territory; he'd thought he'd known heat. But this was something different. This was a sticky heat, a heat that soaked you through, clogged your lungs, and fogged your brain.

Some people dropped. Others just got silly.

Paul and Thede Miller, drunk on adrenaline, had begun warbling, *"Bright college years with pleasure rife / The shortest gladdest years of life . . ."*

"You all make more noise than a train going through a tunnel," shouted Stephen Crane, the correspondent from the *World*, trudging along behind them.

"What?" Paul hollered back.

"STOP!" bellowed Colonel Wood. "Everyone, stay where you are—and BE QUIET."

He rode off ahead as the men dropped where they stood, collapsing with relief, fanning themselves with their hats and taking thirsty slugs from their canteens. It looked like a picnic, with men reclining at every possible sort of angle, hunting through their packs for food, indulging in a quick chew of tobacco, or throwing spitballs at each other with holiday abandon.

Next to them, Lieutenant Colonel Roosevelt, in cool contravention of Wood's order for quiet, was chatting with one of the Cuban officers and Edward Marshall of the *New York Journal* about a lunch they'd all attended at the Astor House in New York.

Paul scrambled to his feet, utterly unconcerned about the sort of target his six-foot-plus frame made, peering at the Cuban officer.

"Carlos de Almendares! Paul Randall. Remember? From the Union Club. What are you doing out here? Last time I saw you you'd just gotten engaged to Minnie Walsh!"

The officer stood. "I was. I am. I offered to release her from our engagement when I decided to enlist—but she wouldn't hear of it." He smiled, a smile so full of pain it hurt to look at it. "I'm worried she may be sadly disappointed in me when I return. If I return. I'm not the man I was."

"A shave and a visit to your tailor and you'll be back to your old self," said Paul encouragingly, kindly ignoring the scar that kept one eye half-closed and a series of powder burns that puckered the skin of one cheek.

"No," said de Almendares, politely but firmly. "I have three bullet holes in me that weren't there before. The Mauser bullets are not so bad—you scarcely feel them going in and they leave a good, clean hole. But I was struck by a shell last year, and that—it tears through your flesh."

Paul was looking a little uncomfortable. "We'll do our best to avoid them."

"The Spanish use smokeless powder," said de Almendares. "Not black powder. You won't be able to see when they fire. But you can hear it—the Mauser bullets make a sort of whining noise, like a hum. If you hear that, throw yourself down."

"I don't think we're going to see any Spanish closer than Santiago," Edward Marshall of the *New York Journal* said, fanning himself lazily with his hat. "They've all run off."

Major de Almendares shook his head. "I shouldn't be so sure of that," he said somberly. "Allow me to tell you from experience. It does not do to underestimate the Spanish."

And then the humming started.

Major de Almendares flung himself to the ground as the rest of them stood there, gaping like idiots.

It sounded like telephone wires vibrating, louder and louder, buzzing in Holt's ears as the forest exploded in bullets and the first man fell beside him.

Guantanamo Bay, Cuba
June 25, 1898

"AS YOU CAN SEE, WE have our own telephone system on board," said the doctor whose name Betsy had already forgotten. "You can call the dispensary from any part of the ship."

For want of anything better to do, Miss Clara Barton and her Red

Cross nurses were touring the US military sloop the *Solace*. Betsy trailed along after Kit and the other nurses as the doctor led them through the main ward, down in the lower deck of the United States naval ambulance ship, making the appropriate noises of admiration (at the latest in modern hospital equipment) and distress (at the state of the men).

Miss Barton, of course, was up ahead, pacing deliberately beside the doctor and doing a very good job of looking like Elizabeth I deigning to visit a minor courtier and not a woman who had been repeatedly ignored and rejected.

Again and again over the past week, Miss Barton had offered their help to the military, only to be answered by resounding silence. As soon as the troops sailed, Miss Barton had sent a telegram to the secretary of the navy, informing him that the Red Cross contingent would be sailing to Key West, where they would await further orders—and, if no orders came, they would sail directly to Cuba.

No orders came.

So they had sailed to Cuba. They hadn't been sure where to go in Cuba, but the rumor was that General Shafter meant to land in Santiago de Cuba, so they had made for the Bay of Santiago, where the American navy had the Spanish fleet bottled up.

Miss Barton had sent her compliments to Admiral Sampson. Admiral Sampson sent his compliments back and suggested they go elsewhere.

He hadn't put it quite like that, of course. He'd told them that General Shafter had landed at Daiquirí and that they'd find good anchorage in Guantanamo Bay, where they might await better intelligence.

So here they were, after nine days of sailing from place to place, trying to get someone to take some notice, shunted safely out of the way.

There was still no word of Ava. The promised contingent of nurses from New York hadn't joined them before they left, but two more reporters had: Mrs. Trumbull White of the *Chicago Record* and Miss Janet Jennings of the *New-York Tribune*.

Right now all three of the reporters were trailing after Miss Barton, dutifully recording statistics as the doctor showed them the wonders of the *Solace*, which made the *State of Texas* look like the hastily converted, elderly tramp steamship it was.

Everyone on board paid Miss Barton the utmost deference. The sort of deference you'd pay to a slightly deaf, elderly maiden aunt. The condescension was so thick you could practically wipe it off the walls.

And Miss Barton knew it. Betsy could see the way her lips thinned beneath her carefully applied lip rouge, the repeated attempts to remind the doctor just who had been saving lives on the battlefield before he was even born.

"What methods do you have of treating gangrenous wounds? I find the habit of amputation both wanton and wasteful. You cannot imagine what it was to see limbs piled in great heaps behind the hospital tents on the battlefield. Why, sometimes the piles of discarded limbs would reach higher than the tents themselves. And the smell—"

"No, no," said the doctor, cutting her off before she could go into detail about the smell. "That was a very long time ago. We have nothing like that here. We haven't had to amputate a limb yet. That's not to say we won't, but we do everything in our power to save them. A lot has changed since your day."

"Indeed. I am glad to hear it." Miss Barton's voice was distinctly frosty. Thwarted by the doctor, Miss Barton turned to a patient. He had one arm in a sling, a hand in a plaster cast, and a leg entirely swathed in bandages. "How have they been taking care of you, young man?"

"Very well?" he croaked.

Miss Barton made a show of smoothing back the hair from his brow. She turned to make sure all three reporters in her entourage were watching and intoned, "You are helping to make the history of your country now, poor fellow."

"Yes, yes," said the doctor, his smile rather fixed, as all three reporters diligently took down her words. "Shall we?"

Back on the *State of Texas*, Kit regarded her portable writing desk without enthusiasm. "I'd better write up my story so I can file it before Mrs. White and Miss Jennings get the scoop on me."

Betsy gave a very unladylike snort. "I think the reporters traveling with the actual army have probably already done that."

"Do you think I don't know that?" Kit balled up her white cap and threw it across the room with unexpected violence. "Here I am writing about Miss Barton touring a hospital ship when somewhere out there the real stories are happening. It makes me sick. I'd be out there if they'd let me."

"Of course you would, but . . ."

Kit glared at her. "Don't you care? Don't you mind that we're not allowed to do our jobs? They stop us getting the good stories and then they say we only cover trivialities because our minds are trivial. They refuse to give us passes and then they tell us we mustn't be dedicated enough because if we were we would have gone where the story was. There's no way to get it right. Whatever we do they'll find a way to make sure we don't do it."

"Kit." Betsy felt awful. Kit, usually so composed, was near tears. "I thought you were the one who told me all it took was sticking a foot in the door and keeping it there."

"My foot is sore." Kit dragged in a deep breath, mustering an entirely unconvincing smile. "Don't mind me. I just can't stand sitting around. It makes me wonder what I'm doing here."

She was missing her children. She never said as much, but Betsy saw her, sometimes, taking out a much-handled photograph, two children, a boy and a girl. The boy, uncomfortable in his sailor suit, squirming to get out of the picture, looked an awful lot like Kit, right down to the freckles.

Betsy's chest hurt. She wrapped her arms tightly around herself, struggling for control.

"What you're doing is writing about the Red Cross visit to the naval ship *Solace*," said Betsy briskly. She posed in her bulky uniform. "Aren't we glamorous enough for you?"

"No one wants to read about the Red Cross. Not when the real action is over there." Kit waved vaguely in the direction of Santiago. "Anything could be happening and we won't know until we read the news in week-old papers written by other people."

It felt very odd to be bucking Kit up rather than the other way around. "You'll still have been to Cuba. We're here, aren't we?"

"Yes, moored in a bay like nuns in a convent." Kit dropped her face into her hands, scrubbing her cheeks with her palms. "I have a daughter. I've always told her she can do anything she wants to do. That by the time she grows up, there'll be women in all the professions. She was so proud that the paper was sending me to Cuba. What am I meant to tell her when I get home? That they sent me but they wouldn't let me there on the ground because I'm a woman? At that rate, I might as well have stayed home with her and baked pie."

"Do you bake pie?" asked Betsy, diverted.

"Sometimes. Doesn't everyone like pie?" Kit shook her head as if to clear it. "I just—I feel like I've lied to her. I lied to myself. I thought it meant something that they were letting me come out here. But we're just sailing around and around going nowhere. Our big excitement is a visit from our ship to another ship."

"You didn't lie. You just only told her part of the story. And you don't know how this story is going to end yet."

"With Teddy Roosevelt inviting me to ride with the Rough Riders?" Kit made a face. "I always knew it wasn't going to be that easy. I just hadn't thought it would be this hard. I thought I'd get a shot."

Her words hit Betsy right in the gut. She remembered fighting with Ava back in Athens, accusing her of being defeatist, of just not wanting to try. It had never occurred to her, back then, that Ava might have been right

Betsy bit her lip. "You never know. Miss Barton seems determined to get us in on the action. She's a national heroine. The Angel of the Battlefield."

"Men prefer their angels cast in porcelain and set on the mantelpiece, not butting into their business," said Kit bitterly. "You saw how they treated her back there. Like a joke. This whole plan—I should have known better."

"Kit—" Betsy paused, not sure what to say.

Kit turned away. "I'm just having a fit of the doldrums. If this were my daughter, I'd tell her to stop feeling sorry for herself and get on with it. You can only do what you can do and you can't fix what you can't fix."

Betsy cast about for a more encouraging aphorism. Unfortunately, she'd never been much for aphorisms. All she could remember was "least said, soonest mended," which didn't exactly seem applicable.

"Fortune favors the bold?" she ventured. It sounded better in Latin.

"Fortune favors the male. What?" shouted Kit, as someone banged on their door.

"Your presence is desired upstairs," came the muffled voice of Sister Bettina. "Miss Barton has called a meeting."

The Clara Barton waiting for them seemed like an entirely different person from the unhappy woman who had blustered and postured her way through their tour of the hospital ship. This Clara

Barton seemed a good decade younger, her color high with excitement rather than rouge, her eyes snapping.

"A friend has brought word of a severe engagement that occurred today at Las Guasimas, where a Spanish contingent was guarding the road to Santiago." Next to her, Betsy could see Kit grab for the notebook that lived in her apron pocket. "The wounded are even now being brought into the village of Siboney. He says they lack every necessity. The wounded need help. They need *us*."

This angel wasn't on the mantelpiece anymore. Even knowing what she knew, even having seen the things she'd seen, Betsy couldn't help but feel the thrill of that call to action down to her toes. For that moment, she would have been willing to follow Clara Barton anywhere.

"The captain has his orders. We sail at once for Siboney."

Miss Barton surveyed the room, making sure to look every person there in the eye, so that each doctor, each nurse felt sure that she was talking to her and her alone.

"It is to the Rough Riders we go. The relief may also be rough, but it will be ready. *You* will be ready."

And with that, Clara Barton turned and swept out to begin the thousand necessary preparations, leaving Betsy feeling not the least bit ready at all. But having set events in motion, she had no idea how to make them stop.

CHAPTER EIGHT

Darling Ava,

Delphi was most informative. I cannot be persuaded that the god speaks out of the rock—or that the French know how to excavate properly—but I did come away knowing a great deal more about myself and my place in the world. γνῶθι σεαυτόν, quoth the oracle according to Pausanius. Know thyself.

Just because I don't believe the Greek gods existed doesn't meant they didn't sometimes speak sense.

I can just imagine the look you would be giving me right now! I'll stop writing rubbish and just say I came away from Delphi more determined than ever to make my mark on Corinth. It's what I'm meant to do. I'm sure of it.

Professor Richardson will have to change his mind about letting me excavate. I won't let him do otherwise.

Aren't you proud of my resolution and purpose? And wouldn't you like to come over here and see for yourself?

> *All my love,*
> *Betsy*

—Miss Betsy Hayes '96 to Ava Saltonstall '96

Delphi, Greece
November 1896

"STOP," BETSY MURMURED.

She couldn't quite remember why they needed to stop; it was hard to remember anything with Monsieur de Robecourt kissing a spot on the side of her neck she'd never known she had. She could feel the sun on her face as she tilted her head back, her body wanting more even as her brain was starting to come out of its stupor and remind her that there was something not quite right about this, even if it all felt quite right, better than right, Monsieur de Robecourt's hands beneath the jacket of her walking suit, burning through the fabric of her chemise, making her feel as though there were no fabric there at all. The bow at her neck had come untied; it slithered to the ground, her shirt gaping open, providing more access, at the base of her neck, the top of her chemisette. . . .

"Stop. We have to stop," Betsy gasped, although the gasp was a different sort of gasp altogether.

She could feel herself pressing toward him even as she pushed away. Somehow, she'd wound up sprawled against one of the plinths of the stoa, half standing, half reclining, her legs wrapped around Monsieur de Robecourt's, her hands beneath his shirt, charting the fascinating geography of skin and muscle beneath her fingers.

"Stop," he echoed, lifting his head, so that his face was above hers, his hat long gone, his hair tousled, his eyes glowing like warm brandy. His mouth was partly open, his lips swollen with her kisses. Betsy knew if she leaned her head back just the littlest bit and closed her eyes he would kiss her again . . . and again . . .

She yanked her hands out from under his jacket and pressed them against his chest, as much to stop herself as him. "What—what just happened?"

A lock of hair fell over Monsieur de Robecourt's eye. "I believe one would call it a kiss."

A kiss? A kiss was a peck one exchanged under the mistletoe. This—Betsy could feel the cold air on the exposed skin of her chest, making her shiver with something other than cold, as if she could still feel his lips and hands on her, waking up bits of her she'd scarcely known were there.

"But . . ." It was hard to muster the words when all she wanted was to slide her arms back around his neck and draw him down to her. His eyes had drifted to her lips. Betsy licked them, forcing out the words, "Aren't you—aren't you married?"

Monsieur de Robecourt pressed his eyes shut hard. "Ah."

"Ah?" Betsy's stomach lurched.

He opened his eyes, looking at her ruefully. "I suppose Aikaterini told you."

For a moment, Betsy could only stare at him. She'd been waiting for him to say—oh, something. His wife had died and Aikaterini hadn't heard of it. His wife had run off and the Pope was in the process of annulling the marriage.

Not this.

Betsy scrabbled out from under him, clutching the open ends of her collar together. "So . . . it's true. You are married."

An expression of great pain crossed his face. "A business contract. Nothing more."

A business contract? One could have many business contracts but only one spouse. There were nasty names for women who weren't wives. Betsy felt suddenly painfully aware that her shirtwaist was gaping open, her skirt was twisted the wrong way around, and her hair had come out of its pins. Betsy yanked her skirt back around.

"Where's my necktie?" she demanded, in a strangled voice.

Monsieur de Robecourt leaned over and scooped it off the ground where it had fallen, shaking off the dirt before holding it out to her.

"Here," he said tenderly. It was that tenderness that broke her. He had no right to sound like that, like he cared. Not when he was already engaged in a *business contract*.

"Were you not going to tell me?" Betsy's voice broke. She fumbled with the tie.

"Let me," he said, and took the tie from her clumsy fingers, looping it gently around her neck, beneath the points of her collar. Betsy knew she should protest, but she couldn't seem to find her voice.

"These past weeks . . . with you . . ." Monsieur de Robecourt bowed his head, tying the bow around her neck with infinite care. Betsy shivered as his fingers brushed her neck, wanting him and hating him all at the same time. "They have been a time outside time. They don't belong to the rest of the world—the part of the world that has my wife in it."

Betsy stared at the top of his head, the light streaks carved by sunshine in his dark hair, overcome by a tidal wave of grief and rage and shame so intense that she could barely breathe. *My wife*. It was the first time he'd said it straight-out.

Monsieur de Robecourt finished tying her bow and took a step back, raising his eyes to her face. "I knew, eventually, a reckoning would come. But was it so wrong to dream a little?"

"Yes! If you're going to try to make the dream flesh!" His flesh against her flesh, the way it had been a moment before.

He'd touched her as though he were free. He'd touched her as though he had a right to touch her. And heaven help her, she'd touched him back.

Betsy ducked her head so he couldn't see her face, although she wasn't sure why she bothered; he had seen enough of the rest of her. "Did you think that because I was American and independent you could—you could dally with me and it wouldn't matter?"

"No." His denial was immediate and absolute. He made a move toward her. "I may have thought many things . . . I may have wished many things . . . but it was not dalliance. It was never a dalliance."

Betsy shied away from his outstretched hand, not trusting herself.

"It was never anything," she said.

Clamping her hat down hard on her disordered hair, Betsy wandered unsteadily up the Sacred Way, feeling strangely light-headed, as though she didn't belong in her own body.

The coffee drinkers, it seemed, had been on their way in search of her. They found her halfway up the hill.

"There you are!" said Ethel, bright-eyed with caffeine and virtue. "Our donkey driver is getting restless. He wants us to move on to our village for the night."

Betsy was very glad that she already had a reputation for being disheveled; no one would be able to tell any difference between her usual state and her state post-kiss. "That's fine with me. I've seen enough of Delphi."

"The oracle didn't speak to you?" teased Wingate.

"It spoke to me," declared Jenks. "It told me I need supper and soon."

She hadn't needed an oracle, thought Betsy miserably. Just a modicum of common sense, which, apparently, she hadn't got. She should have walked away the second she saw Monsieur de Robecourt at the stoa.

"Where's Monsieur de Robecourt?" asked Ethel.

"Oh, somewhere about," said Betsy vaguely. "Goodness only knows."

It took all her abilities to maintain an expression of polite disinterest. And they still had four days together. Four days they'd be forced to travel in close proximity. Longer if they ran into any delays. The itinerary that had seemed so exciting, so full of promise—so short!—in Athens now seemed painfully long.

The mountainous terrain was a blessing. No one could question why she no longer rode next to Monsieur de Robecourt if they could ride only single file through the rough passes, where firs began to replace the olive trees. They were hardy trees, clinging stubbornly to the rock as the path angled up and around. Betsy had a fierce fellow-feeling for them, defying the elements, standing their ground.

What would have happened if she hadn't walked away today?

Outside time, indeed! What he'd meant was "far enough away not to be caught." And if they'd been caught? There would have been no consequences for him.

But Betsy—Betsy would have been ruined. The reality of it hit her hard. If anyone had seen them—if the others hadn't been so far away—it wouldn't matter that she hadn't known he wasn't free. She'd be used goods—and, even worse, it would be taken as an object lesson in the dangers of admitting women into previously male provinces. Just look what had happened to that little American girl who thought she could be an archaeologist.

It was horrifying how close she'd come to ruining her future, everything she'd always planned, and all for a man.

Well, it wasn't going to happen again. Betsy wrapped her righteous anger around herself like the armor Monsieur de Robecourt's ancestress had supposedly worn on crusade. Most likely he was lying about that too. Lies, all lies. She had to remember that. She had to remember that when her treacherous body wanted to remember the feel of his lips against her neck, his hand on her breast. Every look, every touch, a lie.

Aikaterini had tried to warn her. She had no one to blame but herself. She wouldn't be that foolish again. No matter how compelling he was, how intoxicating his touch.

BY THE TIME THEY REACHED Mount Helicon the following day, Betsy was quite ready to pit herself against the elements. Never mind the historical significance, the myths of the Muses; she just wanted to climb something, to make her legs and lungs work so hard there was no room left for thinking.

"This will be," their guide told them, "the first time barbarian women have climbed the mountain."

"Barbarian?" Jenks guffawed, with a grin at Ethel and Betsy, even though he knew as well as the rest of them that *barbarian* was simply the Greek word for all non-Greeks. Betsy looked coldly back at him.

"European," the guide hastily corrected himself.

"We're not European," said Betsy sharply. "We're American. And we're equal to anything. Particularly a measly old mountain."

"Er, Betsy?" whispered Wingate. "Please don't insult the mountain of the man we're trusting to lead us back to civilization."

"Why? Are you scared you can't make it to the top?"

"No," said Wingate. "I'm scared we won't make it back again. Skulls are very picturesque, but I don't want to be one."

"We're all bones eventually," said Jenks philosophically.

Because no one had ever said that before. Betsy turned her back on them all and focused her attention on the slope. She wasn't quite sure if their guide had tried to punish them for her flippant words by leading them up the steepest way possible, but if he had, she welcomed it. Her legs burned; her throat burned; her cheeks burned; the palms of her hands burned from pulling herself up the rough side of rocks. She felt as though she were being scoured clean.

The others ambled their way up the mountain, arguing about the festival of the Muses, pausing to examine the Hippocrene spring. Betsy didn't need to hear Wingate quoting Keats—or Jenks going on about Pausanias. She was sick unto death of Pausanias. Betsy charged ahead, driving their guide half-distracted. He compromised by showing her to the summit and then hurrying back down to the rest of the party, who were picnicking by the sacred spring, taking turns sampling the famed waters to see if it brought out poetic inclination or just gas.

Betsy planted her feet firmly on the rock, the first American woman to stand where she stood, to stare out over Greece laid out like a map before her, mountains and valleys, wilderness and villages. The Gulf of Corinth lay below her, and there, on the far side, the American excavation. Her excavation.

She'd climbed to the top of Mount Helicon, thought Betsy fiercely. Who was Rufus Richardson to say she didn't have the stamina to dig?

This was why she was here in Greece, here on top of the world, looking out at her destiny, not a French archaeologist, chance met and just as quickly forgotten.

"It does put things into perspective, does it not?" It was hard to forget someone when they insisted on creeping up behind you and stealing the thoughts out of your head.

Monsieur de Robecourt took his place at the summit beside her. He didn't look at her, didn't touch her, but it didn't matter. He didn't need to touch her to make her treacherous body tingle. "Standing up here, we are but tiny specks of dust in the sweep of time."

Betsy kept her eyes trained on the Gulf of Corinth. "I might be a dust mote in the eye of time, but I don't mean to be swept away."

She could hear the whisper of his hair against his collar as he turned to look at her. "I cannot imagine anyone would be such a fool as to attempt such a thing."

Why did he have to sound so tender? "Then you'd better not try it, had you?"

"Or account myself even more a fool than I am?" he said quietly. "What can I say to make things right?"

"You can't." Betsy dug her feet into the rock and her hands into her pockets, bracing herself against the winds. "You can't close Pandora's box. It's all out already."

He drew closer, using his body to block the worst of the wind. "Might we not . . . go back to what we were?"

"Do you mean the bit where you pretend you don't have a wife?" Betsy turned to glare at him. A clump of hair blew into her mouth. Betsy spat it out again. "Or the bit where you pretend that you have an interest in my opinions?"

"That was never pretense." Reaching out, he gently tucked her hair back behind her ear for her. "You have a quality of mind—of thought—that is something entirely out of the ordinary. Most of us, we plod along—we accept what we've been told—but you, you look at everything fresh. You examine it, you interrogate it, you turn it upside down to find missing truths. Some day, every Hellenist in the world will know your name. When I am a very old man, I can brag that I knew you when you were first come to Greece, that I knew you and knew what you would be."

Betsy hated herself for the way her cheek turned toward his hand, seeking his touch. She jerked her head away. "And what will I be?"

Monsieur de Robecourt looked at her face as though memorizing it. "A triumph. A credit to the field. An inspiration for those who come behind you."

Betsy folded her arms tightly across her chest. "If it's my mind that's so attractive, why kiss me?"

He touched his finger gently to her lips. "Just because a man knows he'll be burned doesn't mean he won't reach out to the flames."

"So now I'm a conflagration?" Her lips burned where he'd touched her.

"*Qui a la tête de cire ne doit pas s'approcher du feu.*" Betsy didn't need him to translate for her. *He who has a head of wax must not go near fire.* "With you, I have the head of wax. I have no thought, no sense. I know the flame will burn and yet I cannot keep away." Abandoning metaphor, Monsieur de Robecourt said simply, "I was married when I met you. I cannot help that. Any more than I could help falling in love with you."

"You can't say you're in love with me." Betsy could feel herself starting to panic. All the hours she'd spent daydreaming about his falling in love with her—but not like this. This was a warped and twisted version of the dream. "You can't be married and in love with me."

Monsieur de Robecourt raised a brow. "Whoever said marriage and love went hand in hand?"

"The Bible?" Betsy grasped at straws. She wasn't sure who had said it; it was just something she had always known. One didn't love outside marriage.

"This—this was all here before the Bible was ever thought of." Monsieur de Robecourt waved his hand across the summit of the mountain. "From the very beginning of time love has wreaked havoc on the plans of man. Originally, Eros was the son of Chaos."

"I thought Aristophanes said that Eros was the lover of Chaos." Blast it. He was doing it again. In a moment, they'd be deep in a discussion of competing myths and she'd forget herself, let herself be drawn in again, drawn into his banter, drawn into his arms. Betsy dug in her heels. "It doesn't matter. It's all a myth. You can't use a myth as an excuse."

"Not an excuse so much as . . . an explanation."

"Eros made you do it?" Betsy snorted. "Next you're going to tell me he flitted by on his feathery little wings and shot an arrow into your hide and that completely justifies everything. Like those love potions in operettas where everyone acts like idiots but it's all right because they weren't in their right minds so none of it counts."

"Love potions and arrows . . . those are a momentary madness. This is something deeper. Elemental, like that spring. One can try to dam it up, but there's no containing it." As he spoke, Betsy could feel the force of it, like a volcano, unstoppable. Any moment now, she was going to be swept away again. "Think of Paris and Helen."

Betsy wrapped her hands in the folds of her skirt. "They're not an example to follow. They cast the world into war and ruined thousands of lives, and for what?"

"For love." Monsieur de Robecourt was deadly serious. "We've tried to make love into a chocolate box wrapped up in lace and ribbons and bonds of matrimony—but it isn't. It's a madness, a glorious sort of madness, that makes everything else seem without savor or meaning."

Betsy glared up at him, small and fierce. "You can just find your glorious madness elsewhere. I don't want any part of it. I won't topple towers or launch ships. That's just selfishness masquerading as sentiment."

"Then what do you want?" It wasn't a rhetorical question. He genuinely wanted to know. That, thought Betsy helplessly, was what was so horribly disarming about him.

As for what she wanted . . . she wanted this. Endless hours of arguing over whether Eros was the son or the lover of Chaos. Passionate embraces among the ruins. Grubbing in the dirt together and coming back at night to the privacy of their tent. His lips on that newfound spot on the side of her neck.

But that wasn't an option, Betsy told herself brutally.

"I want to be allowed to pursue my work in peace." Betsy's throat felt raw. From the wind. Not from tears she couldn't cry. "I want to be treated as a scholar—as an equal."

It wasn't a lie. It just wasn't totally true.

She should have left it at that, but she couldn't help herself. Turning, she said hoarsely, her voice half-lost in the wind, "I might have loved you—if you had been free. I could have been your friend—if you had been honest."

"And now?" Monsieur de Robecourt was half hope, half fear.

She couldn't unknow what had passed between them, the feeling of his lips on her skin; she would never be able to look at him, talk to him, without remembering.

"Now I don't think we can be anything at all," she said, and turned and walked away against the force of the wind before he could see her face buckle.

CHAPTER NINE

News reached the Red Cross on Friday morning that the first battle had been fought and the list of wounded was a long one, with no proper facilities established to take care of those who had fallen in battle. Our readers will be saddened to see many well-loved and familiar names on the lists of the dead and the wounded.

Miss Barton and her party immediately set sail for the small village of Siboney, where the wounded were being brought down from the hills where the action had taken place. The hospital ships being full, the wounded were taken to an old warehouse and left there on the floor, with only such blankets and gear as they had with them, and the scantiest of care.

The night was dark, and the water choppy, but nothing could keep Miss Barton and her crew from the service of these men who needed their ministrations so dearly. . . .

—*Miss Katherine Carson for the* St. Louis Star Ledger, *June 25, 1898*

❧

Las Guasimas, Cuba
June 24, 1898

HOLT BUCKLED AS SOMETHING HIT him, hard, just above the knee.

The whizzing, whirring sound was everywhere, followed by strange, wet thuds, like the sound of a carpet being beaten. But it wasn't a carpet beater. It was Mauser bullets, pounding into flesh.

They didn't scream, the men who fell. Just that wet thud, and then they pitched over.

"Down!" shouted Captain Capron. "Everyone down! On your bellies!"

Holt dropped. His leg was damp. Not sweat. Blood. His hand came away red. He yanked the bandana out from around his neck, twisting sideways to tie it tight around his leg. De Almendares had been right. It made a nice neat hole, these Mauser bullets. Straight through, and barely ripped his trousers.

Holt gripped his Krag, trying to make out the distinctive conical hats of the Spanish soldiers, but it was hard to see anything through the smoke. Not the Spanish smoke. The Spanish, professional soldiers, had smokeless powder. Their own smoke, clouding their vision, giving away their location. Every time they fired, they announced their presence as surely as a flag.

Not that the Spanish needed any announcement. They had them pinned. Fire was coming from not just ahead of them but both sides. They'd walked right into a deadly trap. They'd skipped into it, gossiping away like schoolgirls at a picnic.

Holt's leg protested as he slithered forward.

Next to him, Paul was lying flat on his belly, squinting through the haze. "Where the devil are the bastards?"

"In front of us. On either side of us. Take your pick." Holt chambered a round and fired. Chambered another, fired again, trying to ignore the pain in his leg and the buzzing around him, that horrible buzzing, the buzz and thud and thud and thud.

The Spanish were firing: organized, rapid volleys, one after the other after the other. Bullets dropped like hail, biting, stinging, killing. It felt like all of Spain was massed against Troop L. Where in the devil was the rest of the regiment? Where were the army regulars?

Ham Fish gasped. "I'm wounded." He sounded more surprised than alarmed.

Paul turned. "Ham?"

Fish didn't answer.

"Ham?" Paul started to lift himself, and then dove facedown again as something exploded, raining down bark and leaves and shrapnel. Shells. The shells de Almendares had warned them were worse than bullets.

Up ahead, Captain Capron jerked and stiffened.

The next in command, Lieutenant Thomas, jumped up to take his place, and almost immediately fell, trying desperately to stand and falling back down again.

"Hell!" Paul rose to his feet and dashed to the lieutenant, as if those were Harvard linebackers coming at him, not scraps of shell.

Cursing, Holt ducked and dodged after him, hunching his shoulders against the rain of bullets and leaves, flopping onto his stomach next to Paul just as the welcome sound of hoofbeats interrupted the buzz of bullets.

Colonel Wood, impervious to his own safety, galloped up next to his fallen subordinates and swung down off his mount.

There was an odd pinging sound. Wood looked down with an expression of mild surprise on his face. The gold cuff link that had been on his wrist a moment before lay in two halves on the ground, neatly shot off by a Spanish gun.

Ignoring it—and all the bullets whispering around him—Wood looked to Thomas. "Mount up. You're losing too much blood. You need the surgeon."

"Not on your horse." Lieutenant Thomas's voice was so faint Holt could hardly hear him. "The men need to see you up there. They need to see their commander in front of them."

"Fine." Wood snapped his fingers at Holt and Paul, the two nearest. "Take him to the rear."

"What?" Lieutenant Thomas struggled against their hold as Holt grasped him under the armpits, Paul by the ankles. "You can't take me back there. They killed my captain. Those Spanish bastards killed my captain. Take me back to the front! You're going the wrong way, damn you!"

"Orders," Holt rasped, his own leg hurting like the devil as they shimmied backward, jerking their faces to the side to avoid falling debris.

It seemed to take years to reach Dr. Stringfellow, the air thick with that buzzing, twigs and bits of leaves raining down around them, Thomas struggling until he finally passed out from the loss of blood. They tripped over vines and the bodies of the fallen, Holt sweating and shivering, his leg aching, his mind refusing to comprehend what he was seeing.

Dr. Stringfellow had set up a temporary infirmary right behind the lines, just out of range of the Spanish guns, moving rapidly from patient to patient, binding wounds and barking instructions all at the same time.

"Put him here." Dr. Stringfellow's sleeves had been rolled above the elbow and his forearms were coated with red. It looked like paint.

But it wasn't. Dr. Stringfellow frowned at Holt. "You. You've got a hole in your leg."

"It's clean." Instinctively, Holt moved back. Never show weakness, never show wounds. He was an expert at avoiding doctors. Because sometimes they asked questions. And sometimes they didn't.

"Nothing's clean. Come see me later." The doctor dropped to his knees beside Thomas, cutting away at the bloody fabric around his leg.

Paul looked at Holt in alarm, suddenly very young under his stubble and dirt. "You all right?"

"It's just a scratch." It wasn't a scratch. It had gone clean through, just like de Almendares had warned him. Holt had no idea what it had gone through in the process, but it hadn't broken bone and he could walk on it—mostly—so that was all that counted. "I've had worse."

Paul's eyes lit with admiration. "Of course," he said. "I'm sure you have."

Holt cursed himself. He hadn't meant to feed this crazy idea Paul had that he was some sort of rough and tough cowboy.

He'd had worse, all right. But it hadn't been outlaws or wild horses or whatever romantic tale Paul was telling himself.

His worst wounds had happened in a mansion in Springfield, Massachusetts. He'd had his head knocked against the polished mahogany of a sideboard, swallowed the taste of his own blood lying flat on his face on a Turkish carpet, and seen his black eye reflected in a sterling silver tea service. Holt could scarcely remember a time when he hadn't been afraid, when he hadn't known how to carry on through the pain, hiding bruises and cracked bones beneath starched linen and thick knickerbockers.

A Mauser hole was nothing to that.

"You all right? Maybe we should get you to the doc after all."

"No. No, I'm fine." Just ten years and a thousand miles away. Holt wasn't that kid anymore. He'd earned his calluses, not with a pen but with whatever tools came to hand, working his way across the country, pure physical labor, as if he could sweat out his past. And if he died now, here, in this jungle? There was no one left on God's green earth to mourn him.

Paul on the other hand . . . There was a whole family back in New York. Father, mother, doting siblings. Undoubtedly a girl, or ten. That Miss Hayes. She looked like a girl who didn't need another tragedy in her life.

"Someone should stay with Lieutenant Thomas," said Holt abruptly. "See him patched up, and get word to Colonel Wood."

"And let our men go unavenged?" Paul's amiable face was strangely stern. It was like watching a golden retriever turn into a Doberman. "They killed *Ham*. What did Ham ever do to anyone?"

He'd been doing his darnedest to kill as many Spaniards as possible. But Holt didn't think Paul would appreciate that point.

And maybe, just maybe, he wasn't doing Paul any favors trying to keep him out of the battle. He'd tried to save his mother. Get away, he'd said. It will be better for you, he'd said.

But it hadn't, had it?

"All right, then." Holt put his weight down as hard as he could on his injured leg. It hurt but it held. He checked his Krag. He chambered another round. *"Once more unto the breach."*

Paul gave him a strange look, but Holt was already limping forward into the fray, quick as his injured leg would take him.

It wasn't until Holt had flung himself onto his stomach at the front of the line, shooting and running and dropping and shooting again, that he remembered that cowboys weren't supposed to quote Shakespeare.

Siboney, Cuba
June 25, 1898

"THEY CALL THIS A HOSPITAL?" whispered Kit.

It was full dark by the time Clara Barton's bedraggled relief force reached Siboney, after a harrowing ride to shore in a rowboat that saw them nearly wrecked against the rocks. Betsy had seen more than one of the doctors retching as they crawled out onto the sand, then hastily wiping their mouths with their handkerchiefs.

They'd managed to collar a passing Cuban soldier, who had offered the information that both the Cuban and US Army hospitals lay just to the right of the beach. They had struggled through the sand, their wet skirts hampering their legs, the nurses in their white aprons and caps, ghostly in the dark. Betsy wasn't sure if she was holding Kit's hand or if Kit was holding hers, but she was glad of the human contact in the strange, dark night.

At the head of the group, Miss Barton strode confidently onto the verandah, demanding in ringing tones, "Is this the army hospital?"

One of the men on the verandah detached himself. "Who's asking?"

He addressed not Miss Barton but the man behind her, Dr. Lesser.

Miss Barton did not take well to being overlooked. "I am Miss Barton of the Red Cross and I would like to speak to the surgeon in charge."

Kit tugged on Betsy's arm. "While she's busy up there, I want to go take a look."

"Kit—" Betsy had a bad feeling about this. It smelled wrong, she realized. There was none of the familiar hospital tang of carbolic that stung the nose and proclaimed a ward from yards away. Instead, the stench of human waste and decaying flesh assaulted her nose.

Kit was already halfway down the verandah. Betsy hurried after her.

"Hey." There was a man sitting in his shirtsleeves on the verandah, in a rickety wooden chair. He waved his cigarette at Kit and
Betsy without bothering to rise. "Don't go in there. There's sick men
in there."

The open door next to him let the air in and the stench out. The
ward was dimly lit by a few hanging lanterns, but that weak light
was more than enough. The men lay where they had stumbled. Or
been dumped. There were no pillows, no sheets; they lay on the bare
boards of the floor. Even in the dim light Betsy could see the filth
that coated it, the things crawling about.

"I'm a nurse," said Betsy sharply. The words came out of her
mouth before she could think them through. *I'm a nurse.* She had
been one, at least.

"Yeah, so am I," said the man, cigarette dangling from the side of
his mouth. "That's my ward."

Betsy saw as red as the glowing circle of his cigarette. "Then why
aren't you in there?"

The man tipped back his chair, his hat slouching down over his
face. "There's not much can be done."

Betsy could see a million things that could be done, starting with
getting those men off the bare floor and onto pallets. "They're dirty.
They're thirsty. You could wash them. You could give them something to drink."

The man looked horrified. "You give one something and then
they'll all want it. What's one nurse to forty men? If there were ten
of me . . ."

They'd be doing as little as one of him. Betsy didn't trust herself
to speak. She turned on her heel.

"Look, what do you expect me to do?" the man called after her.

Betsy stalked straight to Miss Barton. "I just spoke to one of their nurses. I saw better in field hospitals in rural Greece. This isn't a hospital; it's a pigsty."

There was a faint cough behind her. Kit was making horrified eye-popping faces in the lantern light.

"Miss Barton?" Betsy turned to see a very official-looking figure standing there. He did not seem pleased. "I am Major Havard. May I ask to what we owe the pleasure of your company at this unusual hour?"

"The wounded wait not on clocks," said Miss Barton sternly. She stepped in front of Betsy, who subsided into the background next to Kit. "The Red Cross stands ready to serve. I have with me three doctors and four nursing sisters. We can begin immediately."

"That is very kind of you, but I'm afraid you've had a wasted journey. We're not in need of your assistance."

In the ward behind him, a man moaned in pain, cursing the government, the army, the Spanish. Betsy could smell the nurse's cigarette smoke against the salt of the sea and the stench of human waste.

Miss Barton drew herself up to her full height. "Major Havard. My nurses tell me you lack the basic necessities. We have a ship full of supplies and trained workers."

The major brushed that aside. "We have transports with supplies of our own. They'll be here soon enough."

"Will it be soon enough? We are here now."

"With all due respect, Miss Barton, an army hospital is no place for a female nurse."

Miss Barton didn't flinch. "With all due respect, Major Havard, I have spent much of my life in army hospitals."

"In the Civil War, perhaps." Major Havard casually consulted his pocket watch, waiting a moment to let the insult fully sink in. "We have doctors and nurses of our own."

"As I see." Miss Barton looked pointedly at the nurse smoking stolidly away. "And how many men do you expect to survive their ministrations?"

Major Havard snapped his pocket watch closed. "Are you criticizing my arrangements, Miss Barton?"

Miss Barton took a step forward, her starched petticoats rustling. "I am offering my assistance."

"And I," snapped Major Havard, "am refusing that assistance."

Miss Barton looked Major Havard in the eye, and Betsy wondered how she had ever thought her vain or silly. "What about your duty to the men in your care? Will they thank you for refusing aid?"

"That's army business—not yours. If you'll excuse me?"

And with that, the major did them the vast discourtesy of turning his back and walking away.

"But—they can't do that." Kit stared blankly after the major. "I was there with Nurse Hayes. I saw—it's a mess!"

"The army has spoken," said Miss Barton. It was the sort of tone that commanded lightning bolts and turned men to stone. "You. Miss Carson. You will write down every word of that exchange and print it in your paper. I want the world to know what happened here."

"Yes, ma'am!"

Miss Barton gave a curt nod. "Now. All of you. You heard what Major Havard said. Our services are not required. Come."

"We're leaving? Just like that?" Betsy didn't know what to do. She hadn't wanted to be here in the first place, but now that they were, they couldn't just walk away.

"Of course not." Miss Barton's voice was calm, but there was a militant gleam in her eyes. "We're merely diverting our mission. If our own people won't accept our aid, perhaps our Cuban allies will."

The Cuban hospital, housed in General García's headquarters, was on the same side of the harbor, only a few minutes' walk away.

If the surgeon in charge was bemused at being accosted at midnight by a party led by the legendary Miss Clara Barton, he recovered from his surprise with admirable speed and led the entire group directly to General Calixto García.

General García was a wonderful old man with a bushy white mustache and a great scar in the center of his forehead.

"He's a legend," Kit hissed in Betsy's ear. Betsy could tell she was dying to whip out her notebook. Her fingers moved on Betsy's arm as though she were holding a pen. "When he was only twenty, he was already a freedom fighter and shot himself through the head so the Spanish wouldn't catch him. Under the chin and out the forehead. He shot himself and survived it and kept fighting. He spent years in a Spanish prison. . . ."

Kit was whispering to her about this war and that war, but Betsy just couldn't stop staring at that scar, where a bullet had gone through his chin and out his forehead. And he'd survived. He'd survived and lived and fought again. He was fighting still.

It was incredible what the body could bear. For some.

Not so much for others.

"The stories he could tell . . ." Kit hastily straightened, pasting on a serious expression as Clara Barton introduced their party to the general.

"We stand ready to offer whatever aid we can."

"I accept with gratitude," said the general solemnly. At their surprised expressions, he smiled at them. "I know a godsend when I see one. My men have suffered much in three years. I will do anything I can to alleviate their pain. And," he added, with a courtly bow, "your reputation precedes you."

"We do what we can," said Miss Barton modestly, although Betsy could tell she was blazing with triumph and relief and more than a bit of I-told-you-so.

The chief surgeon murmured something in the general's ear and the general nodded, the lamplight playing off the shiny skin of his scar. "My doctors ask only that they might have a day to make the hospital fit for your presence. . . . He says it is no place for ladies."

Miss Barton gave a sharp laugh. "My dear sir, if there's one thing we don't fear, it's dirt! Dirt fears us. Show us your buckets and brooms. We'll have your hospital fit for health by morning."

"I should not wish to be a dirt speck in your path."

"Nor I a Spanish soldier in yours." The two old warriors smiled at each other in perfect accord. "Sister Bettina, Sister Minnie, Nurse Carson, Nurse Hayes, to your mops! We have a battle to be won."

Chapter Ten

Darling Ava,

I have been a model student. You would be amazed by my new powers of application, which have lasted for the better part of a week and possibly more. I have maintained a regular presence in the library. I have attended every lecture. I haven't scandalized the populace with my bicycle for at least a week. I don't see how Professor Richardson can fail to be impressed, can you?

Please do come, Ava. You know you could do with a season in Greece after the winter you've had. I've enclosed tickets and a bank draft. Mrs. MacHugh's coachman will fetch you from Piraeus. You don't need to worry about a thing. It's all arranged.

Don't tell me you can't accept. If you do, I'll bestow the tickets on some thoroughly unworthy individual who won't be nearly as good an influence on me as you.

All my love,
Betsy

—*Miss Betsy Hayes '96 to Ava Saltonstall '96*

Athens, Greece
January 1897

BETSY BATTLED IRREGULAR VERBS AND her own worse nature.

She attended every lecture by Dr. Dörpfeld of the German School, dutifully trailing him around the Acropolis every Saturday as he pointed out this inscription and that statue. She sat in the library of the American School, poring over her tattered copy of Jane. She haunted Dr. Richardson's office.

And yet. The answer was always the same.

"I don't understand," Betsy complained to Ethel. "Professor Sterrett commended us especially. He even said our pluck and courage deserved high praise. We climbed Mount Helicon! What more is Dr. Richardson waiting for? The oracle at Delphi to speak?"

"Or for you to get tired and go away." Ethel looked pointedly at Betsy over the book that she had been trying to read, unsuccessfully, for the past half hour. "Have you ever thought that Professor Richardson would be more likely to give way if you battered at him a little less?"

"Don't tell me you catch more flies with honey than vinegar. I don't want to catch flies. I want to be treated with the basic professional courtesy that Richardson extends to the men."

Ethel narrowed her eyes at Betsy. "The men don't bang on his office door."

"The men don't *need* to bang on his office door."

Ethel controlled herself with an effort. "All I'm saying is that you might want to take . . . a more diplomatic approach. Don't pester Professor Richardson quite so directly. Let Professor Sterrett intercede for you. Or Monsieur de Robecourt?"

Just hearing his name unsettled Betsy. She'd tried so hard not to think of him. Which, of course, meant she thought of him constantly.

"Maybe I should just make Professor Richardson coffee," Betsy shot back.

Ethel closed her book and looked long and hard at Betsy. "The boys like it when I make them coffee. It makes them more comfortable with having me here."

"Because you're skivvying for them!"

"I'm being part of the group," said Ethel, through gritted teeth.

"Is any of them making coffee for you? Is that what you want, to be kept on as a sort of cook-housemaid?"

"At least I'll still be here!" Ethel was on her feet, her knuckles white on the spine of her book. "Whereas the way you're going— Did you ever stop to think that you might be ruining it for everyone else, pushing the way you do? After you, we'll be lucky if they ever accept another woman to the school!"

Betsy gaped after her as Ethel stomped off, her book clamped under her arm. She hadn't—all she had done was asked to be treated as an equal. Was that what Ethel wanted? To be accepted on sufferance so long as she made herself pleasant and useful? Ethel would undoubtedly publish her articles using only her first initial and last name, because heaven forfend a male academic read something by an Ethel rather than an Edward. What kind of career was that?

An actual one. Betsy bit down hard on her lip, feeling shaky and more than a little like crying. What if Ethel was right? What if she was ruining it for herself and everyone else, all those girls at Smith behind her?

The boys didn't invite Betsy to lectures with them. She wasn't one of the crowd around the coffeepot. Professor Richardson hid when she knocked.

The only person who had listened to her, who had taken her seriously, was Monsieur de Robecourt.

And look how that had turned out.

She hadn't seen him since Delphi. Family matters had called him away, Aikaterini said, not quite meeting Betsy's eyes as she said it. Betsy didn't know what Aikaterini knew and couldn't bring herself to ask.

Betsy alternated between hating Monsieur de Robecourt and hating his wife and hating herself, none of which was terribly pleasant.

In a moment of weakness, Betsy sent off a set of first-class tickets to Ava.

Yes, she knew Ava had steadfastly said she couldn't leave her position as a companion, but how could she not, when Betsy needed her so much? And it was for Ava too, she told herself self-righteously. If she didn't intervene, Ava would be stuck winding wool forever. But it was mostly for herself. She couldn't talk to Aikaterini about Monsieur de Robecourt—they'd been friends long before Betsy had ever come to Athens. It wouldn't be fair.

Betsy knew what Ava would tell her. Ava would tell her he was just a distraction and she should focus on her studies. But now— after what Ethel said, Betsy felt painfully self-conscious in the school. She'd known Ethel didn't exactly love her, but she'd never realized just how much Ethel disliked her. No, worse than disliked her, thought she was a threat to female scholars.

Betsy found herself shirking the unfriendly halls of the American School for the far more receptive atmosphere of Aikaterini's salon, thronged with government ministers and court ladies, where one could hear the latest news before it made it into the papers. And was there news! The Greek-speaking world was in foment, the bits of it still under control of the Ottoman Empire on the point of rebellion. Anti-Turkish secret societies were forming in Macedonia; the Turks were oppressing Greeks in Crete; there were rumors that the king of Greece, in defiance of international accords, was secretly sending arms to Crete.

Betsy cringed at the memory of her own ignorance on the boat to Nauplion, when she'd asked Monsieur de Robecourt about the soldiers, and he'd looked at her in such surprise, that she should know so little—all right, nothing—about the recent history of her adoptive country. Just another naive American gadding about Europe.

She wasn't going to make that mistake again. She pored over the papers and tagged along after Aikaterini to the ladies' gallery at Parliament.

"The Great Powers all side with the sultan," complained Aikaterini's friend, the minister of war. "All of them: the British, the French, the Russians . . ."

"Not the Americans," protested Betsy, although she wasn't actually sure where America stood on the matter. "You're the birthplace of democracy. We wouldn't exist without you. Greece can't bow to tyranny! We can't let it!"

Poky old Britain and France, hidebound and decadent, might side with the sultan for the sake of world order, but she was American and she knew better.

The world was kindling just waiting to be lit, and Betsy wanted nothing more than to wave the torch.

It wasn't just Crete that was up in arms. In Athens, the medical students went on strike, furious at their professors delaying conferring their degrees. They were forced, they complained, to twiddle their thumbs in idleness for a year or more after finishing their requirements because their professors couldn't be bothered to read their theses. For days Aikaterini's salon could talk of nothing else, some siding with the students, others with the professors.

"Silly children." Aikaterini dismissed them, but Betsy's blood was boiling.

"They've done the work, why shouldn't they have the degree?"

"They would, if they'd wait for it."

Waiting. Betsy was sick of waiting. Sick of pounding on the door of Dr. Richardson's office, knowing he was in there and hiding from her. She'd done all the work; she'd done more than had been asked of her. And where was she? Twiddling her thumbs in Aikaterini's drawing room because no matter what she did, Professor Richardson was never, ever going to let her get closer to an excavation than the reports in the library.

Ethel was right. The most she could do was make coffee for the boys and hope to be allowed to publish under an initial.

It made her feel sick. It made her furious. At least the medical students were *doing* something about it. When the word arrived that the students had stormed the university, occupying it by force of arms, Betsy took her freshly polished bicycle and set off to wave her flag at the barricades.

She could hear the shouting before she got there. The university looked very different with armed students standing guard at the entrances and a cordon of police blocking them on all sides. Betsy swung down from her bicycle, wheeling it toward the fray. She checked as a stone hit the cobbles, sending up a dash of pebbles and spooking a horse. The police in front of her ducked and shouted as more projectiles came at them.

A hand closed over Betsy's shoulder, pulling her back. She dropped her bicycle, an angry exclamation in Greek on her lips— that stilled as she saw who it was.

"You should not be here," said Monsieur de Robecourt.

He was in his town clothes, a high starched collar, a dark morning coat over narrow gray trousers. Betsy tried very hard to pretend to herself that she didn't remember the way his body felt beneath those sophisticated layers, the play of his muscles against the palms of her hands.

Betsy shook his hand off her shoulder, thrusting her bicycle between them like a chastity belt. "That's none of your concern."

"It isn't safe for you here." He leaned toward her, his voice low and urgent. "Didn't you hear the students shot a schoolboy earlier today? It was an accident—but I should prefer such an accident not happen to you."

Why did he have to act like he cared? It just made it all so much harder. "I should prefer such an accident not happen to me either. But that's no concern of yours."

"Isn't it?" There was a wistful expression on his face that made Betsy's insides do strange things. "If I could cure myself of caring for you, I would. Even if I am not . . . eligible . . . your happiness, your well-being, your safety, they matter to me."

Behind them, stones were being thrown and insults were being shouted, but it was all curiously muted. This was what always happened; whenever Monsieur de Robecourt was near it was as though everything else faded away; there was nothing but him in the world.

Betsy looked at him despairingly. "What am I to do with you?"

"Forgive me?" he suggested. "Allow me to begin again—as your friend?"

Betsy's hands clenched on the handles of her bicycle. She wasn't sure that was possible. On the other hand, trying to cast him out of her life hadn't worked very well either. She was damned if he was there and damned if he wasn't. It was so tempting, the prospect of beginning again—knowing it would go nowhere, she reminded herself firmly.

"If I do, there's to be no romantic nonsense," she said, as much for her own sake as his. "I know you can't help flirting, but do try not to get carried away."

"I shall guard my heart as best I can." But the way he was looking at her made Betsy worry about her own.

Her heart was made of sterner stuff, Betsy told herself. Iron. Or granite. Or something of the sort. Science hadn't been one of her better subjects.

"All right, then," she said gruffly. "You can stop avoiding Aikaterini's salons and everything can be normal again."

"In that case . . ." With a glance behind them at the rioters, Monsieur de Robecourt offered her his arm. "May I escort you back to Academy Street?"

It was only what any gentleman would do. But Betsy was very afraid that, with him, she was no lady.

Monsieur de Robecourt let his arm drop. "If you won't take my escort, will you at least return yourself? I hope we can be friends, and you will accept the well-meaning advice of a friend."

Betsy knew what Ava would tell her to do. To walk away. As she ought to have walked away at the Stoa of the Athenians.

But Ava wasn't here. Betsy wasn't even sure if Ava would accept the tickets she'd sent.

It would be different this time, she told herself. No more embraces in the ruins. No more talk of love.

Pushing her bicycle out of the way, Betsy slid her arm through his. "I can't say I'll accept the advice—my friend Ava will tell you I seldom do—but I would be a fool to refuse a friend."

CHAPTER ELEVEN

After a harrowing landing through the surf, the sisters of the Red Cross discovered no lack of need for their services. The first battle had been fought on the Friday, and the number of sick and wounded far exceeded expectations. The most seriously wounded were taken to the hospital ship *Olivette*, but that left over a hundred still without care. No hospital had been established, no preparations made. Instead, the wounded were taken to an old warehouse and deposited on the hard floor, not a cot among them.

The Red Cross immediately offered their services and supplies, but the surgeon in charge declined, claiming they were in no need of assistance. The Red Cross then went to the Cuban hospital, where they were met with the warmest welcome. There is no need to describe how quickly sleeves were rolled up, aprons pinned back, and men made comfortable, with clean linens and heartening gruel. When asked if they were glad to see the Red Cross sisters, one man told me, "Glad to see them? We were never so glad to see anyone."

The surgeons of the US Army fail to share that view. Although we had been refused admittance, the Red Cross sent supplies to

the US Army hospital, only to discover that the blankets and pillows were left in a heap on the floor as no one had issued an order to distribute them and the men lay still on bare boards, beset
by vermin, the flies buzzing about them, sweating in the merciless
heat, some sharing a blanket between them, others without even
that meager comfort. It strains my pen to describe the horror of
that place. The men have had no food but army rations, no change
of clothing, no baths. They lie in their own filth and blood. The
stench is indescribable. One man told me, "It is hard to be sick in
this place."

Our hearts break for our suffering countrymen and the severe want of management that has caused their current crisis.
The Red Cross stands ready to aid them should the opportunity
arise. . . .

—*Miss Katherine Carson for the* St. Louis Star Ledger, *June 30, 1898*

❧

Las Guasimas, Cuba
June 25, 1898

"TO LOST FRIENDS." PAUL RAISED his tin cup in a salute to the
night sky.

The Rough Riders clustered in small groups around their tents
and campfires, mourning their own in their own way. Some talked.
Some sang. Many drank.

"Lost friends," echoed Holt, although they hadn't been his
friends, not really. *Lost acquaintances* didn't have quite the same ring
to it. Comrades in arms. That was better. They'd eaten together, slept
together, fought together, but he hadn't known any more of them
than they had of him.

If he fell, Paul would mourn him as a friend, not realizing he'd never known him in the slightest. Not even his real name.

Holt tipped his cup back and was surprised when the rest of him tipped back too. He was, he realized, more than a bit drunk. Paul had traded a can of bully beef for a generous portion of rum. Holt had drunk too much too fast, trying to silence the pain in his leg and his head.

It hadn't worked. He could still see Ham Fish lying there on the trail, Dr. Stringfellow red to the elbows. And above it all, the hectoring voice of Paul's old Yale prom date.

The man next to you might be the one to fall. Or it might be you.

Behind them, one of the men at the campfire had started singing in a pure, clear tenor, one of the old ballads of the Civil War. Everyone knew "The Vacant Chair." It was a commonplace of after-dinner entertainment, one of those songs girls sang when they were trying to make an impression on the company.

But he'd never heard it like this before. Not with the tang of blood fresh in the air, the dirt newly turned.

"We shall meet, but we shall miss him . . . There will be one vacant chair."

There wasn't one vacant chair but seven. Seven men laid in a common grave, wrapped in blue blankets to thwart the vultures that circled above.

"We did what we had to do," Holt said, hoping it was true, that those men in their graves felt it too. "We did what was right."

Even if you win you lose, chided Miss Hayes. Holt wondered why she had taken up residence in his head and how much rum it would take to make her go away. Too much, he suspected.

Paul waved his tin cup in the general direction of Las Guasimas. "We'll get our revenge. We'll make 'em pay tenfold for every friend we've lost. Don't you worry."

Fireflies danced in front of Holt, the shifting lights making him blink. "Revenge? We're soldiers. That's what happens in a war. We knew the risks going in."

Paul looked at him like he was crazy. "They *killed* them. The Spanish killed them."

"We killed a fair few of them too." Holt rubbed his forehead, trying to put his jumbled thoughts in order. His tongue felt too big for his mouth, making the words come out slow. "The way I see it, I can hate the Spaniards for what they did to the Cuban people. But I can't hate them for shooting at us. We're here to shoot at them. It's war. They have every right to shoot back at us. As much as I'd prefer they miss."

"They're the enemy," said Paul stubbornly.

"What *is* an enemy?" Time wobbled, and he was back at the law school, standing up in the middle of the room in Austin Hall, trying to work his way down through the tangle of common and civil law to first principles. "Is it someone who's done you a wrong? Or just someone who happens to be on the other side of a conflict?"

Paul squinted at him owlishly, nine parts rum and one part skepticism. "Does it matter?"

"It matters why you do things, not just that you do them." Or else they'd all just be running around killing because they could. "I'm not shooting the Spanish because I want to shoot them. I'm shooting them because I want to stop them doing what they're doing. There's a difference."

"Don't see it," said Paul stubbornly.

He should just let it be, Holt knew. But it felt, in the strange intensity of the tropical night, his emotions raw with rum, very important to hold to that difference. The line between vengeance and purpose. Between God's law and man's.

Maybe because he'd come so close to toppling over into the wrong side of it.

After his mother died, when no one would believe him, when they patted him on the shoulder and told him that grief did strange things, it had been tempting, so tempting, to consider an "accident" of his own, payback for all the "accidents" his mother had endured over the years. If grief did strange things, a grieving widower might lean too far out a window. A grieving widower might drink a bit too much, slip, fall, and bash his head open on the sideboard.

But he couldn't. Holt's spirit recoiled. He couldn't right murder with murder, even if his soul cried for justice. That wasn't justice. That was revenge.

Instead, he'd done what he knew would hurt his father more. He'd dropped out of law school.

Holt's head felt like a balloon, floating above his body. He clasped his hands on either side of his forehead to try to keep it steady. Paul was saying something but it danced in and out of his hearing.

Holt cleared his throat, searching for some middle ground. "Look. Ham Fish and the rest of them—they died for a cause." Not like his mother, who had died to bolster a weak man's pride. "They died knowing they were doing something good."

"Does that mean we're supposed to let their deaths go unavenged?" Paul demanded indignantly.

Holt was tired. So tired. He didn't even realize he was listing backward until he felt the ground beneath his back. It was too much trouble to get up again, so he just stayed there, his cup balanced on his stomach. Above him, the tropical stars quivered in their spheres, shimmying like showgirls. Men might die, but these stars would still be here, shining impartially on whoever won or lost.

Holt lifted an unsteady finger. "Look. There's Scorpius. And there's the Southern Cross."

Paul hesitated for a moment and then decided to take the olive branch. He lowered himself back so he could see too. "You must rely on the stars out on the range."

Forget the range; he'd been a member of the Harvard Natural History Society.

But it would be cruel to strip Paul of his illusions. Holt missed illusions. He settled for a half-truth. "I wasn't much of a cowboy. More a jack-of-all-trades. I only lasted three months on a cattle ranch."

"Roaming the West, rounding up bandits," said Paul dreamily, and Holt didn't correct him.

"Join you?" Paul's Yale friend Thede Miller flopped down next to them, stretching out his legs to display muddy boots.

Paul struggled up to a sitting position. "How's Teddy?"

"Still playing polo in his head. Doc says it's typhoid. I left him at the field hospital in Siboney." Thede looked down at his legs as though surprised they still belonged to him. "It's been a long walk back here."

"Lie down and rest your legs," said Paul generously. "Holt over here was just pointing out the constellations. Does that look like a scorpion to you?"

"Constellations." Thede's brow wrinkled and then his mouth dropped open. He jabbed a finger at Holt. "That's it! That's where we met! I knew I'd seen you before."

A sick feeling settled in Holt's stomach that had nothing to do with the rum. He lurched to a sitting position, feeling the world lurching with him.

"It was the mustache," Thede went on obliviously, delighted to have finally remembered. "You didn't have the mustache then. I was visiting with my brother-in-law. The Harvard College Observatory. You showed us the Great Refractor. Almost made me want to go to Harvard."

Thede grinned as though that were too absurd to be contemplated.

Paul hooted at the very notion. "Holt at Harvard? You must have a—what do they call them? A doppelgänger. That's it."

"No," said Holt. The rum he'd drunk made his mouth sticky. "Not a doppelgänger."

Paul stared at him, too confused to be upset. "What would you be doing at Harvard?"

"College." He could omit, but he couldn't lie, not straight-out. Holt gave up. So much for a new life. Sometimes, the old one just wouldn't let you go. "That's what I was doing at Harvard. I was an undergraduate there."

Siboney, Cuba
June 30, 1898

"MEN. THEY JUST NEVER LEARN." Kit came into the Cuban hospital, setting down a bundle with a decided thump.

Betsy glanced over her shoulder from the man whose dressing she was changing. "Aren't those the blankets Miss Barton told you to take over to the US Army hospital?"

"They sent me back with them. Apparently the army's quite self-sufficient as they are," said Kit drily. "Even though they can't seem to rustle up cots or blankets or even a jug of water."

"That's ridiculous. All right, you'll do for the moment," Betsy told her patient, tucking in the ends of the fresh dressing. Dropping the soiled bandages into a basket for boiling, Betsy went over to join Kit at the washstand. "That's worse than ridiculous."

"That's men. Sooner die than ask for directions. Or a blanket." Kit scrubbed her hands furiously with the lye soap. "I feel filthy just having stepped inside there. The boys asked me why we'd deserted them for the Cubans. I told them don't blame us, blame their doctors. You should see the difference between that hellhole and here."

Here wasn't exactly a picnic in the park, but Betsy had to admit to herself that they'd done a pretty good job. All right, a very good job. They'd meticulously scrubbed each room, boiled everything that could be boiled, and provided fresh bedding and supplies from the stores in the hold of the *State of Texas* before moving the men back in, in clean shirts, on clean sheets, with clean bandages, and with an organized rota that made sure each man got his share of care in a timely fashion. Betsy found Sister Bettina a bit of a pill, but the woman knew what she was doing. The ward stank of carbolic, not rotting flesh.

Betsy felt . . . proud. It was a strange thing to feel, but there it was. Looking at her ward, at her patients, there was the satisfaction of knowing she'd actually done something for them, that there were men who'd go home because she, Betsy Hayes, had changed their dressings rather than letting them fester.

Betsy wasn't used to feeling like she'd done something right.

"You're going to wear off the skin if you keep that up," Betsy said. Kit's already chapped and calloused palms had gone lobster red, but she kept scrubbing away at them all the same, as if there were something more than dirt she was trying to eradicate. "Are things as bad in the army hospital as they were before?"

Kit shook the water off her hands and turned away to look for the drying cloth. "Worse. Sixty-odd men lying on the floor in their own filth, packed in like sardines. Some of them have been lying there since last Friday. You can smell their flesh rotting. It's a disgrace."

Betsy thought of all those men in Tampa, fighting over who got to go to Cuba, so proud in their brown uniforms and blue bandanas. Paul telling her how they were going off to fight Spain. His friend strong-arming her back onto the train. Officious man.

Betsy didn't like to think of them lying on the floor of that squalid shack, wounded, helpless. "Did you see . . ."

Kit glanced sideways at her. "That Rough Rider we met outside the hotel? No sign of him. Although those men were so close-packed it was hard to tell."

Betsy absentmindedly washed her own hands, breathing in the sharp scent of lye. *"He hath no drowning mark upon him / His complexion is perfect gallows."*

"Huh?" Kit put down the drying cloth. "Where did that come from?"

Somewhere from the recesses of her distracted mind. Betsy shook her head. "I just meant that he's too annoying to die. According to Herodotus, whom the gods love die young. *Not* the other ones." Belatedly, Betsy remembered Paul. If ever there was a man whom the gods loved, it was Paul. "What about a tall, blond Yale man?"

"Honey, the place is packed with tall, blond Yale men. I didn't notice any in particular."

There was a peculiar note to Kit's voice. Her banter seemed strangely flat. Betsy followed her as she went to collect the basket of dirty linens for boiling. "Is something wrong?"

"You mean other than all the dying men?" Kit brooded over the basket for a moment, before saying, "I saw Edward Marshall there. From the *New York Journal.*"

Ah, that was it. "Getting the scoop on you?" asked Betsy sagely.

Kit shook her head, stopped, and then shook it again. "Yes. But also no. He has a bullet through the spine. His legs won't move. They're not sure if he'll make it. But he wrote up his story all the same."

Betsy had no idea what to say. "Oh, Kit."

"I didn't even particularly like him." Kit pressed her lips hard together, her face contorting before she got it back under control. "I offered to file his story for him but he said Stephen Crane of the *World* had already done it."

"Well, that was nice of him," said Betsy cautiously.

"Betsy, am I crazy? Are we all crazy? He might die. He'll never walk again. And I can't decide if I'm scared or jealous. What are we *doing*?"

"Your job?"

"My job is writing about hat trim. And this season's sleeves. They let me do this because I begged them, because I convinced them it would be a stunt to have a girl reporter at the front." Kit breathed in deeply through her nose and out through her mouth. "Marshall got a bullet through his spine and his first thought was making sure his story made it in."

"Wouldn't you do the same?"

"*Yes.* And that's what scares me." Kit kicked the laundry basket. "I don't know if I'm a bad reporter because I look at him and wonder what would happen if I didn't make it home, or if I'm a bad mother because I would have been in his place in a heartbeat."

Betsy offered the only comfort she could think of. "You're smaller than he is. The bullet might have missed you."

Kit dropped her face into her hands.

"Think of it this way," said Betsy encouragingly. "You could get hit by a tram going to look at this season's sleeves. Or poisoned by the mercury in hats."

"I wrote an article about mercury poisoning from hats," said Kit in a muffled voice. "They told me to take out the depressing bits and put in more about the shape of the hat."

"All I'm saying is, there are dangers everywhere. My father caught a chill coming to visit me in Northampton." Because she'd been flouting authority, skipping classes, sure she was smarter than everyone. Just innocent high spirits, but her father had died for it. Betsy hastily tried to think of something else. "I knew a girl at Smith who broke her arm falling *up* the stairs. Just tripped and crack! And a friend told me about her cousin who choked to death on a billiard ball. He put it in his mouth for a dare and . . . that was that."

Kit lifted her head. "This is meant to cheer me up?"

"Did it?"

To Betsy's surprise, Kit grabbed her in a fierce hug. "Thank you."

Betsy froze. She couldn't remember the last time anyone had hugged her. Her family wasn't much for displays of affection. Then there was Ava. As much as she loved Ava, embraces weren't at all Ava's sort of thing. A swift pat on the arm represented the extremes of emotion.

For a moment, Betsy stood stiff, not quite sure what to do. Then, tentatively, she put her arms around Kit and hugged her back, resting her head against the other woman's shoulder, breathing in the familiar scents of bleach and lye.

"It will be all right," she whispered, even though she wasn't sure of anything of the kind.

"Nurse Hayes, Miss Carson! Touching as this is . . ." Sister Bettina sounded more weary than angry. They were all weary. "Miss Barton wants us all. Out front."

Kit released Betsy and stepped back, straightening her apron. Her eyes were suspiciously bright. "Thanks," she said.

Betsy suspected she looked equally pinkish around the eyes. "Think nothing of it. I'm happy to share more tales of disaster whenever you need them."

Kit gave a snort and turned to follow Sister Bettina to the front of the building, Betsy trailing behind, feeling, strangely, better than she had in a long time.

General García and Miss Barton were standing on the front porch, the rest of the nursing staff gathered around.

"I apologize for interrupting your labors," said General García, "but I wished to thank you personally for your service before you move on. We know how to appreciate such friendship as this. You have given the men new strength."

"We're moving on?" Betsy yelped.

"We have been summoned." Miss Barton did her best to sound impassive, but the expression on her face might, in a person of lesser stature, have been termed a smirk. "I have received a communique from Major Louis La Garde respectfully requesting our assistance in caring for the patients of the so-called hospital near the port."

No one cheered. They were too well-trained for that. But a palpable fizz of excitement ran through the group.

"It appears they anticipate a major engagement in the next few days and lack the beds, the supplies, and the personnel to manage a new influx of wounded. And it seems the men have raised a clamor about their condition compared to that of their Cuban allies."

She looked to General García, who essayed a half bow in response.

"I did tell them to complain to their doctors," murmured Kit to Betsy.

Miss Barton lowered her voice thrillingly. "I needn't describe to you the magnitude of the work. General García has been kind enough to help us secure a dwelling to use as a hospital."

"What about the current hospital?" asked Kit, back in reporter mode. Betsy could tell she was itching for her notebook.

Miss Barton's face hardened. "It does not deserve the name of *hospital.* It is a noisome, foul place fit for use only as kindling. I pity the men who have been forced to suffer needlessly in those walls."

"I agree," said General García. His voice was mild, but there was an edge to it that made Betsy stop squirming and pay attention. "It is a pity the government of the United States did not recognize us sooner and let us do our own fighting. We are sorry to sacrifice your soldiers. It is a great pity—and a great waste."

It had never occurred to Betsy that the Cuban revolutionaries might not be happy to have them there. From the looks on the faces around her, she wasn't the only one.

She thought of Paul's officious friend, with his droopy mustache and his thin, interesting face, talking about saving the women and children of Cuba. But what about the men of Cuba? And why assume it was always women and children who needed saving? Betsy would generally prefer to save herself.

"War is always a waste," said Miss Barton briskly. "What is past is past. One can only grapple with the present. We shall do our best to make sure as few young men as possible make the ultimate sacrifice—now that the army has deemed it fit to allow us to do so."

General García bowed. "I wish you the best of success. If I may ever be of assistance . . ."

"We shan't hesitate to ask."

When the general had taken his leave, Miss Barton turned back to her troops. And by troops, Betsy meant nurses.

"We have a great task ahead of us. I refer not just to the battle against dirt and disease but to the ridiculous prejudice that attends female endeavor."

Betsy glanced sideways at Kit. Kit grimaced back, completely and utterly in accord, without a word needing to be said.

She'd never had that before. Ava understood her, but it was a different kind of understanding. What would it have been like to have someone like Kit beside her in Greece? Betsy pressed her lips shut hard against a sudden, burning surge of grief.

She couldn't let herself think that. Not about what might have been. And certainly not about what was.

What had Miss Barton said? The past was past. They could only tackle the present. Betsy drew in a long, deep breath, forcing herself to focus on Miss Barton, who was still speaking, two bright circles in her cheeks that had little to do with rouge.

"The surgeon in charge told me that if he had his way, he would send all of us home. It is thanks entirely to the extremity in which they find themselves and the outcry of the men that they have summoned us at all—and they await any opportunity to send us away again."

Miss Barton's voice was rigorously controlled, but Betsy could hear the anger underneath. Betsy could feel that anger burning, spreading; they were all burning with it, all of them, every single one who had been told she couldn't do a man's work, couldn't dig for antiquities, couldn't write for the papers, couldn't nurse on the front. Catch more flies with honey than vinegar. Keep your voice down. Don't let the men know you're smarter.

"They can't do that," Betsy heard herself saying. "We won't go."

Miss Barton looked at her, those old, hooded eyes meeting hers, seeing straight through her. "That, ladies, depends on you. It is incumbent on every one of us to prove him wrong. Every one of us."

Betsy dug her nails into her palms to stop herself panicking. This wasn't Greece. She had Kit. And Miss Barton, who, in her passion, seemed roughly seven feet tall and possessed of a flaming sword. One couldn't imagine anything, including infection, defying Miss Barton.

Miss Barton regarded them all solemnly. "It is a double burden we bear: not just the lives entrusted to our care but the weight of proving ourselves capable, equal to this and any other situation. We shall and we must rise to the occasion. Not just for ourselves but for our sisters at home."

There was no going back. But at least she wasn't alone this time.

"What do you need us to do first?" asked Betsy.

Chapter Twelve

Darling Ava,

All is in readiness for your arrival! Aikaterini has the third best guest room aired; Herakles has polished my bicycle to a fine sheen; and everyone is agog to meet you, particularly the Harvard boys. I've told them to be very afraid, which only intrigues them more.

I can't wait to show you off to everyone and to introduce all my new friends to you. Athens has been all aflutter over the news from Crete—you should see the deputies in Parliament twirling their conversation beads like anything—and martial sentiment is running high, so we shall have exciting times for you. They've let me join the Union of Greek Women even though I'm not. Greek, that is. My feminine state is something of which Professor Richardson never ceases to remind me. I've tried scowling him into a standstill but I just don't have the eyebrows for it, the way you do.

I'm writing nonsense, aren't I? I know it's rather silly writing to you when by the time this letter reaches Concord you will have reached me, but I'm giddy with the thought that in just a day, or maybe two, you'll be here with me. The world feels

*like it's spinning around me faster and faster and I need you
and your calm good sense to keep me from spinning with it. You
will, won't you?*

*I can't wait to show you my Athens. . . . I hope you adore it
as much as I do.*

All my love,

Betsy

—Miss Betsy Hayes '96 to Ava Saltonstall '96

Athens, Greece
February 1897

"SHOULD YOU REALLY BE SPENDING so much time with him?"

"With whom?" Betsy asked innocently.

Ava was not fooled. Ava was never fooled, but that was part of the fun of it. Or at least it had been. Since she'd arrived in Greece, Ava's constant disapproval had felt less like part of their old routine and more like actual disapproval.

Ava was suspicious of the food, horrified that Betsy had a maid to help her dress and a servant assigned to shine her bicycle, appalled by the opulence of Betsy's new wardrobe, and more than a little wary of Aikaterini, whose openhanded good nature was blunted against the granite of Ava's unyielding self-sufficiency.

Right now Ava was standing in a corner of Aikaterini's grand salon, looking decidedly out of place among the crimson velvet and palm fronds in her one decent afternoon dress, which was made of a sensible twill in a sensible deep brown with leg-of-mutton sleeves that had already been outmoded by the time the dress was made. The sleeves did no favors for Ava's square-shouldered frame.

With her dark hair and dark brows and firmly marked features, Ava would be decidedly handsome if properly dressed. Betsy had offered to introduce her to Aikaterini's dressmaker. Ava had refused. Firmly. Her pride had already been bent out of shape by accepting the ticket Betsy had sent her—which, she insisted, she had used only because Betsy had already paid for it, and it would have been worse to let it go to waste.

Never mind that Betsy could afford to send Ava back and forth ten times over without it cutting into her pocket money. Pointing that out hadn't seemed to help.

Betsy couldn't help feeling a little hurt. She'd been so eager to show off her new world and her new friends to her old one. Couldn't Ava pretend to enjoy herself? Just a little? The only person Ava showed any interest in talking to was Aikaterini's husband, the dour Dr. MacHugh, who had unbent so far as to show Ava the dispensary he kept for the use of the household. That was the one time Betsy had seen Ava truly herself since she'd arrived.

She'd had an idea that once Ava was here . . . well, everything would be different. That it would be like Smith again, except with fancier clothes and more men. She would drag Ava to balls and routs, show off her Greek, parade her friend triumphantly through the halls of the American School like her own particular trophy, and spend long hours sprawled in Betsy's boudoir eating Turkish delight and rearranging the world to their satisfaction.

Nothing about this visit was going as Betsy had planned. Nothing at all.

Even the city itself refused to cooperate. Thanks to the death of the Austrian minister in Athens, the Athens social season had come to an abrupt halt, with the more elaborate entertainments canceled, including a ball to be thrown by the officers of the HMS *Nile*, upon which Betsy had been particularly counting. Balls as a rule weren't Ava's preferred pastime, but she might have found a cantankerous British naval doctor with whom to discuss the more gruesome sorts of cases, which might at least have put her in a somewhat better mood.

Without other outlets to divert them, Aikaterini's salon thronged with the bored and fashionable.

Including Charles.

Not that Charles ever allowed himself to be bored. He found amusement in everything, and his lively sense of the absurd acted on Betsy like strong coffee, making everything brighter. All it took was

Charles walking into the room and she could feel herself straightening, smiling, already rehearsing the amusing observations she meant to share with him, anticipating the way his eyes would crinkle at the corners, the feeling of his breath tickling her ear as he leaned over to whisper a witticism.

Ava had not taken to him. Betsy suspected the feeling was mutual although Charles was too worldly and too polite to show it.

"Monsieur de Robecourt is a friend of the household," said Betsy virtuously.

"Monsieur de Robecourt is a married man."

Betsy had forgotten just how New England Ava could be. Betsy, at least, had the benefit of being an upstart with new money, but Ava's family were Boston Brahmins all the way down. Impoverished Brahmins, which was even worse. They clung to their principles as they hadn't to their fortunes.

Betsy gave the taffeta skirt of her fashionable peacock-patterned tea dress a swish. "Don't be so Boston, Ava. This is Europe. It's quite permissible to talk to a man to whom one isn't married. Or would you rather we all be put in zenanas?"

Ava cast her an exasperated glance. "You know that's not at all what I meant."

"You'd probably have more freedom in a zenana than you do in Concord," persisted Betsy. Anyone could see that being a companion to a cantankerous elderly cousin didn't suit Ava in the least. Except Ava, that was. "Life isn't all mustard plasters and improving sermons. Don't you want to spread your wings a little before you have to go back to ministering to that cousin of yours?"

Ava's dark brows drew together. "You spread your wings too far, they burn."

"Only if they're made of wax," retorted Betsy.

It made her remember Charles, what seemed like a lifetime ago, telling her that with her he had the *tête de cire*, the head of wax.

She turned to look at him and found him already looking at her. Betsy felt her cheeks go pink.

All right, maybe Ava wasn't entirely wrong. Maybe she was dabbling her fingers in the fire, just a bit. But not enough to burn. They'd come to an understanding, she and Charles. They could be the best of friends, and that was all. Anything else was just . . . a *frisson*, Betsy told herself, feeling very European and worldly.

She grinned at Charles, just to show that she was a woman of the world and not some blushing schoolgirl, even if she was both blushing and currently in school.

Ava, of course, did not miss the exchange. "That," she said, "is exactly the sort of thing I'm talking about."

"I can't smile at a friend?" Betsy bared her teeth hideously at Ava.

Ava refused to be amused. "Maybe," she said, "if you would actually attend to your studies, you might not feel the need to distract yourself with flirtation with married men. If you had gone to the library yesterday instead of running off to Piraeus to see the troops . . ."

"That wasn't with Charles," Betsy protested. "I mean Monsieur de Robecourt. The colonel's wife invited me, and, oh, Ava, I wouldn't have missed it for anything. You should have seen the evzone soldiers in their red caps and blue coats, singing away like anything, the strangest, saddest song I've ever heard. It made me want to run out and fight the Turks single-handed."

"This isn't our war."

"If Lafayette had thought that, we might still be a colony."

"Lafayette was a military commander. What do you mean to do, recite Homer at them until they beg for mercy?"

"That's not fair. My pronunciation isn't that bad." Betsy grinned at the thought. "I could always hit them with the bits of Herodotus about the defeat of the Persians."

"This isn't . . . whenever that was." The only history that interested Ava were the bits involving scientific developments. She had dutifully memorized dates for exams and then just as promptly excised them from her head.

Betsy allowed herself a smirk. "There were multiple defeats of the Persians. Would you prefer 479 BC or 449 BC?"

"Well, then. Isn't that where you're meant to be spending your time? Didn't you say that Professor Richardson gave you a bunch of inscriptions from Eleusis to go through? You haven't gone once to the American School in the past week."

"I've had you visiting."

"Ha," said Ava eloquently. "You've been to Piraeus to see off the troops. You spend half your time in the ladies' gallery of Parliament—"

"I thought you might like to hear the debates," protested Betsy.

Events were moving so quickly Betsy could scarcely keep track of them all. The prime minister was accused of betraying Greece to foreign interests; the king took over the government and sent his own aide to Crete at the head of a force of three thousand men; the Turks went crying to the Great Powers; reservists were being called up; the Union of Greek Women was outfitting a hospital and organizing the sewing of uniforms for the war that everyone was certain was to come.

By the time the papers were out, the news was already old. Parliament was the place to be.

"I can't understand a word of it!"

"I translated for you. And rather nicely too. Hasn't my Greek improved?"

"Yes, your modern Greek has progressed remarkably. But aren't you meant to be pursuing a career in classical studies? Isn't that what your fellowship is for?"

Yes, but they wouldn't *let* her. It didn't matter how much she had worked, how many hours she had spent sitting conspicuously in the library diligently engaged in the interpretation of inscriptions; it hadn't even mattered that she'd climbed to the top of Mount Helicon. Betsy was beginning to suspect that if Athena herself were to appear to Professor Rutherford to demand Betsy be given permission to participate in excavations, the director would probably shake his head and inform the goddess of wisdom that men belonged in the field and women in the library.

But Betsy couldn't say any of that to Ava. Not when she wanted Ava to get up the nerve to pursue her own ambitions.

"Pericles said that just because you don't take an interest in politics doesn't mean that politics won't take an interest in you," Betsy argued. "Herodotus will still be there a month from now. But the rising on Crete is happening *now*. How could I be here and bury my head over my books and ignore it?"

"You said the same about the dramatic society, the hockey team, the *Smith College Monthly*. . . ." Ava began ticking off extracurricular activities on her fingers.

"Yes, yes, I know."

"And the Philosophical Society, the Banjo Club, the Voice Club, the Gymnasium and Field Association . . ."

They had all seemed so important at the time. So much more urgent than her classwork. Until her father had been called up to see the dean in the frostiest of frosty Februaries and the cold had settled in his lungs.

Betsy hugged herself. "This is different." It wasn't any use fighting with Ava. It never had been. The only thing that ever worked was distraction. "The Union of Greek Women is getting up a first aid class. Would you like to come with me?"

Ava eyed her narrowly. "When have you ever shown any interest in nursing?"

"Aren't you glad I am? You can tell me how I'm rolling my bandages wrong. They've got a woman doctor to teach it." Betsy let that sink in. "She did go to Radcliffe, but no one's perfect."

"Hmm," said Ava, which was Ava for "I know exactly what you're trying to do, but it's too much bother to argue with you." Besides, Betsy had known Ava could never resist if she dangled the prospect of mutilated limbs in front of her. This was a woman who splinted the legs of stray birds and stopped passersby to peer down their throats.

Ava never liked admitting when she was wrong. Or accepting help. But here was a way that Betsy could help without seeming to help. Once she was immersed in medical texts, Betsy had no doubt Ava would be herself again—and they could be as they had been at Smith. Although, if she were being honest, the distance between them had started at Smith, somewhere around the end of their final year. Betsy wasn't sure if it was because Betsy was grieving her father, or if the awkwardness had come of knowing that when they left Smith, Betsy would be pursuing her chosen career while Ava would be going on to Concord and genteel servitude rather than medical school.

Betsy had great hopes for the nursing class.

So, apparently, did a lot of other people. On the day of the first session, Betsy trailed after Ava up the steps of the Grand Theatre, which had been donated to the Union of Greek Women for their war efforts, nodding to acquaintance after acquaintance. Half of Athens appeared to be there. No one wanted to be seen as behindhand in the war effort, even if they had just about as much interest in nursing as Betsy.

Betsy came to an abrupt halt. She clutched Ava's arm. "Do you know who that is?"

Ava dutifully turned to look. "A woman and her daughter?"

"*That* is Sophia Schliemann. And her daughter." Ava looked blank. Betsy bounced up and down on the balls of her feet, flapping her hands excitedly. "She and her husband discovered Troy. She smuggled Priam's jewels out of Hissarlik by dead of night wrapped in her shawl. Can you imagine?"

Ava was craning her neck to try to see the stage at the front of the room, where Dr. Kalopothakes, the Radcliffe woman, had placed chalkboards with various drawings of the human form on them. "Oh, yes. I remember your talking about that."

Betsy stared at Mrs. Schliemann, fashionably attired in a walking suit of plaid banded with velvet like any Athenian society lady. Twenty-five years ago, before Betsy had been born, the very young Mrs. Schliemann had been photographed wearing the jewels she had discovered at Troy, a gold diadem around her forehead, gold streaming past her ears, draped around her neck. Wearing the ornaments that had last graced the brow of a woman who had lived centuries ago, before Herodotus, before Homer.

Mrs. Schliemann was older now—and not completely covered in ancient jewelry—but it was unmistakably the same woman. "She's been involved in—oh goodness—more major excavations than we've had hot dinners. It's not just Troy. There was the treasury at Mycenae . . . and the tholos tomb at Orchomenos. . . ."

"I'll just go find us seats," said Ava, and did.

OVER THE NEXT MONTH, AVA worked diligently at bandaging, splinting, making plaster of Paris casts, caring for gunshot wounds, and properly applying anaesthetics. Betsy daydreamed and doodled through her anatomy lessons, failed to locate her own kidneys, confused the femur with the fibula, and secured an invitation to tea from Mrs. Schliemann.

Mrs. Schliemann's mansion made Aikaterini's look like a humble Boston brownstone. It was an enormous, rectangular building with a double colonnade and gratuitous statuary on the roof. Inside, the walls were rich with murals depicting scenes from the Trojan War. Of course, thought Betsy, craning her neck every which way so as not to miss any detail and tripping over her own feet in the process. What else would they be? This was the woman who, with her husband, had found Troy.

Even Ava couldn't object to her spending an afternoon calling on one of the great names in Betsy's field. Admittedly, it was her husband who had been the great name, but everyone knew that Mrs. Schliemann had been by his side every step of the way, had wheedled the workmen, transcribed the reports, and become, in her widowhood, a focal point of the classicist community, hosting gatherings and giving lectures on her—er, their— discoveries.

Here was a woman who could teach her more about excavations than Professor Richardson had ever begun to imagine.

"Is it true that you carried Priam's gold out wrapped in your shawl?" Betsy asked eagerly, as soon as the proprieties had been observed.

Mrs. Schliemann, respectable and surprisingly ordinary, smiled kindly at her. "No. I wasn't even there when they discovered it."

"But—" Her father had loved that story, had repeated it to Betsy with such relish that she felt she'd been there, had seen young Mrs. Schliemann stooped protectively over the precious bundle in her arms.

Mrs. Schliemann handed her a plate of cakes. "It does make a pretty story, doesn't it? My husband could never resist spinning a good story, whether it was true or not. Men are such romantics. Just look at them all go swoony over the notion of Helen."

Betsy goggled at her, speechless.

"In real life, most of them probably couldn't abide a Helen," said

Mrs. Schliemann thoughtfully. "But they all like the idea of her in theory. Goodness only knows to whom those jewels belonged. But once you claim they're Helen's, the world takes note. It made a nice symmetry, my smuggling the jewels out of Troy, just as Helen herself was once smuggled to Troy."

"But you weren't actually there?" Betsy was still trying to wrap her head around the fact that what she had always taken as truth was instead a prettily arranged fiction.

"I had been called away to Athens upon the death of my father and missed all the more exciting parts of that particular excavation." Taking pity on Betsy, Mrs. Schliemann added, "But that doesn't make the find itself any less valuable. Just a bit less . . . romantic."

Betsy had a moment of panic that everything she thought was true might not be. "But—you did excavate, didn't you?"

"Oh, my dear, yes. I was supervising crews of workmen by the time I was eighteen."

Thank goodness. Betsy scooted eagerly forward in her chair. "At the American School—they've as good as told me that they'll never let me into the field. But *you* worked in the field. How did you do it? How did you make them listen to you?"

"I had the authority of my husband. I spoke with his voice." Betsy's face fell. Mrs. Schliemann regarded her with tolerant sympathy. "If you truly want to excavate, the easiest way to go about it is to find yourself an archaeologist to marry."

Betsy couldn't tell if she was joking or not. She suspected not.

If Charles were free . . .

No. Not only was it wrong to think that way—although she did catch herself daydreaming about it more often than not—it was a betrayal of everything she believed to accede to the notion that a woman's position depended on her husband.

"But what if I want to be someone in my own right?" Belatedly,

Betsy realized how offensive it sounded, implying Mrs. Schliemann wasn't. But hadn't Mrs. Schliemann just said as much herself? "What if I want to excavate on my own account?"

The amusement drained from Mrs. Schliemann's face. She pressed her lips together, making lines appear on either side of her mouth. "It is not an easy thing, being a woman in the field. I missed several seasons due to the care of my children. For a time, I could only dig in the vicinity of Athens, in case one of the children should fall ill or need me." A glimmer shone in her dark eyes. "But I did still dig."

"I don't know if I'll ever have children." If she couldn't marry Charles, Betsy wasn't sure she wanted to marry anyone. There couldn't be that many Charleses in the world, men who would love her for her mind and not just for the dowry she would bring or the children she might bear.

Mrs. Schliemann shook her head. "Even before I had children . . . it was hard, making the men listen. I had to show them I could get in the dirt like them, dig like them, appeal to their egos, tell them the great part they were playing in uncovering our heritage. I recited Homer to them." Her slight, ironic smile reminded Betsy eerily of the expression found on ancient statues. The *archaic smile* they called it. "They were less impressed by that than I might have hoped."

"But you kept digging," said Betsy stubbornly.

"I kept digging. It was my husband's work—and my own," she admitted. "I remember the day we found the side chamber of the tholos at Orchomenos. The workmen struck away some stone, and there, beneath it, was the top of a doorway, so beautifully worked you can hardly imagine. A door where we expected no door! And inside . . ." Mrs. Schliemann's face seemed lit from within, looking at scenes Betsy had seen only in smudged newsprint and artists' renderings. "There is nothing to the feeling of uncovering a piece of the past, bringing it back to light out of the rubble."

Betsy clasped her hands tightly together, practically bouncing on the chair in her excitement. "That's what I want. To uncover the past. To find those hidden doorways."

"Then that is what you must do. But do it knowingly." Mrs. Schliemann fixed Betsy with a serious look. "If you wish to control your own excavation, you must show no weakness, either to your men or to your peers. If you falter, even for a moment, the men will shirk—and your colleagues will say they always knew you weren't up to the task."

Betsy lifted her head high, thrilled by the fact that Mrs. Schliemann—Mrs. Schliemann!—had taken her into her confidence. "I won't give them the opportunity."

Some of the happy glow faded as she bicycled back to Academy Street. *Then that is what you must do*, Mrs. Schliemann had said, and Betsy thrilled to it. But how could she do what she needed to do without permits, without workmen, without being allowed to be part of a dig?

Get a husband, Mrs. Schliemann had said—and that was what Mrs. Schliemann had done, marrying a man thirty years her senior, who spun pretty fancies around her presence at their digs, turning her into something between a mascot and a heroine from an epic.

It all seemed deeply unfair, and Betsy would have felt much better if she could tell herself that was a generation ago, another time entirely, and of course things were different now. But they weren't, were they? Yes, the schools accepted female students, which they hadn't in Mrs. Schliemann's youth, but they hadn't seemed to get any further with fieldwork.

Unless they happened to be married to an archaeologist.

"How was your tea with Mrs. Schliemann?" Ava was buried in one of the anatomy books Dr. Kalopothakes had given her, studying for her first aid examination. Betsy was meant to be studying too, but there were always too many other things to do.

"It was . . . not entirely reassuring." Betsy plopped down on Ava's bed, as if they were back in Northampton, when life had felt so much simpler and the stakes so much lower. "When I asked Mrs. Schliemann how to get them to let me into the field, she told me to marry an archaeologist."

Ava closed her book carefully over her finger. "Did she have one in mind or was this a general theory?"

"A general theory." They both knew Charles was out of the running. Avoiding Ava's eyes, Betsy said brightly, "Which of the Harvard boys should I seduce, Jenks or Wingate? Maybe that was Ethel's strategy all along and I just didn't see it."

"Somehow I doubt that," said Ava drily.

"I just don't know what to think." Betsy hugged her knees to her chest. "I'm not sure Mrs. Schliemann's wrong, but . . . what if I don't marry? Why should my being be wrapped in my husband's? My property is my property. Shouldn't my work be my work? Why should my work be my husband's work? Why should I need a husband? Aren't I enough by myself?"

"More than enough," said Ava, with feeling.

Betsy looked at her friend suspiciously. "You make it sound like that's a bad thing."

Ava laid her medical text facedown on the bed, choosing her words carefully. "Have you ever thought that maybe it isn't that you're enough, but whether anything is enough for you?"

"What do you mean?"

"I mean . . . you're always looking for the next challenge. By the time you're halfway up a hill, you're already looking for a larger, more interesting hill."

"Are you saying I'd get bored with excavation? Or with marriage?"

"Neither!" Ava gave her head a little shake. "I just mean that anything you do will have boring bits. Bits you don't like, but that you'll have to get through anyway."

"Is this about those inscriptions I was meant to be analyzing?" Betsy asked warily.

"Not specifically—but yes, maybe." Ava paused for a moment, before saying, "I don't think marrying an archaeologist is a magic solution—even if there were one you wanted to marry who was free to marry you."

"It would get me to an excavation," said Betsy in a small voice.

"But at what cost? And what happens when you get there and you have to deal with the boring bits?"

There they were again, back to the same old argument. Betsy felt on firmer ground here. She sat up on her knees. "But they wouldn't be boring—not to me. Just the same way all that"—she wafted a hand at Ava's medical text—"isn't boring to you. It's what I've always wanted. It's what my father and I used to dream of together. We used to joke that someday it would be my excavation reports he would be reading—and then he could write me cranky letters about how I was doing it all wrong."

Betsy blinked hard. He would never write those letters now. But Betsy liked to think he could still see. Her father's version of heaven probably looked something like his study.

"I'm sorry, Betsy," Ava said awkwardly.

Betsy sniffed unattractively. "I am too."

"I—" Ava broke off, looking thoroughly torn.

"I know," said Betsy miserably. She'd been responsible for her father getting sick. Well, sicker. If she'd behaved herself he could have stayed and coughed comfortably by his own fireside.

Ava looked like she was about to say something, and abruptly changed her mind. "It's getting late. I should finish this chapter before supper."

Betsy hauled herself off Ava's bed. "I should probably look at an inscription." And then write up an analysis that Professor Richardson would never bother to read.

"Betsy?" Ava looked up from her book as Betsy drifted toward the door. "Don't seduce any of the Harvard boys."

Betsy smiled crookedly at her. "I'll try not to."

CHAPTER THIRTEEN

When the American wounded at the army hospital heard of the care being lavished on their Cuban comrades, they immediately accused us of neglect. We explained to them it broke our hearts to be unable to render assistance and the fault lay not with us but with their own commanders. One can only imagine the hue and cry that must have arisen, because within a few hours, the official position was entirely reversed and our assistance formally solicited.

For those acquainted with the classics, I can only tell you that Hercules's labors in the Aegean stables had nothing on what we discovered in that US Army hospital. While we nurses turned up our sleeves and went to work with carbolic, a force of men on the Red Cross ship the *State of Texas* braved the surf to bring out cots, blankets, food, and bandages.

No sooner had we made those men comfortable than word came of a great engagement between our men and our Spanish foes. . . .

—*Miss Katherine Carson for the* St. Louis Star Ledger, *July 1, 1898*

Sevilla, Cuba
June 25, 1898

"YOU WENT TO *Harvard*?"

"It's not really as bad as you New Haven boys think." Holt had loved it there. He'd loved the lectures, the laboratories, the learned discourse, the way you could talk about everything without ever saying anything. Most of all he'd loved being a hundred miles from home. He'd felt free, really free, for the first time since babyhood, and probably not even then.

Paul stared at him like he'd grown an extra head. "But—you're Hold 'Em Holt. You're a cowboy."

"Briefly." Holt was having trouble getting the words out. He was, he realized, extremely drunk. He tried to stand and lurched on his injured leg. He might have fallen, but Thede Miller helpfully jumped up and grabbed his arm. So helpful, Thede. Why'd he have to go and remember him?

"Briefly?" Paul spat the word out. He'd risen to his feet too.

Holt shrugged, which was a mistake. "I left Harvard. I went West."

"But—the papers—they said—they said you'd been born on the range. You were the child of settlers killed in an Injun attack. You'd been roping steers by the time you were eight."

By the time he was eight, Holt could read the *Aeneid* in the original. And his father had broken his wrist for the first time. Snapped it, like a twig.

Holt broke into Paul's indignant litany. "The papers say a lot of things."

Not Holt. He'd never claimed any of it. He'd just omitted. A whole lot of omitting. As if he could omit away everything he'd been before. Just a blank slate with a new name. Wasn't that what America was all about? Individual initiative, that's what Colonel Roosevelt had said.

Paul glared at him, his face flaring red and orange in the light of the campfire. "You lied."

Holt rubbed the back of his hand across his eyes, which refused to focus. Paul was going in and out like a funhouse mirror. "I never lied." He just hadn't shared. There was a difference. He thought. Maybe. "Look. It's complicated."

"Like our being here is complicated? No wonder you took sides with the Spaniards." Holt's rum-soaked brain couldn't quite make sense of the logic. Paul seemed to be suggesting that Harvard was in league with Spain. "Why are you even here?"

Holt's mouth felt thick and gummy. "Same reason as anyone else." Just don't ask him what those reasons were.

"Impersonating someone you're not?" Paul turned abruptly away from him. "Thede. You got room in your tent now that Teddy's gone?"

"Sure," said Thede slowly. "But . . ."

"Good." Paul stalked toward the tent he'd shared with Holt. "I'll just get my things."

"Paul . . ." Holt began, but the other man didn't hear him.

Miller patted him tentatively on the shoulder. "Sorry about that. Didn't mean to make trouble. Paul'll simmer down."

"Uh-huh," Holt said, and sat down abruptly on the turf.

He must have passed out that way, because he woke up lying next to the remains of the campfire, soaked through with rain or sweat, it could have been either, with a filthy mouth and a filthy head and a vague feeling of dread in the pit of his stomach, the sort of dread he hadn't felt since leaving his father's house for Harvard. Waking up in the sure knowledge that something bad was going to happen, and, somehow, you'd brought it on yourself.

But this wasn't Springfield. It was Cuba. Cuba and his head ached like the devil and someone was blowing reveille and the camp was a flurry of people packing up and bolting down what breakfast they could, because everyone was on the move, and Holt was going to have to move with them even if his head and his leg and his guts didn't agree.

They moved their camp to the banks of the Aguadores River. There was a curious unreality about it, their days on the banks of the Aguadores, this strange pause in time, knowing a battle was coming, but not sure when it would come. There were times when Holt felt that they'd fallen into the pages of *Robinson Crusoe*, building lean-tos out of palm fronds, foraging for food. The men experimented with cookery, boiling mangoes to make a slush rather like applesauce, soaking hardtack to create a sort of gruel that could be fried up with bacon grease into something vaguely edible.

When they weren't trying to fill their bellies, the men wrote home, some scratching out messages on empty boxes of quinine pills for want of paper.

Holt didn't know who he would write to even if he had the paper. His father? His sisters? All the friends of his Harvard days had melted away along with his real name; since then he hadn't stayed anywhere long enough to attach any more than the most casual acquaintance.

Except Paul.

Not that they'd been friends, really. You couldn't befriend a fiction, could you? And that was what Paul saw in him, the imaginary person the papers had created, not the person he was, whatever that might be. Holt wasn't sure anymore. Sometimes he felt like a paper doll, a flat facsimile of humanity, just the outline of a man.

But it was hard not to glance over at the campfire where Paul sat with Miller and the other Yale men, their voices loud as the rum flowed, listening to their camaraderie and feeling an aching emptiness at the lack of it.

Mostly, he just ached. Rain always brought on his headaches and it rained here daily, a hard downpour that lasted a few hours and then evaporated. Some men traded belongings for rum; Holt traded for coffee rations, trying to dull the growing throbbing in his skull. The beans were green and hard. Holt roasted them over his campfire and made a makeshift mortar and pestle out of a dried coconut and a stick. That earned him a brief modicum of popularity. But not with Paul.

He should—not apologize. Explain, that was it. But Holt couldn't muster the energy. Even with the coffee, he felt slow and logy. In the mornings the men burned in a fierce heat worse than Florida; in the afternoons, the rains came and froze them. They hadn't changed their clothes for weeks; the fabric was stiff with sweat and dirt. Holt suspected he might have a tinge of fever. But even if he didn't, so what? What was he supposed to explain? Holt couldn't even explain it to himself.

Impersonating someone you're not, Paul had accused him.

They were all impersonating someone. The millionaires' sons were playing soldier. The cowboys were playing the Wild West as imagined by Buffalo Bill, coming soon to Madison Square Garden. And Colonel Roosevelt—well, he was playing himself, and doing it to the hilt. Possibly with a touch of Pericles thrown in, and maybe just a dash of Alexander the Great, if Alexander the Great wore spectacles.

As for Holt . . . he'd been so many people. He wasn't sure which one he was anymore. A scared boy in an opulent house. A law student convinced he could right the world. An angry young man boarding a train headed West.

And now . . . he'd thought he was here to help, to do something good. To atone. That, somehow, he could set the balance right. And go home.

Holt wasn't sure where that thought had come from. He didn't have a home. But the yearning was there all the same. To be a person again, have a place, a purpose. Not the home he grew up in—but someplace. Someplace that was his.

It was a moot point. Up on the hills, the Spaniards waited. The scouts reported that they could see the tops of their sombreros popping up and down as they dug trenches, fortifying their positions.

"You'd think they'd have us do something about that," said Holt to Paul, nodding in the direction of the new Spanish fortifications. "With every trench they dig, the harder it will be. Assuming that's where we're headed."

Paul glanced sideways at Holt but didn't respond.

"Look." It was early morning, but the ground was already steaming as the day's heat burned off the evening damp. Holt wiped his face with his bandana. "I wasn't trying to con you. I haven't been that Harvard man for a long time. I suppose he's still in there somewhere— but he's a long way buried."

Paul gave a stiff nod and turned away. But then he stopped, scowling back over his shoulder at Holt. "You could have just said, you know."

Could he? Paul was gone before Holt could point out that he wouldn't have thanked him for spoiling his illusions. Or maybe it was just that it had been easier to be that newspaper etching, flat and crisp, rather than too, too solid flesh that ached and bled and stumbled.

Holt tried not to stumble, but his left leg didn't seem to want to hold him properly as the men lined up, ready to march. Wagons rumbled past, holding their precious Colt machine guns, but with no room for anything else. The men of the 1st Volunteer Cavalry could bring only what they could carry on their backs.

The column started and stopped and started again. The Camino Real was too narrow for more than ten men abreast, and the whole of Shafter's army was trying to trudge their way through a road turned to sticking, sucking mud from a brief, hard rainstorm. Stop and start, stop and start. The jungle closed in around them, like something out of an Edgar Allan Poe story, pressing in on either side, the air so thick and oppressive that every breath was an effort. Stop and start, stop and start. Sitting, walking, sitting, walking. Men shared out their scant rations; they were marching empty, a skeleton army.

The light faded from dusk to dark, and still they walked, broken only by a pause for something like sleep in the deserted grounds of an older sugar plantation.

When reveille sounded, they choked down their breakfast as best they could, alone or in quiet groups, as they waited for orders. There was no singing, no loud conversations. There was no Ham Fish, amiably drunk. No "Bright College Years," no glees. It was only the first of July, just a week since Las Guasimas, but there was almost no resemblance between the men, thin and tense, who hunched over their hardtack and the boisterous, laughing crew who had capered their way to the Spanish lines.

They knew what they were facing now.

Holt rather wished he didn't. He would have preferred to have clung to his illusions about the romance of battle, Cavaliers and Roundheads facing off at Naseby. The Light Brigade charging forward with sabers raised.

They can write a lovely poem about you when you're all rotting beneath the palm trees.

For a moment, Holt thought he saw her there, Paul's Miss Hayes, like a wraith between the vines. His own personal oracle.

Holt rose, taking a lurching step toward her, then another—when
the sky exploded in a confusion of bullets and metal fragments, right
over the place where he had been sitting a moment before.

Siboney, Cuba
July 1, 1898

"NO TIME FOR SITTING." SISTER Bettina made shooing motions at
Kit, who had just finished her shift and was frantically scribbling in
a tiny pocket notebook. "We've got wounded coming in."

"More?" Betsy set down the bedpan she'd been holding with a
thump. Fortunately, it was empty. "There are more?"

They'd only just got their new hospital in order, all spick-and-span
with the Red Cross flag flying proudly above it, just so no one would
forget who was actually in charge here. They'd inherited eighty patients from the army, eighty men who hadn't been fed or bathed for
days, eighty men who were sicker than when they'd arrived, suffering
from everything ranging from heatstroke and dysentery to measles.
And wounds, of course. All sorts of wounds. The shell wounds were
the worst.

But no typhoid. Not yet.

"There's been a major engagement," said Sister Bettina briefly.
"Everyone's needed. Didn't you hear the noise?"

Betsy and Kit followed her out the door, where a scene of chaos
greeted them. Men were staggering alone or in pairs down the road,
clutching each other for balance, faces grimed with mud and powder
smoke, their uniforms torn and bloody. Crude carts disgorged men too
badly hurt to move under their own power. Orderlies were carrying
men out on hastily contrived stretchers, putting them on the ground
wherever they could find room, in the full glare of the afternoon sun.

"Get those men out of the sun." With the supreme confidence of someone who had seen it all before, Miss Barton was supervising the erection of two large tents. "I want six tables in there. That will be our surgery. Cots in this one. Put plenty of straw down in each. We'll shovel it out and replace it as needed."

People were scurrying back and forth doing Barton's bidding, some dispatched to fetch supplies from the ship, others putting down straw or putting up cots. Orderlies had been dragooned into dragging out cots and kettles, scrounging up blankets and bandages.

"You. Tell them on the *State of Texas* we need everything. These men don't have a cot to lie on or a kettle to boil a bit of gruel in." Barton turned toward her nursing sisters, who had already lined up, ready for service. "Sister Bettina, Sister Minnie, Sister Isabelle, Sister Blanche, you'll assist the surgeons. Nurse Hayes! These men need feeding."

A man pulled himself up by one arm over the edge of a wagon. "That's Clara Barton," he rasped. "Now we'll get something to eat."

A feeble cheer went up from the men.

"I'll start the cider," said Betsy, and ran off to find their largest kettles to make Clara Barton's own special Red Cross Cider, a fortifying slurry of dried apples and prunes. Miss Barton swore by it.

With little time for meals in between shifts, Betsy might have taken a few stray swigs of it herself and found it . . . well, not exactly what the Ritz Paris would be serving next season, but certainly sustaining.

Gruel, cider, malted milk. As fast as she brewed it up, it was gone, and there was always another hand reaching out, another cultivated voice asking, "Please, if I could just have a drop of something . . ."

"What were they thinking?" Betsy fumed to Kit as they passed each other between tents. "They let these men march empty!"

"That's men," said Kit, clutching cans of condensed milk to

thicken the gruel. "Can't trust them to do the packing. They'll bring the cannon and forget the picnic basket."

Betsy gave a snort of laughter, which quickly faded as she re-entered their open-air ward. Patients were packed as tight as they could reasonably put them, and still the wounded were coming. Just what kind of battle had this been, anyway? Not that it took a major battle to cause major harm. She knew that. She'd seen too many skirmishes in Greece not to underestimate all the ways a man could be hurt.

"I've got a head wound that needs special care." It was one of the regimental doctors. What was his name? Stringfellow. It suited him. He was thin and grim, pale brown hair receding from a high forehead. "Captain Mills. Do you have room for him?"

There wasn't room for a reasonably sized flea. "If we move this cot a few inches this way and that cot a few inches that way . . . There you go."

"It's those blasted Spanish snipers. They shoot for the head." Dr. Stringfellow waved the orderlies forward, snapping at them to set him down gently. "This man requires the constant application of cold compresses to his eyes. Ice wrapped in a bit of cotton works best. Do you have ice?"

"I'll find it," said Betsy, but Dr. Stringfellow didn't hear her. He was already gone, back into the fray of arriving casualties.

Night fell; lamps were lit and brought to the surgeons and still the wounded kept coming, some making their way on foot, goodness only knew how far, others piled into wagons, jolting and jostling down the road to Siboney. Betsy couldn't feel her feet anymore. Her legs seemed to move without her volition. Up and down the ward. Spooning gruel, changing dressings, giving sips of cider to those well enough to drink it, sponging foreheads, sneaking outside to chip ice where the men wouldn't hear it and be tormented, back inside to refresh compresses on the eyes of the worst head wounds. Moving cots to make room for more. And more.

There weren't enough lamps to spare. The surgeons needed them. So Betsy worked by a single lantern and the light of the moon, which was brighter than any moon she had ever seen, even in Greece, where everything had seemed sharper and clearer. The moonlight bathed the ward in an unearthly glow, as if everything had turned to mother-of-pearl or suffered a sea change to something rich and strange.

Captain Mills thrashed in his bed and Betsy hurried over to his side. "Have you ever seen anything as bright as this moonlight? I hope it's not keeping you awake."

Captain Mills stopped thrashing. He was horribly, painfully still. "I can't see the moonlight."

Of course he couldn't. He had a bullet in his head and bandages and a compress over his eyes. Betsy felt awful, like the sort of person who pulled wings off flies and kicked puppies.

"You will. Soon," she gabbled. "I'll—I'll just go get more ice for you."

And she hurried out of the tent, trying to make it look more of a brisk walk and less of a run. The men couldn't see her breaking down. It would be bad for morale. Never ever show doubt or weakness, even if she was so tired she could barely see straight, even if her face hurt with smiling at men who couldn't see it, even if her heart broke a little more every time someone asked for ice and she couldn't give it.

She made it a yard away from the tent before she broke down, covering her face with her hands, her shoulders shaking as she tried to muffle the sobs that racked her body, angry, tearless sobs, sobs of rage and frustration and helplessness.

"Betsy?" It was Kit, sitting on the steps of the hospital, her pocket notebook in her lap, her pinny hideously stained and her hair straggling down, dark with sweat. Betsy suspected she looked much the same.

"What are you doing?" Betsy managed.

"Sister Minnie told me to take an hour and get some rest."

"Then you should." In the moonlight, Kit's face seemed composed entirely of angles and hollows. "Really, Kit. Get some sleep."

"I can sleep when I'm dead—or back in St. Louis." Kit's eyes were too bright in her too-thin face. "The stories, Betsy—the stories these men have been telling me! I have to get it all down before I forget. Or before one of those men out there does it first."

"You mean like your friend with the bullet in his spine?" said Betsy, and wished she hadn't. "Don't make yourself sick, Kit."

"I won't." Kit looked up at Betsy with a shadow of her old grin. "I'm a mother. We're the toughest people on earth."

"Hmm," said Betsy, and realized, with horror, that she sounded just like Ava. When had she turned into Ava?

That was something to be grateful for, she supposed, that Ava wasn't here. Although perversely, she rather wished she were. An extra pair of trained hands would mean the world.

The work was relentless, endless. The healthier men were released from the hospital so the most severe of the new cases could be brought inside in their place. Dawn brought another influx of men, swelling the number of casualties in the tents. Betsy stopped counting after four hundred.

Betsy felt like she could sleep on her feet, like a horse. She had no idea how the surgeons were still operating. At this point, she could barely tell her ankle from her elbow, much less anyone else's. Between her rounds, Betsy brought black coffee and hard crackers to the doctors, who gulped it down without looking at it while probing for bullets and splinting shattered bones.

"Bless you," Dr. Stringfellow said, as he put out a hand for his mug, and Betsy thought of Ethel the Coffee Angel and how she'd mocked her for it.

There was a lot she would change if she could go back.

But she couldn't go back. She could only try to do the best she could in the moment. She felt so painfully inadequate to the task, half-asleep, matted with blood and sweat and heaven only knew what. But the men still cheered when they saw her making the rounds, and that was something, wasn't it? "Sister," they called her, and clung to her hand, the ones who could talk talking, trying to smile for her.

There was no talk of shifts. They needed every nurse they could spare. Betsy gulped some coffee, grimaced, and dumped a spoonful of condensed milk in it to make it taste less like burnt toast. And that's when she saw Clara Barton hurrying past in her traveling cloak, holding a bag of supplies.

Betsy stood, swaying slightly, by the opening of her tent. "You're going? Miss Barton?"

"General Shafter has called upon us for our assistance." Miss Barton glowed like a girl who had just been asked to Yale prom. "His message was of the utmost urgency. He instructed us to send food, medicines, anything, and to seize wagons from the front for transportation."

Betsy gaped at her. The army had been resolute in not wasting wagons or men on medical supplies. If General Shafter was authorizing the commandeering of carts, the situation had to be dire.

"Do you need me—do you need me to come with you? I've worked at the front before." It took everything she had to make the offer.

"I need you to stay here." Miss Barton gestured grandly at the tent, filled to the brim with wounded. "This is *your* ward, Nurse Hayes. Serve these men well."

"But—" Betsy looked helplessly at Miss Barton, too tired to think straight. It was one thing to do the rounds under direction. Another entirely to be told she was in charge. She couldn't be in charge. "What if I don't know what to do?"

"You know what to do." Miss Barton took Betsy's hands in both of hers, gazing deeply into her eyes. "These men's lives depend on you. You cannot fail."

CHAPTER FOURTEEN

Dear Ava,

~~*I know you don't agree with the decision I made*~~

~~*You made your feelings quite clear about my plans*~~

What makes you think you always know best?

—Miss Betsy Hayes '96 to Ava Saltonstall '96 (letter unsent)

Athens, Greece
March 1897

"YOU HAVE FAILED, MISS HAYES," said Dr. Kalopothakes.

Failed? She couldn't have failed. Betsy looked wildly from the examining board to the little urchin standing next to her, a gloopy mixture that looked like porridge dripping down his leg.

It wasn't meant to be drippy.

It should have hardened into a cast. She'd done everything just the way Dr. Kalopothakes had showed them—well, mostly the way Dr. Kalopothakes had showed them. Betsy had been a little vague on the exact quantities of gypsum and water involved, so she had just guessed at it as she went along.

Apparently, she had guessed wrong.

"But . . . but . . . if you'll let me try just one more time," Betsy offered. Behind the examiners sat the queen and Crown Princess Sophie, who had come to lend their countenance to the examinations. Betsy looked to them for help. "I can do it again. I'll get it right this time. You'll see. Or ask me to bandage him! I'm excellent at bandages."

All right, maybe not excellent, but at least passable. How hard could it be to wrap a strip of cloth around a leg? Easier than mixing up a plaster of Paris cast, at any rate.

"On the battlefield, Miss Hayes, there are no second chances," said Dr. Kalopothakes.

She didn't have to sound quite so smug about it. But wasn't that just Radcliffe for you? Betsy wouldn't be surprised if she'd chosen a deliberately impossible task just to trip her up. She'd bet the next woman along got something simpler.

"Maybe there was something wrong with this batch of plaster of Paris," said Betsy desperately, catching at straws. "Maybe it was diluted with . . . something. If I were to try again another day . . ."

"Goodbye, Miss Hayes," said Dr. Kalopothakes firmly.

Queen Olga and Crown Princess Sophie offered Betsy identical expressions of polite sympathy as the doctor called up the next candidate for examination.

Betsy wandered out of the theater in a daze. Failed? She never failed. No matter how little she studied, no matter how fine she cut it, in the end she always came out in a blaze of glory and her teachers shook their heads and said they didn't know how she did it.

But she hadn't done it. Not this time.

Who would have thought they'd have her making a plaster cast? How many casts did you make on a battlefield? What was she supposed to do, lug along a little tub of gypsum and water from man to man? Tell the enemy to wait while the plaster set?

Betsy wasn't going to be telling the enemy anything. She wasn't going to be anywhere near the enemy. She wasn't even going to be helping at the Evangelismos Hospital back in Athens. It appeared her usefulness to the war effort was over. Because she had failed. Failed, failed, failed.

She was supposed to be meeting Ava for chocolate and cakes to celebrate the successful completion of their course. Betsy stood for a moment, in the city where she had lived these past six months, the city whose every street she had traversed on foot or on her bicycle or in Aikaterini's barouche, completely disoriented.

Around her, all the buildings were decked with bright blue-and-white bunting in honor of Greek Independence Day, just a few days away. The streets bustled with refugees fleeing the Turks and volunteers heading in the opposite direction, toward the Turks, eager to fight for a united Greece in which Crete and Macedonia could fly the white-and-blue flag and pledge themselves to the king of the Greeks.

Who was actually a Dane. With a Russian wife. But that was

immaterial right now. The king had stood strong against the Great Powers, had sent his own son the crown prince off to fight just yesterday, which made him the Greekest of the Greeks, a national hero.

Volunteers flocked to Athens from all corners of the Greek-speaking world, from Cyprus, from Samos, from Bulgaria and Egypt and Smyrna, making the streets bright with their colorful native costumes. Why, just over there Betsy could see the blue bloomers and high boots of someone fresh from Crete, and, on the opposite corner, a cluster of bright red-and-green sashes that marked their wearers as coming from the Levant. There were even Italians come to town, Garibaldians, followers of the son of the great Garibaldi, in their iconic red shirts and caps.

It made Betsy's heart swell with vicarious pride, that the whole world had come to Athens to celebrate the independence of Greece and fight for the freedom of Crete.

Except the Great Powers, of course. They were thoroughly on the side of the sultan and had declared that Crete should have local governmental autonomy while remaining nominally part of the Ottoman Empire, which everyone knew was nothing short of maintaining the status quo and a world away from what the Cretans really wanted, which was, of course, to be Greek.

What sort of American would she be if she didn't support self-determination?

The prime minister, a namby-pamby man, had refused to let the minister of war send more troops to Crete, so the minister of war had resigned in protest and had to be comforted with tea and cakes at Aikaterini's, while Aikaterini and Betsy had patted his arm and assured him he had done exactly the right thing. He had blinked tears from his eyes and told Betsy that with women such as she fighting for their cause they could never fail.

There was that word again. Fail, fail, fail.

Maybe if she had just put in a bit less water . . . or a bit more gypsum?

Oh, bother it. What did any of that matter? Her heart was in the right place; surely that counted for something. Hadn't someone or other said that kind hearts counted for more than coronets and simple faith more than detailed medical knowledge? She might just possibly be paraphrasing a bit, but she felt she'd got the essence right. Unlike that Dr. Kalopothakes, who seemed determined to nitpick.

What was she going to tell everyone? Betsy felt sick to her stomach just thinking about it. Even the bunting didn't seem to fly as bravely in the breeze. She'd already announced to everyone that she was going to the front. She'd rubbed it in a bit, really. The Harvard boys were openly jealous. Ethel was unimpressed—but that was only because Ethel had no imagination. Professor Richardson had waxed positively effusive and offered his help and support in anything that was needed to get her off to the front and away from the American School of Classical Studies.

She had even gone so far as to telegraph Alex and Lavinia. Lavinia's chapter of the Daughters of the American Revolution had sent a congratulatory note and a donation to the Union of Greek Women. A small donation, but it was the thought that counted. It was the one time Betsy's sister-in-law had ever approved of anything she'd done, and then only because she was hundreds of miles away, and possibly just a little because Lavinia probably hoped she'd be caught by the Ottomans and thrown into an oubliette and thus out of Lavinia's hair forever. But maybe she was being unfair. Maybe even Lavinia was moved by the cause of Greek democracy. Or just moved by the fact that Cretan independence was popular at the moment, and Lavinia never liked to be behind on anything, whether it was the new, narrower sleeves or freedom from despots.

In retrospect, perhaps she ought to have waited a bit before sending in a notice to the *Smith College Monthly*.

But it was more than that. Betsy had counted on this not just for herself but for Ava. She stood up a bit straighter at the thought. That was it, really. Ava would never go to the front without her, and if she didn't, how was she going to prove to Ava that she was wasting her life by not going to medical school?

Betsy could just see it, the two of them together, like twin Florence Nightingales, moving soothingly from bed to bed in a moonlit hospital ward, bringing comfort and hope and perfectly mixed plaster of Paris casts.

There had to be a way to fix this. If Dr. Kalopothakes wouldn't let her retake the test . . . she'd tell Aikaterini—Aikaterini had the ear of the queen. She'd explain. Everyone knew the queen had the final say. A direct appeal to the queen, from as many sources as possible, was the only way. Why, Betsy could find dozens of people in Athens, across a spectrum of nationalities, to vouch for her character, stamina, and determination. What was a leaky plaster cast against all that?

Ava was waiting for her already, at a marble-topped table, reading her way through a dog-eared copy of the *Lancet*.

"Have you been waiting long? The streets were so crowded I could barely thread my way through. Chocolate, please," Betsy said to the waitress in Greek, flinging herself into one of the small cane chairs. "And some of those little cakes with the honey and nuts in them."

"Betsy?" Ava had known her far too long. She put down her journal. "What happened?"

Betsy concentrated on drawing off her purple leather gloves. "I might possibly have not quite passed. But don't worry!" she hurried on, before Ava's open mouth could turn into words, words Betsy didn't want to hear. "I've come up with the perfect way to fix it. I'll just ask Aikaterini to intercede with the queen and send me anyway."

Ava stared at her. "You can't do that."

Just like Ava, to assume that failed meant failed. "Of course I can. Aikaterini won't mind," Betsy said merrily, her mind teeming with possibilities. The examination that had seemed so crushing an hour ago had receded into the mere minor setback it was. "I'm sure Mrs. Richardson will write for me if I ask. And possibly Mrs. Schliemann. No one can say no to Mrs. Schliemann."

"They should. No, no cakes for me," Ava said to the waitress, who put them in front of her anyway. Ava shoved the plate away. "You can't do that, Betsy."

"Why not?" Betsy pulled the cakes toward her. She was suddenly very hungry and the cakes looked very good.

"You failed your exam," Ava said, very slowly and clearly.

"What's in an exam? It was utterly arbitrary. They had me make a plaster of Paris cast. Really, of all the things." Betsy picked up the biggest pastry and took a huge bite out of it. "I could ask them to let me take it again, but it's much simpler this way. Goodness only knows what they might ask me to do next time. Something utterly irrelevant, most likely."

"Something utterly necessary to the health and well-being of the wounded, you mean?" There were two bright patches of color in Ava's otherwise rather sallow cheeks.

"The red of these walls suits you," said Betsy. "You should really get some dresses made in that color."

"Oh no," said Ava, sitting up very straight. "You are not going to distract me with trivialities."

"Dress isn't a triviality. It affects how people see you." This was one of the many fascinating things Betsy had learned from Aikaterini.

"But not your actual capabilities. You can't dress your way into competence by putting on a nurse's uniform, Betsy." Ava cast a glance over her shoulder to make sure no one was listening. She leaned forward across the tea table. "It would be criminally irresponsible of you to take a place you haven't earned."

"Criminal? That's putting it a bit strong." Ava always did take herself a little too seriously, and she'd been even worse since that first aid course.

Ava's dark eyes fixed on Betsy's, deadly earnest. "Not if a man dies because you don't know what you're doing. That's murder, or the next thing to it. I understand you're disappointed, but you can't just go and talk your way into a job you can't do just because you think you want it."

There were so many things wrong with that statement that Betsy didn't even know where to begin, starting with the "thinking she wanted it" bit. Of course she wanted it. Would she pursue it if she didn't? And as for the rest . . . "Why can't I do it? I took that course just the same as you."

"No, you didn't." Ava sat back hard in her seat. "I actually listened. I took notes. You doodled pictures of the Parthenon and scribbled lines of Greek poetry and ran off to meet that Frenchman of yours when you ought to have been studying!"

Just because she had formed a habit of walking with Charles in the afternoons—it was all perfectly respectable, and it was hardly running off. Everyone in Athens promenaded on Stadium Street between the hours of three and five in the winter. It was a social commonplace. Besides, Charles was a colleague, so, really, it counted as work.

"But it's not just that," Ava went on, with the air of one determined to get through the worst of a bad business. "It's not just that you paid no attention to the course. You shouldn't have been there in the first place. You should have been at the American School attending to your real work! The work you're here to do. Remember that?"

"That's not fair!" Betsy protested. "You're visiting, and I thought the first aid course would be something for us to do together."

An ironical expression spread across Ava's face. "So it's all for me, is it?"

"You're my *guest*."

"Because you begged me to come!" Ava took a deep breath, placing her palms flat on the marble tabletop. "Betsy. Please understand that I am truly grateful for the opportunity to be here. And I do—I do want only the best for you. But I can't sit here and watch you destroying yourself. Again."

"Again?" Betsy demanded, offended, before realizing that really, she ought to be offended at the idea she would destroy herself at all.

Ava was pale but resolute. "You're doing everything except what you're actually here to do. It's just like Smith."

It was not just like Smith. Betsy blurted out her cunning plan. "If I come back a war hero, Dr. Richardson will have to let me excavate!"

Ava blinked at her. "Is that what this is about? Betsy—that's the most harebrained scheme I've ever heard."

"What's so harebrained about it?" demanded Betsy, stung. "Dr. Richardson thinks women don't have the stamina to excavate? Fine. I'll show him stamina. When I come back, he won't be able to tell me I'm too delicate to wield a shovel. We've both agreed I can't marry my way into a dig. What other options do I have?"

Ava took a deep breath. "Have you considered putting in the work?"

"I've been working!" Betsy thought of all those months of haunting Richardson's office, going on treks, climbing Mount Helicon, transcribing endless epigraphs. The hideous unfairness of it rose up to choke her. Or maybe that was just the pastry she seemed to have forgotten to chew. Betsy gulped it down in one furious swallow. "It doesn't matter what I do. Dr. Richardson won't listen!"

"Maybe because you don't *try*."

Betsy's throat closed up. She couldn't, she wouldn't cry in the middle of a tea shop on one of the most fashionable streets in Athens. "I don't try?" she choked out. "You won't even apply!"

Ava pressed her eyes very tightly shut. "We're not going to start that again."

"Why not?" Betsy demanded recklessly. "If you get to pull my character to shreds, then I get to shred yours too."

"I'm not shredding—"

"Aren't you? But let's just have a word about glass houses, shall we? What are you going to do, be a companion your whole life? Go from elderly relative to elderly relative until you're elderly yourself? At least I came out here, Ava! I applied! I tried! You won't even put in an application to medical school."

Ava's dark brows drew together. "So I can throw away money I don't have on a job no one will let me pursue?"

"How do you know they won't? Look at Dr. Kalopothakes."

"Dr. Kalopothakes trained in Paris. Do you think she could have found someplace to take her in the US?"

"Yes! And even if she couldn't, what's wrong with Paris?" Betsy could just see it, *la vie bohème*, a garret with a pile of medical textbooks and a skeleton named Pierre, Ava joking in French with weedy French medical students. "Your French is beautiful, much better than my Greek."

"What's wrong with Paris?" Ava repeated. Something in her seemed to snap. "What's wrong with Paris is that not everyone is an heiress! Not everyone can jaunt off to Europe on a whim! I have eight younger siblings, Betsy! My parents can't afford to throw away money on a profession I'll never be allowed to pursue!"

Betsy decided to tackle the easier bit of that objection. "What makes you think you couldn't pursue it?"

"Don't you think I haven't thought of that?" Ava breathed in deeply through her nose. "How many women doctors do you know? I don't mean Dr. Kalopothakes. I mean back home."

Betsy scrounged for any vague recollection. "There's Elizabeth Blackwell."

Ava folded her arms across her chest. "She moved back to England."

"I'm sure there must be others."

"Yes, women with means. Women who can afford to work without pay. Women like you." Ava glared at Betsy as though Betsy were personally responsible for being a carpet heiress. It wasn't Betsy's fault that Ava's grandparents had frittered away their fortune on short-lived communes and the publication of transcendentalist essays that no one wanted to read. "No one would let me practice on them. No one would pay me to practice on them. I was barely tolerated trailing around after my father holding his medical bag."

"That's why you shouldn't lose this opportunity." Betsy leaned forward, feeling on firmer ground. "This is your chance to do what you love to do. All right, maybe no one will pay you for it, but you'll get to wallow in wounds all you like. And then if you hate it you can go back to winding wool or whatever else it is that companions do, but at least you'll know you aren't missing anything. And it won't cost you anything. You're already here."

Betsy had her, she knew it. She could see Ava thinking it through, weighing her words.

"When will a chance like this come along again? You'll be able to work with the best doctors in Greece, doing real work, not practicing on paupers paid to lie on a pallet. We'll go together," Betsy said persuasively, swept away by her own eloquence. "It will all work out, you'll see. I'm doing this for you."

Ava's eyes went hard and her lips went tight. "No, you're not. And don't you dare try to wheedle me into thinking you are. You're doing this for you. Because you can't bear that the professors at the American School haven't thrown themselves at your feet and declared you their natural heir—without your having to bother to put in any of the work."

Betsy felt hot and cold all at once. "That's not fair."

"No. It's not. It's not fair that you've always had more than your fair share—of money and talent—and you don't seem to *care*." Ava blinked hard. "You've been given everything. You've been given everything and you're throwing it away."

Given everything? She didn't have what Ava had. She didn't have a house full of siblings and a mother who packed her hot lunches for the train ride to Northampton. "I'm not—"

"Oh, aren't you? Instead of staying and trying to make it right, you're grabbing the first excuse you can. I won't do it. I won't be your excuse."

Betsy saw red, and not just the wall hangings. "You mean you don't have the backbone. You'd rather huddle in a mansion in Concord, grooming your cousin's pet poodle, than risk the fact that you might not be as good at something as you think you could be."

Ava stood up abruptly, the back of her fragile chair knocking against the wall. "I'm not the one who failed my first aid exam."

Betsy stood up too. "I'm going to the front," she said stubbornly. "Because some of us aren't afraid to take a risk."

"It's not just your own life you're risking. But you can't see that, can you? All you can ever see is yourself. What *you* want, what *you* need—never mind if you kill a few people in the process. Never mind that the man who squires you about is another woman's husband."

"Don't you dare bring Charles into this!"

"Fine. I won't." Ava's voice was very flat, her face very set. "You can do what you want. You will anyway. But if you do something this monumentally selfish, this catastrophically irresponsible, then I want nothing more to do with you. Not here. Not in Boston. Not ever."

Betsy felt like she was being ripped up into little pieces. But there was nothing she could do about it. "I'll buy you a ticket home."

Ava lifted her chin. "You needn't bother. I'll find my own passage back."

CHAPTER FIFTEEN

The tents were soon filled to capacity. Hay and blankets were set out on the ground next to the tents, and to these "beds" were sent the less desperate cases, although what seems less desperate in a crisis of this magnitude would seem desperate indeed back at home.

Tonight, by special order of General Shafter himself, Miss Barton was called to serve at the front, in conditions even more dire than those that confront us here on the coast. In charge, she has left Sister Bettina in the surgery tent, Sister Anna in the hospital, and Nurse Hayes in the tent ward. At this point, we have in our care four hundred and seventy-five patients, with more coming in from the front with every passing hour.

Some are brought in loads in army wagons, the only ambulances to be had. Others make the trek on foot eight miles over a harsh, mountainous road, using what little strength they have left to stagger into our care. . . .

—Miss Katherine Carson for the St. Louis Star Ledger, *July 2, 1898*

Somewhere in Cuba
July 2, 1898

"WE'LL HAVE YOU BACK SOON. Just another few miles."

Only a few miles. That's what their commanders had told them. But a few miles stretched into endless misery when you had to stop and lie on your stomach while the Mauser bullets peppered the air around you and in front of you a ford was piled high with bodies and the mud turned purple with blood.

But you couldn't move. Oh, no. You couldn't even crawl. You had to lie there and wait, not moving, not firing, just waiting.

"Holt, come on, we have to move." Someone tugged on his arm, trying to pry Holt up off the ground.

What was Paul doing standing up like that? He'd be shot.

Holt grabbed Paul's arm, dragging him down. "Stay low, stay low. Hold your fire! They'll get you if they see your smoke."

Paul crouched down beside him, sliding an arm around his back and hauling him up by main force. "Holt, it's all right. I'm taking you to the hospital. Remember? We're on the Siboney road."

The Siboney road. They'd marched down the Siboney road. When? When? Holt couldn't remember. Everything was blurring and running together, like a painting left out in the rain.

Holt put up a hand over his eyes, squinting at the sky, at the glowing yellow ball bobbing overhead. A giant balloon, a balloon made of silk and air. The signal balloon. Damn them, damn them. Didn't they know it was like sending up a flare to tell the Spanish they were there, that great, big yellow balloon bobbing along over them as they marched?

"Idiots. They're marking our trail." Holt staggered and would have fallen but for Paul's arm around him. Any moment now, that balloon would pop. They'd shot at it, the Spaniards, and who could blame them, a tempting big target like that. And the two men in the basket, calling for help as they drifted, target practice for every Spaniard in Cuba. "Do you see it? Do you see the balloon?"

"That's the sun, Holt, the sun. The balloon was yesterday. The battle was yesterday. Do you remember it? The battle?"

Running and falling, running and falling. Colonel Roosevelt, holding up an arm to show a red furrow on his wrist. *See here, boys. I've got it too.* Bucky O'Neill, blowing out rings of smoke from his cigarette, bragging, *The Spanish bullet isn't made that will kill me.* It got him right through the mouth, that bullet. Right through the mouth. Sometimes the Fates had a sick sense of humor. They'd made him eat his words, and quick too.

Thede Miller, on the ground, at the crest of a hill, lying flat on his back, fighting for breath.

I'm going, Holt, but it's in a good cause, isn't it?

Dammit, Thede. Get up, get up.

"Get up, Holt. Get up." He was on the ground again. On his back. Like Thede. How had he come to be on the ground? Paul was hovering over him, a very stubbly Paul, two Pauls, in fact, now apart, now blurring together again. "Try to drink something."

"No water." Holt's tongue felt furry. There was no water in his canteen. They'd tried to stop, at the ford, fill their canteens up. A hundred degrees in the shade and getting hotter by the moment.

But Tom Hall had told them it was against orders. Keep marching. What did it matter if they were parched? The Spaniards were picking 'em off anyway. Might as well die thirsty. Die thirsty.

Like Tantalus. Holt was back in the schoolroom, that narrow room at the top of the house, hot in summer and cold in winter, translating the *Odyssey* from the Greek for the benefit of a tutor in a rusty black coat and a ruler that hit hard if he missed a word. It was summer; it was hot; he tugged at his collar to try to get some air. He was thirsty, so thirsty, but he couldn't stop and drink, not until he finished his lines. Tantalus, standing in a pool, the water up to his chin, but when he tried to lap at it, the water would all drain away.

And wasn't that always the way? Water, water, everywhere and not a drop to drink.

"Bother." Water was trickling around Holt's mouth. Someone was wiping ineffectually at it with a blue bandana. "We don't have so much water we can waste it. Try to swallow, will you?"

Holt tried, but his lips didn't seem to want to work properly.

"Holt!" It was Paul again, shaking him, slapping him lightly on the cheeks to wake him up. "Can you stand? I think you might have a fever. We have to get you to Siboney."

Siboney. The word echoed around Holt's skull. So bony. Bones. Nothing but bones, bones walking, bones dancing.

He could see them, wearing the tattered remains of brown uniforms, waving at him with hands made of bone. Holt dragged his weary bones along with them, down the Siboney road, stumbling and shivering.

How had it gotten so cold? Holt was shivering so hard his teeth clattered together. Maybe this was all a dream. Maybe he was back in his father's house, hiding up a tree in the January cold, too scared to shiver, because if he shivered someone would find him.

He had to stop shivering.

"Holt." Paul's face was disturbingly close, going in and out of focus. "You can't sit now. We're almost there."

"No. No sitting," Holt agreed. They'd been sitting when a shell struck. On some hill or other. But Holt hadn't. He'd gotten up because he saw something in the tangle of vines. Someone. Paul's friend. That Miss Hayes. She'd beckoned to him and he'd followed and behind him men had been blown to bits. "Can't sit."

But his legs didn't seem to want to hold him.

"It's only a few more yards," Paul pleaded.

And there she was again, that woman, that Miss Hayes, only this time she wasn't clad in diaphanous white robes but in a none-too-clean white pinny over a blue dress with the Red Cross band on one sleeve.

In the twilight, she seemed to film over like hot breath on a cold window, shivering in and out of his vision, blurry around the edges, as if she were a ghost, as if she were that figure in the vines, warning, warning. . . .

"Look." Holt tried to pull Paul's arm, tried to point. "Look where she comes again."

"Oh, thank goodness," Paul said, and dragged Holt forward toward the apparition. "It's Betsy. Betsy! I've got a casualty for you!"

Siboney, Cuba
July 2, 1898

"PAUL?" BETSY BLINKED IN THE twilight, hoping her tired eyes were playing tricks on her.

But no. There Paul was, arm in arm with another man who was slumped forward so that his hat covered his face. She couldn't tell who was supporting whom. They were both covered with mud and blood.

It was Betsy's worst nightmare. Well, one of her nightmares; she had so many, it was hard to tell which was worst. But seeing Paul wounded was definitely high on the list. Paul was one of life's golden people. Nothing bad was allowed to happen to him.

Betsy hurried toward them. "Are you all right? Are you—"

Paul gave himself a shake, like a dog. "Don't fuss, Bets. I'm right as rain. It's not me. It's Holt."

"Holt?" That was Holt? That was the man who had bullied her back onto the train tracks that night, who had loomed over her at the Tampa Bay Hotel, this bag of bones and canvas? But then he looked up at her, and she saw those surprisingly blue eyes in that thin sun-burned face, and she felt a weird sense of grief, which was strange, since this man was nothing to do with her or she with him.

Betsy dealt with her emotions by snapping, "What did you do to yourself, you ridiculous man?"

"S'nothing. I'm fine," rasped Holt. His eyes rolled back in his head and he went limp against Paul's supporting arm.

"He's not fine," said Paul.

Trust Paul to state the obvious. "What happened?" Betsy made wild arm motions at a couple of orderlies. "You! Make up another pallet. Over there on the end. What do you mean you can't fit an-other pallet in? If I say you can, you can. *What?*"

"You asked me what happened," said Paul in injured tones.

"Yes, yes, I did." She snapped her fingers at the orderly, who might have muttered something about her under his breath, but came all the same, taking some of the burden from Paul as they half dragged, half carried the unconscious man to the waiting pallet. "What hap-pened?"

"It's a head wound," said Paul, as though Betsy couldn't have inferred that from the sizable quantity of dried blood caked on the side of Holt's face.

Betsy knelt beside him, smoothing the matted hair carefully away from his brow. Fine, straight hair, grown a bit too long, so that it brushed the edges of his collar, or would, if it weren't clumped with blood.

The wound was on the left side of his head, Betsy could tell that much, but he was such a mess that it was impossible to see more. She took a pair of scissors from her apron and began neatly clipping the hair away from the area, revealing a long furrow from just to the side of his left eye all the way up to his temple.

"Water," she said, holding out a hand. "*Paul*, the basin. Hand it to me. Oh, never mind."

Paul trailed after her as she fetched the basin and began carefully sponging the area around the wound, talking all the while. "I was running straight at this Spaniard at the crest of the hill, and the ba—er, the fellow aimed his gun at me, and I thought for sure I was going to be singing glees with the heavenly choir, but then out of nowhere, there came Holt flinging himself at the man. Grabbed the gun with his bare hands."

"How very noble," said Betsy acidly. "I presume the weapon went off?"

Paul squatted down next to her. "Well, it was all a bit of a blur—a lot of people shouting and shooting and running—but I think that's what happened. Bullet hit Holt in the head, and then the man clobbered him with the stock, but by that time I'd got my knife out and—well." Paul belatedly remembered that one didn't talk about dismembering people with one's former dancing partners.

Sure enough, as Betsy swabbed an impressive amount of dried blood, there was not only a deep and painful-looking furrow but a truly impressive bruise beginning to bloom into blue-and-purple majesty.

Since Holt wasn't awake to be yelled at, Betsy took out her spleen on Paul instead. "Did it never occur to you that it's a bad idea to run straight at men holding loaded weapons?"

"That is what we're here to do," said Paul. "Be gentle with him, Betsy. He saved my life."

She was being gentle. She was being extremely gentle. Even if she wanted to shake him for being such an idiot. But she wanted to shake Holt the most because everyone knew Paul didn't have an iota of common sense in him, and this Holt creature clearly did, and if he'd used just a modicum of it, she wouldn't be dealing with what was most likely both a head wound and a massive concussion.

"When did this happen?" The wound was relatively shallow, but it looked as though it had bled, clotted, ripped open, and bled again. There was also more dirt in it than there ought to be.

"Yesterday. When we took San Juan Hill. Did you know we took San Juan Hill?" Paul bounced on his heels in excitement. "It was—well, you don't want to hear about that, do you?"

Given that she'd been patching up the men from that engagement for the past twenty-four hours and more, no, no she didn't. "It took you over a day to bring him here? Why didn't you put him in one of the wagons?"

"I couldn't do that!" Paul looked deeply offended. "They were just throwing men in any which way! Holt saved my life! I wasn't going to leave him to be jostled at the bottom of a pile of enlisted men. I brought him down myself. It took us a while—he can't walk much—so we had to sack out in the open last night. . . ."

It all began to make sense now. Including the dirt in the wound, which must have been from lying on the open ground with his head rolling into the dirt. Or banging into Paul's shoulder as he hoisted him along. Or both.

Keeping her voice very, very calm, Betsy said, "So instead of putting him in a wagon, which could have brought him here within a few hours, you took a wounded man on a ten-mile walk through inhospitable terrain?"

"It's only eight. Or maybe nine. What was I supposed to do? Put him in one of those wagons?"

"Yes!" exclaimed Betsy in exasperation.

Paul turned big, wounded eyes on her. "I couldn't do that. He saved my life."

He wasn't just wounded; he was burning up with fever. His head was so hot it practically sizzled when the cloth touched it. It was too soon for wound fever, even if Paul had practically dredged the man's head through the mud. Unless . . . Betsy peeled back an eyelid. Bloodshot but not jaundiced. Not yellow fever, thank goodness.

Betsy rounded on Paul. "Has he been coughing? Did he complain of stomach upset?"

"N-no? No coughing. Not that I remember."

"What about the stomach? Does he have the runs, Paul?" she demanded impatiently. Not typhoid, please, not typhoid. "*Think*, Paul."

Paul's sunburned face went red and he shifted uncomfortably. "Er. We all have the runs, Betsy. It's the mangoes. Or maybe the bully beef. But no more than anyone else. I don't think. He's been limping for a while," Paul added hopefully, grabbing at straws to distract attention away from his digestive system. "He took a bullet in the leg at Las Guasimas. But that was over a week ago. So it's probably not anything to do with anything. Betsy? What are you doing?"

"Cutting away these trousers." Stony-faced, Betsy clipped the fabric away, and, sure enough, there it was.

Not anything to do with anything, he said.

In the interest of not killing Paul, Betsy made herself focus on the task at hand. Under Holt's uniform trousers, a dressing the consistency of cement had glued itself to a wound that had started small but was now red, distended, and bulging with pus.

"When was the last time he changed this dressing?"

"We've been in battle, you know," said Paul indignantly.

"When. Was. The. Last. Time. He. Changed. This. Dressing," demanded Betsy, biting out each word like a bullet.

"I don't know. What am I, his nursemaid?" Paul looked as shifty as he was capable of looking, which wasn't much. He hadn't been made for dissembling. "If you must know, we had a bit of a falling-out."

"I don't care whether you quibbled about who won a game of marbles. I care about whether this was cleaned or not."

"This wasn't the Ritz Paris, Betsy. None of us had much chance to bathe. We weren't allowed to go in the river, you know. One fellow made himself a makeshift bathtub by digging a hole in the ground and lining it with some oilcloth, but it didn't work so well." Betsy fixed him with a hard look. Paul hastily summed up, "Um, yes. I don't think he's done anything with it since, well, Las Guasimas."

"It's infected." Betsy forbore to add "you idiot," although she didn't do much to hide the fact she was thinking it.

"Will he lose it?"

"Possibly." Instead of beginning to close, the wound gaped stubbornly open, distended by a large abscess. The area around it was visibly swollen and red streaks marred the skin above and below. How had the man been walking on this for a week? Cussedness, she assumed. Pure cussedness. But there were, thank goodness, no signs of the blackened flesh that signaled gangrene. It stank, but not of putrefaction. Not yet, at any rate. "Possibly not. But if he keeps it, it won't be through any fault of his own. What idiot doesn't change a dressing for a whole week?"

"I told him you'd scold him," said Paul complacently.

"You." Betsy glared at Paul, overcome by a combination of affection and exasperation. "If you get yourself shot, I'll kill you. Now stop clogging up my tent. You're so filthy you're probably infecting my patients just by being near them."

"You tell 'im, sister!" called one of her wounded. The men adored it when she yelled at people. They kept score and cheered her on. Men were very strange sometimes, but it seemed to work, so she wasn't going to question it.

Paul beamed at her. "I knew I could count on you." He started to go and then stopped, dragging a very muddy booted foot through her nice, clean straw. "Um, Bets. About Holt. Look. He's not what he seems. But he's a decent sort. Just—don't be alarmed if he starts spouting French poetry. Some of it's pretty risqué stuff."

Paul was worried about *poetry*? She was surrounded by men maimed in all the ways men could possibly be maimed. Over the past two days, she'd picked shrapnel out of hairy backsides, dealt with punctured private parts, and helped clear an impacted bowel— and a little French poetry was supposed to offend her sensibilities?

"He can quote poetry in Swahili for all I care as long as we get that leg cleaned." There was no point in arguing with Paul. Paul was, and would eternally be, Paul. Betsy sighed. "Go find Nurse Carson. She'll give you a cup of coffee and pump you for your recollections of the battle. Make sure to spell your name for her so she can quote you."

Right now she needed to deal with that leg. Dr. Stringfellow was passing by on his way back to the surgery tent, so tired he was swaying as he walked. Betsy grabbed his arm and dragged him into her tent.

"Can I save this leg?" she demanded.

She had to give Dr. Stringfellow credit. He didn't take her to task for waylaying him or not waiting properly as some of the other doctors might.

Of course, it might just have been that he was too exhausted to argue with her.

Dr. Stringfellow squinted at Holt. "Oh, him. I remember him. Have him come to me a week ago to have it cleaned the way I told him to. That should do the trick."

Given that she didn't live in a novel by H. G. Wells . . . "Do you have any other suggestions?"

"If you drain the abscess and clean it properly, there's a chance. Now if you'll excuse me, I have a dozen casualties waiting for me in the surgery tent."

He staggered off. Like the nurses, the surgeons hadn't had much sleep. Or any.

Drain it. She could do that. She'd done that before. There had been a time, in her first posting in Greece, when she'd had to go running to the doctors for every little thing, but not anymore. There were only six tables in the operating tent and eight surgeons. The doctors were too busy with major casualties to deal with anything less pressing.

Clean the patient, wash her hands, sterilize the knife, prepare the fresh dressings. Sometimes Betsy felt like her hands were moving without volition from her brain. A Red Cross uniform without a body in it, going through the motions by rote.

At least the influx of wounded seemed to have stopped for a moment. It was dark again, her lantern the only light. The men wheezed and tossed in their beds. The air stank of carbolic, sickness, and the salt of the sea.

As she knelt beside him, Private Holt's eyes slitted open. "You," he rasped. "It's you."

Betsy wondered what he was seeing. Did he see a disheveled nurse in a dirty apron or someone else entirely, some Fate or Fury or face from his past?

He would have to wake up now, with no chloroform to be had.

"Nurse Hayes," Betsy said matter-of-factly. "We've met. You have a nasty abscess in your leg and I need to drain it. I think you'd be better off going to sleep again. This is going to hurt."

CHAPTER SIXTEEN

Dear Ava,

I'm writing from a little makeshift hospital in an old schoolhouse in a town you've never heard of.

It's the night watch. I've found I rather like the night watch. It's quiet and the men are mostly sleeping and there are no fresh casualties coming in.

I'm not much of a practical nurse, but I like to think I'm still doing my bit. My bandages may be lumpy, but I'm very good at arranging wards and jollying the men. They like to be scolded. It makes them feel safe.

If you'd been here, we could have made such a team.

Are you still upset with me? Please don't be upset with me. You know I meant it all for the best. And I am doing my best for these men, whatever you might think.

Please write me back.

All my love,
Betsy

—Miss Betsy Hayes '96 to Ava Saltonstall '96

Athens, Greece
April 1897

BETSY TRIED TO PRETEND IT didn't hurt.

She tried to pretend it didn't hurt when Ava packed her bags and left, with the stiff-lipped thanks for her hostess that basic courtesy demanded. She tried to feel the elation she ought when the letter arrived from Queen Olga, commending her enthusiasm and inviting her to join the other nurses in their departure for the front.

And now here she was, standing in the hubbub of Omonia station, off to war! History was being made; the Greeks were rising against the barbarian as they had so long ago. The Persians had underestimated the Greeks, just as the tottering old Ottoman Empire was doing now. It was a noble war, Betsy told herself. A war of self-determination, all the Greek-speaking peoples throwing off the Ottoman yoke.

But Betsy couldn't quite muster the right martial spirit. It was tainted. It wasn't supposed to be like this; she and Ava were meant to be going together. If Ava hadn't wanted to go, she ought to have just said so and not used Betsy as her excuse, Betsy told herself loftily, although deep down, deep in the squirmy part of her stomach, there was a bit of her that knew that hadn't been it at all, that she had touched some hard, immovable part of Ava that truly believed Betsy was breaking an immutable ethical code.

Ava would forgive her. Wouldn't she? She always had before.

She'd never looked like that before.

She'd never said things like that before.

Betsy shivered, even though it was warm on the train platform, warm with the press of bodies as nurses and soldiers and journalists and civilians surged toward the front.

Betsy fidgeted a bit, turning up the collar of her jacket, trying to pretend she didn't feel terribly out of place. All the other nurses wore their uniforms: a gray dress and matching gray cloak, both with the Red Cross insignia, and a white bonnet with a thin gray veil.

Betsy wore purple: her favorite purple traveling costume with purple scrollwork. She stuck out like the proverbial sore thumb.

She hadn't known they would be traveling in their uniforms.

For the first time, she wondered if maybe Ava had been right, if maybe she was making a mistake charging off to battle in a country that wasn't her own in a war that wasn't her own. But it was everyone's, Betsy told herself hastily. Just the way ancient Greece was everyone's. She was doing her bit for the birthplace of democracy!

It sounded better when she thought of it that way, and less as though she was a lone American on a train platform wearing the wrong clothes and not quite sure where she was meant to be going.

Someone tapped her on the shoulder, and Betsy whirled around, trying to stand straight and look martial and alert and whatever else it was nurses were meant to be.

But it wasn't one of the doctors. It was Charles.

"Have you come to tell me not to go?" Betsy demanded belligerently.

The skin around Charles's eyes crinkled. "Does one ask the Seine to cease its flow? The winds to forbear to blow? No. I am not such a fool as that. I came only to wish you *bon courage*. It is a good thing you go to do," he added quietly. "A valiant one."

"I'm glad someone thinks so," Betsy said, and bit her lip, hard. She didn't want to talk about Ava. Charles had tactfully refrained from mentioning Ava's abrupt departure, but she knew he had noticed. "Not quite the same as riding bare-breasted on Crusade, but I'll do my best to keep my end up."

"I cannot imagine your ever doing otherwise." There was something about the way he looked at her as he said it, the tenderness of it, that made Betsy duck her head and take a great interest in tucking in a loose strand of hair.

"You haven't met my college professors," she said indistinctly.

Charles laughed. "My tutors would have much to say of me, little of it good." He paused, the bustle of the station carrying on around them, smoke drifting past them. "I brought something for you— you may think it foolish, but I should like for you to have it. If you will."

He held out his hand, palm up. In it was a single golden coin. A hole had been bored through one end, and a ribbon strung through it.

"It is—I suppose you would say—a good-luck charm. *Un talisman.*"

"It's the same in English. Talisman. But you know that. Your English is better than my French." Charles lapsed into French only in the grips of emotion.

Betsy tentatively reached out and lifted the coin, the ribbon dangling down behind, brushing Charles's outstretched hand. On one side, the words *Liberté, Egalité, Fraternité* were scrolled around a prosaic statement of the value and the date: 20 Francs, 1848. On the other, an angel—one of the avenging sort, not the small and fluttery kind—consulted a long scroll.

"This coin—it is said an earlier version of it saved one of my ancestors from discovery and the guillotine during the Terror. This coin itself has been handed down in my family since the *révolution de Février.* My father wore it into battle against the Prussians. And I have worn it since."

It felt warm to her fingers, warm from Charles's body. "You can't mean to give it to me. What if I lose it?"

"If you lose it, then I have lost you, and what is a coin to that?" While Betsy was still working out the implications of that, he added,

"You do not need to wear it—I know you do not agree with all my superstitions."

"No! No, that isn't it at all. It isn't as though you're asking me to disembowel a pigeon or dance around a campfire widdershins." Betsy was babbling, but it was because she couldn't quite fit her mind around the magnitude of the gesture encompassed by this one tiny coin. "Don't you—shouldn't you—save this for your family?"

"I have no son to carry it. No daughter either," he amended, forestalling Betsy before she could say it. "I should be honored if you would take my luck with you."

"I—I don't know what to say. Thank you. Would you—would you put it on for me?"

With as much ceremony as though he were crowning her empress, Charles solemnly tied the ribbon behind her neck, while Betsy craned her head down to try to see the coin, now lying somewhere awkwardly in between her high shirt collar and the top button of her purple jacket.

"Goodness," she said, swiping at the hair that kept escaping from her chignon, "I feel as though you've just invested me with the order of something or other. I—I will do my best to bring this safely back to you."

"It is not the coin that matters." Reaching out, Charles tucked her hair gently behind her ear. "Do what you need to do and return safely to me. To us," he hastily corrected himself.

Betsy was seized by a horrible sense of injustice. They shouldn't have to keep a polite distance; he shouldn't have to pretend he was wishing her safely home to Aikaterini and the American School; she should be able to kiss him goodbye properly and swear to come home to him and only to him. But she wouldn't, they couldn't, and all because twenty years ago, when she was still in pinafores, he had married an unknown woman of his family's choosing.

It wasn't *fair*.

But it was what it was, so Betsy took a step back and clutched his coin in one hand and tried to rearrange her face along properly indifferent lines. "You'll see, we'll thrash the Turks and be back within a week."

Charles raised a brow, making a valiant effort to sound equally detached. "Even Themistocles didn't prevail in a week."

"Yes, but Themistocles didn't have *me*." Betsy gave him an impish grin, flapped a hand in his general direction, and fled into the crowd before he could see her cry.

A holiday air prevailed upon the *Thrace*, the boat detailed to take twelve hundred soldiers, twelve volunteer nurses, and one Swedish cavalry officer to the front. On deck, the men expressed their exuberance in strange dances involving making a line and holding the ends of a knotted handkerchief. In the captain's dining room, toasts were drunk to the king, the queen, the crown prince, Greece, Greek independence, the Swedish officer, the nurses, and, with a charming nod at Betsy, the United States of America.

Betsy toasted back to life, liberty, and the pursuit of happiness, which went down rather well, as did the rather good French wine someone had brought. She had tucked Charles's coin down deep beneath her collar, and took courage from the press of it in the hollow of her throat. Not that she was going to need anything like the luck Charles had promised; everyone knew the Greek army would be victorious, and Vólos, where the Red Cross had a hospital, seemed like a friendly, charming seaside town, and everyone delighted to see them.

Betsy waved her handkerchief like anything at the men marching out toward Larissa, where the Greek army was encamped, ready to defeat the Turks, confident she would see them marching back in triumph in a day or two at most.

The Red Cross hospital had been set up in a private house in the town, and wasn't at all the fearsome thing she had envisioned. There was a small operating room, sparkling clean and entirely empty, and forty empty cots, like the little beds for the dwarves in the Grimm fairy tale. Their task was only, the nurses were informed, to provide the most basic care to the wounded, who would then be transferred to hospital ships and sent on to Athens.

Ha. She wished she could show Ava. Betsy anticipated a quiet and rather dull week sitting in an empty ward, waiting for the odd grazed hand, campfire burn, or broken leg to show up.

Everyone bustled about, of course. Make-work, Betsy decided, to make them feel useful. Betsy was tasked with acquiring cradles for broken legs, which might have been easier if (a) the carpenter had been able to understand her Greek, which apparently wasn't as clear as she thought it was, and (b) she had any idea of what those cradles were meant to look like.

Betsy was arguing with the carpenter, trying to communicate with him in a combination of broken Greek and elaborate hand gestures, when Dr. Kalopothakes stalked in.

"We need to set up an additional hospital in an old schoolhouse," she announced, which seemed rather silly to Betsy given that they didn't yet have any wounded in the hospital they had. "We will need five nurses. You. Miss Hayes."

Betsy noticed she didn't say "Nurse Hayes." "Yes?"

"You will be in charge of the new hospital."

"But—" She hadn't the slightest idea of what was needed to set up a hospital. And she suspected—no, she *knew*—that Dr. Kalopothakes was fully aware of it. "But I'm meant to be seeing to the acquisition of splints," she finished lamely.

There was a decided glint in Dr. Kalopothakes's eye. "I am sure they can spare you here. You *did* want to be useful, you said."

Yes, but to be in charge? Of a hospital? Well, there would be four other nurses, and hopefully they would have a better idea of what they were doing. Dr. Kalopothakes was just trying to scare her. It was punishment for elbowing her way in after Dr. Kalopothakes had failed her. That bit about being useful was straight out of her petition to the queen.

"Lead the way," said Betsy brightly.

Her determined cheer faltered a bit at the sight of her new domain. It wasn't a hospital; it was a hovel. The ground floor was packed earth, and damp. The second story was accessible only by a rickety external staircase. Betsy would have thought it all an elaborate practical joke but for the fact that villagers who had been conscripted to help were rushing about, setting up makeshift cots out of iron supports, wood planks, and straw. Lots and lots of cots.

Betsy stared.

"The people of the town have provided sheets, blankets, and towels," said Dr. Kalopothakes. "An army doctor will call once a day to see the patients. Send to the Red Cross hospital for anything else you need. Good luck."

Her tone implied Betsy would need it.

Betsy wandered into the ground floor of the hovel, absently touching her fingers to Charles's angel beneath the high neck of her new gray uniform.

The other nurses filed in after her. Not a one of them spoke a word of English. They weren't the society ladies with whom Betsy had trained with the Union of Greek Women. These were the old school of nurses, illiterate and innumerate. Although they had undoubtedly seen a great deal more practical nursing than Betsy had.

Yes, but how were they to communicate any of that to her? Betsy looked around the rows of cots that had been set up, at the pile of pajamas donated by the Red Cross and the supply cupboard sparsely stocked with bottles and jars labeled in Greek.

She didn't know any of the words.

No, this wouldn't do at all. She would have to go back.

Back to Charles, who thought she was doing something good and valiant. Back to Dr. Richardson and Ethel and the Harvard boys, who had been all too happy to see the back of her. Back to the exams she hadn't bothered to study for.

Betsy felt a surge of raw panic.

She couldn't go back. Not to the glint in Dr. Kalopothakes's eye, the glint that suggested the other woman knew she'd break and run, not to Charles, not to the American School, not back to Boston, where Ava would say "I told you so" and Lavinia would make her go with her to meetings of the DAR.

"The what?" One of the nurses was saying something to her, in a thick Cretan accent that Betsy had trouble understanding. "They're coming? Who's coming?"

Betsy turned and saw someone shoving open the gate of their courtyard and muscling his way through carrying something, one end of a stretcher. The wounded. They came pouring in, one after another, man after man, each smellier than the last, some unconscious, some shouting out, others whimpering in low, helpless tones that went straight to Betsy's heart.

She stood there, frozen, horrified, as the stretcher bearers eddied around her, depositing their burdens, while the Cretan nurse, in the absence of an actual leader, directed them to cots.

This wouldn't do; she had to do something. "Water," said Betsy, remembering something of her training. "We need hot water. We need to shave them and clean them."

They didn't have a single pot on hand. One of the nurses went running to a neighboring house to beg some boiled water. Another staggered over with a pile of towels. Betsy kept one eye on the other nurses, following what they were doing, trying to imitate their assured, quick motions. They shaved the men, cleaned them, eased off their clothes when they could be saved, and cut them off when they couldn't, some so soaked with blood that the sight and smell made Betsy's stomach turn, and she had to swallow hard and look away.

She'd never thought herself squeamish before.

She'd never seen anything like this before.

One man had been shot through the cheek, the bullet splintering his jaw before going out the other side. Another had been blinded by shrapnel, his eyes shredded past saving, delirious with pain.

Thank goodness, there was the army doctor that Dr. Kalopothakes had promised. Betsy ran to him, grabbing him by the arm.

"Tell me what to do for them," Betsy begged in Greek.

So he told her, in rapid Greek. Betsy understood roughly a quarter of it. When she tried to question him, the doctor winced.

"En français?" he suggested in desperation.

So much for her hard-won Greek. French wasn't much better. Betsy could declaim speeches from Racine, but medical terminology was beyond her.

Her entire education, it appeared, had been largely useless.

One of the Cretan nurses took her by the arm and led her to the supply cupboard, handing her a tin of boric acid and miming at her mouth, then pointing at the soldier with the gunshot wound. *Lait*, the doctor had said. That word she knew. She was to give the man milk and have his mouth cleaned with boric acid. He cried out horribly as Betsy tentatively began to swab the wound; she fell back, wanting to cry.

One of the other nurses took the cloth from her and showed her how to do it, quick and sure.

Eleven. There were only eleven men, but it felt like so many more. The light faded, the gloom broken only by the tiny specks of light provided by wicks floating in oil in jars of water, set into recesses of the wall.

Betsy had no idea where she was meant to sleep or put her things, but that didn't matter, because it didn't seem like she was to sleep; these men needed care, constant care, and there were dressings to be prepared for tomorrow, when more wounded were to come. More? Betsy couldn't imagine more. Her apron was bloodstained; her hair was coming out of its pins. She wanted to be back in her room at Aikaterini's house. She wanted to be anywhere but here.

"Mother," called one of the men, thrashing restlessly on his cot.

He had been shot in four places, each bullet going straight through, eight separate wounds to be dressed and dressed and dressed again. They were in such terrible pain, these men. Where was the laudanum? The chloroform? She wished she had something to give him. She wished there was something she could do, anything. She was helpless, so helpless.

"Mother, Mother . . ." His voice rose with his pain. He was going to wake the other men.

Betsy hurried over to him, kneeling by his cot. "Shhhh."

She took his hand. It felt so odd, holding a stranger's hand. She didn't know his name or where he was from or anything about him other than that he was hurt and delirious and missed his mother. So she patted his hand and made soothing noises until he fell asleep, with tears leaving tracks on his cheeks.

There were tears on her cheeks too. Betsy swiped them off and went back to join the other nurse on duty, preparing dressings for tomorrow.

Although, surely, tomorrow couldn't be so bad as today.

It was worse. The stretcher bearers seemed to go on forever, one after the other after the other, until their beds were almost full. Twenty-five new casualties, on top of their eleven. But this time, Betsy knew what to do. Shave, wash, change.

The army doctor came by on his rounds, a soldier behind him with a basket of antiseptic and dressings.

"Chloroform," Betsy blurted out. She had no idea what it was in French. *"Le chloroform? Le chose qui fait l'oubli?"*

"Nous n'en avons pas."

None? How could they have no chloroform?

It had to be a linguistic issue, Betsy decided. She had just asked wrong. They couldn't possibly be without anaesthetic.

But they were. There was, it seemed, a very small amount of chloroform and it was being saved for the worst cases. These were not the worst cases. In fact, they had been sending her the easy cases, given her youth and inexperience.

These were the easy cases?

There was no time to argue. There were too many men to tend to. Her fellow nurses taught her by example, slowing their motions so she could imitate them, positioning her hands for her, guiding her to the right cures in the cupboard. They took turns sleeping, so that two were always on watch in the night and three fresh for the day. As head nurse—oh goodness, what Ava would say, what a painful joke that was—Betsy tried to do with as little sleep as possible, to be there both for the day and part of the night watch.

Betsy worried that she was going to wear Charles's angel clear off the coin for rubbing it.

A good thing you go to do, he had said, and maybe it was a good thing, maybe she could make it a good thing. She entertained the men with her broken Greek, letting them correct her. She lied and told the man with the shattered mouth that she'd seen worse and that he'd be right as rain after an operation or two, just wait until he got to Athens; he'd be kissing his children with that mouth in no time. They told her, in the still of the night, about their families, their mothers, their children, in simple words she could understand, and Betsy squeezed hands and patted shoulders and changed dressings—she was getting very good at changing dressings—and told them they were coming along nicely.

By the fourth day, every bed was full and the army doctor came with the unwelcome news that three of the nurses were needed elsewhere. They were to pack their things and accompany him immediately.

Betsy did her best not to howl, although she wanted to. "Why? *Pourquoi?*"

"*Besoin*" was all she was told. There was need for them. Elsewhere.

"Right," Betsy said, and turned up her sleeves. It didn't seem quite so impossible as it had four days ago. She knew the routine now. She knew the care the men needed, although goodness only knew how they were going to manage with two nurses instead of five and the scantiest of supplies. The doctor had taken the basket with the antiseptic and bandages away with him again.

Betsy sent her one remaining nurse with a list—in English, but how different could it be?—to the Red Cross hospital and the orderly with money from her own pocket to the market to obtain food for the men, proper, nourishing sick food.

Which they absolutely refused to eat. Some of them wouldn't even touch the water, turning their faces away when she put the cup to their lips.

"What's wrong? They're not eating." There was nothing wrong with the food. She'd had some of it herself.

Although her one remaining fellow nurse wasn't eating either, which was rather worrying. Maybe there was something about the food she didn't know?

"It's Good Friday," her Cretan friend explained patiently. "Holy Week."

"Oh." That would explain the priests in procession she had seen tottering down the street the night before. Betsy shook her head to clear it. She'd lost all sense of what day it was, what month it was. She'd forgotten that the Orthodox church ran on a different calendar.

"But they need to eat. Or at least take some water!"

Her colleague only looked pityingly at her and quoted something in Greek about faith being better than bread. At least, Betsy thought that was what she said. The Greek of Crete was very different from that of Northampton.

Faith was all very well, but bread was bread. Betsy was about to say so when the old caretaker hobbled in, carrying a saucer of burning incense.

As he walked between the rows of beds, the men, even the very sickest, rose as far as they were able, fanning the smoke into their faces, murmuring prayers, prayers for victory and for peace, lifting their faces to the heavens, even the man with bandages over his eyes, with expressions of such beatitude that Betsy found herself, simply, speechless.

Betsy meekly knelt with the rest, breathing deep of the scented smoke. According to the orderly, who had picked up what he could in the market, the news from the front was bleak. They needed all the prayer they could get.

The doctor didn't come that day or the next. Instead, Betsy found her courtyard thronged with desperate, exhausted men, retreating soldiers who had been told to go to the docks for a ship that never came and didn't know where to go. Betsy didn't know where they were to go either, but they clearly needed food and a place to sleep.

Before she knew it, Betsy found herself running a makeshift hostel and canteen for retreating soldiers, using all their remaining blankets and straw to create rows of pallets in the courtyard and digging deep into the money she'd brought with her to keep the household in food.

A few of the men had terrible coughs. Betsy didn't like the sound of that at all. She wasn't nearly experienced enough to know if they were tubercular or merely suffering from what Charles might call *la grippe*, but either way she didn't want her wounded exposed to it. She made them their own enclosure on the far side of the courtyard, as far away as she could from the convalescent and the merely exhausted, and sent to the market for honey to make them soothing syrup.

And still the doctor didn't come.

Instead, the priest came, moving up and down the rows of recumbent men, his censor swaying, sending out the sickly sweet smell of incense as he chanted, "Christ is risen," and the men called back, "He is risen indeed."

It was Orthodox Easter. Easter Sunday. Betsy had lost all track of the days. There were nearly seventy men in her care now, in her care and that of the Cretan nurse, and the news from the outside was grim. The Greeks had broken at Larissa.

The Turks were coming.

On Monday the evacuation started. There was no warning. There was never any warning, Betsy thought crossly, as she shouted in Greek at the stretcher bearers to be careful, for heaven's sake, these were wounded men they were carrying. It would be nice if someone would actually *tell* her things before coming and taking away her wounded. But apparently there was a boat waiting and all the wounded were to be conveyed to Athens.

Betsy watched as her courtyard emptied and then her wards,

running after stretchers with instructions for the orderlies, making sure the men had their things—they got so upset if you gave them someone else's cap—sternly telling one man that, yes, he did have to go to the boat, no, he couldn't just leave and go back to his village, couldn't he see that leg wasn't ready to walk on yet?

Dr. Kalopothakes arrived just as the last stretchers were being borne off, and the building had gone, in the strange way of buildings, from being a hospital, a busy, useful thing, to an empty shell. It was very disorienting.

"Are we losing?" Betsy asked bluntly, so relieved to hear an American voice again that she hardly minded that it was Dr. Kalopothakes. "Are the Turks really coming?"

"We don't know. Some of the nurses are going back to Athens with the men. You can go with them, if you like. You've certainly done more than your fair share." Dr. Kalopothakes looked around at the empty cots, soon to be dismantled, at the neatly folded stacks of blankets and sheets. Looking directly at Betsy, she said, "You did well here."

She didn't need to sound so incredulous. "It was only what anyone would do. Are you evacuating?"

"No. We've evacuated our wounded, but there'll be more coming." A lot more, if the doctor's grim expression was anything to go by. "You can, if you choose, go back to Athens. Or you can stay here at the Red Cross hospital."

Not her own little hospital. Betsy looked back over her shoulder at the tumbledown building that had been her home for the past week. It was ridiculous how quickly one became attached to a place.

"If you stay, there is the risk the Turks will overrun Vólos," Dr. Kalopothakes said coolly. "The Turks have not agreed to respect the Red Cross as a neutral party."

So, in other words, she could go back to Athens and comfort, as she had wanted from the beginning, with enough nursing under her belt to say "I told you so" to Ava. Or she could stay here and risk a fate worse than death. Or possibly just death.

Betsy touched two fingers to her throat, feeling the familiar outline of the angel through the fabric. "I'll stay."

"Good," said Dr. Kalopothakes.

CHAPTER SEVENTEEN

It is impossible to overstate the terrible condition of our men. These brave boys, who set out so proudly to liberate Cuba, have been reduced to mere skin and bone by the failure to provide them proper rations and the harsh effects of the local climate. Heatstroke, dysentery, and malnutrition stalk our boys, doing what the Spanish could not.

The Red Cross has worked marvels, providing nourishing gruel, "cider," and beef stock for those in their care, but their mandate extends to only those men weak enough to fall into their care. Meanwhile thousands of others continue to crouch in damp encampments within range of the Spanish guns. Are these the men who will storm Santiago?

It is the duty of every feeling person to call for immediate relief for our hard-pressed army here in Cuba. . . .

—*Miss Katherine Carson for the* St. Louis Star Ledger, *July 3, 1898*

Siboney, Cuba
July 3, 1898

"GOOD," SOMEONE WAS SAYING, WHILE committing indignities to parts of Holt's anatomy.

Good was not the word Holt would have used. Whatever was happening, it hurt. He tried to explain; he tried to explain to the doctor, in his rusty black coat, that he hadn't fallen while sliding down the banister, that wasn't what had happened at all, but the doctor just clucked at him and wagged a finger and told him lads would be lads and not to be so reckless, eh?

Holt's leg burned. It was his arm his father had broken, not his leg. Why did his leg hurt?

Someone was gently stroking his head. Water trickled down his face. Tears? No, water. Or maybe water and tears. Holt tried to lift a hand to wipe whatever it was away and saw his hand come away red with blood.

"Oh, for heaven's sake," someone said. "If you don't stop pulling at it, it will never heal."

There was something about that voice, so crisp and sure and aggravated, that was strangely reassuring, that made the fog fade for a moment. Holt tried to smile but it made his face hurt.

He had a black eye. Cook had put raw steak on it and the juice had run down his face like something that might happen to the hero in a story in *Boy's Own*. Holt gobbled up the story papers as quickly as they arrived, not the drawing lessons and contests and instructions on how to build your own birdhouse, but the stories, stories of boys like him, boys who weren't afraid of anything, who could wrestle a grizzly bear or make a shelter out of two sticks and a blanket or who thwarted gangs of robbers and emerged triumphant.

He wished he could be strong like them. He tried to be brave like them, but it was hard, when he knew that any sign of defiance was going to be met by punishment, not just for him, but for his mother, whose fault he was. Maybe he was doing it wrong. Maybe it was him, maybe if he were braver, stronger, smarter . . .

Someone was lifting him, putting a hand to his cheek, cupping his face. "Private Holt. *Holt*."

Who was Private Holt? His mother called him "Bobby," or she did when his father wasn't listening. His father referred to him only by his full name. Or more frequently just "you."

"*Holt*. Private Holt. You need to drink this."

Whoever was speaking sounded rather urgent and there was a cup to his lips, so Holt obediently opened his mouth and drank, or tried to. He choked some of it up again and felt a cloth against the side of his mouth, wiping up the spit, someone's hand rubbing his back.

"Carefully now. You don't have to drink it all in one gulp."

Sometimes you did have to drink it all in one gulp before it was taken away. Holt had learned to squirrel food and water away in his room, for when he was sent there without supper. They'd forgotten him once for two days. His mother had been indisposed; she'd knocked her head. The servants didn't remember his father had locked him in, not until his mother finally woke up and went looking for him, staggering up and down the hallways, clutching the walls for balance.

He should have done something; he should have protected her better.

But he was away, in Cambridge, getting his degree. No, not Cambridge. Cuba. He was in Cuba and there in the vines was Paul's friend, that girl, clad in white samite like the Lady of the Lake, reaching out a pale hand to him holding a . . . sponge?

"Your fever should have broken by now," said the apparition. "Holt? Can you hear me? Private Holt? Drat."

He was drifting on his back in a lake, staring up at the sun through the foliage. The rustling of leaves sounded like voices, voices close by.

". . . mending nicely."

". . . fever?"

"Should break soon. I'd tell you to apply cold compresses, but we can't spare the ice."

"I'll think of something." For a tree, it sounded very determined. The rustling faded and Holt drifted away along his river, the water carrying him gently up and down.

Until he woke and found himself flat on his back on a rather lumpy straw mattress, staring up at a canvas awning. Holt tried to turn his head and found the movement exhausted him. His eyes burned as though they had grit in them. He was ravenously hungry. And his leg itched.

Holt reached down to investigate the itch. There was a flurry of fabric and a hand closed over his, quite firmly. "Stop that!" scolded a fury in a Red Cross uniform. "Don't you dare pull at that dressing. Your wound is only just beginning to mend and I won't have you tearing it open again."

Holt blinked at her. "Miss . . . Hayes."

So he really had seen her. It hadn't all been a hallucination. Although he rather suspected some bits of it were. Like the white samite.

"That's Nurse Hayes to you," she said, but he could hear the relief in her voice. "You've been out for two days—no, three days."

"Three *days*?" Holt made an attempt to sit up that ended with Miss Hayes having to grab him to keep him from toppling sideways off the cot. He didn't remember being on a cot. The last he remembered, he'd been on a pallet. The last he remembered, sitting up didn't feel like major physical exertion.

He vaguely remembered Paul dragging him all the way from San

Juan Hill, but beyond that . . . everything was murky. A lot of what had happened before that was murky too.

"Don't fuss, Rip Van Winkle. You haven't missed much. Unless you wanted to see Private Jones over here do his guppy imitation."

"It's not a guppy, it's a halibut," protested the patient on the next cot in wounded tones.

"They all look the same on a plate," Miss Hayes shot back.

This appeared to be a routine of some standing. Holt tugged at Miss Hayes's sleeve. "Paul?"

"Full of coffee and prunes and back with the regiment," said Miss Hayes crisply. "Undoubtedly flinging himself in front of people with firearms."

". . . news?" Holt's tongue felt thick and fuzzy. It didn't seem to want to form words properly.

Miss Hayes—Nurse Hayes—propped him up expertly with one arm and put a cup to his lips. "Last I heard, your lot were still holding San Juan Heights. Oh, and the Spanish fleet has been destroyed."

"Well, that's something," Holt murmured, and fell asleep again, dreaming of ships on fire, buccaneers and conquistadors and Paul in a feathered hat.

Nurse Hayes appeared at some point in the guise of Elizabeth I, which, in his dream, made perfect sense. Holt tried to shake out his cloak for her across a ford filled with blood but she told him to stop that and keep his blankets on or he'd freeze in the night air, and Holt wasn't entirely sure whether it was Queen Elizabeth talking or Betsy Hayes or both.

The next time he woke it was dusk. Paul's Betsy—Nurse Hayes—was kneeling by his cot, unwinding cloth from around his thigh. His very bare thigh. Which was next to very bare other bits of him. Holt made a grab at the sheet.

Nurse Hayes grabbed back. "Stop that. There's really no need for that sort of thing. This leg and I are old acquaintances. Once you've seen the inside of someone's abscess . . . If you could just release your grip on the sheet—thank you."

Holt did as she ordered, wishing that the unnamed Spaniard who had wounded him had aimed just a little lower down his leg. Or, of course, not hit him at all. But if he had to wound him, couldn't he have done it in a more socially acceptable place?

Nurse Hayes rolled her eyes. "There's no need to be missish, Private Holt. I've seen far worse. There. All done." She pushed herself to her feet, then looked back down, a lock of fair hair falling out of her cap. "What sort of name is Holt, anyway? It's halfway between *halt* and *hilt*."

"My mother's maiden name," Holt said hoarsely. Damn. There went any pretense that it was his own. "If it were between *halt* and *hilt* it would be *helt*."

"Details." Nurse Hayes picked up her basket of dirty dressings. "I'm trying to cure you, not shelve you."

"Thank you." Holt surprised himself as well as her by grabbing her hand. There was something he needed to tell her and he didn't know how else to say it. "Before you go— You were right."

"I frequently am." Nurse Hayes gently extracted her hand, but she paused all the same. "About what?"

"All this. You told me—you told me even if we win we lose. We're winning and we're losing. So much—so much didn't have to happen."

Without saying anything, Nurse Hayes set down her basket.

"Our weapons weren't as good as theirs." It hurt to talk. The words rasped his throat. But once he started, Holt couldn't seem to make himself stop. "We didn't have the right powder. It gave us away every time we fired. The Spanish—everything we thought about them—we were wrong. They know what they're doing. We're like farm boys with sticks compared to them. We've been marching on empty stomachs. Our rations go bad. Or they forget to bring them at all. Colonel Roosevelt had to buy us beans out of his own pocket. Everyone's sick to his stomach all the time."

There were men sleeping all around Holt, men who had fought and paid the price for it. Holt kept his voice low, partly because he didn't want to wake them, and partly because his voice didn't seem to want to work properly. His brain felt cloudy too, crammed with overlapping images like a poorly exposed photograph.

"I've seen so many men die—men who didn't have to die, just mown down because we were in the wrong place with the wrong weapons doing the wrong thing. They put a balloon up over us! A great, big, yellow balloon! For reconnaissance, but they might just as well have put a big sign up saying 'get your enemy here.' We were stuck. There wasn't enough room on the road, so there we were, jammed up one right after another with that blasted big balloon floating over us. We were easy pickings. They didn't even have to aim. No matter what they did, they were sure to hit someone. Talk about shooting fish in a barrel."

"Food for powder," murmured Nurse Hayes. "Just numbers on a report."

For generals who couldn't even be bothered to get out there with their men. "Did you know Shafter didn't even come to the front with us? He's like the Duke of Plaza-Toro," Holt finished bitterly.

"He led his regiment from behind / (He found it less exciting)?"

She was the one person he could say this all to, the one person who understood. Holt tried to look up into her face, but the light was too dim; she was half shadow. "How did you know?"

"My father enjoyed the odd operetta," Nurse Hayes said softly. "We saw *The Gondoliers* twice when it opened in New York."

Holt blinked at her. "I meant—how did you know—it would be like this? That it would be—such a shambles?"

"Oh, that. I consulted the oracle, of course, and poked about in the entrails of pigeons. No, I'm sorry, that wasn't fair." Nurse Hayes rubbed her temples with her fingers. "I've been here before. Not here. I've never been to Cuba before. But I nursed. In Greece. It was not—it was not what I thought it would be."

She looked defiantly at Holt, as though daring him to fault her for it.

"What did you think nursing would be?" he asked curiously.

Nurse Hayes bristled. "What did you think war would be?"

She had him there. A chivalric battle of armor and lances and banners. Riding to victory with pennants flying. A romanticized image of a past that never was. Even Tennyson had known it, in his *Idylls of the King*. He'd painted a world in which the reality never matched the ideal. But it was the ideal one came away remembering, the dream of it, not the flawed execution, the chaos and shame and loss.

"*When every morning brought a noble chance, / And every chance brought out a noble knight*," Holt said woozily. Deeds noble and base, that was what Tennyson had said. And there had certainly been plenty of both. No, that wasn't the problem. "I'd thought—I'd thought it would be more organized."

Two armies squaring off across a field and may the best man win.

"Ha," said Nurse Hayes inelegantly. She squatted down beside his cot. "Be grateful you're on the winning side so far. It's far worse the other way."

"You've seen it." Holt looked at Paul's friend, at the snub-nosed face that was thinner than it ought to be, at the stubborn chin and wide-set gray eyes, ringed with deep purple circles.

Not a vision. Not an oracle. Not a pair of arms in a Red Cross uniform. A woman. A very tired woman, with ghosts of her own.

"Yes. I've seen it." She hesitated a moment, before looking him squarely in the eye. "I was at Vólos when the Greeks were routed at Larissa. And then again when they were routed at Velestinon."

The names meant nothing to Holt. But they clearly meant a great deal to her. "That sounds like a lot of routing."

She shrugged, looking away. "There was a lot of routing and not a lot of winning. As they like to say, mistakes were made. The people in charge . . . they didn't quite know what they were doing. The crown prince's chief of staff was better known for his ability to lead cotillions than to lead troops."

Why hadn't he asked her any of this back in Tampa? He'd been so smug, so sure. He'd never imagined she might have experienced something he hadn't.

"Why were you there?" Holt rasped.

Nurse Hayes plaited her arms defensively across her chest. "In Greece? Classics. I'm a classicist. I was a classicist."

"A *classicist*?" As soon as the words escaped his lips, Holt wished they hadn't. It was just that one didn't expect a nurse to be a scholar of classics. "It must have been something—being in the land of Odysseus."

Nurse Hayes wasn't mollified. "You can keep your Odysseus. I never liked him. He could have got home much faster if he'd wanted to."

"But then there would be no story," murmured Holt.

Nurse Hayes snorted. "Now you sound like Kit. Nurse Carson, I mean." She sighed, looking away over his head, out the tent and far away. "That wasn't the sort of story I was interested in. I had an idea that I was going to bring back the lives of normal people—the sort of people who got trampled when Odysseus passed through. Nausicaa washing her laundry on the rocks. Penelope at her loom. All the everyday things and people that are there in the background, ignored. A whole new sort of archaeology, a quest not for treasures but for vanished lives."

This was a whole new Nurse Hayes. Holt was fascinated. "Then why didn't you?"

"Because I went to war." Nurse Hayes pushed herself up to her feet, reaching down for her basket, the conversation clearly over. "I should have stayed in Athens and studied for my exams. Instead I took a nursing class and went off to the front. I was foolish. And arrogant. And that's the end of it."

Holt's hand brushed her sleeve. "But you did it."

She looked sharply back over her shoulder. "What?"

"You nursed those men. The ones in—wherever it was."

"Well, yes, but—"

"Not so foolish for them. Not so foolish for me." It was an effort to speak, an effort to keep his eyes open. But he had to make sure she knew. "Whatever—went wrong, I'm sorry. But I'm glad you're here."

Siboney, Cuba
July 6, 1898

PRIVATE HOLT WAS ASLEEP ALMOST before the words were out of his mouth.

I'm glad you're here.

Betsy bit down hard on her lower lip to keep it from wobbling. She wasn't the wobbling sort. She was just tired, that was all. But she paused to tuck the blankets more snugly under Private Holt's chin. It got cold at night in Siboney, by the sea.

She hadn't meant to talk to him about Greece.

About the men who had died who hadn't had to, not because of necessity, but because of arrogance and pomposity and self-importance.

War she could understand. Not approve, but understand. Men had always settled their differences by seeing who could punch hardest; *war* was just another name for the same impulse. But what had happened after Velestinon—it was pure waste. Criminal irresponsibility.

That was what Ava had said to her, all those months ago, but Ava didn't know the half of it.

Ava had no idea of just how right she'd been. About so many things.

Betsy looked at Private Holt, his face oddly peaceful in sleep. She'd shaved off the mustache while he was sleeping—not just because it annoyed her, but because that was what they did, they shaved off unnecessary havens for dirt and, all right, also maybe because it annoyed her—and his face looked younger, less tough. The fine-boned face of a scholar or a philosopher.

Not what he seemed, Paul had said.

She certainly would never have expected Hold 'Em Holt to quote Gilbert and Sullivan. Or Alfred, Lord Tennyson.

But as he'd pointed out, no one expected a classicist in a nurse's uniform either.

You can't put on a uniform and pretend you know what you're doing, Ava had told her, but she didn't have much choice, did she? Betsy wasn't much, but she was what they had. She'd failed her men on the hospital ship *Albania*. And then, later, even worse . . .

Maybe this was her chance to redeem herself. Betsy wasn't foolish enough to think that a life could balance a life. But it might help. A little.

She could help these men.

Or at least bring the dirty dressings to be boiled. Betsy made a face at herself and went back to doing what had to be done.

There was a great deal to be done over the next few days and very few people to do it. Sister Minnie and Sister Anna were both feeling poorly; there were rumors that a man in the Cuban hospital was suffering from yellow fever, but, then, there were always rumors about yellow fever. It was like the bogeyman, under everyone's bed, and hopefully just as insubstantial.

But the men still stumbling in were real. A truce had been called, but even if the guns were temporarily silent, fever, heatstroke, and dysentery did the Spaniards' work for them. The men being brought in for care were nothing like the hearty boys who had thronged the transports in Port Tampa only a month ago. They were walking skeletons, swollen with bug bites, infested with lice, debilitated by festering scratches, teeth loose from malnutrition.

And the truce wouldn't last forever. They all knew it was a matter of days, at best, before the guns started up again and the carts jolted back down the Siboney road filled with men in even worse shape than last time.

Kit's pen had been busy, writing indignant essays that her editor would probably never print. They wanted only guns and glory, Kit had complained to her. But she wrote her articles anyway, pouring out her indignation and frustration at the mismanagement, the mishandling, the sheer waste. Betsy was terrified Kit was going to burn herself out, doing two jobs at once, and putting too much into both.

As Betsy finished yet another endless shift, she saw Kit wobbling down the steps of the hospital building, there to relieve her.

"Betsy—oh, darn." Kit slapped at a mosquito with both hands, swayed, and grabbed the side of the tent for balance. "Horrible things. They're everywhere."

"We need those big mesh hats beekeepers wear," Betsy said. There were red welts across Kit's forehead, as there were on the men, no matter how much she slapped the bugs away. The rainy season had brought out the mosquitoes with a vengeance. "Are you all right?"

"Just tired," said Kit, with a shadow of her usual jaunty smile. Beneath the livid bites, her face was an alarming shade of gray, her eyes glassy.

Given the way they were all working, Betsy suspected she looked equally corpselike. She wanted nothing more than to flop down on her pallet and close her eyes. The urge was so strong, she could practically feel her eyes closing where she stood.

But she had done this before. Kit hadn't. And Kit had people waiting for her at home. Children waiting for her at home.

It took all her resolve to say, "Why don't you go lie down a bit? I can take your shift."

Kit rubbed her eyes with the back of her hand. "Are you sure you couldn't use the rest yourself? I can—"

"I know, I know, you can sleep when you're dead," said Betsy sharply. Behind Kit, the detail from the 23rd Michigan Volunteers who'd been sent to dig graves for them was filtering past, muddy shovels over their shoulders. "But being dead is highly overrated and I'd prefer to send you home to your children on your own two feet, not in a box."

Kit blinked at her. "I was only going to say I can use the nap, if you're sure you don't mind. You've been on your feet all day."

"Oh." Betsy felt like an idiot. She made a valiant attempt at flippancy, spoiled slightly by a massive yawn. "What's a few hours more? I'm fine. You go."

She hoped Sisters Minnie and Anna were back on their feet soon; it wasn't clear how long they could keep going on like this. She performed her tasks by rote, in the state of fatigue where everything felt vaguely floaty.

There was a new man in the ward, annoying his neighbors with a high-pitched whistling noise.

"Can you gag him?" one man begged. "Or at least make him hold a tune?"

The man whistled again, louder and harder.

Private Holt was the last man on Betsy's rounds. He was always the last man on Betsy's rounds. It was, of course, entirely because he was next to the end of the ward and not because she deliberately arranged it that way so she could stop and spar with him for a few moments.

"How'd you get that man to be quiet?" he asked, as Betsy knelt down to gently pry off his old dressing.

"It was quite simple. He thinks he's a steamboat on the Mississippi River. Named the *Clara Belle*," she added, dropping the soiled dressing into her basket.

"Is that right?" She could see Holt trying not to grin. He was looking considerably better. There was color in his cheeks and the head wound had healed enough that the large bandages had been replaced by a small patch. Any day now, he was going to be well enough to discharge. "So did you explain to him he has no paddle wheel?"

"Of course not." Betsy sat back on her heels, allowing herself just the slightest moment of smugness. "I told him he'd been taken in for repairs and there's no coal in his scuttle."

Holt gave an abrupt bark of laughter. Betsy knew that laugh by now. It was the laugh of someone not used to laughing and it always felt like a small, personal victory.

"How's the leg?" he asked, as Betsy bandaged him back up. He'd stopped clutching the sheet a few days back, although she could tell he still wanted to. "Will I keep it?"

"Through no fault of your own," said Betsy severely. "You're lucky we're not planting you over there."

Holt grimaced. "I'm hard to kill."

Betsy gave his bandage one last twist. "Don't make me want to try."

Holt smiled at her. Not a grin, not a grimace, but an actual smile, of surprising and unexpected beauty. "Thank you."

"Just doing my job," said Betsy, and stumbled out of the tent, dizzy with more than lack of sleep.

CHAPTER EIGHTEEN

Dear Ava,

I'm just going to go on writing to you until you write back,
you know. I'm back in Athens, but only for a few days. We had
to pack up our hospital at Vólos when the Turks broke through
the lines. They were very complimentary about our work and
even offered us positions with the Red Crescent—as if any of
us would! But even though we had to evacuate, we remain
undaunted, and by "we" I mean both the nursing staff and the
army. This is just a minor setback and I'm sure we'll still prevail
in the end. One can't imagine the Greeks losing to the Turks.
The Greeks always defeat the Turks in the end.

All right, maybe not always. There was that long
occupation. And I suppose I'm thinking of the Persians rather
than the Turks. But if you'd met the soldiers I've met and
bandaged their wounds and mopped their brows, you would
understand my faith in them. It's like that song about the
British tar being a soaring soul, except instead of "British tar"
put "Greek infantryman."

In three days I'm off to my next post. Dr. Kalopothakes
personally recommended me for the new Red Cross hospital in

Lamia, if you can believe it. She's a bit of a stick-in-the-mud, but fundamentally a good sort. She reminds me a bit of you.

If Dr. Kalopothakes can forgive me that disaster of an exam, can't you forgive me too? I've been making up for it as hard as I can. You'd know if you saw my hands. Calluses upon calluses and boiled red with carbolic!

Can't you just see Miss Swenson pointing with her ruler and intoning, "These are not the hands of a lady"?

Write to me, please.

> *All my love,*
>
> *Betsy*

—*Miss Betsy Hayes '96 to Ava Saltonstall '96*

Athens, Greece
May 1897

AFTER BETSY'S WEEKS ON THE front, the normalcy of Athens was dizzying.

Carts and carriages careened around her. In the cafés, men were sitting and drinking coffee and reading papers as if men weren't fleeing and dying on the front. Women shopped in the boutiques on Ermou Street, giving great consideration to their next hat, and children ran and shouted and got underfoot.

It was, in short, life as usual, except it wasn't usual, any of it.

She'd gone from the hospital ship *Albania* straight to the house on Academy Street to find the knocker off the door and covers over the furniture. Aikaterini was not at home. She'd gone off to take the waters at a wonder-working spa somewhere in one of those small German places that invariably began with Bad-something-or-other.

Of course, she hadn't known Betsy would be back. Betsy hadn't known Betsy would be back. The servants assured her it wasn't the least bit of trouble. Despoinída Elisavet's room was always ready, and her bicycle had been kept at a high polish by Herakles, who Betsy suspected had been polishing the seat, as well, and good for him if he'd mastered it. She would offer him a lesson, if she weren't afraid it would spoil his fun.

The servants had run about heating water for tea and whisking the protective sheets off the drawing room furniture, while Betsy had wandered up to her room feeling entirely disoriented. All her things were still in the wardrobe, those fantastical, frivolous dresses she had worn to balls and routs and teas. It had been only three weeks, but they felt like they belonged to another lifetime. Betsy peeled off her Red Cross uniform hesitantly; it felt like it had grown into her, like a second skin.

It felt almost obscene to bathe in the heavenly deep tub Aikaterini's servants filled with scented water, to rinse the dirt and stench of
the *Albania* out of her hair, to put on a tea gown and be served little
cakes in the empty drawing room. They were too rich; they turned
her stomach, although she would never have told the cook so.

She tried to write Ava—she'd decided she was just going to go on
writing Ava until she wrote her back—but she found her pen didn't
want to shape any of the words that mattered. She couldn't make
herself tell Ava the truth of it, only the enthusiastic platitudes the old
Betsy might have written. It felt a bit like playing a part, mimicking
the person she had been a month ago.

Betsy didn't sleep much that night back at Academy Street. It
wasn't just that her bed was too soft or the covers too thick or the
room too quiet.

Every time she closed her eyes, she saw them. The refugees, fleeing the Turkish advance. All those people who had thought themselves safe behind the Greek lines until there was no line anymore,
nothing to protect them from the Turkish army pressing forward,
ever forward, reportedly capable of the most unspeakable atrocities.
The children, so many children, hungry, bewildered, stumbling after
donkeys loaded with their families' possessions, waiting to be loaded
into ships to take them somewhere, anywhere. The sound of battle,
so close, the pounding of the guns and the cry of the Turkish bugles.

But the Turks had been—well, not kind, that wasn't the word
for it; war wasn't kind. They had been civilized. The nurses had been
warned that the Ottomans hadn't signed the Red Cross accord and
might not respect neutral parties. But they had. They'd offered them
work with the Red Crescent and, when the nurses refused, let them
leave in peace.

No, they had been gentlemen. That wasn't where the horror lay.

It was in the *Albania*, the hospital ship chartered by a British newspaper, sponsored by a British member of Parliament, hastily laden with the Greek wounded. So hastily that the ship's crew hadn't time to wait for necessary hospital supplies. The chief medical officer refused all advice. This was his ship, and he didn't need a bunch of Red Cross nurses telling him what to do. He locked their supplies in the hold. They wouldn't need them anyway, he said; he had his own people.

None of the staff on board spoke Greek. They wouldn't even let Betsy translate. Her work was done, the medical officer had told her, puffing out his chest at her. She was to leave it to them now.

Yes, leave it to them to kill her patients.

They'd packed the men in like sardines on the deck, exposed to the elements, and those who wouldn't fit on the deck they'd shoved onto wooden shelves next to the stench and heat of the engines. One man, who'd been out of his mind with fever, they'd locked in the hold, to shut him up. They left him there. Without care. Without food or water.

All that night, all that long, terrible night on the *Albania*, Betsy had heard the priest moving from man to man, offering the last rites. Offering the last rites to men who by rights oughtn't have died. If they'd had their supplies . . . if they'd been allowed to care for their patients . . . if the medical officer hadn't been such an arrogant ass . . .

They lost six men. Six men who didn't need to die. Betsy could see them still, every single one. Every man she had bathed and bandaged and jollied.

One of them had flung himself from the mast. He'd been mad with fear of the Turks; he'd thought he was escaping them. If she had been with him—if she had been allowed to be with him—

She'd tried. She really had. They just hadn't *listened*.

And six men were dead because of it.

And here she was now, not in her Red Cross uniform, but in her most elaborate Parisian walking dress. Battle armor, just of a different sort.

As soon as it was decently light, Betsy had dressed and sallied out to beard Aikaterini's friend the minister of war. He had, of course, been delighted to see Miss Hayes—one always had time for Miss Hayes! Coffee, perhaps? He was clearly miffed at being interrupted at so early an hour, having to shrug rapidly into his coat before she could glimpse the bands that held his sleeves, but he was gentleman enough not to show it.

Betsy had forgotten that there was a world where that sort of thing still mattered, where men still wore their hair slicked and parted in the middle and had starched high collars and gold pocket watches.

The minister, bless him, had done an admirable job of not consulting his watch as she'd poured it all out, the mismanagement, the waste. But when she was done, he only spread his hands and said, what could he do? The ship was the gift of a foreign power. The medical officer, the staff, the British MP who had chartered it . . . they were well outside his jurisdiction. It would, of course, be noted. She might write a letter to the men in question, a strongly worded letter— although perhaps not too strongly worded. One didn't want to discourage acts of charity in future.

Would she like to tour some hospitals while she was in Athens?

Betsy left with letters of introduction and a feeling that her time had been wasted.

And here she was now, in the middle of Syntagma Square, trying to figure out what on earth to do with herself. She could go straight to the hospitals, she supposed. The wounded from the *Albania*—the ones who had survived the voyage—had been transferred to the military hospital. Some of her boys were there. She should see how they were getting on.

"Betsy?" The sound of steps quickening as they approached her, a familiar hat yanked off a familiar head. "Betsy!"

As always, her name sounded foreign and exotic and altogether more special when Charles said it, the emphasis on both syllables rather than just the first.

"Charles," she said, and couldn't seem to make herself say anything more. *Hello* might have been appropriate. Or *goodness, fancy meeting you here!* But she was numb with grief and guilt, still half on board the *Albania*. Charles was like a vision from another world, in his gray suit, with his ivory-topped walking stick.

"You did not tell me you were at home."

"I'm not. I mean, that is, I just got back last night." Betsy gave her head a little shake. "I've just been to the war office to complain about the shambles on the *Albania*."

"The *Albania*?" Charles cocked his head, prepared to listen.

Of course Charles wouldn't know what the *Albania* was. She wouldn't either, if she hadn't been on it, if she'd been here in Athens, translating inscriptions and going to teas.

"It's a ship." Betsy found she didn't want to tell Charles about it, not any of it. Charles was Athens. Charles was Delphi. Charles was mystery and wonder and sophisticated banter; he was ancient digs and modern drawing rooms, and Betsy didn't want to sully that. "How has Athens been since I left?"

"Dull without you." Charles offered her his arm and she took it, strolling down Panepistimiou as if this were any other day in any other time. "Athens has been . . . unsettled. The people blame the retreat from Larissa on the crown prince. There have been marches and demonstrations and the usual cries for heads on a pike."

Betsy wasn't above picking up a pike herself.

When she thought about the men in her care, what had happened to them, even before the *Albania*, she felt decidedly bloodthirsty. If the crown prince had bothered to acquire proper advisers—if he'd consulted anyone who had half an idea how a battlefield worked—so many of those men might have been spared. She was still as much in favor of the cause as she had ever been, but the manner of its execution was another matter entirely.

But Betsy found she couldn't say that any more than she could tell Charles about the *Albania*.

So she said instead, "Shall we see a revolution, then? Is there a Bastille to storm?"

Charles shrugged. "Not at present. If they lose the war . . . perhaps."

Betsy tilted her head up at him. "Don't you mean if we lose the war? This is your adopted country too."

"I am still a citizen of France. France sees this as a rather awkward little squabble and hopes it will go away." He said it as if it didn't matter at all, as if this weren't a grand struggle between democracy and tyranny but just another European war, a skirmish for the history books. "The king has called on the opposition leader to form a government, in the hopes that Monsieur Rallis might prove even less popular with the people than he is himself."

Betsy couldn't get those words out of her head. A rather awkward little squabble.

She didn't realize she had stopped walking until Charles stopped with her, one hand on her arm. He leaned over to see her face beneath the brim of her hat. "M'amie, what troubles you?"

It wasn't Charles's fault. He didn't know; he hadn't been there. The world was still all camellias and champagne for him. And he was French. The French saw things differently. Betsy drew in a shuddering breath, trying her hardest not to cry, but it was so hard, so very hard; the tears kept threatening despite all her best efforts.

"I'm just tired," she managed. Her face crumpled. "Oh, Charles."

He took her quickly by the arm, hurrying her out of the path of other pedestrians. "Did you eat anything at all this morning? Or did you go immediately to bedevil the minister?"

"The latter. I didn't even give him time to get his collar adjusted properly." She pressed her eyes tightly shut, remembering, feeling it as if she were reliving it. "I just needed to talk to him—right away—to make him see—"

She swayed on her feet, and Charles put an arm around her, too worried for propriety. "My rooms aren't far from here. Come."

Betsy had never thought of where Charles lived. She knew he lived somewhere, of course, but it had never occurred to her to inquire. His rooms took up an entire floor of a neoclassical mansion. The nicest floor, of course; what the French called the *bel-étage*. That was hardly a surprise. Charles's *étage* couldn't be anything other than *bel*, thought Betsy, stifling a hysterical burst of laughter. The effort made her sway slightly.

Charles tightened his grip on her arm. "Is Aikaterini not looking after you?"

"She's in Bad-somewhere," said Betsy vaguely, as Charles brought her through a tiled foyer into a grand salon, the sun from long windows glinting off a truly staggering quantity of gold leaf.

Gold-framed portraits leered down from the walls; women in puffy petticoats swung in eternal glee over eighteenth-century shrubbery; devoted swains wheedled shepherdesses; and imposing Greek gods, not at all in the Greek style, disported themselves on the ceiling.

Betsy wandered in circles, reaching out a hand to touch a gilded clock, running her fingers across the marble top of a bombé chest, craning her neck to stare up at Aphrodite. "Good heavens. It's like being in Paris. You've brought Paris to Athens."

"It's not at all like Paris," said Charles decidedly. "Let me ring for coffee."

"Where is Ethel when one needs her?" It seemed so strange to think that Ethel was undoubtedly still back at the American School, trying to figure out who stole Jane.

It seemed even stranger that the man who lived among these gilded relics had crouched over a campfire with her. This was all pure ancien régime. Betsy had no doubt that the powdered and bewigged characters who stared at her with pursed lips from the walls were actual ancestors and not the sort one bought secondhand to lend an impression of antiquity to recent wealth.

Betsy poked at a large bronze Hercules. "Did you leave anything in Paris?"

"Nothing that mattered." Charles gave a sharp tug on a braided rope. He looked at Betsy. "Everything I care about is here in Athens."

Betsy wasn't entirely sure he was talking about the furnishings anymore. She seated herself carefully on a petit point settee far older than she was. "Doesn't your wife mind?"

"Ah, Georgios." The door opened, admitting a male servant. Charles spoke to him in rapid Greek that was much better than Betsy's, ordering coffee and cakes. "We should have sustenance for you quite shortly."

Sustenance. What was sustenance? Betsy shook her head distractedly. "How can I sit and eat cakes?"

"Much as you are," Charles suggested, coming to join her on the settee, but Betsy was already on her feet, prowling distractedly around the room, pacing an uneven track across the Aubusson carpet.

"Yesterday—yesterday I was on a ship. Yesterday I was on a ship where six men died." Betsy felt like an inkblot, the one disorderly note among all the harmony. She didn't belong here in Charles's jewel box, where everything was orderly and calm. "Six men."

Charles leaned forward on the settee. "What happened?"

Betsy wove an erratic path around the furniture, faster and faster, as if she could outpace her own thoughts. "The medical officer on the *Albania*—he treated us all as though we were nothing, as though we didn't matter. The Greek nurses were just peasants to him. And I— I was just a woman and an American and therefore of no account."

"That I cannot believe. You are always of account."

"You ought to have heard him. *My dear girl.*" Betsy viciously mimicked the officer's veddy veddy British accent. "*Do us the courtesy of assuming we know our own trade.* But they didn't. They didn't. It was the *arrogance* of it."

"Would you have been better off if there had been no ship at all?" Charles asked quietly.

"Yes! No. I don't know. That's what the minister said too, that it was a kindness of them. But if they hadn't chartered a ship, maybe someone else would have. Or having chartered the ship, they might at least have *listened* to us." Betsy stopped short next to a bust of a seventeenth-century worthy on a marble pedestal. "It was just so un- necessary. They didn't have to die. It was such *waste*."

"*Il est défendu de tuer,*" murmured Charles. "*Tout meurtrier est puni, à moins qu'il n'ait tué en grande compagnie, et au son des trom- pettes.*"

It is forbidden to murder unless one does it in a large company to the sound of bugles.

"Yes, but that's the point," said Betsy impatiently. "This wasn't an act of war; this was an act of stupidity. These men survived the war. They fell prey to—oh, goodness, what does one even call it? Pure nitwittery! That's what it was."

"Folly has killed more men than cannon."

Betsy narrowed her eyes at him. "Is that also Voltaire?"

"No. Merely an observation of my own."

"Well, I won't have it. Not if I'm there to stop it." Never mind that Ava thought her the most foolish of all. At least Betsy knew better than to leave sick men lying exposed on the deck of a ship. "Next time. I'll just have to speak louder, fight harder. I may not be much of a nurse, but I do know how to be a nuisance."

Much good it had done her. Betsy blinked back another betraying wave of tears. She couldn't, wouldn't give in to them, to any of it.

"You go back?" Charles asked.

Betsy swallowed hard. "In two days."

Charles gestured to the seat beside him, silently inviting her to sit down. "You don't have to. No one would blame you if you didn't."

"I would blame me. I've started this, I need to see it through." Betsy plunked down on the settee, feeling the exhaustion seeping through her. "It's all right when I'm in it. It's when I step away from it—here with you—back in civilization—"

She broke off as Georgios came in with the coffee tray.

Charles fixed her a cup the way she liked it, with a great deal of cream and sugar, before pouring his own, more Spartan beverage. "Shall I slurp my coffee from the saucer to make you feel less *à l'ouest*?"

"In English we would say 'less at sea.'" Betsy didn't want to think about being at sea, the rocking of the ship, the stench of the dying. "No, there's no need to go to such lengths as that. I don't think you could do anything inelegantly if you tried."

Betsy sipped her coffee in silence, under the watchful gazes of Charles's ancestors. The house boy had brought with him a little plate of macarons. Betsy nibbled a corner of one, just so Charles wouldn't fret. When it didn't taste entirely of ash, she took a second nibble, feeling the warmth return to her fingers and toes.

Betsy finished off her coffee, feeling infinitely restored, and set the elegant cup back down on the tray. "Thank you. I needed desperately to say all that to someone."

"I'm glad I might be that someone." There was a note in his voice that made Betsy turn sharply to look at him. He countered her with smooth urbanity. "Would you like more coffee?"

Betsy leaned closer, looking searchingly at him. She had hurt him and she hadn't meant to. She never meant to, but she did anyway, that's what Ava would say. "I didn't mean it that way. That you were just any someone. You do know that, don't you?"

A wry expression crossed Charles's face. "Perhaps it is safer not to know."

There was no safe. Those villagers thought they were safe—a hospital ship was meant to be safe—Betsy was sick of safe.

Betsy cupped Charles's face in her hands, so he couldn't avoid looking at her. His skin was very smooth. He smelled faintly of expensive shaving soap, overlaid by the insistent aroma of very strong coffee.

"But you *do* know," she said seriously. "You know what you are to me."

He lifted his hands to her wrists, as if to draw her hands away—but didn't. "I know what I cannot be to you."

"Why not?" Betsy demanded recklessly, the vision of all those men rising before her eyes. In three days—no, two now—she'd be back at the front. In two days. Facing death and suffering.

Charles closed his eyes, removing her hands with a great effort of will, leaving them clasped in his own. "You know why." A faint smile touched his lips. "You've said it to me yourself. With great force."

And so she had. But Betsy couldn't remember now why she'd felt it was important. Ava would, she knew, but Ava wasn't here. Ava wasn't even answering her letters.

Betsy leaned forward and kissed his lips, right on that smile. "I was wrong."

"No—no." Charles's hands tightened on hers, whether to hold her close or hold her back, she wasn't sure. "You can't—I can't—"

"Why not?" All the frustration and fear Betsy had been feeling spilled out of her. "I could be dead tomorrow. You could be dead tomorrow. And we'll have let everything we could have had go to waste for the sake of a woman in Paris!"

"Not just a woman. My wife. I can't wish her away." With a sigh, Charles let go of Betsy's hands. He traced the path of a loose lock of hair against her cheek. "I wish I could. But I can't. If I could . . ."

"I know." Betsy turned her head and kissed his palm. "I don't care."

"Betsy." She could see him trying to stay firm and the effort it was costing him. His chest rose unevenly beneath his expensive waistcoat. "You say that now . . ."

"And I'll say it tomorrow"—Betsy punctuated her words by leaning forward and kissing him—"and the next day"—another kiss—"and the day after that."

"I can't think. *Tu m'éblouit. . . . Tu m'enivres.*"

"Am I melting your head of wax?" Betsy asked huskily, pressing a kiss to somewhere in the vicinity of his ear. He was right; it was intoxicating, intoxicating being this close to him, getting to touch him, kiss him; it drove everything else away, all the death and defeat and despair.

"Like Icarus next to the sun. Such a fall as that . . . I will not ruin you," he said desperately, holding her and holding her away at the same time. "Betsy! I will not make you a—how do they say it? A fallen woman."

"You don't need to," Betsy murmured, nuzzling his cheek as his arms slid around her, in direct contradiction of his words. "I've decided to ruin myself."

"Head of wax . . ." he murmured, his lips discovering a particularly tender spot along the side of her neck, as Betsy found herself suddenly a great deal more horizontal than she had been a moment before.

"I'll take that as a yes," she gasped, and lost herself in the feeling of falling.

Chapter Nineteen

For a week now, the battle has continued. Not the battle for Santiago, but the battle for the lives of our men, here, in the hospital tents of Siboney. Away in the hills, our boys still gallantly guard their garrison beneath a flag of truce. Who knows what messages pass between the commanders, what demands and refusals? All we know is that here, beneath our canvas shelters, the struggle continues.

For twenty-four hours I have been on duty with the assistance of one orderly, tending to forty patients suffering variously from fever, measles, and dysentery as well as those wounds meted out by our foes. There are a remarkable number of head wounds, for which treatment with ice is crucial, but ice is scarce and hard to come by. Miss Barton has sent her ship, the *State of Texas*, to Kingston for urgently needed ice, but we can only pray it will return in time for these men, whose lives depend upon constant cool applications.

Never in my life have I felt so helpless. . . .

—Miss Katherine Carson for the St. Louis Star Ledger, *July 8, 1898*

Siboney, Cuba
July 9, 1898

"YOU SHOULD BE SLEEPING." NURSE Hayes set down her lantern by Holt's bed.

Holt had come to like this quiet time when everyone else was snuffling and snoring around him. There was something comforting about watching Nurse Hayes on her rounds, her sure, decisive movements as she took temperatures, held glasses of water to parched lips, applied poultices, soothed away nightmares. In the day, her progress was marked by sometimes raucous commentary as the men vied for her attention. But in this last dark before the dawn, the tent was quiet except for the ever-present slapping of the waves against the shore, the labored breathing of the men, and the swish of Nurse Hayes's skirt as she moved steadily from bed to bed, a small light in a great darkness.

Holt was always the last, the final stop before the light passed out of the tent. "Morning and night don't seem to make much difference when you never get out of bed."

"You mean, aside from that big glowing thing in the sky shining in your eyes?" Nurse Hayes felt his brow with the back of one hand. "No fever. I can tell you that even without the thermometer. I think you're on the mend, Private Holt. You and that cot can part ways soon."

"I don't know. I've gotten kind of attached to it." The strangest part was that Holt wasn't entirely joking. How many days had it been? He'd lost all track of time. It felt like he'd been in this tent, in this cot at the end of the row, for something approaching an eternity. He'd been lying here watching the play of lantern light against the canvas while Noah hammered away at his ark; he'd lain here somewhere between sleep and waking while Drake routed the Armada; he'd followed the progress of Nurse Hayes on her rounds while em-

pires rose and fell. Centuries had come and gone; the world outside
was a vague, hypothetical thing. Anything might lie out there. He
might wake, like Rip Van Winkle, to find himself in a world changed
beyond understanding.

He wasn't quite sure who he was anymore: not the new man he'd
tried to be, but not the old one either, a kaleidoscope of fragments,
shifting and whirling.

Nurse Hayes made a face at him. "You mean this cot's gotten kind
of attached to you. We'll have to peel that mattress off you if you don't
get moving. We need to get you up and walking soon, putting some
weight on that leg. I don't know how you managed to walk as far as
you did on it before."

Holt mustered a weak grin. "Sheer cussedness, I imagine."

Nurse Hayes looked at him sternly. "I would have said idiocy.
Who spends a week tramping around on a leg with a hole in it?"

"It wasn't a big hole."

"Ha," said Nurse Hayes. She paused, hesitating. "I never did
say—it was a good thing you did, saving Paul. A foolhardy thing—
but a good one."

"Anyone would have done the same," Holt mumbled.

"No. They wouldn't. So . . . thank you."

She leaned forward just at the same moment that Holt turned his
head to say something to her and her lips, which had been aiming
for his cheek, brushed his lips instead. What happened next was just
a reflex. Anyone would have done the same. Anyone encountering
a soft pair of lips would have kissed them back. It was just human
nature. Nothing conscious about it. For a whole few glorious seconds
there was nothing in the world but the softness of her lips on his,
flavored with the lingering taste of strong coffee.

And then the coffee was gone. The lips were gone. Nurse Hayes
took a step back, her hand pressed against her mouth. In a muffled

voice, she said, "You can't kiss your nurse. It's contrary to regulations. And if it isn't, it should be!"

"You were the one who kissed me," Holt protested, feeling his honor at stake, although if he had to stake his conscience on it, he wasn't entirely sure he could swear he hadn't. Kissed her that was. He would rather have liked to have gone on kissing her, and that was the most alarming bit of all, and not just for the coffee.

"I kissed your *cheek*." Holt couldn't be quite sure in the gloom, but he thought she was blushing.

Holt put his hand to his cheek. His very smooth cheek. He seized on the welcome distraction. "You shaved me!"

Nurse Hayes removed herself safely to the foot of the bed. "Days ago. You've only just noticed?"

"I haven't been entirely myself." And if he hadn't been entirely himself before, he was even less so now. Every time he looked at Nurse Hayes, all he could think of was that kiss. That very brief, accidental kiss. "And now I know why."

Nurse Hayes folded her arms across her chest. "Yes, because you were battling wound fever from the bullet hole you hadn't bothered to get cleaned when the doctor told you to. *Not* because I removed that hideous growth from your face."

"Was it really that hideous?" Holt had rather liked it. Particularly the way it hid his face. The way it made him feel like another person from that clean-shaved, brushed, and combed Harvard man.

Nurse Hayes snorted. "Are you looking for compliments? Let's just say that your chin isn't weak enough that you need to hide it."

It wasn't precisely the most fulsome of compliments but suddenly the air between them crackled and hissed like damp wood on a campfire. Holt couldn't seem to look away. Neither could she.

Outside, something large crashed and someone cursed with great and inventive fluency.

"What's going on back there?" he croaked.

"Oh, Miss Barton sent the *State of Texas* to Kingston for ice and to Tampa to pick up supplies. It must be back. *Finally*," Nurse Hayes said with feeling, and Holt wasn't sure whether the feeling was for the ice or something else entirely.

"In the middle of the night?" It was a perfectly natural question. It wasn't as though Holt was trying to keep her talking, just so he could keep looking at her, at the way her hair exploded in wisps around her face, at the way she swished back and forth where she stood, as though keeping still were too much effort, at the bright spots of color on her cheeks.

"It's hardly the middle of the night. It's"—Nurse Hayes consulted the watch pinned to her breast—"four seventeen. They can only land the boats between three and six in the morning because of the tides. They figured that out *after* we came over and nearly wound up as matchsticks on the rocks. Going out to the boat isn't such a problem; you can go out there pretty much as you please, but coming back here is another matter entirely." Nurse Hayes bent over to retrieve her lantern, talking all the while. "I'll just go see what's come in, shall I? Private Clark still needs that ice on his eyes and we're down to a fragment of a fragment."

Holt pressed his eyes shut, wishing he'd been asleep when she made her rounds, wishing he hadn't turned his head, wishing he could go back to yesterday.

"Nurse Hayes?" He wasn't sure if saying something would make it better or worse, but he had to try. She paused, turning toward him, poised for a speedy exit. Holt didn't know what to say, so all he said was "I'm sorry."

"For what?" Nurse Hayes bared her teeth at him in something like a smile. "Nothing to be sorry about. Except for getting yourself wounded in the first place. Do try not to do that again."

"Not much chance of it flat on a cot, is there?" Holt nodded at the figure who'd just entered the tent by the flap nearest his bed. "Looks like your relief is here."

"But Kit's not supposed to take over until—" Nurse Hayes turned and went very, very white. *"Ava?"*

The lantern swung wildly as Nurse Hayes swayed on her feet. Holt tried to scramble up to grab her and wound up flopping back flat against his pillow, prone and useless.

"Stop that," said Nurse Hayes, in a voice that didn't sound like hers. "You'll rip your stitches."

But she wasn't looking at Holt. She was staring over him, at the woman who had just come in.

"Hello, Betsy," the new nurse said, in a voice that spoke of chowder and the bean and the cod, where the Lowells spoke only to Cabots and the Cabots spoke only to God.

Nurse Hayes lifted the lantern so it shone directly at her, illuminating a strong-featured face with a wide, thin-lipped mouth and a pair of the most emphatic eyebrows Holt had ever seen. Her uniform, with the white band on the arm, was pristine and crisply ironed, her dark hair pulled close back beneath her cap. This new nurse was taller than Nurse Hayes by several inches, but wiry, in a way that made her seem shorter than she was, while Nurse Hayes's constant motion always made such small considerations as inches seem an irrelevancy.

Nurse Hayes gawked, the lantern trembling in her hand. "But you're—how did you—I'm not hallucinating you, am I? Or dreaming? I might just be dreaming I'm on my rounds and none of this is actually real. I hope I'm not feverish. We don't have enough staff left for me to be feverish."

"You're not dreaming—or feverish," said Holt roughly. "I see her too."

The other woman glanced down at him, taking in his various bandages with a clinical eye. "Who is this?"

"Holt. Private Holt. You might know him as Hold 'Em Holt. Scourge of the bandits of the West. Never mind," said Nurse Hayes, never taking her eyes off the other woman. "Ava—you're not meant to be here. You shouldn't be here. I came to try to save you from all this. There's malaria—and possibly yellow fever—and goodness only knows what else. You didn't need to do this. I never meant—well, maybe I did mean—but . . ."

Holt had never seen Nurse Hayes at a loss like this. Not when she was haranguing him on the verandah of the Tampa Bay Hotel. Not with wounded coming in by the wagonload.

"You did. You meant it. And I'm here." The newcomer spoke in a low, quick voice, so as not to wake the patients. "I got your last letter, Betsy."

Nurse Hayes went very still. She didn't say anything. She appeared to be incapable of speech. "I—Ava . . ."

Holt didn't like the way she looked, not at all. "Maybe you should sit down," he said brusquely.

"No. No. I'm fine." Nurse Hayes gave a little shake, like someone coming out of cold water. She didn't look fine; she looked like someone had punched her in the gut. She looked down at Holt and then back at the new nurse. "Not here. I need—I need to finish my rounds."

Her voice was steady enough, but next to her, Holt could see the way she was shaking, shaking and trying to hide it.

"I'll let you get on with it," said the other woman brusquely. "When did you become so responsible?"

"After you left." Nurse Hayes's face wobbled for a moment before she composed herself. "I'll meet you on the hospital steps."

Holt waited a moment, letting her compose herself, before asking, in what he hoped was a casual tone, "Who was that?"

"My oldest friend."

Holt wanted to say that, even in his limited experience of friendship, friends didn't treat friends like that, they didn't mock them like that—but what did he know? He'd never had a friend he hadn't driven away. The closest he'd ever come to one was Paul, and that under false pretenses.

"Why did you say you weren't finished?" Holt asked bluntly.

"Because I don't know what to say." Holt always thought of Nurse Hayes as formidable, but she looked very young: young and shaken and vulnerable. "We parted so badly. . . . I made such mistakes."

"Well, you're both here now," Holt said.

"Yes. We are." That thought didn't seem to bring her much comfort. She scrubbed a hand over her eyes and then turned to Holt with a shadow of her old sass. "Shouldn't you be sleeping?"

There was something so gallant about it, about that unconvincing attempt. Holt felt something clench uncomfortably in the region of his chest.

"If you say so." For all her bravado, she looked so forlorn. Holt found himself possessed of an entirely impractical urge to slay dragons for her. But he was stuck on this cot, so all he could do was say, "And—don't worry. You'll be all right."

Siboney, Cuba
July 9, 1898

IT WAS PROBABLY, BETSY REALIZED, a bad thing if her patients were trying to reassure her.

Not patients. One patient. A patient she'd kissed. Accidentally.

Sort of. Mostly. She couldn't think about that now. There was no room in her head for it. Betsy's brain felt like a beehive, everything buzzing all at once. She was too tired to think. She felt like she'd been stripped bare and spun around in circles.

And there was Ava, sitting on the steps of the hospital.

Betsy sat down next to her, drawing her knees up to her chest. The view from the porch was beautiful: the jagged peaks of the distant mountains, the moonlight on the sea. One would never know that away up there past the roofs of the hospital tents, up among the distant hills, men were fighting and dying, every step of every trail steeped with the blood of the wounded.

"I can't believe you're here."

"Neither can I," said Ava drily. "They refused us permission to land, you know—the army. No nurses needed at the front, they said."

"No nurses needed?" Betsy didn't know whether to laugh or cry. They were all worn thin. "Yes, you can see we're just twiddling our thumbs, nothing to do here. I've only been on shift for eighteen hours."

"They sent us on to Tampa. There's a place called Picnic Island, where they've put typhoid patients."

"Typhoid?" Betsy could feel every muscle in her body tighten. Her vision blurred, fragmenting into red spots. Of all her nightmares, Ava, exposing herself to typhoid, falling ill, dying. "But—typhoid—Ava . . ."

Ava eyed her curiously. "It's work that needs to be done. But there were plenty there to do it—and you were here. So when I heard that Barton's ship was in port, I got them to take me along with the dried beans."

That was enough to shake Betsy out of her private panic. "You stowed away? *You?*"

"I didn't stow away; I asked the captain nicely," said Ava primly.

"I wanted to spare you all this."

"I know," said Ava. "You said that in your letter. What I could make out. What were you writing with, a quill?"

"A pen with a broken nib." They hadn't been allowed to have pens at the place she was then. Betsy was meant to avoid any exertion, mental or physical, but particularly mental. Total rest, that was the rule. No papers. No letters. But Betsy had managed to find them all the same. Because they didn't seem to understand that the silence was worse than anything else; in the silence, there was too much time to think. And remember. And mourn.

Betsy wrapped her arms around herself, around the emptiness where there had once been another someone, her throat clogged with all the things she couldn't say, all the things she wasn't ready to explain, not to Ava, not now.

"You didn't have to try to take my place," said Ava.

Betsy fought the tears back down, finding her voice with difficulty. "You wouldn't have signed up if I hadn't taunted you into it."

Ava looked at her levelly. "I wouldn't have signed up if I hadn't wanted to sign up."

"But if you knew—if you had any idea—"

"Yes, yes," said Ava, without heat. "Do me the courtesy of believing I know my own mind as well as you know yours."

Betsy gave a hiccupping laugh. "I don't know my mind at all anymore."

"Ha," said Ava. She was quiet for a moment before asking, "Was it really as bad as all that?"

"Worse." There was a hole inside Betsy. It was like Holt's wound, a festering abscess, only this one couldn't be drained; it pulsed there beneath the skin, a constant pain that could be dulled only by pretending it wasn't there. But it was. Always. "I had no idea. You were right about all of it."

"You were right too." Ava kept her eyes trained on the surf, not looking at Betsy. Her back was painfully straight. "I got back to Concord—and I just couldn't make myself settle. I made myself miserable. I made everyone around me miserable too. My cousin finally told me she was sick of having my face sour her porridge, and at that rate she'd rather someone *a little less acute and a little more obliging.*"

Betsy had forgotten what a good mimic Ava could be. She used to have Betsy in stitches parodying the other girls in their boardinghouse. It had been a long time since they'd laughed together like that. A long time since everything.

"What did you do?" she asked hoarsely.

Ava quirked a dark brow. "I found another cousin to tend to her. If there's one thing with which I'm well-endowed, it's an embarrassment of relations."

Betsy stared down at the stained fabric of her apron, like a blotted copybook, all her mistakes written on her for anyone to see. "I didn't mean to make you lose your position."

"I made me lose my position," said Ava firmly. "I shouldn't have been there in the first place. I wasn't suited to it. You were right about that too. So I went home—and when I heard that the DAR was paying women to train as nurses and come to Cuba . . ."

Betsy risked a wobbly grin. "They must not have been able to teach you much. You'd done the course already."

"There's always something to learn," said Ava, sounding entirely like her old self again.

Betsy blinked hard. "I thought I'd ruined everything forever."

"It wasn't you. Well, it wasn't *all* you. I was jealous," Ava said gruffly. "And guilty."

"Guilty? For taking the ticket?"

"No. About your father." Ava sat up a little straighter, with the air of one determined to make a clean breast. "That night he took us to dinner in Northampton. There was a rattle in his breathing I didn't like. I should have said something. I knew I should say something. But I was afraid he wouldn't take me seriously. Or that I was wrong. What did I know? I wasn't even a medical student, just a girl who liked to tag along on her father's house calls. So I didn't say anything. And he died."

"But—" It wasn't Ava's fault; it was Betsy's.

Ava clasped her hands together in her lap, the knuckles very white. "You were *supposed* to have gone to Greece with your father. You'd been planning it for as long as I'd known you. If I'd said something that night in Northampton—"

"I killed him," Betsy blurted out. That's what Alex had told her. She'd killed their father just like she'd killed their mother. She ruined everything she touched. Thoughtless, careless, selfish. "It wasn't you. I killed him by dragging him out to Northampton in the dead of winter."

Ava turned and stared at her, her dark brows drawing together. "He had pneumonia. It was already in his lungs by the time he took the train to Northampton. I heard it." Ava's face was as stern and unwavering as a mask from a Greek tragedy. "His death is on my conscience, not yours. In Greece—how could I accept your charity? I could barely look at you."

Betsy couldn't make sense of it, of any of it. She felt as though the world had flipped on its head. "I didn't know."

"I was jealous too. I was jealous of you and jealous of your new friends. That just made the guilt worse," Ava added, with clinical detachment. "I thought you'd hate me if you knew I could have saved your father and didn't. And even if you didn't hate me, you'd be bored of me."

"How could I ever be bored of you? No one takes me to bits

and puts me back together again the way you do." Betsy looked at Ava, biting hard on her lower lip. "I thought you were appalled by me."

"I was," said Ava honestly. "But also jealous. And guilty."

They sat there together in silence, their shoulders touching, letting themselves lean into each other as the darkness of the sky lightened into dawn. Ava didn't hug. Ava never hugged. But it was enough.

"I don't want you to die."

"I don't want me to die either," said Ava briskly, standing up. "And I don't intend to. Not now, at any rate. Come. We came here to work, not paint watercolors of pretty prospects."

Betsy tugged at Ava's skirt. "But the fevers . . ."

"Betsy." Ava squatted back down again. "I was in and out of my father's surgery before I could toddle. I've had every disease you can name and then some—including typhoid. Why do you think I was never sick at Smith? It's not just because I wrapped up warmly."

"You won't need to wrap up warmly here." Betsy let Ava pull her up. "Well, except at night. It does get cold at night."

"How many patients do you have?" Ava asked, all brisk and businesslike.

But that was Ava. Having once said something, she would never admit to it again. What was done was done. And there were patients to be cared for. Betsy led Ava down the steps toward the tents. "We had nearly five hundred in our care a week ago, but about half that now."

"You've discharged them?"

"Some. Some didn't make it." Too many. Betsy forced herself to focus on the matter at hand. "We have a hospital building, two tent wards, and a surgery tent. We keep the sickest men in the hospital—they're less exposed to the elements there—and the milder cases in

the tents. Oh, this is one of our surgeons." Betsy accosted Dr. Stringfellow as he charged down the well-worn path from the hospital
to the surgery tent, smelling strongly of coffee. "He's on loan to us
from the army. We borrowed him and just never gave him back. Dr.
Stringfellow, this is Nurse Saltonstall."

"Very well, good," said Dr. Stringfellow, trying to navigate
around them.

Ava planted herself firmly in the doctor's path. "Dr. Lawrence
Stringfellow? I read your article in the *Lancet*. The one on the case of
the anteverted wandering liver."

"It sounds like a Sherlock Holmes story," said Betsy brightly.
"The Case of the Wandering Liver."

Neither of them paid any attention to her. Dr. Stringfellow had
stopped and was looking at Ava with the attention he usually only
afforded particularly interesting injuries.

"It was a very strange case," said Dr. Stringfellow modestly.

"Was it?" demanded Ava. "Was it, really? If one were to afford
women's health the attention we afford other branches of medicine . . ."

"You believe this is purely a female condition?"

Ava set her chin in a way Betsy knew well. "The woman had suffered a stillbirth at full term. Surely that must play some role."

Dr. Stringfellow looked distinctly intrigued but also skeptical.
"Yes, twenty-three years before."

"As you yourself pointed out, she had been suffering from an in-
guinal hernia for roughly that same period of time. If one assumes . . ."
Ava rattled off a spate of technicalities in something that vaguely re-
sembled Latin.

Dr. Stringfellow, however, appeared to be utterly electrified by
each and every multisyllabic incomprehensibility. He countered with
gobbledygook of his own. It was like watching a sport for which one
didn't understand any of the rules.

At some point, Dr. Stringfellow had offered Ava his arm. At some point, she had taken it. They wandered together into the surgery tent, arguing fiercely and gazing into one another's eyes.

A *coup de foudre*, that's what the French called it.

That's what Charles would have called it.

Betsy let out her breath, feeling distinctly wobbly. She needed to lie down. She had been on shift for over eighteen hours.

In Lamia, she had worked twenty-four hours at a time.

In Lamia, where she had seen Charles again . . .

Chapter Twenty

Dear Ava,

Did you think I'd given up hope? It's not that I've given up writing at you—I will keep on writing at you, you know, until you write me back—it's just that I've been so busy. I've lost track of what post I'm on. We set up a Red Cross hospital in a place called Lamia back in May. It's a beautiful town, right on the Aegean, with crumbling Venetian walls on a hilltop and the cafés bustling with officers and attachés and international newspapermen. I even met an American attaché who had come all the way over from Vienna so as not to miss the excitement.

And excitement we got. The guns started going, the word came it was all hands to the front, and we nurses rushed off to Domokos.

It was a very different thing nursing men where they fell rather than in a hospital. The villagers looked at us as though we were mad and perhaps we were, but, Ava, some of those men wouldn't have made it back to Lamia to be tended. But we were there and we tended them, right in the trenches. I helped patch up none other than the great Cipriani himself and got him on a stretcher to the coast. I won't lie; I was scared witless. The noise *was like nothing you could imagine. But it would all have been worth it if the Greeks hadn't retreated and kept on retreating. We kept waiting for them to stop and take a stand, but the batteries kept right on going, all the way back to Lamia.*

If the crown prince had only held his ground . . . But that's a whole other topic.

After Domokos, Dr. Kalopothakes invited me to nurse with her at a place on the western front called Vonitsa—you can't imagine how much I've come to adore Dr. K. She scowls at me almost as feelingly as you do. But she admits I've come on rather nicely and the boys seem to like me even if my sheet corners never will tuck flat. It felt just like Vólos again, sleeping on the floor of a dirty old schoolhouse and being grudgingly praised by Dr. K.

We thought the Greeks would make another stand after Domokos . . . but they didn't. And now we're on a sort of pause. They call it a truce, which means everyone stands and glares and keeps their guns trained on the other side, ready to go off at a moment's notice.

You'd think that would mean an end to casualties, wouldn't you? But the fever has taken up where the Turks left off. I'm back to dear old Lamia, where the military hospital has now been largely given over to typhoid patients. . . . It's July now, and I'm rather feeling the heat. Or maybe it's just the twenty-four-hour shifts. I never thought I would miss Northampton in January! But I do. And I miss you.

Write me.

> *All my love,*
> *Betsy*

—Miss Betsy Hayes '96 to Ava Saltonstall '96

Lamia, Greece
July 1897

WHEN BETSY CLIMBED ABOARD THE royal yacht, there was Charles.

The other three nurses to be honored with a royal invitation to supper were clattering around her, curtsying to Queen Olga and Prince Nicholas and the crown prince and Crown Princess Sophie. Betsy hastily bent her knees in a curtsy too, a rather belated and perfunctory one. The queen gave her an indulgent smile; Prince Nicholas made a joke about Americans and their democratic ways.

Betsy smiled by rote and answered by rote, because there, behind the royal family, among the sailors and courtiers, the officers and hangers-on, there was Charles in evening dress, everything formal and correct, his sun-streaked hair sleeked down, every inch the aristocrat, but when he looked at her, as she was looking at him, the corners of his eyes crinkled and he was her Charles again, and they were in his apartment in Athens with the afternoon sun slanting through the bedroom windows.

Betsy could feel her cheeks heat with a warmth that had nothing to do with the setting sun and everything to do with the man across the deck and the weight of a gold coin at the base of her throat.

She had worn that coin—for luck, for Charles—since Athens, never knowing whether it was a promise or a farewell.

That was the good thing about being ridiculously busy: it hadn't given her much time to worry about being ruined. One didn't fret about being fallen when one was surrounded by the actual fallen, with the Turks on the march and the sound of artillery loud in one's ears. And there was very little energy left for musing about what was justified for love and was it love and if so what happened next when one was on shift for twenty-four hours at a time, taking temperatures and soothing the delirious. And perhaps, just perhaps, Charles was part of the reason for it all, because if she was careening from post to post, she wasn't back in Athens, having to confront all the uncertainties from which the exigencies of war had saved her.

There was no future in it. Betsy knew there was no future in it, and yet, she had done what she had done, and now here they were, on the royal yacht, seeing one another for the first time since May under the eye of the royal family and assorted hangers-on. They were on the deck of a ship; there was no privacy and no hope of privacy.

And there was Charles, stepping forward, and the queen saying, with a twinkle in her eye, "But I know Miss Hayes needs no introduction to you, Monsieur de Robecourt." Betsy had a horrible moment where she felt like a rabbit surprised in a field, before the queen added, "Or to anyone who studies the past."

"I'm just a student still," said Betsy, her throat very dry. She knew she should be looking at the queen, but her eyes were only for Charles. "Monsieur de Robecourt."

"Miss Hayes." He bent over her hand in the continental fashion, but he held it a moment longer than strictly necessary.

The queen moved on to be charming to one of the other nurses, an Athenian society girl who had taken the first aid course with Betsy, and actually passed it.

Charles was looking at Betsy. "I see you've kept your luck."

Betsy put a hand to her neck, where the ribbon that held his token was poking just a bit above her collar.

"Yes. Close to my heart," she said, and felt like the worst kind of sentimental fool.

They were *en famille* that night, the queen assured them, utterly informal, although *informal* to the royal family still meant a rather staggering degree of ceremony. The table had been set out on the upper deck, the lantern light glinting off silver and crystal; there was something about eating outdoors, almost a picnic, with the smell of the sea and the shadows settling close around that created an odd sense of intimacy. As a courtesy to Betsy, all the conversation at supper was in English, yet another mark of the queen's regard. The queen had adopted Betsy as a sort of personal pet, her very own American who had chosen to nurse for Greece, whom the queen had championed and sent to the front when the doctors wouldn't.

Betsy felt the pressure of that favor and did her best to be as charming as she could, telling stories of the ward, doing impressions of the men, jumping from topic to topic until she was dizzy with it. Although the queen seemed to approve, Charles just looked and looked and said little and Betsy couldn't tell whether he was charmed or utterly put off and wondering what he'd ever seen in her.

"Did you receive the icon I had sent you?" the queen asked Betsy, as the savory was taken away and jellied sweets set out on the table.

"Oh, yes, the men adore it." To the company at large, Betsy said, "We have a cursed bed, you see. First one man died in it, and then another, and after that . . . well, you can imagine. Even the sickest refused to be brought near it. They'd struggle and upset themselves. And we really don't have the room to have a bed no one will use— they're packed in like sardines as it is. So Her Majesty was kind enough to send us an icon. We made quite a show of installing it. It was carried in procession through the ward, and after that every single man in the place had to kiss it."

It had seemed to her quite insanitary, but they all had typhoid anyway; it wasn't as though they were spreading it beyond the confines of the ward. And it had been wonderful to see those haggard, wasted faces light up as the icon was brought to them. It had done more for them than any of the doctor's doses.

Charles toyed with the stem of his wineglass, lifting it so the liquid within glowed with hidden depths where the lantern light touched it. "I thought you had little tolerance for signs and wonders, Miss Hayes."

Betsy made herself address the party generally and not just Charles. "It isn't my way, but—if there's anything nursing has taught me, it's that the most dangerous enemy isn't the disease or the wound, but despair."

Princess Sophie, who was rather a darling despite being the sister of the kaiser, was nodding thoughtfully. Prince Nicholas looked bored.

"Is it a question of morale?" asked one of the military men. Betsy had forgotten his name, or perhaps she had never heard it, too busy watching Charles while pretending not to watch Charles.

"That's it exactly. We've had men in a reasonably decent state who have fretted themselves to nothing, and others we thought we'd see in a box who had the most remarkable recoveries." Betsy sat up straighter, remembering the many men who had passed through her care, but particularly the ones who had defied the odds to stagger away on their own two feet again. "If kissing an icon makes them believe there's hope, I'll carry it myself and light the incense too."

"And say a prayer to the blessed Virgin?" teased Charles. At least, she thought he was teasing.

"If she'll hear me." Betsy took a gulp of her wine. Perhaps she ought to be addressing her prayers to the Magdalen instead. Not that she could say that. Not here. Why on earth did they have to have this conversation here?

Because she hadn't gone back to Athens.

Because she'd spent three days in his bed—well, the better part of three days; some of it had been spent touring hospitals and sending sharp reports back to the war office, and she'd always gone back to Aikaterini's at night, to avoid the servants talking—and then she'd gone away and not come back, even when she was offered the chance of a furlough.

Because there was a war on, Betsy told herself self-righteously.

But that wasn't the whole reason. Was it because to fall into a man's bed once—well, several times in the space of one week—could be accounted as carelessness, but to do it again would be to form a practice? She loved Charles; she was in love with Charles. But to love someone and to be someone's mistress were two very different things entirely.

It was much easier to run about being noble and avoid the whole question.

Like she ran away from everything, Ava would say. Betsy grimaced into her wineglass. That was only part of what Ava would say if she were here. If she knew. If she had answered any of Betsy's letters.

A servant was making the rounds with a box of Egyptian cigarettes, of the sort the royal ladies smoked—and the faster girls at Smith.

Defiantly, Betsy reached for one too.

"You don't have to," said Charles, in an undertone.

Betsy ignored him, waving her cigarette about in the air. "How does one light one of these things?"

BETSY WAS RATHER THE WORSE for wear the next morning when it came time to appear for her shift.

Mornings always began with the making up of beds, with orderlies helping to shake the great sacks of straw. The mattresses felt even heavier than usual, the sheets more unwieldy. The smells of the ward made Betsy's stomach turn.

That's what she got for drinking too much of the royal family's Burgundy last night. And attempting a cigarette. Betsy grimaced at the memory. She'd done it partly to annoy Ava (even if Ava wasn't there to see it) and mostly to show Charles how worldly she was, although coughing herself sick while half the party pounded her on the back and the other half offered helpful tips probably hadn't made that point quite as well as she would have liked.

At eight, the bell rang, heralding the doctor, there to make his rounds. It was Betsy's turn to escort the doctor, answer his questions, and write down his instructions. They'd just finished their tour of the ward when the bell rang again. But this time it wasn't a doctor or a delivery.

It was Charles.

He stood in the corridor, looking entirely out of place in his summer suit, shifting his hat from one hand to the other.

He smiled crookedly. "I've come to see this cursed bed of yours."

"Not cursed anymore," said Betsy as the doctor barked her name, impatient with visitors. "Doctor, this is Monsieur le Baron de Robecourt, who is visiting with Their Majesties." Nothing averted censure like a few noble titles tossed about.

Charles bowed to the doctor. "Her Majesty and Their Highnesses"— oh dear, she'd got the titles wrong again, hadn't she?—"spoke of their pleasure in touring the hospital and suggested I do the same."

The doctor was clearly not amused, but one didn't controvert a royal order. Betsy couldn't remember the queen saying anything of the kind, but, then, she didn't remember much of the end of the evening, and what she did remember she wished she didn't.

"All right, then," said Betsy. She turned away, wishing her hair were cleaner and her uniform didn't have quite so many stains on it. "This is the typhoid ward. We have thirty-eight patients at present. All the men's personal belongings are taken away when they arrive, particularly hats and belts. Some of these men are so weak that the pressure of a belt or the weight of a standard army blanket would be an impossible burden to them."

Sister Psara called it a white ward. White sheets, white pajamas, everything light and easy to boil.

"Why is that man strapped to his bed?"

"Some of the men grow violent in the extremes of fever." Poor Protopappas was sleeping peacefully now with the aid of chloral. But yesterday he had smashed a medicine bottle and tried to cut his own throat. "They think they're being attacked by the enemy or they try to break out and get home. I was on watch at midnight one night when one of the men tried to get through a window with his mattress and two of the planks of his bed still bound to his back."

Charles looked at her with concern. "You weren't hurt?"

"He didn't appreciate my trying to give him a dose of chloral but it took effect quickly enough. And there's always an orderly to help."

Betsy felt she was giving the wrong impression somehow. The men weren't dangerous; they didn't mean her harm. They were scared and suffering and it was her job to help them. Besides, she wasn't such a delicate flower as all that. Even if she did feel vile just now.

"Here," she said, anxious to change the subject. "Here's the queen's icon."

It had been affixed with all due ceremony to the easternmost wall of the ward. With a mischievous look at Betsy, Charles leaned over and pressed his lips to the bright paint.

"Charles!" Betsy protested, and then looked around to make sure no one had heard. No one but all the men, of course. And her fellow nurse, Sophie, who was also on duty and very studiously not looking. Betsy dropped her voice. "You shouldn't have done that."

Charles turned his hat over in his hand. "Do you believe the saint intercedes only for the sick? There are illnesses other than those of the body."

Was he sick for her or sick of her? Betsy couldn't stand it anymore. "Come into the garden for a moment—and then you really must go. I'm meant to be taking the men their breakfasts and they all need something different depending on their condition."

Betsy led Charles quickly into the walled garden, the sun dazzling after the determined gloom of the ward, the air rich with the scent of roses and hollyhocks, geraniums and begonias, driving out the stench of carbolic and death.

"It's beautiful," he said, looking around wonderingly at the flowers so carefully tended by the gardener, such a wonder after Sister Psara's white ward.

"Yes, like one of your Fragonard paintings," she said, and flushed at the memory of the last time she had been in Charles's apartment, lingering kiss following lingering kiss as they had said goodbye only to say goodbye again and again and again.

"But more beautiful a garden than any of those for having you in it." The compliment sounded awkward. It wasn't like Charles to be awkward. He stood near her but not touching her. "You didn't write."

"I wasn't sure you would want me to. After—well. You know." The morning sun felt very warm, even in the cool of the garden. Betsy traced the contours of a rose, just the right side of overblown. "And I've been very busy."

"I can see that," Charles said drily.

Not too busy to write Ava. Not too busy to go on picnics with the other nurses. But he didn't need to know any of that. Sometimes one had to hide not because one cared too little but because one cared too much. Betsy plucked a geranium, absently shredding the petals. *He loves me, he loves me not . . .*

"What was I to say?" What could she say? Once, they had been friends. One might write a friend. But once that line had been crossed—Betsy didn't know what they were. What she was. None of the options were good.

Charles reached out and took her hands, shredded foliage and all. "May I see you again? Not here?"

What for? Betsy wanted to ask. She wasn't sure they could go back, and, after last night, she knew they couldn't go forward, not as they were.

Betsy's throat felt very raw. "I'm about to start my twenty-four hours on—but I've off on Thursday. If you'll be here that long."

Four days from now. It felt like a test.

Charles didn't budge. "I'll be here as long as I need to be."

Betsy wasn't sure why that made her want to cry. She blinked hard, asking hoarsely, "What about Delphi? Isn't it the season?"

Charles look at her curiously. "The war has stopped the excavations almost entirely. There are no workmen to dig," he clarified.

"Oh." Somehow, Betsy had never quite made the connection in her head. The war seemed a thing removed from that other Greece, the Greece of ruins and treks. It had never occurred to her that the men she nursed might be the same men who sifted the rubble from the buried monuments of Delphi.

It had been some consolation to think that while her world crumbled in flame and fever, back in the rest of Greece the peaceful march of scholarship went on, that tea and cakes were had and inscriptions discovered and debated.

She ought to have realized that was nonsense, but she hadn't, and it hit her like a blow, like discovering what one thought was a solid wall was nothing but a painted backdrop, flimsy and false.

Betsy looked at Charles in sudden panic, not seeing her lover but her friend. "Was this a dreadful mistake? The war? It seemed such a good idea back in March, but . . . I've seen so many hurt, Charles. So many lives wasted. And now this truce! Was it all for nothing?"

Charles lifted his shoulders in a shrug. "Who can say? The history of the world is driven by blunders and misapprehensions—and actions that seemed like a good idea at the time."

That wasn't what she had wanted to hear. Betsy didn't like that at all, the idea of history as an accumulation of accidents. "Maybe your history," she said ungraciously. "Your revolution went all to blood and despotism. But ours stuck."

"You're young yet," Charles said gently, "you and your country both. There is time yet for you to make your grand mistakes."

"That's cynical." Betsy scowled up at him. "Is that how you think of me? In my infancy?"

"Say . . . unspoiled."

"You know better than that," Betsy shot back. She folded her arms across her chest. "Don't you need to be getting back?"

It would have been easier to stay indignant if Charles didn't look so stricken with remorse. "I've offended you."

"I'm tired. And sticky." And queasy. The rich food on the ship hadn't sat well with her. Nothing sat well with her. Betsy suspected it was the heat, turning her stomach, making her lethargic and queasy. She didn't have time to be lethargic and queasy.

"Will I see you on Thursday?"

It was impossible to stay angry with Charles. He was what he was, just as she was what she was, American and prickly. "Did you really think I would say no?"

He smiled ruefully at her. "With you, my thinking is not at its best."

That was strange, because Betsy found the opposite to be true. When she was with Charles, she felt sharp and clever, as if she were a character on a stage playing to an appreciative audience. Not that it was a role, really. The role she was playing was herself, only more so. American, outspoken, just a bit daring. The same sort of role she played for the queen.

Right now the only role Betsy was meant to be playing, she reminded herself, was that of nurse. She had thirty-eight breakfasts to prepare and thirty-eight temperatures to take and she was already late. Taking herself firmly in hand, she marched off to wrangle with the cook over just how many peritonitis patients needed their gruel iced.

True to his word, Charles came for her on Thursday morning.

Betsy felt strange in her walking dress instead of her uniform, strange crossing the courtyard and going out into the street, strange leaving her charges behind, even for the day. Strange walking next to Charles, just Charles, rather than a group of nurses.

"I feel like I'm sneaking out," Betsy confided to him as he helped her into a hired trap.

"Dereliction of duty?" Charles settled himself on the seat beside her, taking the reins in a practiced hand. His voice sounded a little flat.

Betsy snuck a look at him sideways. "No, not that. Not just that. When we first got here, whenever people would see us in our nurses' uniforms, they would come running to us, begging for help." Betsy shivered at the memory of those mothers with their hollow-eyed children, and the tiny bundles that, when unwrapped, turned out to be babies, too weak with hunger to cry. "We sent to the queen and she arranged for a doctor to be brought from Athens and a house taken as a hospital and dispensary. They distribute clothing too. I go there when I have the time. Some of those children . . . those poor children. They've scarcely had time to be children."

"You cannot save everyone." Was it her imagination or did Charles sound more impatient than sympathetic? He guided their trap around a cart. "You'll make yourself sick."

Betsy bit her lip. It was true. She hadn't been feeling her best. But those children . . .

"Did you ever think what your life might have been had your

home been invaded?" Betsy demanded, trying to get some sort of reaction.

Charles smiled faintly. "It was. In '71. The Prussians had Paris under siege. I was sixteen. Too young to fight, but old enough to want to."

Betsy hadn't been born yet in 1871. "Yes, but you didn't lose your home or your livelihood the way these people have."

"Only my honor." His face was bleak. "Ah, look. We arrive."

Charles pulled the trap to the side of the road, looping the reins, before Betsy could ask him what he'd meant.

He never, she realized, as he helped her down from the trap, spoke of anything truly personal. She had told him about her father and a little bit of Alex and Smith and of her wretchedness over the *Albania*, but he never spoke of his father or family or childhood, or if he did, only obliquely. It wasn't just his wife he avoided speaking of; that she could understand, just as she avoided discussing her rift with Ava. It was anything personal.

Maybe she was being silly to break life into boxes like that. Ideas were personal, philosophies were personal. So what if they spoke only in platonic allegories? They were scholars, both of them. The life of the mind was the life of the soul. Or something like that.

"Watch your step," he warned her. "The highway was mined with dynamite. But we should be safe enough on the path into the hills."

"Where are we?" Betsy asked. She felt that she ought to know. But she was so tired, so bleary after weeks of night watches.

"Where else?" said Charles, with an attempt at lightness that failed utterly. He lifted a handkerchief to his forehead. It was still early, but the day was already broiling and there had been little shade on the main road. "Thermopylae."

Betsy looked at the pitted, war-scarred road behind them and the wooded hills ahead with a sudden superstitious chill. They had died to a man at Thermopylae. Gloriously, yes. But still. They'd died.

"I had thought you would like to see it," said Charles a little unsteadily.

"I've wanted to see it, but I've been afraid to," Betsy confessed. "The men talk of going to the hot springs at Thermopylae the way we would—oh, going to Atlantic City. It's utterly mundane to them. But I keep thinking of Leonidas and his Spartans. I guess I don't want to face the possibility of defeat."

A curious expression crossed her lover's face. Something like pity. "Didn't you know it happened long ago?"

Betsy squinted up at him. "Thermopylae?"

"Defeat," Charles said heavily. "Months ago. This truce—it is only a way of saving face. The war is over in all but name."

Betsy didn't want to hear it. If he was right, it had all been for nothing. All the men she'd nursed; all the men she'd seen die. All those children who'd lost their homes, who'd lost their fathers. All those babies, starving.

"Is the path that way?" she asked, without looking back. Her voice sounded high and strange.

She could hear Charles's footsteps behind her as she plunged up the pass, between the encroaching trees. "My darling . . ."

Betsy turned sharply to face him. "Am I? Your darling?"

His face was gray and tired in the morning sun, the lines around his eyes deeper than usual. "Can you have any doubts?"

Her doubts had doubts. She scrunched up her face against the sun. "I was wondering if you had brought me here to tell me to my face that it was all . . . oh, I don't know. A bit of madness."

"A glorious madness." He put his hands on her shoulders and she found herself leaning into him, into the familiar warmth and smell of him, his jacket beneath her cheek. Fleetingly she felt him rest his cheek against the top of her hat. She could feel him trembling; his shirt and waistcoat were damp with sweat. "If this is madness, I have no desire to be sane."

Betsy pulled back and looked at him. That was all very well, but the world didn't see it that way. She supposed they could live in glorious sin, but as wild as she might have been, part of her balked at that. She wasn't sure she had it in her to be a scarlet woman, not really.

"Charles, what do we *do?*"

He sat down on a rock, drawing her down with him. "An annulment, I think. One will have to apply to the Pope. . . ."

Betsy stared at him. She could feel the rock sharp and uncomfortable beneath her skirt and underthings. "You mean—marriage?"

"What else? Why do you think I followed you here? Why do you think I stayed?" He dropped his head in remorse. "I ought to have asked you more elegantly."

"It isn't the manner of the asking that matters." She hadn't expected him to ask her at all. This was what she'd wanted, what she hadn't even dared dream of, spending their lives together, excavating together, being together, but— "What about your wife? Won't she mind?"

"My wife has not been my wife for a very long time," Charles said brusquely. "It would have been different had she borne an heir. But as she has not . . ."

There was something about this that bothered Betsy deeply. "But what if she doesn't agree?"

"I cannot imagine she will." Charles gazed out at the pass along which the Spartans had once marched to death and glory. "It would be easier if she would. She might retire with honor to a nunnery. But even if she does not . . . these things can be arranged."

"It seems . . . medieval. And cruel."

"She would waste no sympathy on you." Charles hunched forward. He was shivering, Betsy realized. The day was hot, but he was shivering. "It will be a scandal. But I have weathered scandal before. And you—I do not think you fear it."

"Charles? Are you unwell?" Betsy asked, with sudden alarm.

"Do I need to be unwell to admit that I love you? I love you with every part of this frail and feeble form. I love you with my mind and my heart and my soul," he said fiercely, and Betsy would have been far more moved by it had she not seen, with sudden horror, the glassiness of his eyes, the sheen of sweat on his forehead.

Betsy's mouth was dry. She was a nurse; she ought to have seen it before. But she'd been too busy nursing her wounded pride. "Charles . . ."

Charles grasped her wrist in an unsteady clasp, his eyes brilliant and unfocused as he stared at her. "You give me new life. You give me my youth back."

"You're not that old." He wasn't that old, but something was terribly wrong. She'd noticed he wasn't himself, but it had never occurred to her to wonder why. "You're shaking."

"*Je vis, je meurs: je me brûle et me noie, / J'ai chaud extrême en endurant froidure . . .*" Charles muttered.

I live, I die: I burn and I drown, I'm hot and cold . . .

It was a poem, a love poem, but this wasn't love he was burning with.

Betsy lifted a hand to his head. "Charles. Charles, *stop*. You're burning up."

"With love," he insisted, and tried to kiss her hand.

Betsy pressed his hand hard against her cheek, trying to still the sudden panic in her chest. "It's a fever, Charles. You have a fever."

Chapter Twenty-One

Yesterday, after a week of tense anticipation, the truce ended, and we braced ourselves for an influx of wounded. The sound of the guns reverberated all the way down to the coast. But before the worst could come, the flag of truce flew again, and not a moment too soon. News has come of relief for our hard-pressed heroes in the form of fresh troops, not yet weak and fevered from months of poor rations and inhospitable conditions.

Fevers stalk our troops. Tertian fever (which some call malaria), typhus, and other infections run rife among our weakened men. There are whispers of the dreaded yellow fever, which claims lives wherever it roams.

Your own correspondent will admit to feeling not quite herself. . . .

—*Miss Katherine Carson for the* St. Louis Star Ledger, *July 12, 1898*

❧

Siboney, Cuba
July 13, 1898

"YOU HAVE A FEVER. HOW can you have a fever?"

Holt would have protested but his teeth were clattering together too hard to speak. He couldn't have a fever; he was too cold to have a fever. He felt like he was encased in frost. He wasn't sure how it had happened. He'd just woken up this way, soaked through and shivering for all he was worth, as if someone had dumped him in a lake in winter.

Nurse Hayes's familiar face swam into view. Holt tried very hard to stop shaking; it felt embarrassing, somehow, which was silly, since Nurse Hayes had already seen him in every possible condition. But he didn't want her to see him this way. Helpless. Unable to control the movements of his own body.

"No. No, no, no. What did I miss?" She scrabbled at the bedclothes, peeling away the sodden sheets. Holt was curled in a ball on his side. She rolled him over to get at his leg, yanking down the bandage to peer at his wound, nose to thigh. "It's not infected anymore. It's closing nicely. What else? What am I missing?"

Holt made an effort to pat her hand. "S'all right."

"No, it's not all right!" She glared at him, then grimaced. "I'm meant to be soothing you, not the other way around."

Holt felt like there was something he should be saying to her, something important, but the cold claimed him again, making his whole body convulse.

Red-hot pincers drove into his brain. "Head hurts," he mumbled, and felt like a baby for admitting it.

Don't tell, that was the mantra of his childhood. Never admit pain. Never admit weakness. Hide until it passed.

But where could he hide? Nurse Hayes had seen him inside and out.

"Stay here," Nurse Hayes said. She appeared shortly thereafter—at least, Holt thought it was shortly; time did funny things—dragging Dr. Stringfellow behind her. Nurse Hayes had the doctor by the hand and was yanking him forward like a very determined tugboat.

"I don't understand it. The wound looks clean. What did I miss?"

"Ah, you again," said Dr. Stringfellow, looking down at Holt.

"Hello," Holt managed. His eyes hurt. Everything hurt.

But his head was clear. Aside from the pain, that was. It wasn't like last time, when he'd been drifting. He knew where he was. It was just his body betraying him this time, not his mind. He wasn't wandering the halls of his father's house. He was here, in a tent, with Nurse Hayes, and aside from the pain and the chills, he would have been content to stay where he was so long as Nurse Hayes was there with him.

Nurse Hayes grasped Holt's hand. He wasn't sure she realized she was doing it, but he liked it there, so he didn't say anything. "Well?" she demanded.

"It's not wound fever. You did a good job with that leg." Dr. Stringfellow yanked the dressings back into place. "He's picked up an ague."

"How?"

"How do you think?" Dr. Stringfellow scrubbed his spectacles against the side of his jacket. "They're weak, they're packed together, sickness spreads."

"Not in my ward!" Nurse Hayes appeared to be taking it as a personal affront. If he could have spoken without his teeth banging together, Holt would have vouched for her. Everything they touched was boiled and bleached. She peeled back one of Holt's eyelids. "Look. No yellow. It's not yellow fever."

"I never said it was." Dr. Stringfellow glanced at his pocket watch, clearly impatient to be gone. "It could be any number of things. It might be a malarial ague, it might be typhoid. . . ."

"It's not typhoid." Holt felt Nurse Hayes's grip on his hand tighten. He tried to squeeze back. "I spent two months in a typhoid ward. I know typhoid when I see it."

"It might be tertian fever. Malaria. If I had a lab I could tell you—there was a fascinating piece in the *British Medical Journal* last Christmas about malarial pigmentation found in cells siphoned from an *Anopheles* mosquito that had fed on an infected patient. . . ." Dr. Stringfellow recalled himself. "But without a lab, the best anyone can do is wait three days and see if the fever recurs."

Nurse Hayes gave an impatient bounce. "Yes, but what can I do for him now?"

"Quinine. If it's malaria, he should respond quickly. And if he doesn't . . ." Dr. Stringfellow shrugged. "I was going to discharge him, but not now. He'll need to go with the rest of them."

"Go where?" Nurse Hayes dropped Holt's hand in her alarm. Holt wished she hadn't.

"Orders," said Dr. Stringfellow in a clipped voice. "Straight from General Shafter. We're to discharge anyone who can be discharged and move the more serious cases onto transports to be sent back to the States for care. These facilities need to be emptied for a new surge of wounded. They anticipate heavy fighting for Santiago—and we need to be ready."

Holt struggled to sit up. "Need to go—need to get back to them—"

Nurse Hayes rounded on him. "Don't you dare. The only person you're fighting is me." She turned back to Dr. Stringfellow. "What's the ship? Is it a proper hospital ship? How is it provisioned? Who's to accompany them?"

"They've sent the hospital ship *Relief* to evacuate them. Other than that, I don't know." Dr. Stringfellow's voice crackled with frustration. "I have goodness only knows how many patients to move and an operating theater to prepare. I'm going to need you to tell me who among your men can be discharged and who needs to be transported. This one we know. What about the rest?"

Nurse Hayes wasn't budging. Holt admired that about her. He admired a lot of things about her. "Who's accompanying them on the ship?"

"Two civilian doctors. Contractors. I don't know them." Dr. Stringfellow perked up suddenly. "They'll need a nurse. Do you want to go?"

"On the ship." Nurse Hayes's voice was curiously flat. Holt wished he could see her face, but her back was toward him. He could see her hands, though, curling into fists at her sides.

Dr. Stringfellow made an impatient gesture. "On the ship. The army doesn't want to spare any of the male nurses. We'll need them all, they say."

"Half of them are useless anyway," Nurse Hayes muttered.

"I'll pretend I didn't hear you say that—and that I don't agree," said Dr. Stringfellow drily. "Think about it. The ship sails tonight."

Nurse Hayes turned and looked down at Holt, her face for a moment unguarded, anguished.

Holt reached for her hand, to comfort her, but the cold claimed him, making his hand shake as he reached for hers, so his fingers only brushed her wrist.

She gave her head a brisk shake. "First things first. I'll get you your quinine straightaway."

Siboney, Cuba
July 13, 1898

IT WAS THE *Albania* ALL over again.

Betsy pressed her hands to her knees, breathing in deeply, breathing in the scents of salt water and bleach and male sweat. Just like the *Albania*.

No, no, it wasn't. This wasn't the *Albania*. Betsy forced herself to straighten, to look out at the harbor, where the *Relief* was already at anchor. This wasn't a broken-down old scow with men piled on the decks and launching themselves in their delirium from the mast. Based on the exterior, it was far more likely that this hospital ship *Relief* was a state-of-the-art wonder like the hospital ship *Solace* they'd toured a lifetime ago in Key West, with an elevator to move patients from surgery to the ward and everything shipshape and carbolic-scented.

Betsy tried to get herself in hand. She needed to get quinine for Holt. She needed to make that list for Dr. Stringfellow and see the able-bodied men discharged and the sicker men readied for immediate transport, and then she needed to go get her four hours of sleep before preparing for the new wounded who would come when Shafter made his final assault on Santiago.

This was where she was needed. They were short-staffed here already. Both Sister Anna and Sister Minnie were desperately ill; they'd been moved to a new fever hospital a way away from the rest, up on the top of a hill. No one wanted to use the words *yellow fever*, that terrible scourge from which so few recovered. But they were thinking it all the same.

If Dr. Stringfellow was right, if there was going to be a final scramble to secure Santiago, then the carts were going to start bumping down that road again, the wounded pouring in faster than they could sort them. There would be pallets on the ground and lights burning in the operating tent, only now, instead of a full complement of able-bodied nurses, they had two down with fever and the rest so broken down with nonstop work that it was a wonder they were still walking.

Of course, there was Ava. Ava was here now, and managing, in her own Ava-ish way, to do the work of multiple people.

But wasn't that all the more reason not to leave? Ava was here and she was Betsy's Ava again, even if now she was also very clearly Dr. Stringfellow's Ava.

Betsy fetched the tin of quinine tablets from the store cupboard, her hand shaking slightly as she pressed the wooden panel back into place. She could feel her secrets like an unexploded shell lodged in her chest. Yes, she knew that was anatomically impossible, but that was what it felt like, a horrible, destructive burden that she carried cradled close to her, something that might someday explode.

She was so tired and so sick of herself. She didn't think Ava would be shocked to hear that Charles had been her lover—Ava was enough of a realist for that. She would beetle her black brows at Betsy, she would probably say something sarcastic, but she wouldn't be surprised, and she would, in her own way, understand.

But the rest? Betsy couldn't bear to make herself think of it. But she couldn't not think of it. It was there in every breath she drew, in every step she took, it was there in every sunset and every dawn.

"Quinine," she said, arriving breathless at Holt's bedside, even though she hadn't been running, at least she didn't think she had. Everyone was running; the camp was in a foment, stretchers being prepared, men being examined before being discharged. "Take this. If it's tertian fever you should feel better shortly."

"Yes, I heard the doctor say," said Holt, his voice weak and scratchy but lucid, and Betsy could have hugged him with the relief of it, but one didn't hug one's patients, even if one had already kissed them. Kissed his cheek. The rest had been entirely an accident.

So many accidents. Sometimes it felt like her life was one big accident, only Ava would say it wasn't an accident if it happened often enough, it was just a way of doing what one wanted to do and then disclaiming responsibility.

"I wish you'd listened to the doctor better the first time and let him dress your leg," Betsy blustered, as Holt struggled to swallow the tablet through the chills that shook him. She held a cup of water to his lips to wash it down. "Why didn't you take any quinine? I thought all the men did. We've had cases in here of quinine poisoning from men taking too much."

Holt tried to smile but his teeth were chattering too hard to manage it. "Didn't think about it."

"Just like you didn't think about running in front of a bullet?" Betsy busied herself fussing with his sheets. "You've soaked through your bedding. I'll get you some fresh. Although they're moving you in an hour or so anyway. . . ."

Holt's hand moved weakly against the bedclothes, his finger brushing hers. "Come . . . with . . . me."

Betsy stared at him. Words jostled on her tongue. There was going to be another battle. It was just a short voyage.

But the *Albania* had been just a short voyage. Just one night. And there had been doctors on board there too.

For a moment she thought she could see Holt there, on the *Albania*, lying on that hard deck on that endless night, the priest's beads clattering as he walked from dying man to dying man.

Betsy couldn't breathe; her chest was tight. She couldn't. She couldn't go and she couldn't stay; she didn't know what to do. She could remember, so long ago, telling Charles that next time she'd be ready, next time she'd do better. What if this was next time?

And what if it wasn't? How was she to know?

And how was she to assume she would do any better? After all, look at what had happened with Charles. . . .

"I'll tell the next nurse on duty that you need clean sheets," Betsy said, and fled, trying not to see the hurt on Holt's face. But he didn't know. He didn't know how often she'd failed or how badly.

The next nurse on duty was Kit, grabbing a nap in the little room they used for rest when they could get it, and to store supplies. Kit was curled up on the cot, her buttoned boots poking out under the hem of her uniform, a uniform that, like the rest of theirs, hadn't been changed in days. They boiled their aprons and put on new ones, but Betsy was pretty sure the dress underneath was glued to her for life.

"Time to wake up, sleepyhead," she said with forced cheer. "You're missing all the excitement."

Kit scrunched herself up further. Betsy didn't blame her. She felt the same way. She wanted to curl in a ball and pull a blanket over her head and not have to make any decisions. She could do that. She could take her four hours of rest and let the ship sail away without her and pretend it wasn't her choice. But she'd know. She'd know she was letting Holt down. But if she went with Holt, she'd be letting Ava down, and Kit, and Paul, and all the men still out there. It was impossible.

"Come on. Arise and shame the dawn! Or is it shame the stars? I can never remember. Kit?" Betsy shook her friend gently by the shoulder.

Kit curled further in on herself, coughing a horrible, dry, hacking cough, like dead leaves in a graveyard.

Betsy knew that cough.

Dreading it, but knowing she had to, her hand went to Kit's head. Betsy didn't need the thermometer to tell her Kit was burning up. Kit had been so tired these past few days—but they'd all been so tired. She'd complained of stomachache—but they'd all been short on food, eating odd things at odd hours.

Betsy's hands shook as she loosened the pin that held Kit's collar. And there, beneath, on the skin of her neck, she could see a constellation of small red dots. She could try all she liked to claim it was heat rash or pimples or just wearing the same dress for two weeks, but she knew better.

"No, no, no, no, no."

"What is it?" Ava bustled in, turning up her sleeves to scrub her hands at the washbasin.

"It's Kit. Nurse Carson." Ever since learning that Ava had been jealous of her new friends in Greece, Betsy had tried to protect Ava's feelings by being more formal with Kit. "She has a fever."

Ava didn't hesitate. "I'll tell Lawrence."

"Wait!" He'd put Kit in the fever hospital. He'd put her in the fever hospital, where there might be—all right, there almost definitely was—yellow fever spreading. They might pretend otherwise all they liked, but Betsy had seen Sister Minnie. Moving Kit there, already weak with typhoid, would be nothing short of a death sentence. "Have you heard about the patients being moved out? They're to be transferred tonight. Onto a hospital ship. Kit should go with them."

Ava's dark brows drew together. "If she has a fever . . ."

Betsy planted herself in front of Kit's cot. "Half of them have fevers. We'll keep her separate. I'll keep her separate." She'd made her decision without even realizing it. She looked anxiously at Ava. "If I were to go with them, could you manage here?"

Ava rolled down her sleeves, pinning the cuffs neatly back in place. "I'll cry into my pillow."

"Ava! I'm serious. I don't want to abandon you—not if you need me." Why did everything have to be so hard? Betsy wished, just once, she could know what was really right, that she could make a decision without feeling like she was failing someone no matter what.

"They need you more." Ava looked directly at Betsy, her expression serious. "Go. I walked out on you in Athens. Now it's your turn."

"To walk out on you?"

Ava made an exasperated noise, somewhere between a grunt and a snort. "No! I should never have said it that way. It's your turn to do what you need to do. Don't worry about me. You told me yourself. This is what I was born to do. Lawrence is teaching me how to sew up perforated intestines."

Betsy didn't know whether to laugh or cry. "You'll invite me to the wedding?"

"Worse. I'm going to make you be maid of honor." Ava grinned crookedly at her. "You'll have to wear orange flowers and simper at the groomsmen."

Betsy's lips wobbled. "You really are getting your revenge."

Ava gave a sharp bark of a laugh. "You don't know the half of it. The place will be swarming with Princeton men. Do you think you can stand it?"

"I will for you." Impulsively, Betsy wrapped her arms around Ava and hugged her, hard. After a moment, she could feel Ava hug her back.

Betsy scrunched her eyes closed, trying to just take this moment and hold it, something to remember, whatever happened next.

Gently, Ava untangled herself, holding Betsy out at arm's length. Her eyebrows were, for once, entirely still. "Betsy? Those patients on the ship—they're lucky to have you."

Betsy wasn't so sure about that. But she was what they had and she meant to do her best for them.

On an impulse, she raided the hospital stores, loading up a bag with quinine tablets, antiseptic preparations, Armour's beef extract, malted milk, oatmeal, bandages, and an extra thermometer, just in case. The hospital wouldn't miss any of it. The *State of Texas* had brought back supplies from Tampa. It was probably coals to Newcastle—she hoped it was coals to Newcastle—but better to have too much than too little, and her experience with the army hospital had taught her that men seldom thought to pack food fit for invalids.

As Betsy bustled out with her sack, feeling like an unlikely Father Christmas, the men were already being rowed out to the boat.

To the wrong boat.

Betsy could see the *Relief*, bobbing at anchor, but that wasn't where her men were being taken. The ship was long and low with one big smokestack in the middle with a large number 5 painted on it. It hardly looked seaworthy, much less wounded-worthy.

Betsy grabbed one of the orderlies. "That's not the *Relief*. There's been some mistake. We were meant to be boarding the *Relief*."

The orderly backed away from her toward the next row of stretchers. "No, ma'am. The *Relief* is to stay here. Orders."

Whose orders? What orders?

"I was told we were going on the *Relief*," Betsy said stubbornly. "Who's in charge here? I need to speak to whoever is in charge."

A man came puffing up to her. He was holding a medical bag in one hand. It clanked reassuringly as he lifted a hand to his hat in greeting. Another man, smaller and slighter, followed close behind him. "Nurse? I'm Dr. Hicks, and this is Dr. Baird."

"Nurse Hayes." Betsy held out a hand, delighted to have someone with some authority to be able to defer the problem. "We're being put on the wrong ship."

"Er, um . . ." said Dr. Baird, looking to his colleague.

"It's only a three-day sail to New York," said Dr. Hicks, the more outspoken of the two. Betsy caught a distinct whiff of whiskey. "This transport should do us just fine. It's no *Relief*, of course. But nothing to worry about."

Nothing to worry about? Betsy would show them worry. "It's been provisioned, I assume?" she demanded.

"Betsy . . ." Behind her, she saw Kit, struggling on her stretcher. "Where are they taking me? Betsy! What's happening?"

Betsy hurried over to her. "You have a little fever," she lied. "We're being evacuated with some of the men."

The boats were waiting to row them out, so tiny against the vast ocean beyond. And there, in the distance, hulked the *Seneca*, looking more like a tin coffin than a hospital ship. Not a coffin. Betsy wasn't going to think of coffins. It was only a three-day sail and they had two doctors on board. And beef tea in her sack.

"Betsy . . ." Kit was coughing again, coughing and shaking, as the orderlies carried her down toward a boat. "I hurt."

Betsy slung her sack over her shoulder and climbed in next to Kit's stretcher, holding the other woman's hand for all she was worth.

"Er—should you be sitting that close to the patient?" asked one of the doctors. The smaller one, with the cowlick that made him look like a schoolboy. "She sounds infectious."

"I've had it already." Betsy glared at the doctors, daring them to defy her. "Don't worry. I'm here. I'm not going to leave you."

The boat pitched, fighting against the waves, as they plunged their way toward the *Seneca*.

One of the young doctors retched, losing his lunch over the side of the launch.

The *Seneca* loomed above them, even less impressive at close range. Holt had been rowed out earlier. He must already be on board. Betsy could hear the sounds of shouting and cries of pain as men were jostled up from the boats onto the ship.

She didn't have a good feeling about this.

Betsy wrapped a blanket around Kit's shoulders to protect her from the salt spray. "It will all be all right," she whispered. "I'm going to nurse you myself. And we're all going to make it home safe."

Chapter Twenty-Two

Dear Ava,

~~Things have gone so terribly wrong~~

~~I've done a terrible thing~~

~~I'm not sure what to do. I wish I could make everything go away and start over again.~~

~~Ava, I don't know what to do. I've made such a terrible mess.~~

—Miss Betsy Hayes '96 to Ava Saltonstall '96 (unsent)

Athens, Greece
August 1897

BETSY WANTED TO NURSE CHARLES herself, but they wouldn't let her.

The hospital was a military hospital and he was a civilian, and what right did she have? What right that anyone would recognize? Just a coin on a ribbon around her neck and a promise of marriage that sounded absurd given that he was quite married already and no one other than she had any idea he was contemplating annulments and papal intercessions. Sometimes Betsy wasn't even sure of it. He'd been in the grip of a fever, a fever of 104. People said strange things in their delirium. Perhaps he'd meant it, perhaps he hadn't, but whatever he'd said was between them and them alone.

And so the court physician had borne Charles back to Athens. Betsy hadn't been with him as he doubled over with stomach pain. She hadn't been with him as he coughed and gasped for breath. She hadn't been with him as the red rash spread across his chest.

She hadn't been with him when he died.

The word came to her in Lamia, in a carefully phrased letter from Aikaterini. The body had been sent back to France for burial. Body. Charles. Dead. Betsy couldn't quite make the words make sense. They buzzed around in her head like mosquitoes, stinging her and whisking away again. Charles wasn't that old. He had decades ahead of him yet. He couldn't be dead.

But he was. He was dead and she had killed him.

Betsy began making mistakes. She was dizzy and confused. She overslept her shift. She stared at a thermometer trying to remember which end went where.

Overwork, they called it. She had been nursing nonstop, in various war zones, often going days without sleep, since April. Everyone was very kind about it, even Dr. Kalopothakes. They spoke about her valorous service and told her to get some rest; she'd done more than her share. Especially in a battle not her own.

They sent her back to Academy Street to recover, back to Aikaterini, the one person in the world who knew that Betsy's collapse was nothing to do with her work—but who knew enough not to say too much.

In its own way, Athens was worse than Lamia. Except for that one brief moment, that one brief visit, Lamia was only Betsy's. But Athens belonged to Charles.

Betsy saw him everywhere. She saw him on the velvet sofa in Aikaterini's salon, helping himself to cakes. She saw him strolling across Syntagma Square, always just a few yards ahead, always just past that next person. She saw him in the hall of the American School in Athens, sprawled on the floor after she'd knocked him down.

He ought to have known after that. That she was trouble. That she would bring him down.

Maybe Charles had been right. Maybe everything was signs and wonders—and omens. Maybe knocking Charles over had been an omen of things to come.

What would have happened if they'd just gone their separate ways after that? What would have happened if Betsy had never gone to Aikaterini's and met Charles over coffee and cakes? She might have ignored Aikaterini's invitation to tea and gone to live with that Presbyterian minister like Ethel and annoyed Dr. Richardson, and Charles would still be alive and well and sifting through dirt at Delphi, looking for the next Charioteer.

Betsy went to his apartment. Not inside, of course. She had no idea who lived there now, if anyone. She stood outside and stared at those long windows, so elegantly draped, imagining that Charles was still there, sitting in his bit of Paris in Athens, beneath those frothy Fragonard romps, with his manservant bringing him macarons.

She could picture him there, writing letters at the escritoire, thumbing through a copy of the latest excavation reports, dressing to go to a reception.

There was a whole world in which they'd never met and Charles was still alive.

If Betsy had stayed where she was meant to be and Charles was still alive, might they have met in future? One day, years from now. Betsy spun an elaborate fantasy. An older Betsy, distinguished, wiser. A reception for—oh, something or other. And Charles there, in his evening clothes.

Looking through her, past her, not knowing her.

But alive. Safe.

Herakles faithfully polished Betsy's bicycle, but it sat unused. Her books and papers lay piled where she'd left them in April. It was September now, and a new term would be starting soon at the American School, but Betsy hadn't done anything about securing a place for herself or making up the work she'd missed at the end of last term.

Betsy felt like a broken watch, stopped permanently at that moment when Charles had died, the hands frozen in place.

After a month of letting Betsy drift about, Aikaterini appeared in Betsy's room with a servant bearing coffee and iced cakes.

She waited until the coffee was poured and half the cakes eaten before delicately working her way around to the question of Betsy's future. "Do you mean to go back to the American School?"

"I missed my exams," said Betsy dully, picking up another cake and eating it. The exams had been in May, while Betsy was nursing in Vólos. Or possibly Vonitsa.

"You can take them again. I am sure if you asked the director . . ."

Betsy shrugged. It didn't matter anymore.

Aikaterini set down her coffee cup. "Is it because of the baby?"

Betsy choked on a mouthful of French pastry. "The what?"

"You didn't know." Aikaterini's face was a study, frozen somewhere between consternation and exasperation. "I've been so worried for you—I thought you knew—that you couldn't bring yourself to tell me—"

"Tell you," Betsy repeated. She had picked up another cake without thinking about it. She'd gone from being always queasy to always hungry. She looked at the cake and then at Aikaterini. "A baby?"

Betsy craned her head down to look at her stomach, which, to be fair, was looking a little rounder than usual in the loose tea gown she had taken to wearing around the house because it was more comfortable than her other clothes and the flowing Aesthetic style felt vaguely like wearing a nightdress. But whose stomach wouldn't be rounder after lying around the house for weeks, eating tea cakes? "But I can't—I don't—"

"When did you last have your courses?" Aikaterini asked.

"Vólos," said Betsy, her mouth suddenly dry. "In Vólos. In April."

"Mmph," said Aikaterini. "Then you are . . . four months along."

Four months. The beginning of May. Sun slanting through Charles's bedroom window, the feel of his skin beneath her fingertips, the taste of his lips. The utter shamelessness of it; the thrill of the forbidden, of giving up and flinging herself into her own ruin.

Her ruin. It had only been meant to be her ruin, not Charles's.

If she hadn't gone to bed with him, he would never have followed her to Lamia. It was all her fault. For not thinking, never thinking, just doing what she wanted to do and letting other people suffer the consequences. Her mother. Her father. Charles.

A baby?

"Oh my dear. There's no need. Shhhhh." Aikaterini scooted off her chair and onto the chaise, wrapping her arms around Betsy, stroking Betsy's tousled hair, never minding the stains Betsy's tears were making on the delicate silk of her dress. Somehow, that only made Betsy cry harder. "Shhh. Don't worry. You're not alone. I'll find a way to make it right."

Betsy shook her head numbly. It couldn't be right. Nothing would ever be right again.

"I would take it myself, say it was mine—but people would know. Even if I claimed it was the waters. . . . We don't look enough alike, you and I. And Charles was fair."

Charles had had brown hair and eyes, although *brown* was too dull a word for either. His eyes had been like whiskey, lit with lamp-light.

Tu m'enivres. You intoxicate me.

BETSY STOPPED GOING TO CHARLES's apartment. September blundered along, one day following miserably after the other. The papers announced an armistice. The war was over. Irreparably, irretrievably over. All those lives lost, all those brave Cypriots and Macedonians who had fought for freedom, the Italian Garibaldians who had come to lend their lives for the cause, the men who had perished on the *Albania*. Charles.

All gone and for nothing, worse than nothing. Not only was the Ottoman yoke still in place, but Greece, chastened, had to cede more territory to the Turks, more Greeks under Turkish rule, and pay a vast indemnity to boot.

September lurched into October. The gatherings in Aikaterini's salon were muted. Betsy didn't attend them anyway. She had better things to do, like write letters and tear them up again, or lie in bed, with Charles's gold coin clutched in her hand. She couldn't stop thinking about all those men, marching off so bravely. All those men who would never go home again. Men who limped home without limbs, men whose bodies had been broken by fever. Children left without homes; mothers with skeletal babies begging for scraps.

Her baby.

Charles.

Betsy tightened her hand around Charles's coin, holding it until it hurt. Charles had given her his luck and she'd turned it against him. Not intentionally. She'd never meant to harm him. But she had anyway.

When Betsy opened her hand, she could see the imprint of the angel on her palm. Marking her. Maybe she should be marked. Didn't they used to do that in France, to murderers? Brand them? Betsy folded her hand closed and opened it again, watching the marks fade. But she knew. She knew what she'd done. She wondered how she could explain to this baby, this child growing inside her, that she had killed its entire family. Its grandfather. And its grandmother.

And now Charles. But for her, he would never have been in Lamia. But for her, he would still be alive. Betsy wrapped her arms around herself, around the space where their child was growing, and rocked back and forth, her head pressed against her knees, her mouth opening and closing in mute misery.

There was only one conclusion. She carried death with her.

"I'm so sorry," she murmured to her baby, Charles's baby. "I'm so sorry."

The baby pushed and kicked inside her. Six months along now and it was already trying to get away from her.

"Elisavet. Betsy? There is someone to see you." Betsy knew it had to be important for Aikaterini to fetch her herself, rather than sending a servant.

Betsy shook out her crumpled tea dress and made a half-hearted effort to stick a few pins into the bird's nest of her hair.

Dr. Richardson, she assumed. Come to make sure she didn't intend to return to the American School. Or maybe Mrs. Richardson, sent as emissary.

But it was neither of those. A woman stood by the mantel, where Charles used to like to stand, a woman in a perfect dream of a dress, the very latest model in cut and color.

Betsy knew who it was, knew it deep in the pit of her stomach, even before Aikaterini pronounced the words. "I would like to present you to the Baronne de Robecourt."

Charles's wife was beautiful. Charles had never said she was beautiful. No, maybe not beautiful, but—lacquered, like an expensive box, all shiny finish and everything locked inside.

She was fair, like Betsy. Or maybe not like Betsy. Her hair wasn't an ash-blond muddle last washed a week ago but smooth and shining, coaxed into curls and gleaming gold.

She was taller than Betsy. That wasn't surprising. Everyone was taller than Betsy. She was tall and slender and wore her Paris gown the way the women in the fashion plates wore them, all long lines and perfect posture and not a seam out of place.

Betsy looked down at her battered Aesthetic gown. There was a dried splotch of honey on the bodice and what she thought might be coffee down the skirt.

From the way the baroness was looking at her, she didn't think much of Betsy either.

"You are Miss Hayes." The baroness's accent was much thicker than Charles's. "I understand you knew my husband."

"Knew. Yes." In the biblical sense. Why was Aikaterini doing this to her? "He was a remarkable man."

"Yes," said the baroness drily. "Remarkable."

Were they just to repeat each other's words like parrots? Betsy cast a look of entreaty at Aikaterini. Aikaterini guided Betsy to the settee, sitting down beside her in a fluid movement of silk and embroidery.

"I believe Madame de Robecourt might be able to help you in your difficulty," Aikaterini said gently.

Help? The woman looked like she wanted to squish Betsy like a bug.

The baroness seated herself elegantly on the most elaborate chair in the room. "My husband left something with you. I will take it."

It took Betsy a moment to figure out what she meant. Charles's most prized possession. His luck.

Betsy's hand went to the ribbon at her neck, fumbling on the bow. The ribbon was getting worn and frayed from the number of times she'd tied and untied it. She held it out by the ends, the gold coin, somewhat smudged from constant use, swaying gently in the middle.

"Here," Betsy said dully. "Take it."

The baroness eyed her askance. "I don't want your trinkets." Turning to Aikaterini, she said sharply, in French, "Is the girl a half-wit?"

Betsy bristled. Strange, what mattered when nothing else did. "I graduated from Smith with honors."

The baroness cast Betsy a look of extreme distaste. *"Les cervelines. Propre à rien. Le cerveau se développe au détriment du cœur."*

Bluestockings. Good for nothing. Nourishing their brains at the expense of their hearts.

If her heart was malformed, then why did it hurt so much?

"I do speak French," Betsy said in that language.

"Good." The baroness was even more terrifying in her own language. "Then let me speak plainly to you. I have come for the child. It is my husband's, and for that it will be mine."

It. Like an object. Betsy put her hands over her stomach.

Aikaterini took one of Betsy's cold hands. "My dear. This could be the solution. Your child will have a home and a name—a noble name. And you can be as you were."

Betsy stared at her dumbly, not sure how Aikaterini thought she could ever be as she was. Once a civilization was destroyed, it couldn't be put right, only excavated from the ruins, a testament to what had been but no longer was.

"It is all quite easily arranged," said the baroness briskly. She might have been talking about ordering a new hat. "There is a place in Switzerland. I will go there for my *accouchement*. A baby, at my age, in a time of mourning—it requires the utmost care and quiet."

Aikaterini squeezed Betsy's numb fingers. "Everyone knows you worked yourself into a decline, nursing our soldiers. There is no shame in taking a rest cure. A few months among the trees and the mountains, in utter peace and solitude—it is precisely what you need. The queen herself suggested something of the kind. She takes an interest in you, you know."

"She doesn't know—"

"No! Nothing of the sort. Her Majesty knows only that you nursed valiantly and has expressed her concern about your health." Aikaterini hesitated a moment, and then added, "Her Majesty has mentioned her interest in seeing you happily settled, here in Athens, if possible. She suggested, perhaps, the court physician."

Betsy stared at her in horror. "I don't want to marry the court physician."

"Then you won't," Aikaterini hastened to reassure her. "No one wants anything but your happiness. You don't need to marry anyone if you don't wish it. But this way, should you wish to marry some-day . . . there will be no bar."

Other than her own conscience.

The baroness rose, in a single, swift motion. She drew on her gloves. They were beautiful gloves. Pristine. "We are agreed, then. I shall make the arrangements and convey them to Madame Mac-Hugh." She looked directly at Betsy for the first time since the interview began. Her lip curled. "There is no need for us to meet again."

And she was gone, leaving a subtle hint of French perfume and a distinct chill in the air. Like the witch in a fairy tale, thought Betsy irrelevantly, come to steal her baby and seal it in a tower.

But she wasn't in a fairy tale. She was a modern American woman and no one could take her child without her saying so. Or could they? Betsy felt hot and cold at the same time. "I haven't—I didn't say I would."

"But, my dear, what else are you to do? You cannot raise the child alone."

"I could find a little cottage somewhere." A hut deep in the woods surrounded by brambles. There she would tend the steaming cauldron while her child went out barefoot to collect berries, until one day a talking bear would appear at the door—or was it a frog? No, Betsy didn't want to live in that sort of story. "Or an apartment in a city. One of the modern sort where you send a dumbwaiter down to the basement for meals and someone comes and cleans for you once a week. I could pretend to be a widow. I could tell my child her father died in the war."

"You would be found out," said Aikaterini, not unkindly. "Do you think there is any city you could go where someone would not know you?"

Betsy didn't have an answer. It was true. In the sorts of cities that had universities where she might study and apartments with staff who lived in the basement, there would always be someone who knew her or her brother or her father. She might try to change her name, but it would come out. And how was she to pretend, as herself, that she had married during the war? Greece was a small place, in its way. Everyone she had nursed with would know that was nonsense. The queen would know that was nonsense.

Betsy had money of her own—but only so long as Alex continued to disburse it. Betsy wasn't sure of the exact terms of her trust. She had never bothered to check. But she knew Alex. She knew how he valued his reputation, his precious respectability, always trying so hard to wash the stench of the Yonkers carpet factory out of his money so his Beacon Hill neighbors wouldn't get a whiff of it. If Betsy were to turn up with a child—Alex would find a way to stop her funds. He'd have her declared incompetent, unfit.

What if he had her put away? He could. Alex was a lawyer, well-connected. Betsy had flouted him—she'd flouted him with glee—but he couldn't very well declare her not of sound mind for studying the classics.

But if she were to come home with an illegitimate child . . . Betsy could feel the cold against the back of her neck. Alex would have her put away. He'd have her put away and her child taken from her.

Betsy crammed her fist into her mouth, trying to keep the panic inside.

"She's not as dreadful as she seems."

"What?" Disoriented, Betsy realized Aikaterini was talking to her. She'd been lost in a nightmare where Alex had her baby stolen from her, given away, brought in a basket to an orphanage, leaving her child alone and unloved. He would, he and Lavinia both. They'd do anything to preserve their good name. They'd never think of the child as a person. Their children were people. Their children mattered. But not an illegitimate child. Not an inconvenience.

"The baroness," said Aikaterini, entirely misunderstanding Betsy's terror. "We took the waters together. Again and again, we took the waters. I may not care for her—not as I care for you—but she's not so bad as all that. I do not think Charles ever knew just how much she minded not having a child. Or it might be that he knew and didn't want to know."

Aikaterini's face was bleak. Betsy wondered if it was the baroness she was speaking of or herself. Either way, she didn't want to think about it. She didn't want to think of Charles and his wife. She wanted—oh, she wanted to go back. Back before Lamia. Back before the *Albania*. When everything was still simple.

"But it won't be hers," Betsy said huskily. She remembered how the woman had looked at her. A *cerveline*. With messy hair. "What if she's cruel? What if she blames the child for me?"

"I think," said Aikaterini carefully, "that Delphine is one of those people with the facility to believe that which she wishes to believe. If she tells the world the child is hers, it will be. And she will never allow herself to know otherwise."

"You mean she'll pretend," said Betsy flatly.

"I mean that she will remember it as she wishes it to have been. A final reconciliation with Charles. The long-awaited heir." Aikaterini allowed herself a moment of cynicism. "There is, of course, also the inheritance to be thought of. Under the *Code civil*, the widow gets a share, but there are other properties which go only to the heir—to Charles's brother should he die without a son."

Betsy's head jerked up. "Charles has a brother?"

"Two of them. And three sisters."

Betsy hadn't known that. She'd thought she knew him, but— what had she known? That he had a fey streak. That he liked to wander. That he was charming. Nothing more. He'd never spoken about his family, about his life before Athens. He'd hinted at it, the Prussian invasion, his experiments with absinthe, his wanderings in Egypt. But he'd never elaborated. And Betsy had never asked. She ought to have asked.

"Your child has a dozen cousins, or more," Aikaterini carried on, not realizing she was grinding salt into the wound. "Some are much older, of course. But this child will be the most senior of them, the head of the family."

"And if he's a girl?" Betsy asked hoarsely.

"Then she will have female cousins to share gossip and male cousins to defend her honor. She will have aunts to tell her what is *comme il faut* and uncles to slip her coins to buy ribbons and sweets."

But not a mother. Not her real mother. But what sort of mother would Betsy be? She'd never had one of her own, not really. She wasn't even sure what they were meant to do, although she had a vague idea, from watching Ava's mother and reading *Little Women* over and over that they were meant to dispense wise counsel and mold character and provide clean handkerchiefs.

Betsy always forgot her handkerchiefs.

"To have a child out of wedlock . . . it would ruin your life and that of the child." Aikaterini looked at Betsy with compassion. "I wish it were otherwise, but it is what it is. A son of the baroness will be heir to a great fortune. A daughter of the baroness will move only in the best circles. Your child will have a name, a history, a family."

Charles's coin lay discarded on a richly lacquered table, the ribbon limp and shabby. Betsy scooped it up, worrying the frayed ends between her fingers. "And if I keep the child—"

She didn't need to say it. An outcast from birth, tainted by the sins of the mother.

"This is the best way. For you *and* the child." Aikaterini put a pin back into Betsy's chignon, her hands gentle. "You will have a holiday in Switzerland. Then you will come back to me and resume your work and we will be as we were."

Betsy nodded obediently, but she knew it was a lie. They would never again be as they were.

And she could never come back.

Chapter Twenty-Three

"The afternoon the vessel sailed I heard that she was to evacuate a number of our wounded to the States. Being informed that no nurse was on board, I volunteered to go with them. I went first to the hospital, where I gathered up a great bag of such necessities as I believed could be spared. Why did I gather such things? I had had experience of evacuations before, in the war in Greece. No, I had no reason to believe the ship would be unprovisioned. I believed we were to sail on the hospital ship *Relief*. It was simply a matter of caution. You might call it instinct. No, I'm not claiming female intuition—just common sense. Oh, for heaven's sake."

[Testimony paused. Debate on whether women can be said to have sense omitted as immaterial to the purpose of the commission.]

"The ship on which we were put—the *Seneca*—was not at all prepared to receive sick and wounded. The poor fellows were put between decks in cattle pens. There's no other way to describe them. Yes, I know they weren't actually meant to hold cattle and that cattle can't lie on bunks. I'm simply trying to describe the inhumane conditions in which these sick men found themselves.

"There was not a surgical instrument or thermometer aboard. . . ."

—*Report of the Commission, vol. 7, p. 3542; testimony of Miss Elizabeth Hayes re: conditions on board the USS* Seneca.

❧

On board the Seneca
July 14, 1898

"WE MUST GO BACK."

Someone was speaking in an agitated whisper. Holt tried to sit up, and promptly banged his head on a plank.

He was lying, he realized, in a coffin-sized space, just long enough and wide enough for his recumbent body. It was roughly a thousand degrees in his impromptu casket, the air heavy with moaning and snoring and snuffling, some of which seemed to be coming from above him.

Holt carefully maneuvered his legs over the side of the plank. Straw rustled beneath him, and the very movement made him sweat, but his legs did what he told them. He slithered out of the bunk and found himself standing—swaying, really—in the very narrow space between rows of similar bunks. There was, he realized, a man who had been sleeping below him and two more piled on top. As far ahead as he could see, and to either side, bunks had been lined up like shelves, with corridors in between rows so narrow that Holt could just fit.

On the plus side, it meant he had two sides to grab when his legs wobbled under him.

"We can't go back." The voice was coming from somewhere down the close-packed row of bunks. Not far away, but the thicket of beds confused him. Or maybe he was just confused generally. Holt felt about as substantial as tracing paper. His legs didn't like the idea of holding him, but Holt forced them to anyway, partly out of—what had Nurse Hayes called it?—bloody-mindedness, and partly because he wasn't sure he could climb back into that bunk even if he wanted to, which he didn't.

"We can't go on, not like this." In her agitation, Nurse Hayes wasn't keeping her voice quite as low as she should. Slowly, Holt followed the sound, until he could see her through the beds, just a row away, facing off against a man in a dark coat. "There's not a single medical instrument on the ship, Doctor!"

The doctor murmured something barely distinguishable.

Nurse Hayes put her hands on her hips. "Oh, pardon me. A forceps. A single forceps. But there are no other surgical instruments and half a dozen men desperately in need of surgical intervention!"

"I am as distressed by the situation as you are—" the doctor began, but Nurse Hayes cut him off, her voice clipped.

"Distress doesn't measure temperatures or stanch blood. We have ninety-four wounded on this boat, and the only medical supplies are the ones I brought in my satchel!"

"We sent a requisition form to the *Relief*," the doctor said weakly.

"It's impossible, you have to see that. We can't in all conscience keep going."

The doctor's shoulders stiffened. "We can't go back. We have orders. . . ."

Nurse Hayes let out a noise like a kettle on the boil. "Orders? Orders that you let these men die on a floating disaster?"

"I'll just do my rounds now," said the doctor, and scurried away, leaving Nurse Hayes staring after him, her face very white and her lips very set.

Holt meant to slip around the side of the bunk, but stealth wasn't so easy when the room tended to wobble. He stubbed his toe, and Nurse Hayes was at his side in a moment, grabbing him to steady him, as though she were a Titan rather than five foot nothing and about ten pounds.

"Private Holt? What are you doing up?" Her face underwent a remarkable transformation, lighting with sudden, fierce joy. "You're up! You're not shaking!"

It was like staring at the lighthouse of Alexandria; she glowed like a beacon. Holt couldn't look away from that small, brilliant face.

"The quinine seems to have done the trick," he said thickly. "Er, mostly."

"Well, what did you expect? First you were bedbound and then you were feverish. If you were steady on your feet, I'd suspect dark arts. Or someone behind you, propping you up." She slid an arm around his waist. Her head came just to his chin. "Come on. Put your arm around my shoulders. I'll brace you. I don't want you falling and breaking something."

Holt looked down at the top of her head. Her spirit was so towering, he tended to forget how little she was. Her shoulder bone felt tiny and fragile beneath his hand. "I don't want to weigh you down."

"You're the least of the weights on me," she said grimly. "Let's get you back to your bunk."

No. The idea of going back there—Holt wasn't sure he'd make it out again. "Would it be possible to get some air?"

He could feel her hesitate. "I'm the only nurse on board."

"You don't have to linger by my side. I'll sit on the deck out of the way. Just drop me anywhere."

"Overboard? Your chances are probably better swimming for shore than staying on here with us." She shook her head. Her flyaway hair tickled his chin. "Never mind. Forget I said that. All right, then. One foot after the other."

"I heard you talking back there. To the doctor." Holt sucked in the salt air as they made their way up onto the deck. He hadn't realized how foul the air below was until he was out of it. "What's wrong?"

"What isn't? I have nearly a hundred sick men and no way to treat them." Nurse Hayes blindly waved a hand. "There's a deck chair for you."

Holt didn't sit. "The doctors—"

"They don't know what they're in for. They haven't a clue. But I have." Nurse Hayes wrapped her arms around herself, trying to stop herself shaking. Her eyes had the horrible blank look Holt remembered from Tampa. "I was on a ship. In Greece. A hospital ship. We were evacuating men from Vólos to Athens. Our supplies were locked in the hold and the medical officer wouldn't listen when we tried to tell him what needed to be done. . . . Six men died that night."

"That was Greece," said Holt.

At least that woke her up a bit. Her eyes focused on his, alive with pain and fear, as if all the demons in the world were burning away in there. "That was a better provisioned ship! And that was only one night! Six men. In one night. How we're to spend four days on here—three days if we're lucky and the weather is fair—with only the medical supplies I brought and one kettle to cook food for a hundred men . . ."

"One kettle?" Holt seized on the least of it. "Isn't there a galley?"

"Whoever prepared the boat stripped the ship. Anything that wasn't nailed down is gone. Except for the passengers. They left passengers on board. Passengers!" Nurse Hayes made a sound somewhere between a laugh and a sob. "We've got wounded stuffed into bunks while the cabins are clogged with foreign observers and newspapermen. I guess we're giving them something to observe. They can go home and tell everyone what a disaster this was."

"Hold on." Holt put his hands on her shoulders. "It's not a disaster yet."

She looked up at him, her eyes huge. "I searched the ship, Holt. I searched it from top to bottom. The only medical supplies aboard are a few quinine tablets and a roll of bandages. Oh, and one forceps."

It was a disaster.

Holt looked down at her. "What can I do?"

"Not get sicker?" She bent forward, leaning her forehead against his chest. He could feel her struggling not to break down.

Holt tentatively touched her back. "I meant more than that. Tell me what to do and I'll do it."

She pulled herself upright, her lips pressed very tightly together. "I don't want you falling and hurting yourself."

Holt didn't particularly want to fall and hurt himself either, not least because the last thing Nurse Hayes needed was more injuries on her hands.

He seized on a sudden inspiration. "You said there are passengers. Newspapermen and foreign observers. They're not wounded. Why not put them to work?"

"As orderlies?" she said skeptically, but he could see the wheels beginning to churn.

"As whatever you need. Or at least see if they'll give up their cabins for the more severely wounded. The bunks below—they'd be hard on a well man, much less a sick one."

"They're not going to go gently," she said thickly. "These are men who are used to the Hotel Grande Bretagne and the Tampa Bay Hotel."

"It's only for three days, you said. They can bear the inconvenience for that long, can't they?" Holt watched Nurse Hayes closely. Her nose was dripping slightly and her eyes were red, but there was a bit more color in her cheeks, and he could see her standing straighter. "This is war. They come to watch a war, they get what they get."

"That'll show them?" She gave a laugh that sounded like a hiccup. "You're right, you know. I don't know why I didn't think of it."

"Because you've been caring for all of us for weeks without rest?" Without thinking, Holt peeled a bit of tear-damp hair off her cheek and tucked it behind her ear for her.

She gave him a wobbly smile. "I've had the odd nap."

"You need more than a nap," said Holt roughly. It was the remains of the fever making him light-headed. Not Nurse Hayes with the tip of her nose red and damp hair clinging to her cheeks. "What needs to be done?"

Nurse Hayes took a gulp of salt air, looking down at her hands as she ticked off items on her fingers. "Food for the wounded. Beef tea for the invalids and oatmeal for those who can stomach something firmer. They need to be made in sequence because we have just the one cookpot, so I'll need someone who can man the galley. I'm also not so sure about the water. When I asked the captain about the tanks, he said they'd last been filled in May. The water's gone brackish. It's drinkable with ice—just—but we don't have enough ice to last."

They really hadn't thought of anything. And they'd left Nurse Hayes holding the bag. Holt tamped down his own simmering rage. "It's a steamship, isn't it? We should be able to use the engine to distill water. It's slow, and it won't produce as much as we'd like, but it will be something."

"But what do we distill it into? There's just the one—"

"Kettle, I know. Let me figure that out." Never mind that the deck wasn't entirely steady under his feet. She couldn't be left to do this on her own. "Point the way to the engine room. I'll deal with the water if you deal with the passengers." She was looking lost again. He chucked her under the chin, doing his best to keep his voice light. "Hey. You're not in this on your own. We'll pull through together, Nurse Hayes."

"Or we'll all fall apart?" She grimaced at him, holding out a hand as if they'd just been introduced. "And it's Betsy. 'Nurse Hayes' makes me sound like someone who knows what she's doing."

Her hand burned in his.

"You know more than you think," said Holt, and escaped to the engine room before she could see how shaky he really was.

On board the Seneca
July 14, 1898

CRAVENLY, BETSY WISHED HOLT WERE still with her when she gathered the passengers together to announce that there might just be a slight change of plans and would any of them mind abandoning their nice, comfortable cabins to sleep on the deck, or possibly on the floor of the smoking room?

He was a patient, she reminded herself. He was meant to be convalescing.

But there was something so wonderfully steadying about him.

Betsy couldn't remember why she'd ever found him an annoyance. That felt like it belonged to another lifetime, that the people they had been on that railway line outside of Tampa had been different people entirely. She'd come barreling back from Greece to rescue Ava, and here she was, on another doomed ship, and Ava was exactly where Betsy hadn't wanted Ava to be. In a strange way, though, her failure was her success. She'd never seen Ava so happy as she'd been in Siboney, up to her elbows in perforated intestines, exchanging sweet medical murmurings with Dr. Stringfellow. Lawrence. Betsy supposed she would have to start thinking of him as Lawrence if he was going to be a sort of honorary brother-in-law, which everyone, particularly Ava, seemed quite determined he would.

She was doing it again, Betsy realized. She was doing exactly what she had done at Smith and in Greece. It was much easier to plan Ava's wedding than figure out what on earth she could say that might move a group of hardened newspapermen and international grandees to give up their rooms. Just as it had been easier to fling herself into Charles's arms than it was to face up to the fact that six men who hadn't had to die had died on the *Albania* and nothing she said to the authorities was going to make any difference or stop it happening again.

What can I do? Holt had asked, calmly assuming that there was something that could be done.

That they could make a difference. That she could make a difference.

Betsy hauled herself up onto a deck chair, feeling like a poorly carved ship figurehead in her stained and rumpled Red Cross uniform.

Betsy waved her hands about. "Hello? Everybody?"

Not exactly "friends, Romans, countrymen," but one had to start somewhere.

"Um, as you may know, this ship has been requisitioned to evacuate the wounded from Siboney to New York, where they can receive medical care."

Some people seemed to be listening. Others were shuffling or whispering or picking their noses. They were a motley lot, the passengers, but they were a motley lot that Betsy recognized from her time in Greece. Not the individuals, but the types. They'd had a Swedish army officer just like that one on the ship to Vólos. The American newspapermen were chomping their cigars with impatience. Unlit, as a nod to her female status.

And, good heavens, she did know that one, the one with the hair slicked down from his part with a strong comb and an excess of cream. A Harvard man. Cabot? No. Coolidge. John Coolidge. They'd danced a polka together. He was squinting at her as though trying to figure out how he knew her.

Betsy didn't blame him. She barely knew herself anymore.

"Many of these men are gravely wounded. They were wounded fighting for freedom, for liberty, for the people of Cuba. Have they been given the care owed such heroes? No. We've crammed them into horrid bunks in the hold."

They were listening now. Betsy could see them lifting their heads, actually paying attention.

"We have two doctors. Two doctors and one nurse. For the care of ninety-four men." Betsy let that sink in. "Some are struggling with fragments of shells still lodged in their extremities. Others are delirious with fever. Crammed into the hold as they are, they have very little chance of making it to New York and the care they need. But—"

No one shuffled; no one whispered. Betsy looked around the group, making eye contact with each man, one after the other.

"If you—any of you, all of you—were to give up your cabins, it could make all the difference. You could save a man's life. Many men's lives. These men have mothers at home, wives, children." Betsy's voice caught as she thought of Kit, Kit talking about her children. "Won't you help them go home to them?"

There was a moment of quiet. Betsy stood there, feeling painfully conspicuous, the cold of exhaustion seeping through her, the weight of failure heavy on her. This had been her one shot at this. If she'd failed—

"You can bet I will!" shouted Coolidge, bouncing on the balls of his feet as he waved his hat in the air.

The Swedish naval officer bowed his head, his face grave. "My cabin is at your disposal, as am I."

"Thank you," whispered Betsy.

The Russian representative didn't want to be behindhand. He cast a dirty look at the Swede before bowing to Betsy. "Mine as well."

The German officer clicked his heels. "I am at your service."

"Sure, you can have mine," said one of the newspapermen. He frowned at the end of his cigar. "But you should know, Sylvester Scovel's wife is laid up in the cabin next to mine and she's in a pretty bad way."

Another newspaperman let out a whistle. "Scovel, eh? That—er." He remembered Betsy's presence. "Don't tell me he's on board."

"Course not," said the first man sourly. "Shoved his wife aboard and left her to fend for herself—he wouldn't miss the fun."

"When you say she's pretty bad," Betsy broke in, before the men could get going, "what do you mean?"

"Fever," said the first man laconically. "She was moaning like anything last night."

The Russian officer cast a sideways glance at his counterparts. "Lieutenant Akiyama, as well."

"The representative of Japan," explained the Swedish officer.

Two more patients for her roster. "Is there anyone else I ought to know about?"

One of the newspapermen shoved the other. "Herbert here was ill over the rail last night."

"That was the bully beef," protested Herbert with an attempt at dignity.

Betsy ignored them. "Right. Thank you so much to all of you who have offered to sacrifice your own comfort for the good of others. I'll look in on Mrs. Scovel and Lieutenant Akiyama as soon as I have the worst cases transferred from the hold."

She spoke as briskly as she could and just hoped none of them could see how she was shaking, from exhaustion and relief and fear.

"Ma'am?" A man stepped forward, the others parting to let him through. He was a distinguished-looking man of middle years, with an impressive beak of a nose. "Captain Robert Dowdy, US Army. You say you are the only nurse aboard. I cannot claim any experience of nursing, but I do have a sound pair of arms and can follow instructions. A few of us back here have had a quiet word, and we'd like to help. Say the word and I'll make a list of volunteers and set up a rota."

Betsy was overcome. Volunteers. A rota.

You're not in this on your own, Holt had said.

"I don't know what to say other than thank you. And yes, please." Betsy cleared her throat, hoping they'd put any suspicious scratchiness in her throat down to the salt air. "Our first order of operations is moving the men up from the hold. If you'll indicate to me which cabins are now free and how many there are, we can designate some for fever patients and others for the most gravely wounded. And now if someone could help me get down from this chair?"

The Turkish military observer retreated into his cabin and pretended not to understand her French, but the rest of them were good-natured about gathering up their personal belongings and the odd pillow or two and making nests for themselves in the corners of the smoking room.

When Betsy went down to the hold to inform the doctors of her success, she found Dr. Baird with a lung-shot patient, examining two open wounds oozing quantities of foul pus.

The doctor didn't look up as Betsy came up beside him. "Sergeant Pagelow—he was shot through both lungs the first day of the fighting at Santiago."

Betsy straightened, ready to work. "What can we do for him?"

"Nothing," the doctor said bitterly.

The man was in so much pain. "There must be something! What if we—" Betsy came up blank. She might have had a fair bit of experience nursing, but there had always been doctors to direct her. And actual implements. Even on the battlefield at Domokos they had been better prepared than this.

"Don't you think if I could, I would?" Dr. Baird turned to face her and Betsy realized he was near tears. "If I had a proper operating theater I could help him—or just a set of sterile instruments. But here? Nothing."

Betsy took a deep breath. "We can move him upstairs." It seemed so little, but it was something at least. "The passengers have agreed to give up their cabins. Almost all the passengers."

The doctor blinked at her. "We'll have to find a way to move them. . . ."

"Don't worry," said Betsy, patting him on the shoulder. He looked like he needed a pat on the shoulder. "We've got that worked out too."

True to his word, Captain Dowdy organized stretcher bearers. The cabins weren't large—the boat had been a coastal steamer, designed to house passengers for one night on the trip from New York to Norfolk, Virginia, not a grand ocean liner like the one Betsy had taken to Greece—but even so, that was thirty men they moved out of the hold.

Thirty men and Kit.

Fever cases and the worst sorts of wounds were given priority for cabins; the rest stayed in the hold or, if they were well enough, had blankets set out for them on the deck. There were some cases that would have made Betsy rage if she'd had time to rage; as it was, she could only do what she could do with what they had, making her rounds with malted milk for the wounded and beef tea for the feverish, bathing foreheads, changing dressings, taking temperatures.

Down in the heat of the hold, one man told her sheepishly it would make such a difference to have a handkerchief to mop his brow. So Betsy took her petticoat and cut it into squares. Another patient had taken a bullet in his left side, a bullet that couldn't be extracted for want of surgical tools. Every time he rolled in his sleep, the pain woke him. Betsy appropriated a pillow and squished it into a sort of bolster, strapping it to his side. Crude but effective. It felt good to be effective, even if only in small ways.

It was the ones they couldn't help at all that hurt; the men with shrapnel in them that could so easily have been removed if they'd only had the tools. Like poor Private Allen, who couldn't straighten his leg because of the metal shards lodged in his knee. They had to move him every so often, so he wouldn't get bedsores, but every movement was such agony that it felt like torture. One of the volunteers came to Betsy in tears, saying the poor man was begging to be left alone. But they couldn't leave him alone, not if he wasn't going to develop other nasty conditions, so Betsy moved him herself. Or did until Holt saw her wrestling with him and took over.

Holt was hardly well himself, but Betsy was too exhausted to complain. Some of the other wounded had quietly taken up places on the rota as well. She would have hugged each and every one if only there'd been time for it and she hadn't been afraid of spreading disease. That was her biggest fear, that the fever patients would infect the rest of them. She'd tried to isolate the fever patients in the cabins, but with her one thermometer giving out on her, sometimes it was more guesswork than actual nursing.

Day bled into night into day again.

Three days. She just had to keep everyone alive for three days.

Malted milk, beef tea, tiny sips of water. Betsy checked in on Kit whenever she could, but it was hard to force herself past the door of the cabin, hard to look at Kit without seeing Charles, Charles as they hadn't let her see him at the end, delirious and muttering.

It was one thing to soothe a stranger in his delirium, quite another to have Kit grabbing at her hand and calling her Dorothy and telling her it was time to put her hat on. There were times when Betsy came in and Kit was having conversations with people who weren't there, and Betsy had to pretend to fit into whatever story was playing out in her mind to get a few sips of beef tea into her.

And then there were the times when Kit wasn't conscious at all, collapsed into a sort of coma, and those were worse still.

Betsy had been through this so many times with so many men. Usually, by the time they came to her, they were done with the first phase: the headache and the cough. Then came the distended stomach, the high fever, the delirium. After that—sometimes there wasn't an after that. The biggest fear in Lamia had been peritonitis, the inflammation of the intestines. They'd had special food for the peritonitis patients. And doctors on hand, to try to save the patient if something ruptured.

They weren't always successful.

The doctors treating Charles hadn't been successful.

"Kit? I've got some beef tea for you." Even with the best attempts at ventilation, the cabin smelled foul. Betsy yearned for Sister Psara's white ward, for the carbolic, the laundry, the comfort of having Sister Psara there to tell her what to do.

Kit blinked at her. "Betsy," she whispered.

"I'm here." Sometimes Kit thought they were in Siboney and she was meant to be on shift. Other times she was helping Betsy find her way to the Tampa Bay Hotel, offering her candy that existed only in Kit's imagination.

"I hurt." Kit's voice was the barest thread.

"I know." Betsy knelt by Kit's bed. In Lamia, they'd iced the food for peritonitis patients. But the ice was the only thing making the brackish water drinkable, and they had almost run out. So instead there was beef tea that Betsy had let sit out until it was as cool as the climate would allow, which wasn't very cool at all. "I'm just going to give you a sip of something. Do you think you can swallow?"

"Betsy." Kit stirred, or as much as she could. She was so weak that even that small movement exhausted her. Her eyes were hollows in her emaciated face. "Betsy, am I going to die?"

Chapter Twenty-Four

Dear Ava,

Please don't go, whatever you do, please don't go. I should never have said what I said back in Athens. I hadn't the slightest notion. I didn't know, I didn't know anything at all about anything, but now I do and I can't bear to think of you going off to nurse not knowing how quickly it can all happen, ~~how quickly you can go from~~

~~There was nothing wrong with Charles and then~~

I couldn't bear it if anything happened to you. I'll go for you, if you like. ~~I'm not worth anything but you are.~~ I'll take your place. I don't care what happens to me, but I care what happens to you. Please don't go to Cuba, Ava. Please. I don't want you to die. Let me take your place.

~~I don't know if this letter will find you in time, so I'm coming to find you too.~~ If you get this, know that I'll be joining the Red Cross so you don't have to. You can tell them I'm going in your place, so it's all settled and there's no trouble about releasing you. And if you don't get this—I guess I'll see you there and I can say this all in person.

*But I hope you do get this and stay home safe in
Concord.*

> *With love,*
> *Betsy*

—*Miss Betsy Hayes '96 to Ava Saltonstall '96*

Loèche-les-Bains, Switzerland
January to May 1898

IT WOULD HAVE BEEN SIMPLER if Betsy could have just died in child-birth, but, of course, she didn't. She couldn't even get that right.

Betsy's baby was born at the end of January, in the midst of a ter-rible snowstorm that howled around the windows of the building that was part hotel and part hospital while being not quite either. A quiet place. A place where people could take the waters and rest. A place where a woman could, in the snowbound days of winter, give birth to an illegitimate child or pretend to give birth to a legitimate one.

It was a boy, that was all she knew. That was all they said before they took him away. They didn't let her hold him. She had only the faintest glimpse of him, skinny limbs, a wrinkled face, a slick of hair dark with goo, as the midwife held him up and wiped him down and bundled him into the receiving blanket the baroness had supplied, a beautiful, soft, woolly receiving blanket embroidered with a coat of arms that dated back to somewhere around Charlemagne.

Betsy took an instant and unreasonable dislike to that blanket.

She wanted to pull it off him and wrap him into her arms instead. She wanted to gather him close and snuggle him and turn her body into his blanket as it had been these past however many months. But she was flat on a bed in a pile of soaking linen, exhausted and dizzy, and before she could sit up, before she could move, the blanket-covered bundle that had been her baby was whisked away, out the door, away to the woman who was covering him with her name as she had with that blanket.

Betsy turned her head into the pillow and wept, which the nurse assured her was an entirely normal thing under the circumstances, and Betsy wasn't sure if by "the circumstances" she meant childbirth or giving one's baby away to be claimed by another.

It was not, apparently, an entirely normal thing to keep weeping for the next month. It wasn't that Betsy meant to; it was just that she couldn't seem to stop, as if the tears were coming out for everything, for her mother, for her father, for Charles, for Ava, for all the opportunities she'd thrown away, for the baby she'd thrown away. Ava had been right about everything. She knew—she *knew*—that this was what was best, that her baby was better off without her, better off being raised as Charles's son, with a mother who didn't sow destruction and hairpins in her wake, but she couldn't seem to convince her heart of that or her tear ducts.

She cried and cried until the doctors came and examined her and pronounced her blooming—only they said it in German, of course, a long compound word that used about sixteen syllables to contain one thought. Betsy didn't want to bloom. She didn't want to be. It felt like an insult that her body should go on being healthy when Charles was in the ground and her baby in a cradle rocked by another woman.

She really ought to have just died.

She had seen so many people die. Why couldn't she have been one of them? Why couldn't she have died of typhoid instead of her mother? Betsy could picture their old house, the one in Yonkers, the one from before they moved to Boston, the one where she had played with the guttersnipes and picked up the infection that had killed the wrong person. Somewhere, there was another version of the story, where her mother survived and had half a dozen other children and Alex didn't grow up angry and bitter and proper and marry that awful Lavinia and Ava had an entirely different roommate at Smith and Charles never met her and never came to Lamia and was there in Athens still, among his parquet and his porcelain, dreaming over the finds from Delphi.

But then her baby would never have been born, and Betsy couldn't quite find it in herself to wish him away, even if she devoutly wished herself away. It was a paradox, and one she couldn't solve.

The doctors argued over how best to treat her. Some thought she needed something to interest her, so they brought her books and papers. They found her American papers, whatever they had been able to scrounge, she supposed. It was kind of them. Kind, but pointless. Betsy had no interest at all in the fog that had engulfed New York, causing numerous rail collisions. She flipped listlessly past accounts of debates on Cuba in the Senate. She stared blankly at the ads. Lister's Dentifrice thought she needed whiter teeth. Ogram's wanted to make her beautiful with almond-and-glycerin cream. Hunyadi Janos wanted to help her with constipation, dyspepsia, and liver complaints.

What about dyspepsia of the soul? Where was the cure for that? No amount of dentifrice and glycerin cream were going to scrub her clean again.

When they found the papers wadded up, flung one by one across the room, the doctors decided perhaps stimulation wasn't what she needed. She needed rest, complete rest.

And why not? That was the story, after all, the story that Aikaterini had put about. Betsy had gone to Switzerland for a rest cure. It was a very good story, in its way, combining the reality of her four months of war nursing with just the tantalizing hint of a total breakdown. People could feel sympathetic and superior all at the same time.

So Betsy rested. And she dreamed. But not of what she had seen. Not of the refugees at Vólos or the battlefield at Domokos. She dreamed of Delphi. She dreamed of Charles dying at Thermopylae, unaccountably attired in Spartan armor and his own panama hat. She dreamed of the angel on the coin around her neck appearing before her with a fiery sword and, for some reason that wasn't entirely clear, an accordion. She had no idea where the accordion came from.

Nothing felt quite real, least of all herself, although that might have had something to do with the drafts the doctors gave her. Her mind and body felt strangely disconnected. Sometimes she imagined herself back in Northampton and woke with her feet already on the floor, convinced she was late for class.

Days drifted like the snow outside her window.

They kept sharp things away from her. Anything with a point, even a pen. Betsy could have told them that was ridiculous. She didn't need to slice herself open; she was rotting from within. Obediently, she went with her attendants to take the waters at the thermal springs, as if the minerals might leach whatever strange toxin she carried within her that brought death to those fool enough to love her.

She'd spared her child that, at least.

Betsy knew that somewhere else in the spa, the baroness and her retinue were housed. While a nurse wrapped yards and yards of cloth around Betsy's chest, binding her breasts tight to stop the milk, somewhere, not so very far away, a wet nurse was suckling her baby.

They caught Betsy once, in the night, creeping down the corridor, trying to find her baby, to look at him, just to look at him. She wasn't going to touch him, hold him, lift him. Just look at him. Just once.

There was a nurse outside her room at night after that. To stop her from sleepwalking, they explained. So she wouldn't hurt herself.

It was all very diplomatic, very tactful. She was a paying customer, after all. Not an inmate, this wasn't that sort of place, Aikaterini wouldn't send her to that sort of place. This was a hotel and spa where people paid exorbitant sums to take the waters and be looked after.

So she let them look after her and she slept and wept and slept again as winter softened into spring and the trees began to develop bits of green fuzz where there had only been bare branches. The fuzz turned into leaves, proper leaves, bright and exuberant. Easter came and went with church bells ringing.

Letters came to her. They let her have her letters. Letters from the Athenian society women she had nursed with, asking when she'd be back, inviting her to teas and lectures. Letters from her colleagues at the American School, tactfully not asking her whether she was coming back. Letters from Aikaterini. Chatty, gossipy, nonchalant letters.

In one, she included an announcement of birth. A son, to the Baron (deceased) and Baroness of Robecourt.

It wasn't meant to be cruel, Betsy knew. It was Aikaterini's way of telling her it was done, it was time to come back and move on. But Betsy couldn't; she was stuck; she was stuck in her mind and her body; she couldn't leave knowing that her child was still here, somewhere, and that if she listened, sometimes she could catch the faint sound of his infant cry.

Or the not so-faint sound of his infant cry.

There, in the courtyard, there were carriages prepared for travel, carriages and servants and trunks being carried out, and, there—yes, there was her baby, wrapped in a blue wool blanket, held in the arms of a woman she didn't know.

Betsy didn't stop to think. She flung herself out of the room, down the stairs, into the courtyard, never mind she was barefoot, never mind it was noon and she was in her nightdress, never mind that her hair was in a braid down her back.

There was her baby and they were taking him away.

Betsy barreled through the door, ignoring the startled noises of the staff. She could see her baby, see the little round head with its tufts of fuzz sticking up out of the blanket that was wrapped around him. It might be May but there was still a chill in the air in the Alps. The nursemaid holding him joggled him up and down, making cooing noises.

The baroness, tall and elegant in a high-crowned hat and a tight-fitting velvet jacket, leaned over and tucked the blanket more comfortably around his neck.

Betsy stopped short. She stopped short there in the mud, her nightdress flopping around her bare ankles. She wasn't sure what she'd intended to do, but whatever it was, her mind stopped and stuttered at the sight of that simple gesture.

The baroness looked up and her face froze. Or perhaps that was just all the makeup, layers of it, beautifully applied to create a perfect mask rather than a face. "Miss Hayes."

I've changed my mind; give him back; I want him back.

The baroness stepped forward, ever so slightly, so that she was between the baby and Betsy. Shielding him.

Betsy felt something inside her crumble.

"Here." Betsy yanked the ribbon from around her neck, the ribbon with Charles's coin, thrusting it at the baroness. "Here. This is for Charles's son."

The bright gold of the coin had been dulled by her rubbing it, by grease, by grime, by the touch of her fingers.

"Please. It belonged to Charles. He called it his luck. He said an ancestor had an angel coin just like it—it helped save him from the guillotine. I don't remember the whole story, but I'm sure one of his family must know."

The baroness took it up gingerly by the end of the ribbon, the grubby, frayed, decidedly dirty ribbon, letting the coin dangle in the air between them. "You tried to give this to me before."

"Not to you. To the baby."

Betsy wasn't sure why but it was suddenly desperately important that he have it, that he have something of her and Charles, Charles's coin, worn next to her heart. She might not have loved Charles as she should but she'd carried his token, and it was only right his son should have it, this last relic of whatever it was that had been between them.

"Charles would have wanted him to have it. He only gave it to me because he didn't have a son to carry it for him."

Somewhere, under all that paint and powder, an expression of pain crossed the baroness's face. But only for a moment.

"Now he has." The baroness closed her hand around the coin and gave a sharp nod. "I will make sure he has it once he is old enough to understand."

Betsy grasped the baroness's hand, the hand holding the coin. "You'll tell him—you'll tell him the story of it? You'll tell him— you'll tell him it was his father's?"

The baroness looked at Betsy for a long moment. "In his home, at Carmagnac," she said slowly, "his father's portrait hangs on the wall. He will sleep in the nursery that was once his father's and rock on the horse that was once his father's and fight battles with the soldiers that were once his father's. His father will be everywhere with him, in the library, in the stables, in the memories of his servants. Does that content you?"

Betsy jerked her chin up and down in a nod.

Tears were rolling down Betsy's cheeks, making damp splotches on her gown. There was a time when she would rather have died than disgrace herself in front of the baroness, but it didn't matter anymore. All that mattered was that Charles's son was going to Charles's home, to be raised as Charles would have wanted.

Without Betsy.

It was best for him, it was. And the baroness—oh, she didn't like Betsy, and Betsy didn't like her, but she was, Betsy knew, being kind.

In her own strange way, she was being kind. She didn't have to tell Betsy any of this. She didn't have to talk to Betsy at all. That hadn't been part of their agreement. It was, in fact, directly counter to their agreement. But she was being kind. Betsy clung to that kindness.

Let him know he is loved, Betsy wanted to say, but maybe that wasn't a gift. Betsy's love was something to be avoided at all costs. She was no one to him now, just the vessel who had borne him. He'd be safer with the elegant propriety of his adoptive mother, his adoptive mother who had known this other Charles, the Charles who had lived in those stables and those woods. And the nurse, the nurse looked kind. She looked like the sort who would get down on her knees and shake rattles and pull wooden toys and make animal noises.

He would be cared for, he would be loved, he would have a family and a home and a name.

Monsieur le Baron de Robecourt.

Betsy took a step back, trying very hard not to look at that little bundle cradled in the nurse's arms.

Not such a little bundle anymore. He was round-cheeked and chubby-armed and lifting his little head to look around with those big, dark eyes.

He was four months old, and in those four months he had known only the baroness as his mother. The baroness *was* his mother.

"Godspeed," Betsy said politely, as though they were strangers at a party, as though she weren't wearing her nightdress in the middle of a courtyard, with tears sticking her eyelashes together and clogging her throat.

"And you," said the baroness graciously. "I trust we will never meet again."

Behind her, the baby caught sight of Betsy and smiled a wide, toothless grin.

Betsy turned and stumbled back into the hotel, not seeing any-thing, not seeing anything except that happy, chubby face. Smiling at her as he left her.

"Come now." It was one of the nurses, Betsy could never remem-ber which was which—they all looked the same in their uniforms—putting an arm around her and leading her gently toward the stairs. "Let's get that mud cleaned off your feet."

Betsy looked down. Her hem was damp and draggled. Behind her, where she had walked, dark footprints marred the carpet.

And wasn't that just appropriate?

She started to shake and couldn't have said whether she was laughing or crying or both. "I'm sorry," she said. "I'm sorry."

"It's no matter," said the nurse soothingly. "Someone will brush it right off."

They'd brushed Betsy right off. Like mud on a carpet. Let it dry and then sweep it away with a stiff brush.

"There's mail for you," the nurse said coaxingly as she scrubbed Betsy's dirty feet and tucked her into a clean day dress and neatly pinned her hair. They all tried so hard. Betsy wished she could be more of a credit to them. "Mail from America."

"Thank you," said Betsy numbly. Outside, the courtyard was empty. The baroness's cortège had departed. They were gone, truly gone.

"I'll leave you to read it," the nurse said, and gave Betsy's shoulder a little pat.

The letter from America sat on the writing desk she wasn't sup-posed to use for writing.

Probably something from Alex. Disbursements from her trust. Invitations to speak at Lavinia's DAR meeting about My Experience Nursing in Greece. Ever since she'd been awarded a medal by Queen Olga—in absentia, but royal recognition was still royal recognition—

she'd become a Credit to the Family, at least on paper. It must be driving Alex utterly mad, which was something at least.

Betsy seated herself, slowly, awkwardly. Her limbs felt like they didn't quite belong to her, the outward detritus of a soul that had died. She wasn't quite sure why she was still here. In Switzerland. In the world.

The letter was a confusion of stamps and crossed-out addresses and the odd splash of mud. Betsy recognized Aikaterini's hand overwriting the original address.

No letter openers. They were on the forbidden list. Listlessly, Betsy pried the envelope open—and sat up very straight, her mouth dry, her hands shaking. She felt as if she'd been zapped by lightning, electricity zinging from the top of her head straight down to her toes, waking up bits of her that had been numb for months.

She knew that writing, that firm, angular writing. No colored inks for Ava. No curlicues and flourishes. She wrote a strong, dark hand. But the words. Betsy stared and stared but the words wouldn't change.

> *I had thought it best you hear from me before you read it in the* Smith College Monthly. *Now that our country has officially declared war on Spain (yes, I know you never read the papers: we're at war with Spain, in case you haven't noticed, which you probably haven't), the New York Red Cross has put out a call for volunteer nurses.*
>
> *I have volunteered.*

Oh no. Oh no, no, no.

She couldn't let Ava go. She couldn't. Frantically, Betsy flipped open the torn envelope, searching for dates beneath the confusion of stamps. April. She'd sent it in April. It was . . . oh goodness, what was the date? May. It was May. May something. The date hadn't seemed important before, but it was now, vitally.

She had to stop Ava. She had to stop Ava before she could get to Cuba.

Betsy scrabbled through the desk, finding some overlooked paper, a pen with a broken nib, some half-dried ink. It would serve. She scribbled her message as fast as she could, the jagged edge of the pen biting through the paper, the ink barely showing in spots. But it was legible, just.

But what if it didn't reach her in time?

Betsy shoved back the chair hard enough that it toppled over. Her coat. Her shoes. Where were they? Passport. She would need her passport. Passport and money. The rest she could buy if she had to.

"I heard a crash." The poor nurse skittered into the doorway.

The desk chair lay on its back on the floor. Had she done that? Betsy dismissed it as immaterial.

Already, Betsy was plotting out her course. Through the mountains to Zurich. What was the nearest port? Ostend, perhaps. Someone in Zurich would know. She could send telegrams and make arrangements in Zurich.

"I need my passport," she told the nurse. "My passport and my purse. And whatever clothes I brought with me. Whatever can fit in a carpetbag. I'm only taking what I can carry."

"But the doctor—"

"Has no say in the matter." Betsy squared her shoulders and looked the nurse in the eye, feeling like she was fully awake for the first time in months. "I came here for a rest and I've rested. I'm done resting."

Betsy could feel the energy coursing through her, so much energy she could barely contain it. She'd wondered why she was still alive. *This* was why she was still alive. To sacrifice herself in Ava's place. It was all very much like a Greek tragedy.

Betsy wondered if her chorus would be made of nurses.

"Go on," she urged the nurse, who was still standing there, looking like she wanted to argue. "I must leave as soon as can be arranged. Every moment matters."

She wasn't going to let Ava die.

Chapter Twenty-Five

"I don't know how the *Seneca* came to be used as a hospital ship, but anyone with eyes in their head could have told you it shouldn't have been. Not the slightest investigation was made of her condition before the sick and wounded were shoved aboard. Many of the men needed surgical treatment when they came on board, but the two medical men sent with the ship were supplied with neither instruments nor medicine. I found Dr. Baird in tears over one man, whose lung wounds might have been treated if only he had had the tools, but was instead smothering in his own pus, purely due to the carelessness of the relevant authorities at Siboney.

"You call that an unfounded accusation? Spend a week on a ship crammed with wounded men you have no means of helping and then tell me if you find it unfounded. . . . Even better, climb into one of those bunks with a chunk of shrapnel in your knee and a fever of a hundred and two, too weak to leave your bunk to relieve yourself, with only the clothes you came on board in, in agony every time you move, caught in your own filth, with men in similar state stacked all around you, and then tell me if you think my judgment is too harsh.

"And that was nothing to the way matters deteriorated once the water gave out. . . ."

—*Report of the Commission, vol. 7, p. 3546; testimony of Miss Elizabeth Hayes re: conditions on board the USS* Seneca

❧

On board the Seneca
July 15, 1898

HOLT WOKE UP WHEN SOMEONE kicked him in the kidneys.

He'd spread his blanket on a nice, quiet corner of the deck. At least, he'd thought it was a nice, quiet corner of the deck.

"Ooof," he heard, and woke to Betsy windmilling her arms over him, flailing wildly to keep from falling.

Holt stumbled to his feet, kicking his blanket out of his way as he went. The motion made the scab on his leg itch. "Whoa. You almost went over the side there."

"Sorry," said Betsy, in a choked voice. "I didn't mean to step on you."

"I didn't think you did." It was too dark to see her face, but when she didn't sass him back, Holt knew something was very wrong. "Betsy. What's wrong?"

"It's Kit," Betsy said thickly. "She asked me if she was going to die."

"Is she?" Holt asked.

"I don't know. That's the thing with typhoid—you just don't know! Sometimes the ones you think won't pull through do, and then the ones you think are fine—" Betsy paced in restless circles in the narrow space between the rail and the wall. "I told her she wasn't going to die but she didn't believe me. I don't believe me."

"You're doing the best you can for her," Holt said to the blur that was Betsy. "You got her into a bed."

Betsy stopped, shaking her head wildly. "She asked me to say g-g-goodbye to her kids for her." Her face crumpled. "Why couldn't I have been the one to get sick? Why did it have to be Kit? She has people who want her back. Not like me."

Holt held out a hand. "That's not—"

"My brother can't stand me. He'd be relieved to be shot of me." Betsy moved in erratic circles, hands waving, skirts swishing, hair blowing, the words tumbling out like a river breaking through a dam. "My father's dead. There's no one else, no one else who matters. Ava would miss me—but she has Dr. Stringfellow now. She'll be fine. And it's not like I have children to care for. I gave my child away."

Holt could have sworn the stars froze. Everything froze. Betsy stared at him, a look of horror on her face.

"I didn't mean to say that," she whispered, pressing her knuckles to her mouth. "I didn't mean to say that."

"I can pretend I didn't hear it," said Holt carefully.

"But you did. And you're wondering, aren't you?" Betsy's voice was unnaturally high. "You don't have to wonder. I had a baby. I had a baby and I gave him away. Now you know. You can hate me now."

"Why would I hate you?"

"Why wouldn't you hate me? I hate me. I had a lover—and I killed him. I had a baby—and I gave him away—"

Her voice broke. Holt watched, horrified, as Betsy folded in on herself. She rocked back and forth, shaking with the effort of keeping the sobs inside, great, gulping, ugly sobs that racked her whole body.

"Hey," Holt said softly. Very gently, he put an arm around her, trying not to crowd her. Her bowed head bumped against his chest; she was gasping, snorting, trying to suck the sobs back in. "Hey."

Betsy made a blubbery noise that might have been words or might not. It was hard to tell.

"Have you been holding this in all this time?"

Betsy lifted a ravaged face. "There should be—there should be a warning on me. *Caveat . . . emptor . . .* Beware. *Lasciate ogni speranza . . .*"

Holt felt a ridiculous surge of affection. Only Betsy would use what little breath she had to berate herself in three languages. He wanted to wrap his arms around her and tell her none of it mattered. But he didn't think she'd believe him. That wasn't how her mind worked. Her diamond-sharp, brilliant mind. Layers upon layers of pains and doubts shoved down, so one only saw the bright surface, hard and glittering.

Holt had guessed that there was something at the heart of it, but he had never imagined that this was what it was. *I had a baby and I gave him away. I had a lover and I killed him.*

"This lover . . ." Holt had a hard time pronouncing the word. "Did he hurt you? If you were defending yourself . . ."

Yanking back, Betsy gaped at him. "I didn't— Is that what you thought?"

Holt felt like a heel. "You did say you killed him," he said apologetically.

"How did you think I killed him? With a blow to the head? A knife to the ribs? Poison? That would have been quicker—kinder." Betsy straightened, holding herself with a sort of tragic dignity despite the snot bubbling out of her nose. "No. I didn't kill him like that. I was nursing—at a typhoid hospital—in Lamia. He came to see me. I didn't ask him to! He just . . . appeared."

Betsy swiped hard at her nose with the back of her hand. Holt handed her a handkerchief. She took it blindly, staring past Holt, her attention concentrated on something only she could see.

"There was an icon on the ward. A wonder-working icon. The

queen gave it to me. All the men kissed it for luck. Charles—it was because he was trying to make a point, trying to impress me, trying to, oh, I don't know."

She wrapped Holt's handkerchief around and around in her hands, twisting it, wringing it.

"Sometimes I wonder if it's because I didn't believe. Maybe God is punishing me for not believing in signs and wonders. But then why did Charles die and not me? Why take Charles?"

"Charles was your, er, lover?"

Betsy nodded abstractedly. She was somewhere else. Back in Lamia. With this Charles. "He didn't deserve to die because of me. It wasn't fair. I keep thinking—if he'd never met me—if I'd never known him—"

Holt couldn't bear it anymore, not the twisting, not the wringing, not this Charles. He clasped her hands in his own. "Did you deliberately infect him with typhoid?"

Betsy blinked at him. "Well, no—"

"Then how was it your fault?"

"Because I was *there*." Betsy pulled her hands out of his grasp. Holt's handkerchief fell to the ground. "Because I destroy everything I touch."

"You didn't destroy me. You saved me. Three times over."

Betsy frowned at him, momentarily diverted. "How do you get three? Never mind. It doesn't matter. You don't understand. If it hadn't been for me— I killed Charles."

"I understand more than you know." Holt bent over to retrieve his handkerchief, taking longer than he needed to. It was hard, so hard, to force the words out. But he had to. For Betsy. "I killed my mother."

That caught her attention. "Did you just say that you killed your mother?"

"By your logic." By his logic too, Holt realized. It was why he'd gone West, trying to outrun his crime, trying to escape his guilt. He jammed his handkerchief down into one of his pockets. "I didn't do it on purpose. Mine wasn't the hand that pushed her. But if I hadn't been born—"

"Childbirth fever?" Betsy said sagely.

"No." Maybe that would have been better. Maybe it would have been kinder. Not to have all those years of fear. Beloved mother on her tombstone. "She was murdered. My father murdered her. He pushed her down a flight of stairs."

"But you said—you said *you* killed her."

Holt tried to back up, but he was trapped. Trapped between the wall and Betsy. "You said you killed this Charles."

"That's not an answer."

Holt was beginning to wish he'd just handed Betsy a handkerchief and confined himself to sympathetic noises. But he'd started this. He had to see it through. "My father was . . . easily frustrated. He liked to take out his frustrations on those who couldn't fight back. Like my mother. Or me, when I was younger." He'd meant to leave it at that, but the words tore out of him, words he never intended to say. "He wasn't like that before I was born. My sisters love him. Everyone loves him. It was just me. It was something about me, about the way I am. I was small, I was sickly, I had headaches. I wasn't the son he wanted."

Holt could feel all the old emotions boiling up, as though he were eight again instead of twenty-eight. Fear and confusion—and guilt. All those nights, lying sleepless under the stars, or in a bunkhouse, or in a train car, trying not to think about it, trying not to remember, trying to persuade himself that it was all done, that he was someone else now. All the running, all the pretending, all undone in a moment. So much for Hold 'Em Holt, scourge of bandits. He was a scared boy in a silent house, listening at doors, lurking by his mother's room, wanting to make it all stop but not sure how. Knowing, somehow, that all this was his fault. For being born. For being himself. He would have given anything to have been anyone other than who he was.

Holt could feel the wall hard against his back. "When I went off to college . . . things were better for a while. I'd finally done something I was meant to do. I was his boy at Harvard. I thought—maybe it was over. But then I did something. I don't even remember what now. Joined the wrong club, took the wrong girl to the wrong dance—it didn't seem like it mattered at the time—but it all started up again. My mother claiming to be indisposed, clumsy, hurting herself. . . . I told her to leave him."

"Of course you did!" Betsy said stoutly. "I'd have done the same. What was wrong with that?"

"Everything," Holt said bitterly. "I was so smug. I thought all I had to do was tell her to pack her bags and it would all be fixed. I was a second year at the law school and I didn't want to be bothered. That's not how I put it to myself, but that was what it was."

"Don't you think your mother had some say in the matter?" demanded Betsy. "You might have suggested it, but it was her choice in the end."

End being the operative word. Acid burned at the back of Holt's throat.

"She wouldn't have made the attempt if I hadn't pushed her into it." Holt had gone over it in his head time and again, blaming himself, hating himself. "He caught her. He wasn't going to let her leave him. An accident, he called it. Just another accident. Everyone knew about her accidents. But this time, there weren't going to be any more. This time she broke her neck. *He* broke her neck."

"Holt. I'm so sorry. That was your father, not you. You're not responsible for what he did."

"There's a thing in law called proximate cause," said Holt slowly, trying to put his scrambled thoughts into words. "It's not just the immediate action but the chain of action that leads to the harm. You have to ask, could you have foreseen that what you did would cause the end result? When I told my mother to leave, I should have known that would set my father off."

Betsy tilted her head to try to peer at his face. "You couldn't know he'd be there when she tried to leave. You couldn't know he'd push her down the stairs."

"I didn't know. But I could have guessed. I should have been there." That was the worst of it. He should have been there. But there had been cases to study and articles to edit for the *Law Review*. . . . Holt felt sick with self-loathing. "Did you guess your Charles was going to follow you to—where was it?"

"Lamia. No. I never—I never thought of it. That's what's so miserable about it. Maybe if I had thought . . . But I didn't, not really. That's how I hurt people, by not thinking. I never mean to do harm, but I do anyway." Betsy scrubbed her nose furiously with the back of her hand. "My brother, Alex, always said I killed our mother. I got sick—and she died of it. I was two years old. I don't remember it. Or her. Alex said I didn't deserve to remember her."

Holt went from wanting to punch her lover to wanting to punch her brother. "Your brother is an ass."

"Well, yes. He is. But that doesn't mean he's wrong."

"He's wrong," said Holt firmly, feeling better now that they were talking about her again instead of him. "It wasn't your fault you fell ill. You were a child."

Betsy looked him in the eye. "So were you."

Holt felt the way he had when that bullet went through his leg.

Nothing at first and then the knowledge you'd been hit. The sting of it. The sense of your own blood leaking out onto the ground.

Betsy pressed both hands flat against his chest, looking up at him, making him look at her. "Whatever happened to your father—whatever changed him—that was him, not you. You're not responsible for his turning mean. He was probably always mean. He just hid it better."

"You didn't kill that Charles," Holt said hoarsely. "He made his choices. They were his choices, not yours. You don't hurt people. You're not bad luck. You're going to nurse that friend of yours and send her home to her kids."

Betsy shook her head. Her lashes were still wet with tears. The moisture glistened in the light of the ship's lanterns. "You don't know that. You don't know typhoid."

"I know you."

He'd watched her over the past few weeks, watched her working cheerfully, tirelessly, making the impossible possible. Shoving down her own hurts to care for others. He couldn't stand to think of her hating herself, blaming herself.

Holt cupped her face in his hands, looking into those great, haunted eyes. Into that expressive face that always said so much.

"If anyone survives this, it's going to be because of you. Do you understand? It's going to be because of you."

On board the Seneca
July 15, 1898

THIS TIME, THERE WAS NO doubt about the fact that Betsy kissed him.

She could tell herself she'd done it to stop him talking. She could tell herself it was easier to stop his mouth than argue with him. She could tell herself all sorts of things but the truth of it was that she had no idea why she kissed him; like most things in her life, it just happened.

Ava would tell her nothing just happened. Things happened because she made them happen, because she wanted them to happen, because she couldn't own up to wanting them to happen.

So maybe, just maybe, she might have wanted to kiss Holt.

Betsy kissed him with the salt of her tears still on her lips. She kissed him with all of the fear and uncertainty and guilt and goodness only knew what else roiling through her, clinging to his shoulders to keep from falling, clinging to his shoulders because she was dizzy with exhaustion and emotion and the constant rocking of this ship, and just maybe because they were very nice shoulders, sturdy shoulders, and the arms that folded around her held her close and safe, so she could let her eyes shut and not worry about falling, because it was Holt and he was holding her and kissing her back, and if there was one person in the world she could trust to hold her up, to keep her from going splat, here he was.

It was strange, but there it was. Betsy had never ever in her whole life, not in Boston, not in Northampton, not in Athens, felt as sure and safe as she did here in Holt's arms on the uneven deck of an ill-provisioned ship stuffed with wounded and fever patients.

She could have kept on kissing him like that indefinitely, but Holt's conscience got the better of him, and Betsy opened her eyes to find him looking at her, looking as bemused as she felt, somewhere between guilt and awe.

Holt ran his hands gently down her arms until he reached her hands. He squeezed them and then let them go. "You're tired—you're distressed. I shouldn't have. I'm sorry."

"I kissed you," Betsy said bluntly. "Don't you dare go all noble at me. I don't think my feeble constitution can stand it."

Holt grinned at her. Just like that. It was like seeing the northern lights or the Southern Cross or some other incredible natural phenomenon one had heard existed but didn't quite believe in until one saw it oneself.

Holt's grin was a wonder.

It made his whole face transform. It filled Betsy with an odd mix of lightness and trepidation all at the same time. As if she were on the threshold of something rather wonderful, but knew that she'd already bungled her chances of getting through the door.

Betsy looked at him through her damp lashes, feeling strangely uncertain, off-balance. "The things I said—can you forget I said them?"

Holt thought about it. "Are you going to forget what I said?"

Every single word of it was burned into her brain. "No."

Holt cleared his throat. "When was the last time you slept?"

Betsy tried to remember sleep. It was something she had once done. In Switzerland, it had felt like she had done nothing but sleep. She had fallen asleep for a few minutes earlier that day kneeling by the side of Kit's bed and woken with the imprint of the sheets on her forehead. "Siboney?"

Holt put an arm around her, guiding her as though she were an invalid. "There's a deck chair. You're sleeping now."

Betsy yanked back against his arm. "I'm the only nurse on board!"

Holt shepherded her to the deck chair. "If you don't sleep, you'll be a dead nurse, and what use will that be to anyone? Captain Dowdy has his rota. There are four men on duty—and a doctor on call. We'll wake you if you're needed."

"What about you?" Betsy asked suspiciously. "Weren't you sleeping when I stepped on you? You're still meant to be healing, you know."

"I'm fine. Don't worry about me."

It was her job to worry about him. She was his nurse. And—

well, his friend. Was *friend* the right word for it? Betsy knew she should object, should go back along her self-appointed rounds, but the deck chair rose to meet her. She could feel her body sinking into the wooden slats like plaster into a mold. There had never been a deck chair in the history of the world as comfortable as this deck chair.

"I'm only going to sit"—her words were disrupted by a giant yawn—"for a minute."

"Only for a minute," Holt agreed.

The last thing Betsy remembered was Holt settling his blanket over her as she slumped into slumber.

BETSY WOKE WHEN HER CHAIR tipped over.

She came to herself sprawled on the deck like a child's doll that had been dropped, legs spraddled and skirts any which way. She hastily clambered up onto her knees, and then onto her feet, realizing, belatedly, that it wasn't just the deck chair that had moved but the deck itself, which was plunging up and down at an alarming rate, while crew members hurried around her, shouting at each other over the sound of the wind, no doubt doing vastly important things.

Spray dampened Betsy's hair and dress; it was nearly impossible to hear over the sound of the wind and waves and shouting and chugging. Gathering up her damp skirts, grabbing on to whatever would support her as she careened from side to side, she stumbled for the hold, slipping and nearly falling on her way down, grabbing herself just in time, feeling the sort of wooliness she'd last had when they'd given her laudanum in Switzerland, but without the pleasant floaty feeling, just the foggy inability to concentrate.

What she saw in the hold woke her up immediately, more effectively than a bucket of cold water in the face.

The portholes had been closed against the spray, and the fog of blood and pus and feces was nearly unbearable; it rose to choke her.

Men were clinging to their bunks, crying out in pain as the ship tried to toss them out. Dr. Baird was rushing from bed to bed as fast as he could; Captain Dowdy and his volunteers were there too, lashing men to their bunks like Odysseus to the mast. Dr. Hicks was swaying down the narrow aisles, but that could have been either the whiskey or the motion; one could never tell with him. In the flickering electric light, Betsy could see bandages reddening where wounds had torn open.

"I'll get the bandages," she said, and raced for the supply cupboard, zigzagging drunkenly with the motion of the ship, grabbing up her meager supply of antiseptic gauze and styptic cotton, the last of the supplies she had filched from the hospital in Siboney.

Broken wounds, broken limbs, sprained wrists, new cases of fever. They worked through a dawn that never dawned, a morning dark as night, as the ship bucked around them. The men who'd been sleeping on the decks had to be moved back to the hold; Betsy could have wept for it.

"Give them the smoking room," she said hoarsely. The newspapermen could smoke their smelly cigars elsewhere. She wasn't sticking her recuperating wounded back in the hold to pick up goodness only knew what. She'd tried to isolate the fever cases in cabins, but it was like emptying the sea with a spoon. For every case she moved, new cases broke out, and there were no more cabins, there was no more space, there was no air in this blasted hold.

"We're out of ice," Captain Dowdy told her bluntly when she sent him for a chunk to dilute the brackish water for her fever patients.

"No ice," Betsy repeatedly numbly.

They'd known it would happen. They'd known the ice would run out. Without it, the water in the tanks was undrinkable; it had been barely drinkable with the ice. Holt's ingenious contraption produced just enough pure water for a fraction of a cup each for the worst of the fever sufferers. How long could they survive without water?

Three days, they'd told her. This was . . . July 16. They'd been on this ship three nights already. Surely they had to be nearing New York.

They weren't.

When they still hadn't made port by the following morning, Betsy put a guard on Holt's water system; dehydration and fever rendered many completely prone, but those who were ambulatory couldn't be trusted not to try to break in and slake their thirst. She'd tried giving the passengers and the wounded the water from the tanks, but it was too vile to drink undiluted; the well lost their lunch over the side of the rail and the sick retched up what little they had in their stomachs.

"Whiskey," Dr. Hicks suggested. That heavy bag that Dr. Hicks had brought on had turned out to consist almost entirely of whiskey bottles. Medicinal whiskey, he had specified, although he seemed to treat himself as liberally as he did the patients.

"Fine," said Betsy. It would only make them more dehydrated, but perhaps then they wouldn't mind as much. She was tempted to take a swig herself.

A fine thing it would be when they made port in a ship full of whiskey-scented wounded. But she didn't care, just as long as they did make port. If they ever made port. Grimly, Betsy toured the ship, whiskey bottle in hand, pouring out a tot each for those who could stomach it.

When they still hadn't made land the day after that, six days after leaving Siboney, Betsy sent Holt to the captain to find out where on earth they were.

"Cape Henry," Holt reported grimly.

"Where's Cape Henry?" Betsy asked, frantically shaking her poor, overused thermometer. They were developing new fever cases by the minute. Her understanding of geography was limited to the Greek islands and the route from Northampton to New Haven.

"Not New York," said Holt. When Betsy gave him a look, he clarified, "Virginia."

"Virginia?"

Even in normal conditions, it took at least a day to get by steamer from Virginia to New York.

They didn't have a day. They had no water, they had no bandages. Oh, they had food, all right. Tinned bully beef cans that bulged suspiciously and exploded on you if you were brave enough to open them, and hardtack, impossible for the sick to chew. Army rations. The passengers had offered to share their food—they'd been provisioned properly—but it wasn't going to spread far among the rapidly growing number of sick. What they needed was beef tea, oatmeal, and malted milk, all of which were nearly gone.

"Captain Decker says it's the rough seas. They've slowed us down."

"We can't afford to slow down!" How much longer could they last on board like this? Not long. And the longer they stayed, the more disease spread. Even one more night could be fatal for some of her patients. Could be fatal for Kit. Betsy bit her lip, hard, using the pain to steady herself. As calmly as she could she said, "Can you go check on the cabins for me? I need to find the doctors."

She found Dr. Baird gray with exhaustion, practically dead on his feet, tending to Sergeant Pagelow, whose lung wounds were producing alarming quantities of pus.

If they'd been on the hospital ship *Relief,* those wounds could have been dealt with within hours. As it was, he was drowning, drowning in the fluids from his own lungs.

Betsy wanted to scream, except it was no fair screaming at poor Dr. Baird, who had been working as hard as she had and seemed on the verge of imminent breakdown.

"Where's Dr. Hicks?" Betsy demanded.

"He's ill."

Betsy had no patience left for euphemisms. Or for Dr. Hicks. "Do you mean drunk?"

"No. Fever." Dr. Baird looked numb, just an empty shell of a man. "It was just a matter of time. . . ."

"We need to make port," said Betsy bluntly. "I don't care where, but we need to make port. The captain won't change orders for me, but he might for you."

"I don't think . . ." began the doctor.

Betsy wasn't having any of that. "I'm out of quinine, I'm out of water, I'm out of bandages—I've already torn up my petticoat!"

There were cheers from the less delirious men in the bunks around them, who were following their conversation with interest.

Dr. Baird's waxy face turned a faint pink. He made a point of not looking at Betsy's skirt. "Er, yes, well . . ."

"It's decided, then," said Betsy. "If you won't talk to the captain, I will."

"Nurse Hayes?" Holt was back. "There's something you need to see. Can you come with me?"

"What is it?" Oh, Lord. She'd sent Holt to check on the cabins. On Kit. "Is it Kit?"

"I'll talk to the captain," said Baird weakly, sidling away.

Betsy whirled back to face him. "Tell him now. We *must* make port. Not tomorrow. Not the day after tomorrow. Tell the captain. Today. It must be today."

If she'd spoken to any of the doctors in Greece like that, they'd have had her up before the matron. But there was no matron. There was nothing but one sick doctor, one broken doctor, and she, Betsy, with a boatload of dying men.

"Kit?" she asked Holt.

Holt put an arm around her as he shepherded her upstairs. He and

Captain Dowdy had taken it upon themselves to make sure she slept, for at least a few hours here and there, but the accumulated exhaustion was beginning to make Betsy feel as though she'd been tippling Dr. Hicks's whiskey. She couldn't quite seem to walk straight.

"You'll see," he said, holding her steady as she swayed on the steps.

Kit was lying in bed, just as she'd been lying for the past six days. Her face was so white it was gray. Her hair hung in sodden strands around her face; her sheets were soaked.

Betsy drew in a ragged breath.

"Go on," said Holt gruffly.

Betsy staggered to Kit's side and put the back of her hand against that damp forehead. That damp, cold forehead.

Betsy dropped to her knees next to the bed, pressing her face against Kit's limp hand as the sobs tore out of her.

Betsy knew she needed to pull herself together; she knew there were a hundred and thirty other people on this boat who needed her, but Betsy just couldn't seem to stop crying.

The fever had broken. Against all odds, Kit's fever had broken.

There was a movement against Betsy's forehead like the flutter of butterfly wings.

"Oh, honey." Kit was too weak to move; her voice was barely audible; but she was trying to pat Betsy's tears away. "What did I miss?"

Chapter Twenty-Six

Miss Elizabeth Hayes

Dear Madam:
The undersigned, United States officers and other passengers on board this steamer returning from Siboney, Cuba, full of sick and wounded men from the Santiago campaign, have observed with admiration the heroic and self-sacrificing manner in which you have cared for those suffering men. We have seen how unremitting you have been in your attentions to these sick and wounded, who were put aboard the steamer without the more ordinary provision for their care and comfort . . . and we have been witness to your devotion in preparing food for them, in watching for their wants, in administering medicines and making them as comfortable as possible.

We cannot see this trying voyage come to an end without giving you some expression of our admiration for your conduct, and our hope that your devotion will meet with a fitting reward.

We are Very Truly Yours,
[Forty signatures follow]

              —From the passengers on board the transport Seneca,
              off Fortress Monroe, July 18, 1898

Hampton Roads, Virginia
July 18, 1898

HOLT WASN'T SURE IF DR. Baird was more afraid of fever or of Betsy, but either way, he made a sufficiently impassioned case to Captain Decker that the word came down that the ship was to put in immediately at Hampton Roads, Virginia, where there was an army base with a hospital of sufficient size to take in the more severely wounded.

The local medical authorities, it seemed, had other ideas.

"Out of the question." Dr. Pettus, the medical officer tasked with inspection, emerged from the hold looking deeply shaken. He rounded on Betsy and Dr. Baird, who were following behind him. "This ship ought never to have been here! The idea—the idea of bringing these passengers to shore— We haven't the facilities for containing yellow fever."

Dr. Baird said weakly, "There's no evidence that we have yellow fever on board."

"There's no evidence you don't!" Pettus's voice rose as he hurried across the deck toward the ladder that would take him to his waiting dinghy. "I noted at least six suspicious cases. This ship should never have been allowed to enter Hampton Roads."

He stopped and turned, facing all of them. He was, Holt realized, shaking. His whole body was shaking. Shaking with anger. And fear.

Pettus raised his voice as he addressed all those on deck, from Captain Decker, standing in the background, looking suitably naval, to those patients who were well enough to take the air, to the American newspapermen, now somewhat less robust than they had been when the voyage began. He glared at them all. "No one is permitted to leave this ship. No one is to approach this ship. All boats will be ordered to lie well to windward until you depart."

There was a horrible stillness. No one could quite take in the idea that their promised haven wasn't a haven after all. They had no water, no supplies, a hold full of men getting sicker by the moment. And they were being sent back to sea.

It was Betsy who spoke. In a high, carrying voice, she said, "So you're signing the death warrant of every man and woman on board."

Holt could see Dr. Pettus bristle. "There's no need to be dramatic about it. I have a responsibility."

"You have a responsibility to the sick." Betsy was standing on the very tips of her toes, terrible in her anger. Holt half expected snakes to start writhing from her hair.

"I have a responsibility to the people of Norfolk," Pettus snapped.

"Hey," said one of the newspapermen. Holt still couldn't tell them apart. He'd made a habit of avoiding newspapers, and he wasn't about to change it now. "Some of us are just here as passengers."

"Doesn't matter," said his comrade, who had long since run out of cigars to chomp. "He'll leave us here to rot with the rest of them."

"This ship," said Pettus angrily, "originated in the village of Siboney. That pestilential place has been so overrun with yellow fever that the army saw fit to burn it to the ground."

Betsy's feet went flat on the ground. Her face drained of color. "Burned. Siboney? But we've only been gone . . ."

"Six days," Holt supplied for her. Six days for yellow fever to go from a vague rumor to a threat so severe that the army incinerated an entire village.

Dr. Pettus made for the ladder. "I saw enough ugly sickness down below to warrant me in my decision not to allow your surgeons to land these men. I myself shall proceed directly to a quarantine vessel for a complete change of clothing before setting foot onshore."

Betsy was white as a sheet, in shock. Holt limped forward. "We fully appreciate that, Doctor. But we can't go back to sea lacking the basic necessities. These men need water, food, and medical supplies. If those items could be provided . . ."

The doctor's legs and torso were already disappearing over the side. "Make a list and wire it to the shore."

Within an hour, the supplies began to arrive. Casks of water bumped up against the side of the ship as they were hauled up one at a time with a winch and tackle, delivered by small boats manned by sailors who kept their faces carefully muffled to avoid breathing in infection. Back and forth the boats went, bringing blocks of ice, cartons of medical supplies, food.

Holt found Betsy in the galley, frenetically sorting supplies.

"There's enough beef tea to keep us for months," she said, in a bright, unnatural voice. "And malted milk too. If we're to be lepers, at least we're to be well-fed lepers."

She turned her back on him, plunging elbow deep in a box full of packages of Armour's beef extract.

Elsewhere on the ship, casks of water were being opened, quinine pills distributed, telegrams sent back and forth between the ship and the authorities in Washington. It wasn't ideal, but their immediate problems had been, if not fixed, at least alleviated.

Holt didn't think that was what was really upsetting Betsy.

Holt wasn't sure when it happened, but at some point, maybe in the tent in Siboney, maybe on board ship, he had found himself translating from Betsy to English, as if she were a tablet scratched with ancient writing and he had, tentatively, found the code.

Having once started, Holt couldn't seem to stop. He found himself absurdly aware of her every mood, every word, every gesture, weighing the meaning of each expression, each half-drawn breath.

Holt propped an elbow against the counter. "You're worried about your friend. The one with the eyebrows."

He saw her stiffen, half-bent over the box. Slowly, she straightened and looked at him. "They burned Siboney. How bad does it have to be for them to burn a whole village?"

Holt shook his head. "I don't know," he said honestly. "People are more afraid of the fever than they are of the Spanish. The fear might be enough."

"Or the fever might have taken hold." Betsy clutched a container of malted milk so hard, Holt was afraid it would shatter. "I don't know whether to be happy about Kit or terrified for Ava."

"What about both?"

Betsy didn't seem to hear him. She was lost in her own terror. "I don't know what I'll do if anything happens to Ava. I know, she told me, she's her own person, and it was her choice to stay in Siboney. . . ."

Betsy broke off, her eyes meeting Holt's. It didn't take much to tell exactly what was haunting her. Someone else who had made his own choice. Charles, who had chosen to follow her to Lamia.

It wasn't fair to hate a dead man. But Holt did anyway.

"If you know that," he said, "why are you blaming yourself?"

"How can you ask that? You, of all people—" Betsy ducked down into one of the cartons, coming up flushed and disheveled. "I'm meant to be her maid of honor. That implies a responsibility."

"I don't think that's chief among a bridesmaid's duties," Holt said mildly, to cover the turmoil of his emotions. She was right; he was a hypocrite. He didn't know how to stop blaming himself any more than Betsy did. "I'll ask the captain to send a cable to Cuba. Someone should be able to tell you what happened to the hospital staff."

Betsy tilted her head, looking at him with something in her eyes he couldn't quite read. "You always have an answer for everything, don't you?"

Except when he didn't. "The captain says we leave for New York at noon tomorrow. We're almost at the end of this."

Betsy breathed in deeply through her nose. "Do you think they'll let us land in New York?"

She looked so tired, with the great circles under her eyes, the hollows below her cheekbones.

"If they don't, we'll just sail the seven seas. You can turn pirate. I can picture you with a cutlass."

"Ha," said Betsy, but her mouth turned up at the corners, just a little. It made Holt feel like king of the world. Or at least ruler of a small principality. She hesitated, frowning at a bottle of beef extract. "What *will* you do when this is over? If this is ever over."

"I don't know," Holt said. He couldn't see himself going back West. It already felt vaguely unreal, his life there. "I suppose there's always Buffalo Bill's Wild West Show."

That won him a snort. "You never made that convincing a cowboy. Even with the mustache."

Holt took the beef extract from her, adding it to the collection on the counter. "I liked that mustache. Maybe I should grow another one."

"Don't you dare."

"A beard like the Ancient Mariner?" There was only so long he could avoid the question that was hanging over both of them. "What about you? What will you do?"

"I don't know." Betsy set down another bottle, turning it so the label faced just so. "I could retake my exams and go back to the American School."

"You don't sound delighted by the notion."

Betsy reluctantly abandoned her bottle of beef extract, not meeting Holt's eyes. "All I ever wanted to do is excavate—and the American School wouldn't let me do that."

"Then find someone who will."

Betsy frowned at him. "It's not that easy."

"Neither was this," said Holt. "That didn't stop you."

"It's different. I couldn't *not* do what I'm doing here." She bit her lip. "I'm so tired I don't know what I'm saying."

But that, thought Holt, looking at her bowed head, was just when the truth came out. When you were so tired you didn't know what you were saying.

Like the other night. The night they weren't talking about.

Holt wanted, more than anything, to just reach out and open his arms to her. To stand there, together, not saying anything at all. Just being. Because they both already knew more about each other than anyone in the world. They could just be. Together. And that would be enough.

But somehow, he couldn't quite work up the nerve to do it.

Instead, he heard himself saying, in a carefully neutral voice, "It's a one-day sail to New York. Only two days left to go."

"If they allow us to land." Betsy let out a deep breath, matching his detached tone. "Could you take charge down here? I need to go and unpack those boxes of medical supplies. Dr. Baird thinks he might finally be able to do something about that shrapnel in Private Allen's leg."

Holt watched her go, thinking of all the things he wished he'd said and hadn't.

Only two more days.

If New York let them land.

Hoffman Island, New York
July 21, 1898

NEW YORK CITY WELCOMED THEM, as it had so many other huddled masses yearning to breathe free.

Wretched refuse, homeless, and *tempest-tossed* did about sum them up, decided Betsy, who had reached the giddy stage of fatigue. She couldn't remember the last time she'd bathed. Or slept in a bed. Or done anything with her hair other than drive a few more pins into it. There were probably tropical birds living in there. Land crabs. Lost tribes. Her dress was so stiff with dirt it could stand on its own. It could probably nurse on its own by now.

Betsy entertained the notion of an autonomous apron, taking temperatures and administering fluids. Relief was doing strange things to her brain. Kit's fever had broken; a telegram from Cuba had assured her that Ava and her Dr. Stringfellow were both alive and well and happily elbow-deep in intestines; and now here they were, with the prospect of an end to their endless voyage, with proper beds and proper food and someone else to look after everyone. Betsy felt thoroughly bewildered by it all and not quite sure what to do with herself, so she fussed around her patients to keep from thinking, adjusting blankets and changing dressings that didn't need to be changed yet and dispensing unnecessary quantities of beef tea.

New York welcomed them, but it inspected them first.

The fever patients came in for particular scrutiny. Fourteen of them were marked off as potential yellow fever cases. Like the authorities at Hampton Roads, the medical officer in New York had been warned about the fate of Siboney. A separate launch waited for the fever cases, to take them to isolation on Swinburne Island.

"They'll be cared for properly?" Betsy demanded.

"We have had fever patients before," said Dr. Doty, not unkindly. "They'll be given the best care possible."

The care she hadn't been able to give them. The sort of care possible in a proper hospital ward.

Betsy nodded and stepped back. These weren't her patients anymore.

It felt very strange not being responsible for everyone.

The wounded and ill, including Dr. Hicks, were sent on to Bellevue Hospital for proper treatment. Betsy could see Dr. Baird nearly break down at the relief of it. Not being able to treat them had weighed on him so. She clasped his hand in silent sympathy and felt him shake with what she hoped were unshed tears and not the beginnings of a new case of fever.

The rest of them—the passengers, the close-enough-to-well, Dr. Baird, Betsy—were sent to quarantine on Hoffman Island, a small, man-made island employed expressly for placing the potentially plague-ridden. The accommodations consisted of barrack-like wards lined with cots.

It wasn't exactly the Hotel Grand Bretagne, but it was a distinct improvement over conditions on the *Seneca*.

Betsy submitted to being scrubbed and having her clothes taken away for disinfection, by which she assumed they meant "utter incineration," which was really the only possible outcome, assuming the dress hadn't attained a state of sentience by which it might fight back.

She took the nightdress that was given her, cleaned her teeth, braided her hair, fell into one of the cots, and slept for the better part of a day and a half.

When she woke, she found Kit sufficiently recovered to lean up against pillows and hold a pen. Kit was scribbling away busily, determined to make up for lost time.

"Go away and stop trying to read over my shoulder," she said, which Betsy took as a sign that she was starting to feel better.

So Betsy went. There weren't many places to go. The island itself was tiny; their corner of it tinier still. Betsy followed an attendant's directions out through a small courtyard to a tiny strip of wind-blasted grass where the *Seneca* passengers could take the air, filtered through the wires of a strong fence.

Among the flurry of telegrams, one had been sent to Kit's family, who were going to come to New York and collect her once she had cleared her quarantine.

In a few days, Kit would have her family. Betsy's wounded were being cared for by doctors with actual surgical instruments and nurses who wore crisp white aprons and didn't smell like the hold of a ship. As for Holt . . .

He'd probably grow a new mustache and join Buffalo Bill's Wild West Show.

Somewhere, on the other side of that fence, across those choppy waters, lay the future. In a day, or possibly two, the medical authorities would release them. But to what? Betsy had no idea where she was meant to go or what to do.

Lavinia, she knew, would be delighted to have her, the same way the Romans had delighted in possessing captive enemies, to show off as trophies. Only instead of being hauled before the populace in a chariot, decked with ornaments, Betsy would be pinned into tidiness and displayed in the drawing room to a select audience of Daughters of the American Revolution. Betsy wasn't a Daughter of the American Revolution. She wasn't even a first cousin once removed of the War of 1812. But she had been decorated by the queen of Greece and nursed in Cuba, so she was a feather in Lavinia's bonnet.

Betsy didn't want to be a feather in Lavinia's bonnet or a thorn in Alex's side or any other kind of protuberance.

She just wanted—what she'd always wanted, she supposed. To dig.

Then find someone who will, said Holt's voice in her head. As if it were that simple, that easy, to just go and set up a dig in Greece. There was funding, permits. . . .

Well, of course, money wasn't really a problem. Thanks to the despised carpet factory her father had sold, she had more than enough money to fund a dig herself.

The queen would see the permit sorted for her. Sophia Schliemann would advise her. There wasn't much Sophia Schliemann didn't know about running a dig. And Aikaterini would help however she could.

She had some ideas about places one could try—not the well-trafficked places, not the legendary cities or major religious sites, but lesser-known places, places where one might find the traces of ordinary lives. . . .

Betsy's nose bumped up against the wire and she drew herself back, feeling obscurely guilty for letting herself even dream about it. It felt like cheating somehow, to think of going back, of starting over, as if none of it had happened—the war, Charles, their baby.

Not your fault, Holt had told her, but then, whose fault was it? How was it fair?

Someone coughed behind her, the sort of cough that said he'd been trying to get her attention for some time.

"Holt," she said. Speak of the devil and all that.

He'd shaved, Betsy noticed, despite his claims about aspirations toward a new mustache. His hair was damp and neatly combed down, instead of sweaty and any which way.

"How are the others?"

"Sleeping. Eating. Bathing. Smoking. Everyone is enjoying the sensation of being on dry land." Holt smiled ruefully. "The authorities here have never been saddled with a group like us before. The foreign observers have been demanding transatlantic cables. The newspapermen have been clogging the wires filing their stories."

Betsy stood with her back to the wire. "Poor Kit. She was worried they'd steal a march on her."

Holt cleared his throat. "As much as I'd like to be here on my own account, I've been sent as the representative of a delegation."

"A delegation?" Betsy frowned at him.

"Of the passengers of the *Seneca*. They'd like you to have this." Holt produced a rather crumpled piece of paper, folded in half. "They wrote it the night we tried to dock in Virginia, but it needed to be passed around for signatures—and then there wasn't a good chance to give it to you. And since we'll all be going our separate ways tomorrow, the consensus was that you should have it now."

That was an awful lot of words saying nothing. Betsy felt strangely unsettled, and not in a good way. "What is it?"

Holt shook his head and flapped the paper at her. "Just read it."

"Fine." Betsy took it from him and made a show of reading out loud. "*Miss Elizabeth Hayes. Dear Madam: The undersigned, United States officers and other passengers on board this steamer returning from Siboney, Cuba, full of sick and wounded men from the Santiago campaign, have observed with admiration the heroic and self-sacrificing manner in which you have cared for those suffering men. . . .*"

Betsy's voice faltered. The words blurred in front of her eyes.

Holt caught the letter before it could fall. "*We cannot see this trying voyage come to an end without giving you some expression of our admiration for your conduct, and our hope that your devotion will meet with a fitting reward.* They mean it, you know. Every word. We all mean it."

They'd all signed it. Everyone. Every passenger, from Captain Dowdy down to the Turkish attaché who had pretended not to understand her French.

Betsy turned her face away, fishing in her sleeve for a handkerchief. Naturally, she didn't have one. She never did.

Holt produced a handkerchief from his pocket. Betsy vaguely recognized it as a fragment of her petticoat, cut into a rough square. He pressed it into her hand. "Not one person died on that ship. Not one. Do you realize what a wonder that is? That was your doing. No one else's. Yours."

Betsy blew her nose noisily into Holt's handkerchief. "You put them up to this."

"I didn't. I swear." Holt stepped back, leaning his lanky frame against a post. "It might have been Commander Anderson—the Swede. He's half in love with you."

"Ha," said Betsy thickly.

"They're all half in love with you." Holt's face had gone blank, his voice strangely flat. "I'm in love with you."

Something about the way he was looking at her made Betsy's stomach do strange things. "Very funny," she said hoarsely, trying to make a joke of it. "Have you looked at me recently?"

"Every day." There was nothing flippant about the way he said it, the way he was looking at her, as though there had never been anything more important or more precious in the world. "It's the best part of my day. You're the best part of my day."

Betsy did her best to brazen it out. "Well, between me and Dr. Baird there's not much to choose between. I suppose there is also Captain Dowdy—and Commander Anderson. I wouldn't want you to have a hopeless passion for Colonel Yermsloff. You might wind up in Siberia."

"Betsy." That was all. Just her name. But it made her stop and swallow hard. "I know I don't have much to offer you. . . ."

"You? Don't have much to offer me?" Betsy could feel the panic rising up in her. Whatever else, whatever had happened on the *Seneca*, she couldn't let Holt throw himself away on her. "I had a lover! I had a child out of wedlock! I do have a large fortune, so I suppose someone might be willing to overlook my other deficiencies. . . ."

"Don't talk about yourself like that."

"Don't tell me how to talk about myself!" The last man who'd declared his love for her had been dead within a fortnight. Betsy glared up at him. "At least I'm traveling under my real name and not some sort of ridiculous nom de guerre!"

"It's not a nom de guerre." Holt looked at her, his emotions so bare on his face it was painful to behold. "Maybe it is. It's my mother's maiden name."

He had told her that before, and she hadn't realized then what it meant. Now she did, and it would have made her feel all sorts of things if she hadn't been working so hard on feeling nothing at all.

Why wouldn't he fight with her? That's what they needed, a blazing row, so she could flounce off and he could storm off and be safe, safe from her, because he might delude himself that he loved her, but he couldn't, not really, and if he did, then, well, it had to be stopped before he hurt himself. Before she hurt him.

"What's your name?" Betsy demanded. Her voice sounded flat and hard. "Your real name."

"Ambrose."

"Ambrose?"

"Ambrose Charles Rutherford IV." Holt's lip twisted. "I didn't choose it."

"Ambrose." There was no way to say it that made it sound any better. It was stuffed leather sofas and the law library at Harvard. It sounded like someone her brother would befriend at one of his clubs. "No wonder you ran off West and changed your name."

He didn't take the bait. "I did it because I didn't want to carry my father's name. I didn't want any part of him. But I was fooling myself, wasn't I? You can't just shed that sort of thing."

Betsy felt like crying. There was no fighting someone who wouldn't fight back. He'd got under her guard; nothing was left but the raw truth.

"No. You can't." There was no just going back and starting over.

There was no putting back the clock. "I'm damaged goods. Not just in the eyes of the world. Inside. In here. If I were a vase, I'd be in a thousand pieces."

"You're not a vase." Only Holt could say that and make it sound like an endearment. "Besides, isn't that what you do? Put broken things together again?"

"Well, yes, pots and inscriptions and . . ." She was losing the thread of the discussion. He had a way of doing that to her. "I know you mean well by all this. I know—oh, I don't know what I know. But these are strange times. We've just been through a ridiculous amount together, and maybe right now you're feeling grateful, and maybe it's just because I was the one who was there—but I don't want you to wake up a year from now and find yourself saddled with me. You could find yourself someone so much better. Someone not so—cracked."

"There's so much wrong with that I don't even know where to begin. Do you really think I'd be proposing to Kit if circumstances were reversed? Or your friend with the eyebrows?"

"You'd have to fight Dr. Stringfellow for her." But that wasn't the real problem. Betsy forced herself to say it out loud. "Somewhere out there—maybe there's someone fresh and new for you. Someone who hasn't made so many mistakes. Someone who hasn't hurt so many people."

Oh, bother. There went the tears again. Betsy blinked them back furiously, not wanting Holt to see.

Gently, he wiped away the tears from under her eyes with a knuckle. "All of that you call mistakes—if I could have spared you the pain of it—I don't know. It's hard to think through what might have happened and who we might have been if our lives had been different. But the idea that having lived and endured makes you less worthy of love—that's pure nonsense. I love you as you are. I love you because of what you are. I don't want to erase your past or pretend it didn't happen. Any more than I can erase mine."

Betsy sniffed mightily. "What if I want to erase it?"

"Do you? Do you really?"

She wasn't sure anymore. Betsy tried to remember the person she had been. But she wasn't sure she had liked that person either. She wanted to scrub the dark spots out of her soul. She wanted to be someone who could be loved and not feel like that love ought to be better spent. She wanted things to be simple.

"I wanted to dig up pots," she whispered. "I just wanted to dig up pots."

"And inscriptions." It was no fair looking at her like that, so tenderly, as though he understood. His hand found hers, their fingers twining together. Betsy clung to the comfort of that hand, even as she knew she should push him away. "I just wanted to go to law school."

How had they both become so derailed? Like that train two miles from Tampa, stuck on the tracks in the middle of nowhere. Betsy remembered that night, the wilderness pressing close around them, the coal smoke everywhere, obscuring her sight, rasping her throat.

But that train in the middle of nowhere brought her Holt.

That was a dangerous line of thought. She couldn't let herself think that way. Betsy shook her fingers free from his. "Then why don't you? Why don't you go back to law school? Finish your degree?"

"Because it was what my father wanted for me. Because when I tried to bring him to justice, the law wouldn't hear me. What was the use of it?"

"Then go back to law school and make them hear you." If anyone could bring good out of evil, it was Holt. He was too good for her. Better to send him on his way to do the things he was meant to do. He'd go his way and she'd go hers. "Go back to law school. Use your power to fight for the people like your mother. Be the one who believes them."

"I believe in you," Holt said simply.

Betsy pressed her fingers to her temples. "Don't. Please."

"Don't believe in you? Or don't love you?"

"Either. Both." Betsy couldn't look at Holt, because if she did, she might weaken, and if she weakened, she might go to him, and if she did . . . "Could you go away now, please?"

And because he was Holt, he did.

Chapter Twenty-Seven

VOYAGE OF HORROR ON HOSPITAL SHIP

Intended only for carrying troops, the *Seneca* was never designed as a hospital vessel. She was in no way fitted for such service. Miss Elizabeth Hawes [*sic*], the Red Cross representative, proved to be the angel of the dreadful journey.

Were it not for Miss Hawes [*sic*], many of the patients must have died on the trip. The woman deserves a medal from the United States Government. She went right down among the wounded in the foul hold of the ship, where they were lying on rough boards, and nursed them. She made gruel and cooling drinks and encouraged them.

—New York World, *July 22, 1898*

VOYAGE FULL OF MISERY

It was a miserable voyage, but made more miserable by the drunkenness on the part of several military officers and by the neglect and indifference on the part of the medical men to whom was intrusted [*sic*] the health of the passengers. . . . Personally, I failed to observe any particular "sacrifice" on the part of anyone, with the exception of Miss Elizabeth Hayes, the Red Cross nurse. Miss Hayes proved to be an angel of mercy.

—*John Maxwell, reporter and passenger on the* Seneca, Chicago Tribune, *July 22, 1898*

JUST A HYSTERICAL WOMAN

"It is really too bad that so much importance is being placed in the utterances of hysterical females. . . . Miss Hayes is a hysterical woman and she is liable to say almost anything. She lies, that is all."

—*Major George Torney, chief medical officer of the* Relief, *quoted in the* New-York Tribune *and the* New York World, *July 26, 1898*

❦

New York, New York
July 22, 1898

A LAUNCH TOOK THE *Seneca* passengers from Hoffman Island to Manhattan the following morning.

This was the end, Holt realized. The final leg of their long, strange journey. Once that launch touched the dock, they would all go their separate ways.

Betsy would go her way and he'd go his.

She'd made her feelings clear. One didn't get much clearer than "go away." "Go away" meant go away.

So here Holt was, standing at the back of the launch, watching all the other passengers thronging around Betsy, thanking her, saying their farewells, wishing he could be there too, but knowing he'd forfeited that right. He'd forfeited the hope not just of her affection but of her friendship. Looking back, Holt wanted to kick himself. He could have just handed over the letter and left. He could have let Betsy bask in her well-deserved accolades. Instead, he'd ruined it all by forcing his feelings on her.

He'd been an ass.

He was as bad as that Charles who'd followed her to Lamia without her asking him. Worse. She'd never invited Holt's affections.

Aside from kissing him. Twice.

But the first kiss had been on the cheek. And the second—Betsy had been in the grip of strong emotion. He'd be a cad to refine too much on it. Or remind her of it. She'd been distressed and exhausted and lonely and he'd been there. That was all there was to it.

If he'd just handed her the letter last night and left, he'd be standing next to her now. She'd be looking up at him with the tilt of the head that was so uniquely hers, depressing his pretensions with a pithy remark. Holt missed that. He missed her. Maybe it was odd to miss someone who was standing right there, but he was missing her in advance, missing all the future hours that could have had a Betsy in them and wouldn't.

Holt hung back as Betsy got her passengers organized. Colonel Anderson, the scoundrel, kissed her hand. Not to be outdone, Colonel Yermsloff kissed both hands.

Captain Dowdy assisted Kit Carson, thin and pale, all freckles and nerve. She gave Holt a long, speculative look as she passed, and Holt felt himself reddening.

The launch bumped up against the dock, a very crowded dock, thronged with people being ineffectually shooed away by police officers. Around the edges of the crowd, newsboys were hawking papers. "Read all about it! Voyage of horror on hospital ship!"

The *World*, the *Tribune*, the *Sun*—they were all there. All with bold black headlines.

The *Seneca* was front-page news.

The reporters and curiosity seekers thronged forward, shouting, pointing, craning their necks, barking questions at the passengers as they stumbled off the launch. On Captain Dowdy's arm, Kit gave a jaunty wave and called back, "You want to hear all about it? Read my feature in the *St. Louis Star Ledger*!"

Only Betsy and Holt were left.

Betsy and Holt and a hundred onlookers.

He wanted to say something, to apologize, but even an apology felt like an imposition, a way of forcing her attention to him, to his feelings, to the emotions she didn't return. He couldn't pretend he hadn't meant it all: he did. Every word.

So he just said, "Go on."

Betsy looked silently over her shoulder at Holt. For a moment, he thought she might say something, but she dropped her head and stepped up on the side of the boat.

A huge cheer rose from the crowd, deafening in its enthusiasm. The crowd thronged the boat, men pushing forward, hands outstretched, fighting over whose would be the hand to help Betsy onto dry land.

Betsy stood there, frozen, staring in bewilderment at all the shouting mouths and waving hands. Some of them were waving papers. There was a very poor line drawing of Betsy, depicted as a cross between an angel and Florence Nightingale, in Grecian robes, holding a lamp.

"ANGEL OF THE *SENECA*!" blared the headline.

"They're here for you," Holt said quietly. "You're a heroine."

Betsy looked horrified. "But I'm not."

Holt smiled wryly. "Don't tell them that. The world needs heroes."

Betsy scowled at him. "Is that right, Hold 'Em Holt?"

Ignoring all the hands, Betsy stepped down herself, wobbling just a little.

The crowd parted in front of her. It was the most extraordinary thing Holt had ever seen. They fell back as courtiers might have at the court of Louis XIV. One by one, the men bared their heads as Betsy passed. A little girl darted forward and pressed a posy of flowers into Betsy's hand before ducking back into the crowd. Holt could have sworn at least one woman dropped a curtsy.

"Miss Hayes! Did you know they're calling you the Angel of the *Seneca*?"

"Miss Hayes! Is it true there was no water on board?"

The reporters were canny. They'd ranged themselves right at the end of the crowd, just before the carriages, blocking Betsy's path.

"Miss Hayes! How does it feel to be a heroine?"

"I'm not." Betsy turned and raised her voice to be heard above the crowd. "I'm not a heroine. I'm just someone who did what was needed."

The crowd adored it. Everyone loved a heroine who claimed she wasn't a heroine. The reporters were scribbling busily away. *As modest as she is kind . . .*

"I mean it!" Betsy said shrilly.

Holt limped toward Betsy as fast as he could, but the crowd had closed in again, following her, and it was hard to get through. Her slight form was swallowed up by the reporters ranged around her, clustering in to catch her every word.

As Holt tried to push his way through, he saw Betsy pull herself up onto the step of one of the waiting horse-drawn cabs, but she didn't duck inside. She stood there, on the step, one hand on the doorframe, and faced the crowd.

"I appreciate your kindness, but I can't accept your accolades under false pretenses. You shouldn't be praising me." Betsy's throat worked convulsively. "What I did on that ship—it wasn't heroic."

Holt watched as the entire crowd went silent, the reporters gripping their pencils, everyone waiting for what promised to be a shocking revelation.

"*I* wasn't heroic," Betsy burst out. "Half of what we call heroics are just people making the best of a bad situation. But we shouldn't have been in that situation in the first place! Whatever you've heard about the *Seneca*? It's true. All of it. The water was brackish; the ice gave out. The men were crammed into pens not fit for cattle. We hadn't a surgical instrument or a roll of bandages on board except what I brought with me—which was precious little. Would you like to know the worst of it?"

Everyone leaned forward eagerly. Everyone desperately wanted to know the worst of it.

Betsy's voice rang out clear and strong. "The worst of it is that it never had to happen. This wasn't an act of God. This wasn't the strange workings of Providence. This was nothing short of criminal negligence by men who ought to have known better."

The newspapermen were writing frantically, desperate to take down every word.

Betsy waved one arm wildly. "Don't look for someone to praise— look for someone to hold accountable! This was entirely the fault of the authorities at Siboney. We ought never to have been on that ship! No one inspected it. No one provisioned it. They just shoved us on board to get us out of the way. It was worse than careless. It betrayed a shocking lack of concern for human life—for the lives of these brave men who risked so much. This entire fiasco—this entire war!—is the fault of arrogant, incompetent men playing with lives as though they were boys playing with toy soldiers and then kicking them aside when they're done."

Betsy pressed her lips together hard. She was shaking. Holt could see her, standing there in her black dress with the Red Cross insignia on the arm, framed in the door of the carriage, swaying slightly, too thin, exhausted, worn to the bone, but determined to have her say, determined to make sure justice was done.

He was so proud of her it hurt.

A reporter broke the spell, shouting out, "Is it true that the captain was drunk and the doctors incompetent?"

Betsy glared at the unfortunate reporter. "I don't know who told you that, but it's nonsense. Captain Decker, the captain of the *Seneca*, was all that was kind and provided every assistance within his power—which was precious little! The doctors on board, Dr. Hicks and Dr. Baird, had ninety-four wounded to care for—and that's not counting the passengers who fell ill. They worked themselves sick."

Dr. Baird was standing with a bunch of the other passengers, waiting to board the cabs. Holt watched as he lifted a hand to scrub at the tears falling down his cheeks. One of the other passengers, the society boy from Boston, patted the doctor on the shoulder.

Betsy surveyed the crowd, quelling them with a look. "This fiasco was purely the fault of the authorities, not of anyone on board. The people on board were *wonderful*. We would never have survived—none of us—without the selfless assistance of the passengers who gave up their cabins and volunteered to serve as orderlies and nurses. Captain Dowdy and—and Private Holt"—for the first time, Betsy's voice faltered; Holt saw her eyes slide sideways toward him before sliding away again—"they were pillars of strength. But they shouldn't have *had* to be. None of us should have had to be."

Her face twisted; she had exhausted herself and was fighting for control.

"Is that the opinion of the Red Cross?" demanded one of the reporters.

Betsy's hand went reflexively to the Red Cross badge on her arm. "It's *my* opinion. It's more than my opinion. It's my true belief." She raised her chin. "If anyone wants to know more, I shall be staying—I shall be staying at the St. Denis Hotel. I will give my statement there, this afternoon."

Her eyes met Holt's for one moment before she turned and ducked into the carriage, shutting the door smartly behind her.

Betsy's salvo appeared on the front pages of all the major papers that evening.

Holt didn't go to the St. Denis Hotel. He didn't go to her press conference. He wanted to go. He wanted to go and stand behind her, to announce himself as her lawyer, to fend off anyone who challenged her—but he wasn't a lawyer. He was just a man who'd dropped out of law school. And she'd told him to go away.

Besides, she'd made it very clear she didn't need Holt to stand up for her; she could stand up for herself.

So Holt went uptown to the Harvard Club on Forty-Fourth Street, venturing out only to buy copies of all the special editions containing Betsy's statement to the press. He didn't have to go far to find them. They were being hawked on all the street corners. The *Seneca* wasn't just news. It was *the* news.

SOME ONE BLUNDERED . . . WOUNDED
SUFFER.

There was a drawing of Betsy as she had been that morning, standing on the step of that carriage, alone and brave in her black dress, the Red Cross insignia disproportionately displayed and her hair inaccurately smooth. They'd got her hair wrong but they'd caught her defiance.

"Miss Elizabeth Hayes, the Red Cross Nurse, Exposes the Disgraceful Neglect Practised on Injured Soldiers Brought from Cuba on *Seneca*."

Holt kicked back on the bed, a real bed, easing the pain in his healed but still not happy leg.

He could hear Betsy's voice through the paper; he could picture her face as she lectured the press, as she said, "I don't want to be a heroine. I don't want your praise. I just want someone to promise me that this will never happen again."

Holt fell asleep in a pile of papers and woke up with newsprint on his cheek.

The counterattack came swiftly.

The surgeon general, George Sternberg, took the train to New York, convening a hurried conference that included the New York medical officer and Doctors Hicks and Baird—but notably not Betsy. After a few hours huddled together, he emerged to pronounce that he had undertaken a review of the situation. No blame was to be attached to the army or the authorities in Siboncy. They had done exactly as they ought, clearing the field hospital to make room for new casualties. As to the ship not being provisioned—nonsense. They'd had quinine pills, bandages, malted milk, and beef tea aboard.

The entire hullaballoo was "absurd and absolutely false." It was all in the fevered imagination of a hysterical woman: Miss Elizabeth Hayes.

Betsy, never one to let herself be cowed, fired back. There were more drawings. Betsy in front of the St. Denis Hotel addressing a mob of reporters: "If it is hysteria to speak the truth and speak it plainly, then I am, indeed, what they say. I have every faith that a formal inquiry will reveal the truth of my statements."

NO FURTHER INQUIRY INTO THE CASE OF THE *SENECA*.

The morning paper came with Holt's coffee. He shook it out, read it once, and then again, feeling sick as he tried to make the little black marks form into words and sentences. General Sternberg, the surgeon general, had made inquiry into the case and concluded that the entire matter was exaggerated. Perhaps they might not have had as many supplies as were needed, but that wasn't the fault of the authorities; it was entirely the responsibility of the inexperienced, junior doctors, who weren't part of the army at all, but only contract workers, and ought to have applied more forcibly for stores before sailing. As for the allegations made by the Red Cross nurse . . . the army placed no importance on the utterances of hysterical females.

Holt thought of Dr. Baird, crying over the patients he didn't have the tools to help.

He thought of Betsy, working determinedly, tirelessly.

He thought of all those men down there, in the hold, in the dark, in the stench, on those horrible, close-packed bunks. The brackish water that was almost worse than no water at all. The fever, the pain, the fear.

Holt wanted to put General Sternberg on that ship, in those conditions, for seven days and see who was hysterical.

Holt drained his coffee without tasting it. He couldn't let this end like this. He couldn't let them call Betsy hysterical.

Something had to be done. And Holt had a pretty good idea of what that something was. Two ideas, actually. Both of them loathsome.

He made himself face the worst first. Going down to the front desk, he dictated a telegram. It was a long telegram. But it wasn't the price that made him grit his teeth. It was the recipient.

Holt felt a bit like he needed to scrub himself with carbolic after he'd sent it—he felt soiled down to his soul—but he didn't have any carbolic and there was one more teeth-gritting-but-necessary task ahead of him.

Holt took his hat and his brand-new cane and headed downtown on the streetcar.

Kit wasn't staying at the St. Denis. She had chosen a smaller, cheaper, less storied hotel, closer to Park Row, where the *New York World*'s gold dome sneered at the spire of the *New-York Tribune* as they both lorded it over the squat building of the *New York Times*. The entire street thrummed with the rhythm of underground printers churning out the latest scandals. Holt had no idea how Kit managed to sleep through any of it, but it seemed to energize her. She was looking considerably better than she had when he'd last seen her, although that might have also been due to the very grown-up six-year-old who asked his name and admitted him, and the somewhat less grown-up four-year-old who promptly took his toy soldiers and crawled under a table.

"You're looking better," said Holt.

Kit snorted. "It would have been hard to look worse. My husband told me he's seen corpses in better shape. He said it with love," she added, as an afterthought. "Thanks for helping to keep me alive on the *Seneca*."

"It was mostly Betsy. Thanks for helping to keep me alive in Siboney."

Kit grinned at him. "It was mostly Betsy. I'm assuming Betsy is why you're here."

Holt hovered next to her chair. "How did you guess?"

"My penetrating powers of observation. Sit down. You're giving me a crick in my neck."

"Yes, ma'am." Holt folded himself into the indicated chair, resting his stick against the arm. "Have you seen Betsy? How is she?"

"How do you think? Furious. Hurt." Kit looked sideways at him. "She comes and visits every day, you know."

Holt didn't know.

Kit looked meaningfully at Holt. "You might go and hold her hand."

"She told me to go away," Holt mumbled.

Kit snorted. "Oh, honey. And you listened?"

Kit's six-year-old was watching with undisguised interest. Holt was strongly tempted to crawl under the table with the four-year-old.

"I take what Betsy says seriously," said Holt with dignity. "That's why I'm here. Because we have to do something about the defamation of her character."

"All right," said Kit, although there was still a glint in her eyes that made Holt distinctly squirmy. "What's the plan?"

Holt gripped his cane and leaned forward in his chair. "You wanted an interview with Hold 'Em Holt? Here's your chance."

Chapter Twenty-Eight

THE ANGEL OF THE *SENECA* SAVED MY LIFE THREE
TIMES OVER:

Exclusive Interview With Hold 'Em Holt

—Miss Katherine Carson for the St. Louis Star Ledger, *July 28, 1898*

❧

Central Park, New York
July 30, 1898

IT WAS THE SORT OF late-summer day that made New Yorkers flee the
city for more salubrious climes.

Horse droppings steamed in the middle of Fifth Avenue. Motor
cars burped exhaust. A vendor wanted to sell Betsy fried oysters; the
smell clung unpleasantly to her brand-new walking dress. Inside the
leafy oasis of Central Park, small children ran and screamed and
were tutted at by pedestrians and tried to shove each other into the
Conservatory Water.

There was a man standing by the edge of the water, a little apart from the madding crowd. He wore a lightweight summer suit and a straw boater, all quite new and quite neatly pressed. With it, he carried a walking stick, which he was using to fish out a rather bedraggled boat that appeared to have come to a bad end.

As Betsy watched, Holt neatly splinted the mast using his handkerchief, and handed the mended boat to the ungrateful owner, who immediately ran off, hollering.

Using another handkerchief to dry his hands—good heavens, did the man have an infinite supply of handkerchiefs?—he turned and saw Betsy.

Betsy had planned this moment. She'd prepared for this moment. She'd arranged this moment. But now that she was here she found she wasn't prepared at all. She'd expected—oh, she didn't know. The same man she'd known in Cuba. The mustache-draped man in his Rough Rider uniform, looking stern on the verandah of the Tampa Bay Hotel while Kit tried to wrangle an interview with him, or the bedraggled patient on his cot in the tent in Siboney, all tatters and hollow cheeks.

Or the man who'd kissed her on the deck of the *Seneca*, sunburned and steady.

Not this perfectly ordinary metropolitan gentleman with his straw hat and his Brooks Brothers suit.

"Hello," he said.

And just like that, Betsy couldn't remember what she'd meant to say, never mind that she'd been rehearsing it for the entire walk over.

The paper under her arm crinkled. Right. That was it. Betsy shook it open, holding it up so Holt could see the headline. "The Angel of the *Seneca* saved my life three times over, says famous lawman Hold 'Em Holt?"

Holt limped slowly over, leaning heavily on his stick. "I say it as it is."

Betsy wasn't letting him get away with that. "You don't usually say it at all. And I still don't understand how you came up with three times. Never mind. That's not the point. I thought you didn't give interviews."

"I don't. This is my first, last, and only." The sun cast his face into shadow beneath his hat brim. "Your friend Kit told me you'd promised her a Yale-man cowboy Rough Rider. She said failing that, a Harvard cowboy Rough Rider would do. I was just trying to make good on your promise. Breach of contract, and all that."

Betsy squinted at him, wishing she could see him better. Blasted sunshine. "You told me you hated being Hold 'Em Holt."

"I did. I do. I couldn't let them say what they were saying about you without saying something back." Gentleman that he was, Holt moved to the side so that the sun wouldn't fall in her eyes. Betsy followed him into the shade of the foliage that clustered around the clearing. "This was Hold 'Em Holt's swan song. He doesn't exist anymore. I followed your advice. I called the Harvard Law School. Ambrose Rutherford IV will be returning for his final year."

Betsy felt a horrible sense of loss, which was silly. She knew it was silly. "So no more Holt."

"No more Holt."

Betsy tried to make a joke of it. "Does this mean I have to start calling you Ambrose?"

"I'd prefer you didn't."

Maybe he'd prefer she not call him anything at all. Maybe he'd recovered from his momentary madness on the *Seneca* and realized she was a bad lot.

"Mr. Rutherford, then." Betsy took a deep breath and gripped her paper. Her hands felt very sweaty inside her charming new gloves. "Did you know, the most remarkable thing has happened? I've been summoned for an audience with President McKinley. He wants my opinion on what happened on the *Seneca*."

The shadow of the leaves made strange patterns on the ground. Holt traced them with the tip of his cane. "That's not surprising."

Betsy narrowed her eyes at him. "Isn't it? I don't usually have heads of state soliciting my opinion." Well, except for the Greek royal family, but that was different.

"You've been in the press." Holt poked at a fissure in the paving. "And then there's the *Concho*. You've heard about the *Concho*."

"Oh, yes." The papers were full of the *Concho*, which had limped into New York Harbor to a universal outcry. Like the *Seneca*, it had been a transport sent with wounded from Siboney, unprepared, un-provisioned.

Holt lifted his head, looking her squarely in the eye. She hadn't remembered his eyes being quite so blue, but they were; they were alarmingly, distractingly blue, like the sky over the Aegean; one could sail off in them and not come back. "They didn't fare as well as we did. Five men died. They might have brushed aside what happened on the *Seneca*, but now the *Concho*'s come into port . . . well, it's clear there's a problem. And that problem wasn't Dr. Baird."

"Poor Dr. Baird," said Betsy, trying to put her scrambled thoughts back together. "I hope this helps clear his name. The ship might have been a horror, but he got everyone through alive."

"*You* got everyone through alive," said Holt quietly. "Do you wonder why the president wants to talk to you?"

"I don't wonder, I know. Holt, I know you arranged it." Betsy was consumed by an almost unbearable mix of fondness and exas-peration. She didn't know whether to embrace him or shake him or both. "For heaven's sake, Holt. How did you ever survive out West? You have the worst poker face of anyone I've ever known."

"Only with you," he said ruefully. "How did you know?"

"Well, the president's aide telling me to make sure to convey his regards to Mr. Rutherford was something of a clue."

Holt winced. "He wasn't supposed to say that."

In other words, she was never meant to know that Holt had been working behind the scenes to clear her name. He was just going to perform his bit of knight errantry and ride quietly off into the sunset—or to Harvard Law, which was pretty much the same thing, only with more books involved.

"I assume the Mr. Rutherford to whom he referred was your father, not you."

"You assume correctly." Betsy stood there, pointedly waiting, until Holt added, reluctantly, "They know each other through political and legal circles. My father gave . . . generously to the president's campaign."

"You hate your father."

"Yes."

Betsy could feel the droplets of sweat dripping down her back beneath her tightly fitted new summer walking suit. "Then why?"

"Because you were right," Holt said quietly. "Would I rather crawl naked over ground glass than ask my father for anything? Certainly. But some things are worth it."

Their eyes met.

Her new walking suit was too tight. Betsy couldn't quite breathe in it.

Holt dropped his head, poking his cane at a crack in the paving. "What happened on the *Seneca* was unpardonable. If you hadn't been there—half that ship would have been buried at sea and everyone would have shaken their heads and called it the wages of war, and it would have been left at that. But you didn't leave it. And neither could I."

"So this is about justice." The breath she had been holding all came out in one deflated whoosh.

"Isn't that what you told me to do? To go off and fight for justice and be a voice for the voiceless? Not that you're voiceless," Holt amended hastily. "You have more voice than an entire men's chorus. But I couldn't let them slander you. Not after everything you'd done."

Because she was the Angel of the *Seneca*.

There were drawbacks to being an angel. The wings, for one. The distance it placed between them.

Betsy had sent him away. She knew that.

She just hadn't meant it to be forever.

Or maybe she had. She wasn't quite sure.

Oh, honey, Kit had said, when she'd come back to the room. *How can you expect him to read your mind when you don't know it yourself?*

It was better this way, she'd told Kit. Better for Holt, better for her, better for everyone. A few days off the claustrophobic confines of the *Seneca* and he'd quickly realize he was better off without her.

And she'd been right, hadn't she? The fact that he hadn't tried to contact her was proof.

But when that man on the telephone had said to give his regards to Mr. Rutherford . . . when Betsy had seen Kit's nauseating headline . . . Oh, it was foolish, but part of her couldn't resist poking. Poking to see if this was, perhaps, Holt's way of letting her know he hadn't changed his mind, that everything he had said to her was all still true, that even after a good night's sleep in a proper bed, even after a return to the normal world, he still saw something in her, in all her cracks and flaws. . . .

Not the Angel of the *Seneca*.

People need heroes, he'd told her. That was what this was about. Not about her. Not about him, not about them. It was about two fictional characters, created by the press: the legendary lawman and the angel of mercy, emblems of honor in a world seething with corruption.

Betsy swallowed her disappointment and tried to pretend that was what she was here about too, and that her motives hadn't been low and selfish.

"I don't care what they say about me," Betsy lied. "But I do care about justice being done. How many men have to die before someone is held accountable? I'm sick of people shrugging and saying it's war. What happened on the *Albania* wasn't war. What happened on the *Seneca* wasn't war. It was incompetence and callousness and—goodness only knows what else. I may not matter, but if I don't speak out, it will just keep happening again and again and again."

Holt took a step back. "Say that to the president. Say all of that to the president."

"I will." The words stuck in Betsy's throat. It felt like goodbye. She wasn't ready for it to be goodbye.

But somehow they had begun walking, walking slowly in tandem along one of the twisting paths that would lead out of the park, a sure sign this interview was over.

"Once that's done . . . will you go to one of the army camps to nurse?" Holt asked politely. They might have been strangers, exchanging commonplaces.

"No. I only started nursing because I was angry that no one would let me excavate." It was hard to say because it was true. And also because it meant admitting that they'd come to the end of their particular moment in time. "You took my advice. I'm taking yours. I'm going back to Greece. I'm going to get my own permit and hire my own workers and run my own dig."

She'd thought long and hard about it during her stay at the St. Denis Hotel. This time, she was going to do it her way. No gadding about on the fringes of Athenian society, no waiting for the men at the American School to let her play with their toys.

Betsy dragged her feet along the path, scuffing the shiny toes of her new buttoned boots. "I don't want to hunt down the relics of battles. I don't want to discover more about the Trojan War or what exactly Hector's armor might have looked like. I want to learn about the lives of normal people. Ordinary people. Women. I want to learn how they cooked, how they dressed, how they raised their children, how they nursed their ill. I want to dig up all the bits and pieces other archaeologists throw away, because they're not big enough, grand enough. Shards of cooking pots and fragments of children's toys." Betsy stopped short, nearly causing a collision with a baby carriage. Holt moved her neatly out of the way, just in time. "Shouldn't we want to find those? Shouldn't that matter too?"

"Yes." Holt leaned on his cane, looking down at her. Betsy could see the shadow of the scar at his temple, beneath his carefully combed hair. "It should."

Betsy thought about him as she had first seen him, on that train platform outside of Tampa, among that boisterous, lively crew of new-minted soldiers, all anxious to get out there and strike a blow against the Spaniards. So many of them dead now. Or wounded.

"I don't want anything to do with war ever again," Betsy said vehemently. "I don't want to study it or teach about it or live it."

"Neither do I." Holt turned his cane over in his hand, examining the handle. "My father always said the war was the making of him. I think it was the unmaking of him. Not that it makes him any less of an, er—um."

Holt reddened, covering his confusion with a cough.

Betsy was afflicted with an absolutely unbearable wave of affection. "I've heard worse," she said tartly. "Did you really think men deep in the throes of delirium mind their language? Even you."

Holt groaned. "I don't know what to say. If I'd known . . ."

"You would have guarded your tongue in your pain? It's not your language that makes you a gentleman." As she said it, Betsy felt the way she had when she'd first looked at her Greek letters and they'd begun to make sense in her head, as though a great truth lay before her and she finally had the skill to read it. "I've known so-called perfect gentlemen who don't have a gentlemanly bone in their bodies. It's not the language or the clothes—although that is a very nice boater."

Holt's hand went instinctively to his hat. "Thank you?"

"Don't thank me. I should be thanking you—three times over, a hundred times over." Betsy didn't understand why she'd been too stupid to see it before. She'd been dazzled by Charles's charm but she'd missed what was right in front of her with Holt. He wasn't even a diamond in the rough. He was just a diamond, pure and simple. "You couldn't stop being a gentleman if you tried. It's your kindness. It's the way you look out for everyone. You looked out for Paul, you looked out for me—even when I didn't want looking after."

"I couldn't have let you walk in the dark to Tampa," said Holt hoarsely. "There were alligators."

"Do you think I didn't notice how weak you were on the *Seneca*? How much your leg was hurting you? But you still did the work of ten men. You held me up even when you barely had strength to stand yourself."

"What was I meant to do, lounge on a deck chair while you worked yourself to the bone?" Holt looked horrified by the notion. "It was what anyone would do."

He genuinely believed that. After everything—after his father, after the army—he still believed that.

And that was why she loved him.

The realization didn't strike like one of Cupid's arrows. It wasn't a blow out of the blue. It felt like looking up and realizing the sky was blue. It had always been there; she just hadn't had the wits to see it.

He was always there, quietly, in the background, propping her up, never asking for thanks. Knowing what she needed before she knew she needed it.

Betsy looked at him, at that familiar-unfamiliar face, with his smoothly shaved cheeks that were still too thin from all the weeks of privation and the scar she had cleaned and dressed. "I wasn't the one who saved us all on the *Seneca*," she said, in a voice that didn't sound like her own. "That was you. You came up with the idea of moving people from their cabins—"

"You were the one who asked them."

"Stop trying to give me the credit! You're the best person I know." Betsy couldn't do this anymore. She couldn't talk around it. She couldn't pretend. A million thoughts and emotions jostled together, but all that came out was "I love you. I didn't want to love you but I can't imagine not loving you and I don't know what to do about it."

"Are you asking my advice on the matter?" It was very hard to tell what Holt was thinking.

Betsy felt strangely exhausted. "Well . . . yes. I suppose I am."

"In that case . . ."

Holt's cane clunked against the ground. He leaned forward and kissed her, right there in the middle of a path in Central Park, to the vast interest of half a dozen squirrels, two fascinated children, one horrified nursemaid, and Betsy.

When the trees stopped revolving around them, long after the outraged nursemaid had shooed her charges away, Betsy held on to Holt—after all, he'd dropped his cane, and she didn't want him to fall—and said breathlessly, "Compromising me in Central Park is the solution?"

Holt grinned at her, resting his forehead briefly against hers. "It's a start."

Betsy scrunched her eyes shut at a particularly mortifying memory. "Kit did tell me I should make an honest man of you while I could."

"Oh, did she?" said Holt. "When was this?"

"On Hoffman Island." Betsy had blundered back into the room and flung herself down next to Kit's cot. "I asked her why things couldn't be simple. She told me if I wanted simple, they'd be simple, but I like making problems and you like solving them, and what could be better than that? There was a bit more to it than that, but that was the main point."

Holt framed her face in his hands, smoothing his thumbs over her cheekbones. "If the problem is that you love me and I love you, then I think there's an obvious answer."

Betsy wrinkled her nose at him. "Does that answer involve orange flowers? I don't know how to be a wife, Holt. All I know is how to translate dead languages." Betsy thought for a moment. "And bandages. I've gotten quite good at bandages."

Holt didn't laugh. He never did when she wasn't really joking. That was part of the joy of him. "All I know about being a husband is that whatever my father did, I want to do the opposite. I think we just go on being ourselves. But we go on being ourselves together."

"You make it sound so simple," said Betsy despairingly. Kit was going to gloat. Kit was going to gloat unbearably. She was probably going to gloat in print, no less.

"Oh, don't worry." Holt's eyes crinkled at the corners as he looked down at her. "I'm sure you can find a way to make it complicated."

"Hush," said Betsy, thinking hard. "If you're going to set up your practice in Massachusetts, I could teach at Smith during the winters. . . ."

She wasn't sure if the classics faculty would be delighted or horrified at the notion. Either way, she was sure she could talk them around. It might be rather nice to have the opportunity to shape a new generation of scholars.

The boys at the American School would have no idea what hit them.

"I've heard Greece is lovely in the summer," offered Holt.

Betsy rested her hands against the soft fabric of his brand-new suit. "It's hot. It's very hot. But you should be used to that after Cuba. And no one will be shooting at you. So there's that."

Holt looked tenderly at her. "If they do, you can bandage me."

"You always have an answer for everything," Betsy said thickly, scrubbing at her eyes with the back of her hand.

Holt reached into his pocket and held out a scrap that had once been part of her petticoat. "Handkerchief?"

EPILOGUE

From the Mixed-Up Files of Mrs. Ambrose Rutherford IV
  (née Betsy Hayes)
Archaeologist, Humanitarian, and War Nurse
Miss Elizabeth Hayes to Miss Katherine Carson
September 2, 1898

Dear Kit,

  *Don't think I've forgiven you for that nauseating article; I
mean to make you pay for that for the next decade at least and
possibly longer. You can start by being my bridesmaid. Yes, Holt
and I are engaged! I followed your advice and made an honest
man of him before he had the sense to reconsider.*

  *I'm not entirely sure who proposed to whom. Let us just say
it was a matter of mutual agreement.*

  *Lavinia is planning an elaborate wedding in Boston
next June with herself as matron of honor and her favorite
Daughters of the American Revolution in tulle with orange
flowers as bridesmaids. I'm not entirely sure for whom she
thinks she's planning this wedding as neither Holt nor I intend
to participate. We plan to be married very simply in May in*

Northampton, which is near enough to Springfield that Holt's older sisters and their numerous offspring can attend. I appear to have acquired three sisters and a substantial quantity of nieces and nephews.

Holt's father will not be in attendance. He suffered an apoplexy, although it's unclear whether it was a result of hearing that his son had been masquerading as a desperado—and a rather famous one!—for the past four years or the shock of acquiring a college woman as a daughter-in-law.

I want only you and Ava as my bridesmaids. I promise not to make you wear anything too dreadful—unless you write a mawkish article about romance upon the Seneca, in which case expect sackcloth and ashes, or at least a particularly unbecoming shade of puce. As for the children, Dorothy can come along and pelt people with rose petals or whatever it is flower girls do and Oscar can carry the ring on a little cushion.

I intend this to be the simplest sort of family affair. We're inviting only family, close friends, some of our fellow sufferers from the Seneca, and the entire faculty of Smith College. Oh, and Ava's doctor, of course. And perhaps some of the nicer undergraduates. I was thinking it might be nice to have something rather similar to an Ivy Day procession. . . . Wouldn't it be charming if someone gave an oration in Greek? Or possibly a Greek play, with strophes and antistrophes and a chorus of fifty or so undergraduates. They could be charmingly draped in white chitons and carry flowers.

Holt refuses to wear a toga. I pointed out to him that togas were Roman, not Greek, and it would be a chiton, or, if he'd rather, an exomis.

He modified his response to encompass any kind of skirted

*garment. This, I suppose, is to be expected when one finds
oneself engaged to a lawyer-in-training.*

*The good thing is that he seems to enjoy it—the training
in the law, that is—and he's far happier parsing contracts and
wrangling about precedent than he ever was back when he was
chasing bandits, or whatever it was he actually did out on the
range. (Apparently the bandits were a brief aberration. Or so
he claims.)*

*My brother is delighted by the match for all the wrong
reasons—but it means he was willing to release a number of
funds to me without asking too many questions. He believes
they're for my trousseau. I can't imagine where he got that
notion. In fact, they're for the hiring of workmen and the
bribing of officials.*

*I mean to return to Greece directly after the wedding.
(With Holt, of course. I don't mean to marry him and then
desert him before the bubbles have gone flat in the nuptial
champagne. He says he can study for the bar exam just as well
from a dig in Greece as he can from rooms in Cambridge.) I
have an idea of where I might like to excavate, if only I can
arrange the correct permits. . . .*

*I would have liked to have gone this year, but the president
has decided to set up a commission to investigate the conduct of
the army and their administration, and I'm to be interviewed.
They haven't told me when they intend to call me, but I don't
mean to miss it for the world.*

*Holt insists I browbeat the president into creating the
commission. I did nothing of the kind. I simply, clearly laid out
the mistakes that were made and the abuses that needed to be
corrected and then allowed him to reach his own conclusions.*

You'll be happy to hear that the president assured me that there will be no recurrence of the sorry affair of the Seneca *and the* Concho. *Official protocols for converting troopships into hospital ships have been sent to those in charge in Cuba, Puerto Rico, and the Philippines.*

And no, I did not dictate those protocols to him. I may have made some gentle suggestions and those suggestions may have been incorporated into the final document, but that is not at all the same thing.

I have found the president to be a very reasonable man and am entirely satisfied to leave the matter in his hands—especially now that he has been told exactly what needs doing.

Any reports that I made the president cry are highly exaggerated. He assured me it was only dust in his eye.

    Warmest regards,

    Betsy

⚜

Report of the Commission Appointed by the President to Investigate the Conduct of the War Department in the War with Spain

February 1899

    ... To two transports in particular, the *Seneca* and the *Concho*, <u>general attention was strongly drawn by reports published soon after the arrival of the vessels at New York</u>. The facts were as stated— the ships had too many sick, and the sick had not enough nurses and doctors; medicines and supplies were in insufficient amounts; beds and bedding neither in quantity nor quality such as the sick should have had; the water supply was not pure and fresh. ...

    ... In the last twenty years the value, the efficiency, and the availability of well-trained women nurses has been demonstrated, and it is much to be regretted that this fact was not fully realized by the medical officers of the army when the war commenced. It is to be remembered though that in military hospitals in the field, women had been employed as nurses, if at all, only to a very limited extent, and there was good reason for questioning whether a field hospital, with a moving army, was any place for a woman. <u>Our recent experience may justly be held to have shown that female nurses, properly trained and properly selected, can be duly cared for and are of the greatest value</u>.

What is needed by the medical department in future is—

1. A larger force of commissioned medical officers.

2. Authority to establish in time of war a proper volunteer hospital corps.

3. <u>A reserve corps of selected, trained woman nurses</u>.

[Excerpts, underlined as shown, found in Mrs. Rutherford's files. Comments in margin omitted for the sake of public decency.]

❧

Madame la Baronne de Robecourt to Mrs. Ambrose Rutherford IV
August 8, 1903
(translated from the French)

Dear Mrs. Rutherford,
    It is very kind in you to take such an interest after our chance meeting in Switzerland all those years ago. My son thrives. You will be pleased to hear that Monsieur l'Abbé declares he has never had a child so quick to learn his Latin. It is a heritage from his father, whom he greatly resembles.

Do enjoy your visit to Paris this autumn. I regret we will be unable to renew our acquaintance. My son and I will be visiting family in the Loire Valley, as we do every October.

I have enclosed a pencil drawing made by one of his cousins. Everyone agrees it is a very speaking likeness.

You must be very busy with your archaeological endeavors, about which I have read in the papers. Please do not feel you need to write again. I should not wish you to disturb yourself.

I shall from time to time send you some small reminiscence as a token of your kind interest.

I beg you to accept my most cordial salutations,
  Delphine de Robecourt

❧

A *Clipping from the* Concord Daily News

June 18, 1904
DOCTOR[S] WEDS*

Dr. Lawrence Stringfellow and ~~Miss~~ [Dr!!!!] Ava Saltonstall were united in marriage at 7 o'clock Wednesday evening at Trinity Episcopal Church. The only attendant was Mrs. A. Rutherford IV, a friend of the bride.

~~Miss~~ [Dr!!!!] Saltonstall is the daughter of Dr. John Saltonstall of Concord. Dr. Stringfellow is a graduate of Princeton and the Columbia University College of Physicians and Surgeons. [Inserted by hand: The bride is a graduate of Smith College and Johns Hopkins School of Medicine—and successfully diagnosed a ruptured appendix at her own wedding reception!]

Dr. and ~~Mrs.~~ [Dr!!!] Stringfellow mean to make their home in Philadelphia.

*The newsprint has been edited in a hand identified as that of
Mrs. Ambrose Rutherford*

❧

Mrs. Ambrose Rutherford IV to Dr. Ava Stringfellow
Gournia, Crete
June 30, 1904

Darling Ava,

Greetings from Gournia! The work is coming along nicely—I won't bore you with what we've found, since I know you don't care in the least, but I've been happily wallowing in Bronze Age Minoan artifacts. After three seasons here, our workers know me and my ways—and they've stopped pointing and laughing whenever Holt climbs on a camel, although there might still be the odd snicker.

Kit and her husband brought Dorothy and Oscar, who have become alarmingly grown-up since I last saw them. They are now twelve and ten. Oscar shows a great facility for digging, although it appears to be the movement of dirt—or the acquisition of it on his person—that interests him more than anything that might be found within it.

We've had such happy times here—I shall never forget our first season here, Holt studying for the bar exam in our little hut by lamplight and muttering about torts and whatnot, while I pieced together pottery—I shall hate to leave it, but it's past time I wrote up my findings. For various reasons (yes, you know very well what it is; I could see that look in your eye at your wedding) it seems prudent to spend the next year or so back in the States. I can bring the baby with me to my lectures, particularly if it's a girl. I can't see why Smith would object. She'll be starting there later anyway.

But I do hate to leave. I know we'll be back—not to Gournia, but to some new site, yet to be determined—but Gournia will always have a special place in my heart: my very first excavation of my own, Holt's and my first home together. You will not be surprised to hear that when Holt tucks in mosquito netting, it stays tucked.

I really don't understand his difficulties with camels.

Goodness, there I go, getting all weepy for no reason. Fortunately, Holt has left a stack of handkerchiefs on my desk for just this purpose.

Are you sure you and Lawrence wouldn't like to spend the rest of your honeymoon in Greece? I can offer you a charming hut and a fine range of minor injuries.

Do think about it. We miss you both. Surely, the sick in Philadelphia can get by without you for a bit?

I've enclosed tickets and a map. You can thank me when you get here.

> *All my love,*
> *Betsy*

HISTORICAL NOTE

This book is based on the lives of two remarkable real women, who I have shamelessly grafted into one person for my own purposes: Harriet Boyd (later Harriet Boyd Hawes) and Janet Jennings.

Those of you who have read *Band of Sisters* may remember Harriet Boyd Hawes as the real-life founder of the Smith College Relief Unit. As I wrote that book, I became increasingly fascinated by the career of that redoubtable woman: archaeologist, humanitarian, and occasional war nurse. What, I wondered, would make a dedicated classicist drop her career to run to Florida to nurse in the Spanish-American War? The question haunted me, and, as I worked on *Band of Sisters*, my fictional version of Harriet Boyd Hawes, Betsy Hayes Rutherford, began elbowing me and dropping little hints.

This book is the answer to that question.

Most of Betsy's experiences are stolen directly from the real Harriet Boyd, who, like my fictional Betsy, won a place as one of two women in the American School of Classical Studies at Athens, electrified Athens by swooping around the city on her bicycle, and locked horns with the director of the school, Rufus Richardson, who shook his head over the notion of women excavating and suggested she try being a librarian. Like Betsy, Harriet was invited by an acquaintance, the fascinating Aikaterini McCraith, to lodge in her home at 4 Academy Street, and through her was drawn into fashionable Athenian circles. Charles de Robecourt was entirely my own creation and bears no relation to the real de Robecourt family, but all the other details of life at Academy Street and the "treks" to Tiryns, Mycenae, and Delphi with Professor Sterrett are taken directly from Harriet Boyd's biography and letters.

Like Betsy, the frustrated Harriet, thwarted at the American School and fired by the cause of Greek independence, took a nursing course, failed, called in favors, and went off to the front, where she nursed at Vólos and Lamia. Dr. Kalopothakes, like most of the other side characters in this book, is real and *did* assign the inexperienced Harriet Boyd her own hospital—possibly as revenge for pulling strings. The debacle of the hospital ship *Albania* was as described, as was the typhoid hospital at Lamia, the royal visit, and the icon sent by Queen Olga, who took a personal interest in Harriet Boyd and unsuccessfully contemplated marrying her off to her court physician. All details of Betsy's nursing career in Greece are drawn directly from Harriet Boyd's recollections. As far as I know, the real Harriet Boyd never had an affair with a fascinating but married Frenchman (although she did have a crush on a doctor in one of her hospitals) and certainly didn't have a secret baby, but those were my only deviations from her remarkable career. I strongly recommend the wry and loving biography written by her daughter, Mary Allsebrook, *Born to Rebel*, where you can read all the incredible exploits I wasn't able to fit into this book.

Trust me, I tried. Many, many details and many, many scenes were deleted during the editing phase. The bits that had to go included a description of stumbling into a wedding party at the village of Arachova and a lot of details about the various excavations, including the fact that Delphi was crisscrossed by train tracks put in by the French to haul away the mounds of dirt they needed to move to uncover the classical site beneath a modern village. (Why, yes, the original draft did include the exact number of cartloads of dirt removed.)

So why did Harriet go to Florida and why is it so quickly glossed over in her biographies? Not, I quickly discovered, because of a broken heart. Nor is the lack of mention because she was hiding something (at least that I was able to discover). In real life, Harriet Boyd arrived on the scene late, nursed in Florida rather than Cuba, and decided that rather than devote herself to nursing, she did want to go on with archaeology after all. The excavation at Gournia, which I attribute to my fictional Betsy, was Harriet Boyd's triumph.

Betsy's experiences in Cuba were drawn largely from the life of another woman, a reporter for the *New-York Tribune* named Janet Jennings who accompanied Clara Barton to Cuba, nursed in Siboney, found herself the sole nurse on the doomed transport *Seneca*—and created a firestorm when she went to the press and then the president, taking on the army and winning. Many of the descriptions of nursing in Siboney, first at the Cuban hospital, and then in a new Red Cross hospital, working around the clock as the wounded poured in, come directly from Janet Jennings.

As described in the novel, reporters from major papers rode with Roosevelt and even bunked with him. Women reporters, however, were not allowed along, and did exactly what the characters in this book did: they hitched a ride with Clara Barton and her Red Cross. While my Kit Carson was fictional, Katherine White (Mrs. Trumbull White) and Janet Jennings were not. Both accompanied Barton as a way to get around restrictions on female reporters and both found themselves undertaking heroic acts of nursing. My fictional Kit was based partly on Katherine White (Kit's dispatches were inspired by White's articles in the *Chicago Record*) and partly on Kathleen Blake

Watkins Coleman, a Canadian journalist sent by the Toronto *Mail and Empire* who wrote under the name "Kit"—and who did her best to cover the Spanish-American War despite resistance from all the males in the vicinity.

I stole Janet Jennings's remarkable ordeal as "Angel of the *Seneca*" for my own heroine. All characters on the boat other than Betsy, Holt, and Kit are real people, behaving as they actually behaved; aside from my fictional characters and their emotional dramas, everything on the boat happened pretty much as described. At the last moment, wounded were sent not to the hospital ship *Relief* but to a transport called the *Seneca*, which still had passengers on board—but no medical supplies. The two contract doctors sent to the *Relief* for supplies but got no response. On an impulse, Janet Jennings volunteered to go with them and found herself keeping a boatload of patients alive in impossible conditions on a journey that took double the predicted time. When the boat attempted to dock at Hampton Roads, they were refused, but supplies were sent on board, enabling them to make it to New York and quarantine.

I made some small tweaks for the sake of my story. Like my fictional Betsy, Jennings on impulse shoveled necessary supplies into a satchel—but she didn't raid the hospital at Siboney. She took her supplies directly from Miss Barton's ship, the *State of Texas*. There was a great more back-and-forth between the *State of Texas* and Siboney than I included in the book—partly because having the nurses constantly rowing out to the ship and being rowed back would take up a lot of narrative time to no purpose. In real life, it was Dr. Baird, not Dr. Hicks, who fell ill in the final days of the voyage. One final note: it was widely reported in the popular press that Jennings tore up her petticoats as handkerchiefs and bandages. A very irate Miss Jennings retorted that she had done nothing of the kind; she had brought bandages with her. Nonetheless, I couldn't resist using the petticoat story for Betsy. It seemed like the sort of thing Betsy would do.

The hullaballoo about the *Seneca* was as described: reporters and spectators mobbed the dock when Jennings was released from quarantine in New York. Janet Jennings was a sensation, the Angel of the *Seneca*. The army quickly struck back, impugning her as a hysterical woman. Undaunted, Jennings spoke out to the papers and secured a personal meeting with President McKinley. Her testimony to the Dodge Commission helped ensure needed reforms. Jennings and the other Red Cross nurses who served in Cuba were instrumental in the creation of a professional army nursing corps, which came into being in 1901, following the recommendations of the Dodge Commission.

Surprisingly, one finds almost no mention of these groundbreaking female nurses—or the *Seneca* debacle—in any of the many, many books about the Spanish-American War. For the activities of the Red Cross, I relied heavily on contemporary newspaper accounts, including the articles of Katherine White, one of the journalists who traveled and nursed with the Red Cross; on Clara Barton's *The Red Cross in Peace and War*; and on reports by the doctors who traveled with Clara Barton. While there aren't any monographs on the subject, there are some excellent articles in both academic and local historical society journals about the women who went to the field in 1898.

All the instances in which Barton was snubbed, turned away, or told women nurses didn't belong in the field were taken directly from the historical record—as were all the instances in which the army then turned around and begged for her help. Clara Barton, I am sure, would be both annoyed and unsurprised to have been written out of the story of the Spanish-American War.

For the plight of the *Seneca*, I relied heavily on the testimony of

Janet Jennings and her shipmates to the Dodge Commission, the lively (if not always entirely reliable) coverage in contemporary newspapers, and John Evangelist Walsh's comprehensive article "Forgotten Angel: The Story of Janet Jennings and the *Seneca*."

Unlike the role of the Red Cross, the more martial parts of the Spanish-American War—and particularly the exploits of the Rough Riders—have been meticulously documented, both at the time, by the participants, who were aware that they were involved in the making of history, and, later, by historians recreating exactly what happened in that crowded hour. Some of the more absurd bits recounted here are entirely true: when the train designated for them didn't arrive, Roosevelt and Wood hijacked a coal car and rode it backward to Port Tampa. Roosevelt also cut out two other regiments for a transport—but let the Vitagraph men board. General Joe Wheeler did deliberately leapfrog General Lawton's troops, and also repeatedly forgot that he was fighting the Spanish instead of the Yankees.

Other than Holt, Paul, and Dr. Stringfellow, most of the characters you meet in Cuba are real people. Ham Fish died at Las Guasimas; Teddy Burke came down with fever and was carried to the hospital at Siboney by his Yale buddy Thede Miller; and Thede Miller (who happened to be Thomas Edison's brother-in-law) died at San Juan Hill. Dr. Stringfellow, while fictional, was based on the Rough Riders' actual junior surgeon, a Princeton man named James Robb Church, and many of his actions and comments (other than falling in love with Ava) are taken from his real counterpart. In real life, Dr. Stringfellow would have served at the field hospital to which Barton was urgently summoned by General Shafter after the fighting at San Juan Hill, but I needed him for my own purposes, so I seconded him to the Red Cross and kept him at Siboney.

While I tried to remain as true to the actual facts as possible (and those facts were pretty incredible), I was forced to cut out a great deal. For that, I offer my apologies to any Spanish-American War buffs who might notice where well-documented discussions or scenes are missing or have been truncated. To the military historians out there, I apologize for any liberties I took with the disposition of battles. There are very detailed accounts by multiple parties of what happened in those two frenzied hours at Las Guasimas. I put my fictional Holt at the center of the action in Troop L, where the first men fell and the Rough Riders took their worst pummeling, but there's a delicate balance between portraying the truth of what we know now, pieced together later from multiple accounts with the benefit of hindsight, and what a man in the field would have experienced at the time. I tried to give a sense of the confusion without doing violence to the particulars of what we know to have occurred. Whether or not I was successful, I leave to you to judge.

For anyone wanting to know more about the Spanish-American War in general and the Rough Riders in particular, there are a plethora of options, from firsthand accounts like Burr McIntosh's *The Little I Saw of Cuba* and Teddy Roosevelt's classic work *The Rough Riders* to recent monographs like Mark Lee Gardner's *Rough Riders: Theodore Roosevelt, His Cowboy Regiment, and the Immortal Charge Up San Juan Hill* and Clay Risen's *The Crowded Hour: Theodore Roosevelt, the Rough Riders, and the Dawn of the American Century.*

One final point: while this book is set around two conflicts that shaped the fates of nations, it became very clear to me while writing it that this was neither a book about Greece nor a book about Cuba. On the contrary, it is a book about Americans in Greece and Cuba, which is a very different thing. By including the conversations with my fictional de Almendares (who was based on a real Cuban officer) and the very real General García, I tried to convey something of the Cuban perspective, which was very different from the American one.

The Rough Riders' motivations for going to war were a mixed

bag. There were some, like Holt, who were deeply moved by the sensational articles in the press about Spanish brutality and the plight of the Cuban people. And then there were others for whom it was a grand adventure, a chance to prove one's manhood by going to war—without much real thought as to what the war might be about. If there seems a great deal of discussion of Yale, Harvard, and Princeton, that's because there was a strong Ivy League contingent in Teddy Roosevelt's volunteer cavalry—and if you read their memoirs, it comes as a bit of a surprise when you learn they're off to war and not the Yale-Harvard game. It appears to have come as a bit of a surprise to some of them too.

For anyone wanting to learn more about any of the aspects of this book from the American School for Classical Studies at Athens in the late nineteenth century through the tragedy of the *Seneca*, you can find a bibliography on my website, www.laurenwillig.com.

ACKNOWLEDGMENTS

This book was meant to be with you a great deal sooner than it was. In March 2020, I planned to plunge straight from finishing *Band of Sisters* into this story about the formative years of the founder of the Smith College Relief Unit. And then a pandemic happened.

I am so grateful to my amazing editor, Rachel Kahan, for offering a year's extension before it even occurred to me to ask for it. I am also grateful to my agent, Alexandra Machinist, for refusing to be deceived by my argument that of course I could write the book in four months while Zooming the six-year-old into virtual school and playing Peppas and dinos with the two-year-old and still get it in on deadline—or, you know, somewhere in the vicinity of deadline. Thank you for making me take that extension. Huge thanks to Rachel Kahan, Liate Stehlik, Ariana Sinclair, Tavia Kowalchuk, Danielle Bartlett, and the rest of the team at William Morrow for all your support, encouragement, and ingenuity in these strange times.

When the world shut down, so did the archives. Thank goodness for my own personal Angel of the Bibliography, my dear friend and super-librarian, Vicki Parsons. The bulging folders of material I used to recreate life in 1890s Athens, on the front in the Greco-Turkish War, in the Rough Riders' camps in Tampa, and in the field with Clara Barton are entirely due to Vicki's research genius. Thank you for the sources, the book recs, the plot musings, and the hand-holding!

Huge thanks go to my sister, Brooke Willig, who—despite having a job of her own and a wedding to plan—responded to my plea of "Help! I can't make the revisions work!" by line-editing the entire manuscript. Equally huge thanks go to my parents, who, when we wound up in quarantine with my preschooler and in virtual school with my second grader, swooped us off to their house to give me time to work—which was only one of many, many swoops, without which this book would still be waiting to be revised and I would have had to come home two days into my last Team W book tour. Thank you, Mom and Dad!

This book took place on multiple continents in several languages. *Mille mercis* to Professor Jessica Sturm and @parisphrase for providing me with *le mot juste* when needed and ευχαριστώ to Aspasia Katerinis for answering my panicked questions about modern Greek idioms. Any mistakes are entirely the fault of the author—and possibly autocorrect.

A thousand thanks to my favorite medical consultant, Dr. Jonathan Romanyshyn, for the painstaking explanations of how gangrene actually works, the X-rays of a wide range of gunshot wounds, and the pictures of your toddler playing with a Teddy Roosevelt bobble-head.

Thank you to Nanci Young, Smith College Archivist; Mary Irwin, Smith College Libraries Development Officer; Lindsey McGrath of Alumnae Relations; and everyone else at Smith College for opening your arms to this Smithie manqué (which sounds slightly better than "Smithie wannabe," but amounts to the same thing). Thanks go as well to the powerhouse founder of the Seven Sisters Alumnae Association, Smithie extraordinaire Jennifer Pollock Mc-

Nally: I so appreciate your support and the giant Seven Sisters coffee mug, which provided crucial caffeination for the writing of this book.

I am so grateful to my support network for always being just a text away. Thank you, Nancy Flynn, for long-distance snark, book recs, and best-friend telepathy; Claudia Brittenham, for epic walk 'n' whines; the Ladies' Caucus—Stella Choi-Roy, Christina Bost-Seaton, Debbie Bookstaber, and Lien Johnson—for being a lifeline of commiseration, All the Articles, and mutual cheerleading; and, of course, the Unibrain, Karen White and Beatriz Williams, without whom my phone would bing a great deal less often.

One of the hardest parts of being in perpetual quarantine with a small person was missing events with my writer friends. Thanks to Lynda Loigman for catch-up Zooms; Fiona Davis, Brenda Janowitz, and Alyson Richman for alfresco lunch; M.J. Rose for that lunch we keep trying to plan (and will eventually have!); and Deborah Goodrich Royce for twilight dinners and fascinating conversation. I owe special thanks to the author friends who generously joined me in hosting Pink Carnation Read Along Zooms. Sarah MacLean, Tasha Alexander, Eloisa James, Deanna Raybourn, Andrea Penrose, Donna Thorland, Francine Mathews/Stephanie Barron, Lynda Loigman, Beatriz, and Karen—you are the best. Ditto the wonderful Sarah Wendell, dowager duchess of the romance novel world, and Bea Koch, chatelaine of the Ripped Bodice.

I am so grateful to the booksellers and librarians who have worked so hard to pivot with the times and find new ways to bring authors and readers together. Whether online or in person, I can't thank you enough for all you do. If I tried to name names (FoxTale Book Shoppe, Poisoned Pen, Litchfield Books, Murder by the Book, Diane's Books . . .), this acknowledgments section would be longer than the book, but I want to send special hugs to my local, Shakespeare & Co. Lexington Avenue, for being my go-to for signed books for virtual events *and* for keeping my preschooler supplied with Who Would Win books.

Thank you so much to the bloggers, bookfluencers, book gurus, and online book worlds that welcomed me both as a reader and a writer. Andrea Katz, Robin Kall, Kathie Bennett, Pamela Klinger-Horn, Ann-Marie Nieves, and Sharlene Moore, thank you for your wise counsel and boundless enthusiasm. I don't know what I would do without you! Huge hugs to the ladies of Bibliophile, esq. (special shout-out to Jackie Vavroch!) and Lawmas Who Make Shit Up. You are my home away from home.

This last thank-you is a big one: thank you to all of you reading this. Thank you to everyone who listened to or contributed questions for the weekly Wednesday Ask Me Anything; to everyone who joined in the epic year-long Pink Carnation Read Along; to everyone who emailed or commented on my website or posted on Facebook or liked a story on Instagram; and to everyone who ventured out in person when I made it out on the road this past summer. Thank you for joining me on all of these adventures. I can't tell you how much it means to me.

About the Author

LAUREN WILLIG IS THE *New York Times* and *USA Today* bestselling author of more than twenty novels, including *Band of Sisters*, *The Summer Country*, the RITA Award–winning Pink Carnation series, and four novels cowritten with Beatriz Williams and Karen White. An alumna of Yale University, she has a graduate degree in history from Harvard and a JD from Harvard Law School. She lives in New York City with her husband, two young children, and vast quantities of coffee.